"A SUMPTUOUS FEAST OF A BOOK.
The sensuous pleasures of eating and cooking
and the tortured ambivalences of a mother-
daughter relationship are artfully interwoven
in this witty, juicy story of a Jewish Italophile
gourmet who has a way of reaching for disaster
and (though she'd never let you know it)
turning it into victory."
—MOLLY HASKELL

"As Ms. Rossner warms to her real subject,
family ties, the book becomes increasingly
rich. The author deftly introduces other
relationships bringing the theme full circle."
—*The New York Times Book Review*

"The fierce ties between mother and daughter
are explored masterfully in this fine novel. A
vintage Rossner."
—JOAN MICKLIN SILVER

"Tickled my funny bone, teased my palate,
and wrenched my heart."
—VICKI GOLDBERG
Author of
Photographs That Changed Our Lives

"Engrossing characters and entertaining riffs
on the importance of traditional meals keep
the pages turning."
—*Kirkus Reviews*

By Judith Rossner:

TO THE PRECIPICE
NINE MONTHS IN THE LIFE OF AN OLD MAID
ANY MINUTE I CAN SPLIT
LOOKING FOR MR. GOODBAR
ATTACHMENTS
EMMELINE
AUGUST
HIS LITTLE WOMEN
OLIVIA*

*Published by Ivy Books

OLIVIA

or
The Weight of the Past

Judith Rossner

IVY BOOKS • NEW YORK

Ivy Books
Published by Ballantine Books
Copyright © 1994 by Judith Rossner

Library of Congress Catalog Card Number: 93-50211

ISBN 0-8041-1246-0

This edition published by arrangement with Crown Publishers, Inc. CROWN is a trademark of Crown Publishers, Inc.

Manufactured in the United States of America

First Ballantine Books Edition: August 1995

10 9 8 7 6 5 4 3 2 1

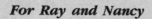

For Ray and Nancy

What did the Zen Buddhist say to the hot-dog vendor?
"Make me one with everything."

It was my intention that this memoir be a light-hearted kitchen romance, *My Life in Food*. I would describe how, the daughter of two professors, I was drawn to cooking as a small child, eventually became a professional chef, and after working for years in Italy, returned to the States to become known as the talky-impulsive host of the TV show "Pot Luck." I meant to glide lightly over my marriage to Angelo Ferrante and life with our daughter, Olivia. If I was supremely comfortable with mishaps before an audience and occasionally courted disaster to liven up my show, I'm far less easy with the mistakes and misunderstandings of real life and had no desire to recount them to strangers.

I was first diverted by the question of names. My maiden name was Sindler. I'd changed it automatically when I married Angelo in 1974, and there'd never been any question of going back to Sindler when we divorced. If Ferrante suggested someone I was not, neither was I a Sindler anymore. A new name would solve the problem in theory even while denying my past. Nor did I like the awkward hyphenated labels many women were choosing. My maiden name, was, after all, not just mine but my father's. Using it seemed to negate my life since leaving home. I finally decided to be Ferrante for publishing purposes because that was who could get a contract. In fact, my professional name would be a useful reminder of what the book was to be about. Settled.

Well, not so settled. For as soon as I began writing, I was swamped by memories that weren't the ones I'd intended to evoke. Stories about Angelo. Good and bad times with Livvy—Olivia, as I'm instructed to call her. And finally I realized I'd made the same mistake I had when she was young, in assuming I had two lives, in and out of the kitchen, and that she would take this for granted as I did. I was an adoring mother from the time Livvy was born, but I was patient and attentive only when I wasn't cooking meals for twenty to sixty people at a time. Now her memories of me are of a kitchen monster, a whirling dervish who never turned from the stove except to scream at her. Nothing I say can make her believe the pleasure I took in her, what wonderful times we had, while her memories of Angelo are of a father who adored her until he remarried and life changed, to an unimaginable degree, for the worse.

It's so much easier to deal with food than with people. The difference between people and food is that if you take identical pieces of food and treat them identically, they will turn out the same way. Eggs whipped for a long time will be frothier, meat will grow tender if you pound on it, sour cream that's separated by heat can be restored in the blender. Results are predictable, damage can be disguised or repaired.

It took me a long time, with Livvy, even to understand that some attempt at repair was in order. At first I thought she was simply a teenager gone haywire. I could pinpoint the moments when adolescent irritability erupted into volcanic rage; they never appeared to be about anything really terrible. One of the worst occurred after the first television show I did, in 1989, when I was called in as a last-minute replacement on the cooking segment of "Johnny Wishbone."

"Hi, everybody. I'm Caroline Ferrante and the camera is visiting my summer cooking class in Westport. We've just finished making a *buridda*, the Ligurian fish stew that you can see in these pots on the stove. I was thinking about a change of pace for 'Johnny Wishbone,' and fresh vegetables seemed like an obvious choice at this time of year. Don't get scared. This isn't going to be one of those, uh, Everything-You-Ever-Were-Scared-to-Ask-About-Sterilizing routines. But I'd like to encourage you to, say, prepare some fresh tomato sauce and freeze what you don't use in a couple of washed-out yogurt containers. Everyone's learned about *pesto geneovese* in the last few years, it's all over the place. But it doesn't seem to occur to people that plenty of other herbs can be frozen when they're fresh and dry. Or pounded or ground up with oil into *pestos*, pastes, and frozen in those little pill bottles you never had any use for, then added to sauces, soups, all kinds of dishes that need to be livened up a little. Including vegetables. I mean, vegetables aren't sexy the way meat is, but meat without any vegetables is . . . is sort of like sex without a mattress. The good stuff is there, but it isn't quite as easy to enjoy. By the way, those little bottles are good for tiny amounts of left-over sauce and gravy, too.

"Anyway, today we're going to do a *salsa verde*. A green sauce. It's usually easy to get the main ingredient, good Italian parsley, the kind that doesn't curl up so hard you can't taste it. Some people use arugula and basil as well. If I have time, I'll do different versions of green sauce, and encourage you to do the same. See which one you like best. Think about which food you'd like to put it on.

"Use your imagination. I don't mean try cinnamon if the recipe says capers or anchovies. But if it calls for basil, and you've got a lot of mint in your backyard, try the mint. Look at whatever else is around that's green. Taste it. Try to imagine how the combination'll taste. If you think it might be good, throw it in. The worst that can happen is it'll be awful, in which case you'll play with it to make it better. Or throw it out."

As I spoke, I'd been chopping garlic, then parsley and basil. Now I started to put them in the Cuisinart, then realized that the bowl was clean, but the blade wasn't in it. I saw the Waring Blender nearby on the counter, pulled it over, took off the cap. I put in the garlic, parsley, and arugula, then measured in the mustard, lemon juice, and olive oil.

"I yield to none in my love of the Cuisinart, but the fact is you're really supposed to do all this with a mortar and pestle, so I don't think you should worry if you have to use a blender. In fact . . ." I pressed one of the buttons, smiled at the camera. I was about to say that it barely mattered which button you pressed, but I stopped speaking because the contents of the blender, the cover of which I had neglected to put back on, were spraying my hair, my neck, and the near side of my face, as well as everything else in the vicinity.

I looked down to find the button to turn off the machine and the green gunk flew into my eyes.

"Oh, my God!" I moaned, trying to find the buttons. "This is like braille!"

I found them and pressed one. The machine stopped. I groped for a dish towel, which one of the women in my class came forward to hand me. They were all giggling. The cameraman turned to catch them, returned to show me cleaning myself off.

"I just remembered—did you ever hear about the Jew who gave a blind man his first piece of matzo?" I pretended to be the blind man, running his fingers over the big, crinkly matzo cracker that is foreign to him. "And he feels it, and feels it, and after a while, he asks, 'Who wrote this sh—junk?' "

As the class laughed harder, the cameraman signaled that I had four minutes to fill.

"Actually, this reminds me, when my daughter was little, maybe two years old, we lived in Rome, and I was the chef in a restaurant there. . . . The Italians do not believe, as the French and Americans do, that women shouldn't cook in an establishment where money changes hands. . . . Anyway, one day Livvy wanted something to eat and she looked down into a bowl of *salsa verde* and asked what the *grasso verde* was. They may sound similar, but one is green sauce and the other is green grease.

"Let's see. Where was I? Okay. We can clean up the mess later. I guess the first thing to do is . . . No, even before that, we're going to *cover* the blender. Then we'll turn it on for a few seconds and see what we've got left." I took off the cover, stuck in my finger, withdrew it, and tasted it. "Hmmm. What I've got is a pleasant blend of some herbs and garlic, to which I'm going to add some oil and a little lemon juice, and I'll end up with a pleasant little salsa that's a little better or worse than the one I usually do. Or maybe it'll make a nice salad dressing. Flexibility is the important thing. . . ."

Two minutes.

"I'm reminded . . . Telling the story about Livvy reminded me of another one. Some years ago, my brother, Gus, came to visit us in Rome during Easter vacation. Gus is a physicist, the kind of person who wants to know everything about a place before he goes there, and he'd read a lot, not just on the museums and the Vatican, but about food. He'd read that *abbacchio*, baby lamb, was a Roman Eastertime specialty. He was delighted because he hated fish and he'd been afraid he'd have to eat pasta all week. He was dismayed to discover that the restaurant owners hadn't read the same book as he had, and almost every good place in Rome was closed for Easter week. Of the open, more modest ones, nobody was serving *abbacchio*, which is not only very expensive, but difficult to hold in its rare and juicy state for any length of time.

"The Italian word for lamb is *agnello*, and *abbacchio* is a word Livvy had probably never heard. Anyway, we were all sitting around in the restaurant, our restaurant, before dinner hour, and Gus was complaining about not being able to find *abbacchio*, and I was saying I'd make it for him, and Livvy asked what *it* was, and Gus explained in his detailed, physicist's fashion, and Livvy sat there staring at him. Something horrible had clicked. I think until that moment, she'd never connected meat to the pictures of animals she'd seen in her books. She ran to me for protection as though Gus might take it into his head to carve her up next! And nothing I said could change her feeling about him.

"It was a while before my daughter would look at any kind of meat. On the other hand, I'm happy to tell you that by the end of that week, Gus was eating two kinds of fish."

The first three phone calls were from Sheldon, my agent, now producer. 1. I was wonderful. 2. I was to get back to my parents' house immediately so he could reach me. 3. If anyone wanted to talk to me about a show, I should just give them his number. Not try to talk to them. And I should please, for God's sake, put on some makeup and comb my hair before anyone saw me on the street. You never knew who ... (I'd had ten minutes to prepare for the show and hadn't been able to worry about my appearance. I am an ordinarily attractive female with light-brown hair and dark-brown eyes who, when I was younger, got looked at on the street no matter what I was wearing. Now I was more likely to have my existence noted by strangers if I dressed up a little.)

I made my way back to my parents'. I hadn't thought to call and tell them to turn on the set. It was just as well; I'm not sure they knew yet that it worked during daytime hours. Unfortunately, the same was not true of everyone else in Westport.

"You think I'm Mickey Mouse or something?" were Olivia's first, furious words as she stormed into the house, having been told by a friend's mother that I'd talked about her on TV. Thank God the friend's mother hadn't repeated the anecdote. "You think I'm some kind of character you made up?"

It crossed my mind that a case could be made for my having, indeed, made her up, but I wasn't about to sacrifice all hopes of peace for a one-liner.

"I can understand if you don't want me to make a habit of talking about you in public. But I was asked to fill in for someone on a cooking show. Last minute. I needed to fill the time—"

"That's what you think I'm here for? When you need to fill time?"

"No," I said, "but the stories were about when you were little and it didn't oc—"

"I don't want you to talk about me!" she shouted. "Ever!"

"I guess I thought I was talking about me, too."

"What's that supposed to mean?" she demanded.

"It means that whether you like it or not, we have a great deal to do with each other."

"Nothing but money! All we have to do with each other is money!"

"Oh," I said wearily. "Well, if you can believe that, I guess there's nothing to discuss."

"Except using me on your show."

I smiled slightly. "Well, I hope I'll have a show to not use you on. If I do, all I ever really expect to talk about is food and cooking. On the other hand, it's not giving away any secrets to say I have a daughter. Hundreds of people between here and Italy know I'm your mother."

"My birth mother!" she shouted back.

"Birth mother?" I hadn't heard the phrase before, though I gather it's widely used. "Well, of course I'm your birth mother. Your birth mother and your nursing mother and your diaper-changing mother and your hugging and kissing—"

"I don't remember you ever hugged me or anything else! I don't believe any of it!"

"Oh. But you do believe I gave birth to you?"

"No." It was so fast as to take my breath away. "I don't really believe it, except my father said it was true."

"I see. Your father acknowledged that I was your mother."

"He acknowledged"—the words were slowly and loftily spoken—"that your womb held me for nine months while I grew into a baby that could be born."

"I see. That's all a mother, a birth mother, is. A womb. A holder."

"That's right. Some mothers." Not a moment's hesitation or ambivalence.

"Well, then . . ." It was coming slowly. I was amazed by the way my tears were staying in my brain and out of my eyes. "Perhaps my reward for carrying you for nine months is that I can say I have a daughter."

From that time on, I didn't refer to Livvy in my classes, or, later, on the show. But I cannot eliminate her so thoroughly from my writing memories. Blood is stickier than desire, less subject to the owner's whim, or to the wear and tear of time. Unacknowledged bonds are no less powerful and may even, like mushrooms, grow better in the dark. There are times when I think that if Livvy hadn't gone so far in her rebellion the trip back would have been less painful.

Whatever else is true, whatever I think is on my mind as I sit down to write, she is with me as the words begin to flow.

When I was younger I was puzzled to hear women talk about cooking as though it were higher mathematics—some arcane field one dare not enter without the brilliance to divine the meaning of 1 C flour or 1 Tbsp. salt. Assurances to friends that some dish I'd served was straight out of a cookbook they could read as easily as I were met with admiring disbelief or uneasy laughter—as though I'd promised that if they'd just glance at a physics text, they would understand instantly why E equaled MC^2.

Aside from its physical pleasures, cooking always held for me the allure of the forbidden. My parents, having passed on to me their strong interest in eating well, resisted the notion that any subject so remote from the academy was appropriate as a life's work. They both taught at Columbia University, my father, European history with emphasis on the Second World War and its aftermath, my mother, art, her strong interest being in the nineteenth- and twentieth-century Italians. Gus teaches physics at the California Institute of Technology. My older sister, Beatrice, is a psychologist—borderline academic but still acceptable to my parents.

I was born in June 1954, my birth cleverly arranged by someone or other to coincide with my parents' summer vacation. If its timing had been arranged, the fact of my conception had not. My brother and sister are eight and six years older than I, and my mother, having put in her years of full-time child care, was back at school, on the tenure track. From the time I was born, a full-time housekeeper always lived with us in our huge Morningside Heights apartment, which was owned by the university.

While my parents appreciated women with other fine qualities, they were kind indefinitely only to those who were excellent cooks. And from an early age I exhibited a strong affinity for those women, a tendency to be with them in the kitchen when the rest of the family was off reading or writing. As I grew up I became increasingly helpful in the matter of training new housekeeper-cooks, increasingly skillful at making a good meal myself.

As I remember battles with my parents over school and homework, it strikes me for the first time that they tried to impose some split in my feelings not unlike the one I later expected of my own daughter. I was fourteen months old when my mother returned to Columbia, having hired a kind and competent woman to superintend me, the apartment, and the kitchen. My parents are good people and they were never awful to me, but during the school year they worked almost as hard at home, on their own papers and their students', as they did at the university, and for a long time it didn't bother them that the kitchen was the center of my home life. How convenient to have a little girl who was more comfortable with the housekeeper's taking her to the doctor than she would have been with either parent; who was more than content to bake cake on a Saturday afternoon when they wanted to take the two older kids to a museum; who, when she learned to play Go Fish, brought the deck to the kitchen to see if the housekeeper would play with her, instead of nudging them. It was a long time before they became uneasy about my attachment to the kitchen and its primary occupant.

My earliest memories are of Caitlin, the lovely Scots-Canadian who came to us when I was about three, who let me "help" her in the kitchen, and who allowed me, if we weren't too close to dinnertime, to lick the bowl when we'd finished mixing and pouring the batter I came to prefer to baked cake. The batter was just for me, while the finished product had to be shared with the family. When Caitlin left to get married, I was heartbroken. She was replaced briefly by a cousin of hers from one of the Northern Canadian provinces whose culinary skills turned out to be of little interest to my parents (she insisted that the roast would not have been tough had my parents allowed her to look for moose or rabbit meat). But then Suallen came to make me and the kitchen happy.

Suallen's grandparents had been slaves, her parents farmers on a small piece of Georgia land where they raised chickens, a few pigs, and as many vegetables as space would allow. My parents had tasted a Suallen meal at the home of friends who could no longer afford a live-in housekeeper, and had hired her on the spot without knowing that she'd left school to help on the farm before she had learned to read. With instruction from my father and help from me, she was reading cookbooks as well as *The New York Times* within a year. In 1961 she was awarded a B.S. in Education by Teachers College and returned to Georgia to teach. In the meantime, I'd learned to cook what had been called soul food by Suallen's family long before the notion that collard greens were edible and sweet potatoes good for more than Thanksgiving hit the cooking pages of the *Times*. (Chitterlings, the wonderful, crackly pigs' intestines, became a favorite in our house and remained one until my parents started reading about cholesterol.)

If I don't recall precisely when announcements about a dish I'd mastered began to be greeted with queries about whether I'd done my homework, I do remember the evening when I came to understand the strength to my parents' disapproval of the reality that food continued to draw me more powerfully than academia did.

Our housekeeper was Anna Cherubini, whom my parents had found in Florence the summer after Suallen left. Anna's family ran a trattoria in Florence, for which she had been the sole chef until her husband died two years earlier, and was still the mainstay now that her sons ran it. But for reasons having to do with one son's wife, she had become unhappy there. She had consented to come to the States to work for my parents "for a few months," tending the apartment and, of course, preparing her lovely meals. The few months had stretched into a few years because her talents, unlike mine, were appreciated unequivocally by my parents, and because she and I developed a strong attachment to each other as I learned Italian from her, and she picked up English from me.

Anna was a Sicilian who'd married a Florentine, whose mother was from Genoa, and who was comfortable with a variety of cuisines. Anna did tripe in the style of Bologna,

Genoa, or Rome, liver Veneziana, or as cooked in Trieste or
Tuscany, fish soup as made in Sicily, Rome, or any of the
more than a dozen regions with their own fish and vegetable
favorites. Within months of coming to us, and with translation
and marketing assistance from me, she could also do a divine
brown sauce, a perfect *tarte tatin*, and various other dishes my
parents adored.

During my last term of high school, Anna got a call from
her son Anthony, who said she was needed desperately at the
restaurant. *Subito.* The call came on Wednesday morning. She
left Thursday night, promising that as soon as she was reset-
tled, I could visit.

I was far more disconsolate than I'd have been if my mother
had left. I was scheduled to begin Barnard in the autumn. I
made a couple of stabs at persuading my parents to let me apply to a good French cooking school, but they were convinced
that in college I'd find an academic subject, an *appropriate*
subject, that interested me more than cooking did. In the meantime, observing my continued depression over the loss of
Anna, they said that if I would cook as they asked, and as my
school schedule allowed, they would give up their live-in
housekeeper and provide me with something between an allowance and a salary.

Which is how I came to make dinner one Friday night for
their friends, the painters Jason and Eleanora Steinpark, who
owned a home in Gaiole, about half an hour outside of Florence. When Jason learned that the meal (*canederli*—dumplings
stuffed with prosciutto, because in those days I couldn't get the
proper ham even at Zabar's or in East Harlem; a *burridda*, the
one with two *d*'s, made with squid and lotte; Parmigiano-
Reggiano with an endive and walnut salad) was my work, he
congratulated me in Italian. I answered in kind and we got into
a conversation about food. He was startled by my knowledge-
ability.

"I must say, Caroline doesn't sound like a student with a
nice hobby," he told my parents at some point, laughing be-
nignly. "She sounds like a professional."

"I'm going to be," I assured him, although I hadn't actually
thought that far ahead. "I'm going to be a chef."

Silence. It was 1972, the height of the era that would later
be called The Sixties. Women were more worried about pregnancy and overweight than about contracting sexual diseases,

and if many parents would have been grateful for an eighteen-year-old who was so discreet about her sex-and-dope life that they didn't have to know it existed, mine were of a different mindset. Dope was no scarier to them than anything else that might keep one of their children from earning a Ph.D. Julia Child was splendid, as was Catherine Deneuve's prostitute in *Belle du Jour*, but you didn't expect your own children to make a living the way either of them did. (In my senior year I had become promiscuous, a word nobody would have used then and which I use now to describe a young woman who went to bed with almost any boy she kissed.)

My parents laughed uneasily. Jason needed help but he wasn't getting any. Eleanora wasn't attending to the conversation; she never did when it wasn't about her.

"Well," he finally said, "I think you're very sensible to be going for a degree. You can . . . sort of . . . have your academic cake and eat it, too." He laughed uncomfortably.

My parents joined him, a tiny bit less apprehensive than they'd have been if I had challenged his words.

But I was as restless at Barnard College as I'd been at Stuyvesant High School, where I'd done fine on the entrance exam, but then just scraped by in the endless math and science classes that were of no interest to me. If language still came easily, there was no Anna waiting at home to joke with about fancy folks' talk, as opposed to the good, idiomatic Italian she'd taught me. I was taking college French, but it was more fun learning Spanish from a Cuban friend at Barnard with whom I ate often at one of the good Cuban-Chinese restaurants that had opened along Broadway.

I was trying to figure out how to persuade my parents to subsidize one year's attendance at cooking school (delaying my second year at Barnard), when the Steinparks, apparently with their consent, asked if I'd like to work as their mother's helper in Gaiole that summer. I would prepare lunch and dinner for the family as well as breakfast for their eight-year-old son, Evan. I would be responsible for Evan six days a week as well as those evenings when his parents wished to go out, and I would make a serious attempt to get him to learn some Italian, which he'd resisted until now. Eleanora would be working particularly hard, and she and Jason would be eating at home more than they normally did, because she was preparing for her first major show. They would pay on the high side for that sort of job.

The summer worked well. Gaiole was hot but very beautiful, and there was a pool on the substantial plot of land in back of the house. The Steinparks also owned a vineyard that lay across the dirt road that passed their home. The dirt road led to a paved one, which, in turn, led to the *autostrada* to Florence. Most often Jason, Evan, and I drove to Florence, since Eleanora was under so much pressure. It was understood that Jason was not under similar pressure, but unless I'm mistaken, there was always some reason for life's being run around Eleanora.

In Florence we usually had lunch at the Trattoria Cherubini. The food was as good as one would have expected, I met Anna's sons and their families, and even if Anna was too busy to spend much time with me, I enjoyed seeing her briefly and knowing she was always nearby. A highlight of my summer occurred one afternoon when Genevra, the difficult daughter-in-law, who was also the better cook, wasn't around. Anna cut her finger badly and I was able, with Jason's consent, to take over. Anna stood next to me, holding clean cloths around her finger and directing me during what remained of the lunch hour.

My absorption in the matter of everyday life made it easier than it might have been to get along with Eleanora. When challenged about food (or almost anything), I became involved in finding the physical solution, whether it was learning why she adored *osso buco* only in Milan (the Milanese use no tomatoes in the sauce), or trying to duplicate the *tiramisù* from the restaurant in Florence that had nothing else of interest (it was their brandy). This also worked with Evan, who got hooked into kitchen matters and began to learn Italian from me very much as I had learned it from Anna.

Finally, I was fascinated by the operation of the Steinpark vineyard, run by Angelo Ferrante, who managed theirs and several others owned by nonresidents. This fascination led me into an affair with Angelo, an attractive-homely Sicilian of thirty-one who, before we ever sat down together on the grass, told me he had a wife and four children in Palermo.

Angelo was casually flirtatious from the beginning. I flattered myself that this was because I spoke a nontouristy Italian he could readily understand. He had English but wouldn't use it, and was given to pronouncements like "All American girls are spoiled." It is easier for me to quote such lines than to admit the corresponding truth, that I enjoyed, and later married, an outline and a cliché. Angelo was the dark, sexy peasant, as smart as he was uneducated, as strong as he was foreign to me. If he was tender only when aroused, this had to do with custom, and if he refused to absorb knowledge of other (American) ways of doing things, this was because rich Americans like the Steinparks always had an upper hand supported by wealth. Ordinary Italians couldn't compete, and so were left with no recourse but to fight domination. Surely there is some grain of truth to this argument, which, like most such arguments, takes no notice of broad variation in individuals, or explains why I hooked up with this particular person.

Our affair began less than two weeks after I'd arrived in June, but our friendship began on the day I told Angelo he should not judge all American women by the bitch I worked for. (He dealt only with Jason.) From then on, I saw him, or so I assumed, whenever he was in or near Gaiole. He taught me all the Italian words Anna didn't know or wouldn't use, often in the course of unburdening himself about Eleanora. As he complained and I sympathized, we grew closer and closer. But if Angelo ever fell in love with me, I would have to say that it wasn't my sympathies or the set of my mind, any more than it was my eyes, breasts, or any part—or the whole—of me he fell for, but, rather, it was my *caponata*.

Caponata is a dish that originated in Sicily and there are important regional differences in its preparation. As Angelo grew up with it, and as I had already mostly prepared it on the fateful afternoon when the Steinparks decided to take Evan someplace for an overnight visit, it contains not only eggplant, celery, olives, and so on, but sometimes bits of lobster, shrimp, or tuna—and here is the point where the tongues of true Sicilians separate them from others—unsweetened cocoa and slivers of toasted almond tossed on at the last minute.

I told Angelo that the Steinparks were away until the next morning and that I'd already made a *caponata*, which we might as well eat. Then, if he wished, he could stay with me in the house *durante la notte*.

When he arrived without having eaten, he usually asked for some bread and cheese. If I offered him a meal, he always said he'd eaten too much for lunch. Now he was sure he wanted to stay over, less certain he wanted to eat the meal I'd cooked. He said he'd take me out to dinner. I told him he should go out if he wanted to, and if he did, he should stay out.

He got it.

I can still hear his heavy step as he came to the table, picture his sudden alertness as he saw the Sicilian bread Evan and I had baked that rainy morning (made with semolina flour, it was heavily sprinkled with the poppy seeds Evan adored), his look of near disbelief when I began to ladle the *caponata* into the big, flat-bottomed bowls, being careful to leave some of the almond slivers on top.

I sat down facing him at one end of the long wooden table in the kitchen. He sliced some bread, bit into it, looked at the slice as he chewed, looked back at me. He moved the bread to his left hand, lifted the fork with his right, prodded various pieces of the *caponata*, raised the sauce-coated fork to his nose, sniffed it, carefully skewered a piece of fish and an olive, pushed the fork gently through the sauce, then, staring at the loaf of bread in front of him, lifted the fork, opened his mouth, and set in the food as though it were a bomb that still might explode. He chewed slowly.

I had become absorbed in the process and wasn't eating, but just watching him. The momentous nature of the occasion dawned on me only as his eyes, more softly focused than I had ever seen them and slightly moist as well, moved to meet mine for the first time. Still looking at me, he speared some more fish and vegetables, mopped up a little sauce, ate.

"Who taught you this?" he finally asked, a hush to his voice.

"I *told* you I could cook," I pointed out. "You should've . . . Anna," I finally said. "She was a Sicilian. *Is* a Sicilian." Anna hadn't added the cocoa and almonds at my parents', but she'd mentioned them, and I'd since found them in a Sicilian cookbook. Angelo had never talked much about his life, and I knew little more than that he'd grown up near Palermo and his wife and children were still there. Certainly he'd never mentioned preferring Sicilian food to all other. I'd thought of myself as taking a chance, preparing the *caponata* in that style. "She's the one I told you about, with the restaurant in Florence."

He nodded. The kitchen's atmosphere had grown close to a church's.

"Next week, we go there," he said. "In the meantime, you eat."

In the meantime, I ate. But our relationship had altered. I don't know if Angelo was in love with me, I know that I wasn't with him, but he couldn't keep his hands off me, became affectionate at times when there was no chance of getting me to bed—or to the blanket he took from his pickup truck and spread on the grass. And he came to the vineyard more frequently. During August he was around much more often than he'd been in July. I assumed this had to do with the ripening grapes until one day Jason winked and said they must have me to thank for the fact that Angelo was tending their vines more closely than in previous years.

Now Angelo and I invariably went into town on Thursdays, my day and night off. I'd introduced him to Anna, with whom he was at once filial and courtly, telling her, after our first meal at the trattoria, that if he hadn't anything else to be grateful to me for, he would always thank me for bringing him to her. He went to the men's room and Anna whispered to me that I should be careful about what Angelo had to be grateful for.

I giggled.

She shook her head, said she was serious, that he was a *damerino* if she'd ever seen one.

I hadn't known the word for ladies' man but could understand what she was saying and wanted to reassure (and deceive) her (and myself).

"Don't worry, we're just pals," I told her. "He has a wife and kids in Sicily."

"All the more reason," she said, "to watch yourself. He's a charmer." (*Incantatore*. Anna hadn't spoken a word of English since her return to Italy.)

At the beginning of my last week in Gaiole, as Angelo and I lay together one night on a tarp spread over hay in the back of his truck, I made a teasing remark about how long it would take him to find another girl for times when he was away from his wife.

"I don't have a wife," he said. "I tell them I'm married so they won't disturb my bachelorhood."

I was not nearly so startled as I should have been. Nor did

it occur to me to question his use of the feminine plural they—
esse—to describe people who might have disturbed him.

"I don't believe you," I exclaimed. "No wonder Anna told
me to watch out for you!"

He rolled back on top of me, looked at me seriously from
a distance of a few inches, and asked whether I would prefer
him to be married.

"I don't know," I said truthfully. "I guess it doesn't make
much difference."

He rolled off me and remained quiet during our brief remaining time that evening, then was alternately loving and
withdrawn during my last week in Gaiole. If he hoped I'd remain when the Steinparks went home, this didn't enter my
mind as a serious possibility. In New York I often suffered
from the feeling that I was the only member of my family who
hadn't a life to call her own. But Angelo seemed even less finished than I. Much too restless to be the sort of man with
whom one could imagine settling into a life.

Would that I had allowed this impression to remain with me!
Would that I had believed what I sensed, that the person between the outlining cultural dots was foreign to me, specifics
all too easily misperceived or misunderstood. Back in New
York, whenever school was going badly or I had no boyfriend
or one I didn't much like, I'd yearn to be with Anna. And
Angelo.

In fact, Angelo and I began a correspondence that subtly altered their order of importance, so that at some point it became
Angelo, and then Anna, I wanted to see again. If my letters
were mostly complaints about school, with discussions of movies I'd seen and an occasional anecdote about a friend or relative, his were rich in details of his past, some of which I later
ascertained to be true. He did have eight brothers and sisters,
all of whom lived, with their families, in Sicily, between
Castellemare del Golfo and Palermo. His father and one of his
brothers had olive orchards. The other brothers were fisher-
men, his sisters all had children. There were wonderful letters
in which he described the harvesting of the olives in November
and December, the green ones before they were fully ripe, the
purple when just ripe, and the black when overripe. All were
cleaned and rinsed in cold water, crushed in stone mortars or
under granite millstones, then kneaded and crushed again for
the first pressing. He wrote lovingly of the way the beautiful

flowers turned into berries; the first time he'd eaten an untreated olive he'd been horrified by the taste. He told me how
he inhaled with greater pleasure than any food or wine the first
pressed oil, and described the tables at the *vucciria*, the
marketplace in Palermo, where there was an olive vendor with
a differently prepared olive every time you took a step. I wrote
back that his description of eating an untreated olive had reminded me of the first time I hid in the bathroom with a stolen
cigarette and choked on the smoke. (Angelo had always
smelled strongly of cigarettes, and his dark skin had been
tough and discolored on his cigarette-holding fingers, but he'd
never smoked in my presence.) I asked what had made him
leave Sicily, when it was so beautiful. He wrote that he didn't
even like to talk about this, but his family's lands were Mafia-
owned and he couldn't abide the thought of being controlled
by the brotherhood. (*The Godfather* was already as well known
in Italy as it was in the States, everyone knew Americans were
infatuated with it, and I think he assumed, correctly, that this
explanation would appeal to me. If there was some truth in his
stories, it probably lay in his inability to get along for any
length of time with anyone who had power over him.) He described how, as a boy of nine, he'd left Castellemare for Palermo, where he worked the cigarette table in the *vucciria*. The
table would hold a pack of each kind of cigarette—Marlboro,
Winston, and so on. Customers would pay the man attending
it for a carton of whichever they wanted and moments later a
small boy—Angelo, or one of his brothers or cousins or
neighbors—would be tugging at a leg of his pants, giving him
the carton. More difficult was the fisherman's job of swimming
out to collect the cigarette cartons in the harbor, in plastic bags
thrown overboard from boats that were part of a chain set up
to avoid the *Guardia di Finanza*, the finance guard whose job
it was to collect the heavy cigarette taxes. Later the same chain
would be used for drugs. Later he had worked for a large land-
holder near Castellemare, but there'd been trouble. The guy
didn't want to pay the tribute, *il pizzo*, extorted by the Mafia
to do business. *Il pizzo* meant the beak of a bird. They always
wanted to dip their beak in your business. This was the life he
had run from when he was twelve, moving to Naples, where
he had been taken in by a woman who knew the owner of the
restaurant where he'd gotten a job washing dishes, though he

was always looking to get back to the wine. It took a long time.

Maybe.

I wrote Angelo that I wished I were in Florence and I was trying to save enough money to visit. (I already had more than enough, but it seemed wise to provide us both with an out.) He answered immediately, promising that if I could manage this, I wouldn't need money to live while I was there. He had begun working as a bartender at Anna's without giving up his vineyard jobs. We'd discussed the possibility of traveling together through Sicily. If only I would return to Florence, he said now, getting to Sicily would be easy. I resisted the increasingly strong pull of his letters for almost a year, perhaps sensing that if I went to Florence, I wouldn't return.

Anna's 1973 Christmas card came in November and contained an invitation to visit during Christmas. She had room for me to stay in her apartment, but I should be warned that I would be put to work along with Angelo and the others. Trattoria Cherubini had been discovered by an American film crew, and had subsequently metamorphosed from a workingman's restaurant into a fashionable café. The other fancy customers had remained when the film crew left. Then the family (the widowed Anna, her two sons, one of whom, Walter, was an engineer not active in the restaurant, and their wives) had been offered the opportunity to expand to the second story of their four-story building in the Oltrarno. With Angelo's help and encouragement, they had installed a large bar on the ground floor that he purchased the wine for and tended along with Anna's second son, Anthony, and which had become known for its extraordinary selection of Italian wines, many of which were not exported. They had nearly doubled the number of tables upstairs. This was all very well except that both daughters-in-law were pregnant, Delfina due in January, Genevra only a month later, and neither was much help. (Delfina was no good at the stove, anyway.) Anna couldn't understand why they'd done this twice in a row now, one getting pregnant right after the other. It wasn't even as though they were close.

My parents, sensing that I was up to something, refused my request for round-trip economy fare to Florence as a Christmas-Hanukkah present, but they'd been paying me fifty dollars a week (I was cooking at least four nights a week, usually more, and doing the shopping) and I had plenty of money saved. On the first day of my Christmas recess I flew to Italy, where, after an intense reunion with Angelo in the airport, then the front of his car, then the back of his car, then the room he rented he brought me to the trattoria.

My Italian, unused since my Gaiole summer, came back in such a way as to convey a sense of destiny about my return. The Oltrarno was a wonderful, lively mix of working people and tourists, expensive places and cheap ones, so that just to walk around it, when I could leave the restaurant for a few minutes, was a treat. (There was never time to travel farther.) I threw myself happily into work. Anna was pleased and grateful for my help and all the members of her family welcomed me in a way that made my visit feel like a homecoming.

It had been arranged in advance that I would stay at Anna's. I'm not sure how much the arrangement had to do with concern for her sensibilities, but as a practical matter, it worked for me to be there, two flights of stairs above the trattoria, able to come and go in a minute's time. During the holiday, when every chair was always occupied and there were never fewer than a dozen people at the bar, most of them waiting for tables, Angelo and I had to steal our times alone. If the person who had written me lovely romantic letters about the beauties of Sicily and the pleasures of my body was not in evidence, there was barely time to make love, much less think about it, and I could believe that my romantic correspondent would become visible when the holiday crowds thinned.

I used my diaphragm most of the time and I don't know precisely when I got pregnant. Pregnancy wasn't yet on my mind during the relatively slow day, December 30, when Angelo and I spent some morning hours in his room, and he laughed when I referred to my departure date, said he couldn't believe I was going to do the same thing again.

"What do you mean, the same thing?" I asked, though it had crossed my mind more than once that there was no law, other than the parental one, that decreed I had to return to New York and school.

Angelo said I had evaded my destiny after our summer together by going home instead of staying and marrying him.

I said, "I didn't even know you weren't married until I was practically gone."

He shrugged.

The message of that shrug, perceived only much later, was that he, Man, could do what came naturally to him, while I, Woman, should do what was right for Us . . . for the Family . . . for the Species. At the time all it evoked in me was the guilty recognition that no matter what else was true, if I had been in love with him, I wouldn't have left Italy the first time. I didn't know if I was in love with him now. I might be in love with the man who'd written those letters.

"How do you even know Anna would want me to stay?" I asked.

"Of course she wants you to stay," he said. "You help her much better than the wives."

"Okay. Anna wants me to stay. And you want me to stay. That doesn't mean we have to get married. We can live together."

"What are you talking about?" he asked in a whisper, this man whom I suspect was never faithful to me for a week at a time after the fourth or fifth month of my pregnancy. "Live together. You live together, you get married."

"Oh," I said.

You live together, you get married.

Life was simpler here. . . . And of course that simplicity had its appeal. I was nineteen years old. Nobody I'd gone to bed with had suggested we live together, much less marry. Not only was life simpler, but marriage would make it more so. Give me chapters and a verse I could bear to live by.

"You know I'm Jewish, don't you?"

It had never come up in our conversations, but then, it seldom came up at home, except in connection with holidays, or something one of my parents was studying—a German Jew's experiences during the war or the way some Italian's Jewish background came to the foreground in his paintings. We were Assimilated American Jews, all of us quite certain that the two *A* words came before the *J* one. If Angelo viewed me as more American than Jewish, this wasn't different from the way I viewed myself.

Angelo laughed shortly. "Jewish. What's Jewish?"

"I don't know," I said. "But I'm it."

"You go to Jewish church on holidays?"

"No."

"Your mama and papa go?"

"No."

"You don't cook Jewish."

"You mean kosher?" I asked, though I'm not certain that was what he had in mind. Anna had told me that *carciofi alla giudia*, artichokes Jewish style, were on the menu at most of the trattorias in season, but that was as close as anyone came to a Jewish cuisine.

Angelo nodded.

"No," I said. "I'm not a kosher Jew."

"Where does a Jew get married in Rome?" I asked a few days later, though it wasn't what was uppermost in my mind.

Angelo shrugged. "The courthouse. A Jewish church. Wherever Jews get married."

I said, "*You're* not a Jew."

He shrugged again. "A church, if you want."

"I don't want. I'm not a Catholic."

The issue bored him. A ceremony that doesn't matter formalizes a marriage that doesn't matter, but my period was a week late and I had begun to suspect I was pregnant. *Roe* v. *Wade* was not quite law, but I had a friend who'd gotten an abortion in Pennsylvania, and if I returned to New York, I'd surely go about finding one. That was my choice. I could return to New York, a place where an abortion and an education awaited me. Or I could remain in lovely Florence, surrounded by a family whose quarrels and problems had nothing to do with my own, and cook, and get married, and have a lovely, cuddly baby who would be like a grandchild to Anna. I could have something recognizable as a life.

When I told Angelo that I thought I was pregnant, he grinned, shrugged, and said he guessed that settled it.

So it did. I was due back in New York three days later. I called my parents to tell them I was getting married. Their reaction was such that I wrote only to ask them to ship me some cookbooks and clothes. I did not mention the immediate reason for the marriage. I told myself I might have chosen to remain with Angelo anyway.

Anna was pleased that we were getting married, delighted that I'd continue to work with her. There were no further warnings about Angelo. It would be three months before she was forced to notice that I was incubating yet another infant to interfere with the workings of her kitchen, and by that time, Genevra would be able to give her some help. I proceeded to fit myself as well as possible into Angelo's room and, with the time and energy left me after cooking at Anna's, to settle into Florentine life.

Actually, Anna's *was* my Florentine life, or, you might say, the trunk of that life, the branches being the various merchants the family dealt with, whom I was gradually getting to know, and of course family and friends of Anna and her children. By the time Olivia was born, on October 24, I felt almost like one of the family. The Cherubini family, if not the Ferrantes, for the first time I asked Angelo about Sicily, he said we'd best wait until the baby was born. At the time I assumed he didn't wish to offend them with our impropriety. Later, observing the distance he kept from most of his family when we were together, I came to think this had not been the only reason.

I waited six months to send my parents an announcement of Olivia's birth. (Angelo had begun chain-smoking in my presence, but he never smoked in Livvy's.) They called to congratulate me, wanted to know if they could visit their first grandchild during Easter vacation. I asked them to wait. If I was happy with my daughter and more comfortable than I had reason to be with the man I'd married, I feared my contentment would not hold up under their scrutiny. I had no sense of the extent to which grandchildren alter the attitudes of parents far more intractable than mine, muting disapproval and softening the ties that bind. When, weeks later, my father called to say they would love to visit during the summer, I told him— not, I'm happy to say, without crying—that I really needed more time. I knew all too well, I said, what they would think of my life.

Whether because of Anna's warm, steady presence, or because Delfina and I had grown close and she was always available for consultations about the baby and gossip about life, my early months with Olivia (whom I always called Livvy, my unthinking recognition that she was half American) were easy to the point of being idyllic. If she had been born red-faced, limb-wavy—*ipertesa*, hypertense, as the family doctor had announced to my righteous rage—it seemed to me that a long and difficult birth was enough to make anyone hypertense for a while, and I was determined to make her happy. I nursed her at the hint of discontent, slept when she did after breast feedings, held her in one arm if she awakened while I was doing chores, sang to her, kissed her, chattered with her when we were alone. No academic mother would I be—dry, distant, without intense feeling. This child would know how much I loved her, would take for granted her importance to me.

I would not be obliged to cook at the Trattoria Cherubini for three months, but our room was only two blocks away, so most afternoons I brought Livvy to the restaurant for a visit. Often I took over at the stove while Anna played with her. Although there was little to do at the vineyards during those cold months, Angelo was seldom around in the afternoon, nor had I begun to wonder where he was.

If there had been a change I didn't like when Angelo became my husband, if sex had survived the wedding but physical affection had not, if he seldom talked to me about what concerned him, and never mentioned Sicily or the wine business that had also intrigued me, he was such an adoring father as to silence any complaints I might have had. No need ever to ask whether he'd mind keeping an eye on his daughter; if he was around and unoccupied, that was where his eyes were. When he talked to me, it was likely to be about her beauty and charm. If I wanted to leave the house, all I had to do was check on his plans. If I asked him to take care of her, he'd want to know what I thought he was doing.

As time wore on, although I didn't allow myself to dwell on it, I grew resentful. If Angelo still turned to me in bed on nights when we came up the stairs together or mornings when there was no rush to go downstairs, nothing in his behavior or actions could have been described as lovemaking. He was like the boys I'd known in early adolescence who weren't yet dope-mellowed and needed only to get off in something alive.

When Olivia was six months old, Doctor Corrado said that Anna, now sixty-two, was showing problematic coronary symptoms and should slow down. I didn't believe him—he was the idiot who'd said my beautiful baby was hypertense— but I wasn't any more willing than the others to take chances. Anna shouldn't be walking up the two long flights from the trattoria to her apartment, so would move in with Genevra and Anthony, who'd drive her to the restaurant every day. Angelo and I would move into Anna's apartment, and I would resume my six-day schedule in the restaurant. There'd be no problem in keeping the baby there. Angelo cleared out and painted the tiny room, separated from the bar by a curtain, that had always been used for storage and in which there was now a fold-away cot. We added a small crib and a comfortable chair to turn it into Olivia's room, the place where she would rest and sleep during the hours when Angelo and I were working, and where Anna would be able to rest when she was tired.

Genevra couldn't imagine a baby sleeping peacefully down there, was sure Livvy would be better off upstairs, being checked on frequently, but I had no anxiety on the subject of keeping an infant in such a lively, noisy place. I'd spent my early years in a household I remembered as deathly quiet because everyone was reading or writing all the time. We hadn't even owned a TV set until the *second* Kennedy was shot. My daughter would grow up with the lively noises of people laughing and glasses clinking, and with two loving parents right nearby, ready to give her whatever she needed.

You will recall that a Sicilian trip had been (unnecessary) bait on the line that pulled me back to Italy. If I was disappointed when Angelo was in no hurry to bring me there, I was much too absorbed in my daughter, my work, and my new family to think much about it. But on the weekend before I was to take over at the restaurant, when Livvy was just past six months old, Angelo brought us to Sicily for her baptism.

His parents were well into their seventies by this time. They had nine children, twenty-six grandchildren, and several great-grandchildren and remembered few of their names. I doubt they knew I was Jewish, but they surely knew I was a foreigner. What seemed clear, as they kissed the baby, pronounced her beautiful in a ceremonial manner, and were as pleasant to me as they might be to a casual friend brought to some affair, was that Angelo was a foreigner, too. Whether this was the cause or an effect of his living so far from them, the family's easy camaraderie excluded him. When I asked him later about family favorites, he gave me one of his You-Americans-have-such-crazy-ideas looks, so I asked no further.

The baptism itself was neither long nor objectionable (two other family babies were baptized with Olivia). I remember little of the ceremony because there was so much else to take in. I'd had ample experience of Angelo's Sicilian chauvinism; often, holding Livvy, he would croon to her not the words of a song but a sort of extemporaneous ode to the island. I'd reacted with amusement or irritation, depending on my mood, but I'd never appreciated the legitimacy of his words.

If Sicily is not the most beautiful place on the face of the earth, it was, is, the most beautiful I've ever seen. As we drove on country roads bordered by gullies of wildflowers, past small farms where newborn goats and lambs were grazing, and craggy mountains with water trickling down their sides, I told myself I could never again be away from Sicily for any length of time. But that reaction was milder than the one I had at the market in Palermo.

The cuisines of Europe are said to have their foundations in Sicily. Whether or not this is true, Sicily has the broadest and richest collection of fish, the most extraordinary fruits and vegetables, ranging from the best figs in Italy to the nearly unimaginable variety of olives, from the best artichokes to the sun-dried tomatoes nobody in New York had heard of yet to the *bergamotto*, the wonderful lemony Calabrian citrus from which Angelo's mother made the world's best marmalade. To walk through the *vucciria* was to know, long before Angelo became fanatical about Sicilian food, that no actual pain would be involved in being limited to it. To sample the oranges and figs at one stand was to understand what America's lust for standardization has done to the taste and texture of our fruits. To bite, when it grows just cool enough, into one of the fried artichokes the vendor has taken out of its hot oil and put in a napkin, is to wonder whether you must leave this place without eating all the others. Many cooked dishes are offered at the *vucciria*, including a range of *fuori tavola*, foods eaten away from the table, both breathtaking and inspirational in terms of my own cooking. (It was part of the charm of our restaurant, when we opened it, that we served *fuori tavola* to people waiting for tables and at the bar.) There are the olive vendors Angelo had written of. There are cheeses and walnuts, candies and pastries, dried fruit and fresh fruit, and a quality and variety of fish unimaginable even by people who shop in excellent American markets. Some can be bought only raw, others—swordfish, tuna, and sardines—can also be found cooked in a variety of ways.

The *vucciria* left me subdued. Angelo and I had been married for a little over a year when we brought Olivia to Sicily. When he had complained about the quality of various ingredients obtainable in Florence, I'd heard him with the ears of someone who has found more and better ingredients there than she'd known to have existed. Now I understood that in Sicily there were foods richer and better than any I'd dreamed of. It did not occur to me then or for some years to question whether he might have remained there without working for the Mafia, or, if he had to leave, why he spent so little time there. The first answer, which I refused to believe until it was forced on me, was that he spent more time there than I knew. That from the early days of our marriage, there was no time when he didn't have a Sicilian mistress. That his lengthier trips often involved a visit to Sicily. And that when Olivia was toilet-trained and he took her with him, it was at one woman's house, or another's, that they stayed.

I wasn't immune, during our early years, to the dreaded What-Have-I-Done? disease. I was not only inexperienced at marriage, but still unwilling to acknowledge the extent of our cultural differences. I remember my confusion at the moment during that visit when Angelo's distance from me came to seem like a virtual blockade.

We'd had our last meal in Palermo at the home of his youngest sister. We'd drunk a lot of the red wine made by the brother with his own grapes and now we were drinking coffee with tiny *cannoli* from the market. Everyone was teasing me about my excitement over the *vucciria*, my desire to go back that morning when we'd spent much of the previous day there. Someone told a joke about a man who married a girl when she lived so close to the *vucciria* that he was intoxicated by its smells, then wanted to give her back when they moved away. We were laughing and I didn't hear Livvy fretting in her car bed just the other side of the kitchen. She might have been crying for a few minutes by the time Angelo heard her, went to get her, and brought her back to the kitchen, handing her to me because she had a load in her diaper, though he changed her as often as I did at home.

Half-tipsy, I took her from him. She wore only a long-sleeved undershirt and a diaper. Her arms and legs waved jerkily, her torso tensed with each outraged cry, her face was so red it was nearly purple.

I giggled, thinking of the purple olives at the marketplace. "Okay, Olivia. *Oliva mia. Mia piccola oliva purpura.*"

I began singing the best-known aria from *Il Barbiere di Siviglia*, substituting *"piccola purpura"* for *"Figaro, Figaro,"* dissolved into giggles, looked at Angelo to find a sign that he thought this as funny as I did, was startled to see that he was angry.

"What happened?" I asked, I think in English. I knew I wasn't supposed to call Olivia Livvy in front of his family, but I didn't think I'd done so. Livvy wouldn't even have led to my little *oliva* joke. I looked at the others; some were amused, some were too much aware of Angelo's reaction to have their own.

He took Livvy from me, resolutely went to the changing table, took care of the diaper himself, as though I'd proved myself unfit to touch his child, then put a drop of wine and a lot of water in a glass and sat down at the table, feeding it to her. The women and older girls were by this time clearing the table and washing dishes. Even the ones who'd been friendliest to me were reluctant to meet my eyes. I was afraid to lift a dish, lest I drop it. Angelo, his eyes steadily on his precious daughter as though to ascertain that she hadn't been irrevocably damaged by my joke, although he wouldn't discuss it with me, then or ever, signaled to me to pack up. Within twenty minutes we had said our good-byes.

While Anna was with us, Angelo's remoteness from me and from family concerns other than Livvy was tolerable. But when she was not yet sixty-five years old and Livvy was two, Anna died of a heart attack. Not only was her death a devastating loss, but before we were even out of the mourning period, it became clear that she had been the hub that allowed the spokes of our family's wheel to turn together. Now Anthony and Genevra had increasingly serious arguments with Angelo about management and expenditures. Walter, from the sidelines of his engineering job and against Delfina's wishes, sided with Anthony as they turned against Angelo and forced us out of the restaurant. Although I held none of what had happened against her, once it was done, Delfina felt she couldn't be my friend.

It was a ghastly time. Angelo was enraged and away from home a great deal as he tried to find a new job. In the meantime, he earned what he could bartending and selling to restaurants and liquor stores for a couple of vintners. I was depressed. I'd been deprived not simply of work but of my best friend in Florence. Of a life. And with this deprivation had come my first more-than-momentary unhappiness over the distance between my husband and me.

On nights when Angelo disappeared, I had told myself he was this *macho* Italian male who couldn't be questioned, never dwelling on the matter of what it was he couldn't be questioned about. Days and nights, watching his tenderness with Olivia, I had asked myself why he'd not touched me tenderly, lover-like, since we'd been married. But I hadn't allowed myself even to question the nature of this trait, whether, for example, it belonged to a group or an individual, and even if I'd had the courage to dwell on such matters, this was hardly the time to raise them with Angelo.

Olivia, accustomed to too many people and too much activity, and finding herself mostly alone with a depressed mother who talked to her at length about matters she couldn't comprehend, grew cranky and difficult. When Angelo was away, she went around looking for "Nanna" all the time, Nanna being Anna, while at some point during those months she ceased to call me Mamma and began calling me Cara, for Caroline, as Angelo and the others did.

Angelo decided to seek financing for his own restaurant. One evening, in a foul mood, he informed me that it was because of my youth that no bank would finance him.

"Dear, dear," I said, with a rage I'd seldom felt and he'd never seen in me before, "it's hard to see what *my* age would have to do with *your* restaurant. Is it possible you told them I was the cook? And they think the cook's the most important person in the place?"

Angelo raised his hand as though he were going to strike me but held it there, above his head, no doubt because Livvy was watching. After a very long time, he lowered the hand and walked out of the house. Livvy called to him. When he didn't return, she began crying that she wanted Nanna. At first, staring at the door, I just ignored her.

But finally, in a voice she'd never heard, I shouted, "No more Nanna! Nanna's dead! Gone! No more Nanna!"

She stopped in her tracks and stared at me for what seemed a long time, after which misery turned to hysteria.

She did not ask for Nanna again and resisted my efforts to talk with her about Anna in a more loving way.

* * *

I wrote my parents a real letter—as opposed to five minutes' worth of birthday or Christmas *merda*—and included a snapshot of Livvy and a promise that I was trying to prepare myself for a visit. I told them that if they'd suspected I knew I was pregnant when we married, they were, of course, correct. I said I hadn't felt I could handle their seeing me because I knew too well what they would think of my life, although some aspects of it were, or had been, just right. I told them of Anna's death and of our subsequent difficulties, and of how Livvy had adored Anna and missed her almost as much as I did. I said that the loss of my adopted family had forced me to feel more keenly than before the absence of my real one. Now I could only hope they would forgive me and come to see us as soon as possible.

They called to say they'd booked air passage for their Christmas vacation, but were having trouble finding a hotel room in Florence. Did we know of a place? It didn't have to be elegant. They were so eager to see us! I asked around but had no luck, and finally enlisted Angelo's help. A week earlier I would have been afraid even to ask him, but something had happened to alter his mood.

Angelo had created a résumé for me that said I was thirty-five (I was twenty-three) and had managed two restaurants in New York. With this résumé, and I don't know what else, he'd been able to get financing from a group of businessmen eager to reopen a once-great trattoria on the Via dei Greci in Rome. He'd told me, as though I should be purely and simply grateful, that we would be moving to that city, where I knew no one, and which, whatever its virtues, was huge, and foreign to me. My reward for making no protest was that within hours of my asking him, he'd arranged for my parents to stay with a woman named Helena D'Agni whose husband had once been Angelo's boss in the wine business, and who had turned her home into a boarding house after his death.

How would I look to them? I had gained about ten pounds in Florence, then lost it during my depression. And I had acquired, almost against my will, the sense of fashion that comes close to being universal among Florentine (and Roman) women. I swept up my hair in the artful fashion shown me by Delfina, used makeup as she'd taught me (I'd never even owned a lipstick in the States), and away from the restaurant, dressed in the bright reds and oranges, the deep greens and browns that became me, with my fair skin and light-brown hair. I'd picked up clever tricks with scarves and clips from women on the street. During my most depressed days I'd moped around the house in my robe, but when I went out, I'd still used makeup and worn decent clothes. I'd done it automatically, but now I wondered whether my parents would notice, and, if so, whether they would like the change.

I need not have worried. Once we'd hugged and kissed, they barely looked at me. Gus and his wife showed no inclination to have children; Beatrice and her husband had not begun trying. Olivia, now two-and-a-half, was their first grandchild. It was immediately clear to them that she was the most wonderful child ever born. They were thrilled to meet her father, who'd brought us to the airport, delighted to find her a blend of our best qualities. She had the biggest, most beautiful eyes and the shiniest black hair they'd ever seen aside from her father's. And so on. They didn't bother to enumerate her points of resemblance to me; for all their excitement, they knew what they were doing as well as they always had when they wrote grant applications.

In the car, as we drove toward the city, Livvy clung to me. When we reached Helena D'Agni's, Angelo helped us in with their suitcases, then left for Rome to negotiate with the contractor over some work on the new restaurant. Livvy and I would remain with my parents as long as we wished, then walk the three blocks back to our apartment. (The family was allowing us to remain there until Angelo had a job and we found a new place.) We'd hook up with my parents again when they were settled in.

It was eight-thirty A.M. by now, and a few of Helena's guests were at the long table in the dining room. My parents, who'd had only juice on the plane, were eager to eat, and as soon as their bags were deposited in the small but pretty room, we came downstairs. Helena invited Livvy and me to join them in the dining room.

The four people at the long table, which was set as for a formal dinner, were Italian tourists. While they were there, even when we were talking among ourselves, my parents and I spoke Italian. Livvy sat quietly on my lap. Every once in a while, one of my parents would ask her a question she'd answer (When are you going to start school? Don't know. Who's your best friend? Papa. What's your favorite color? Red. Now, what do you think of that? We just happened to bring you a red sweater! and so on), always, of course, in Italian. But when the others had left, Helena brought out a few of the lovely rice cakes that were her specialty. My parents adored those cakes and hadn't had them in years. In their excitement they began to speak, in English, about where they'd last savored them.

Livvy came to a different kind of attention. She had seldom heard English spoken outside of the restaurant. Angelo had told her that the people speaking it were Americans. (The English hadn't entered his frame of reference.) I'd explained to her on the way to the airport that my parents, who were coming to visit, were American, as I was, or once had been, but I don't think the idea of them had been solid enough for details to stick.

"Are they from the restaurant?" she asked me now.

My parents stared at her as though she'd just recited the rice cake recipe. Backward. In Cyrillic.

"You are wonderful," my father told her.

"Magnificent," my mother chimed in.

"Do your parents tell you how wonderful you are?"

Livvy smiled shyly.

They explained, alternating in their eagerness to connect with her, that they came from a place even farther away than Sicily, and it was called America, but the language was called English. Et cetera. If much of it was beyond her, it didn't matter. She liked the fact that they wanted to explain, was delighted when they offered to teach her some "American" words. They told her she could call them Grandma and Grandpa, repeating both words and definitions several times, explaining how they were Mommy's mommy and daddy, and so on. They told her that Livvy was sort of an American name, which made her thoughtful.

As we stood to leave, Livvy slid down me to the floor, went to my mother, who had stretched and was smoothing her hair (I noticed, for the first time, a couple of gray ones), and took her hand. Then she turned to my father and reached for his. "Grandpa," she said with a shy smile. "Nanna."

Tears came to everyone's eyes. (Perhaps I need to explain that Nonno and Nanna are Italian for Grandma and Grandpa.)

I said, "Anna was Grandma to her."

My mother kneeled and held out her arms to Livvy, who came into them.

From that moment on, they couldn't be torn away from one another. I thought my parents might want to change and rest. All three thought there was no reason this couldn't be done with Livvy in the room. I asked if they remembered how small it was, but I was thinking that there was room for three, but not for four. We went back upstairs, my father carrying Livvy. I saw my mother look around. Floral wallpaper, a white bedspread, and a cherry wardrobe, with two bottom drawers, which left a foot or so of visible carpet space around the bed. Pretty, but really tiny.

"It was the best we could do," I said, "and I figured better—"

"Talk in American," Livvy ordered me in Italian.

They stared at her in wonder.

"She's incredible," my mother said. "Please don't worry about the room. It's beautiful. And the breakfast was perfect."

It was agreed that I would do some errands and Livvy would remain with them for a while, then I would come back and pick her up so they could nap. The problem was, I had no errands. I'd assumed I would have to make dinner at our apartment, that there was no way to keep my parents from seeing the somewhat dark and dingy apartment where I lived, but they were in no hurry to see it. Maybe they knew what it was like. I stood at the bottom of the steps in Helena D'Agni's, forlorn. Unwanted. Nothing had changed in all the years since those childhood mornings when Gus and Beatrice and my parents all had things to do and places to go—schools, museums, libraries, whatever—and I had only to pass the time, trailing the housekeeper around the apartment until she finally went to the kitchen.

Helena D'Agni was clearing the last dishes from the dining table.

I asked if I could help.

She was startled.

I smiled, said that the grandparents and their grandchild were keeping one another busy, picked up the butter and jam from the table, followed her into the small but neat kitchen, joked about what would happen if I ever dared to put butter on our table, expecting she would ask why.

She nodded. "He's a real Sicilian." She stopped herself. And blushed brightly, *furiously*, red.

Ah.

So that was how Angelo had found a lovely room a couple of weeks before Christmas.

"So you know Angelo's Sicilian," I said lightly, and rattled on, it doesn't matter about what, as though I were in the kitchen and had set something on fire and made it flambé without thinking twice. Helena D'Agni, an attractive but not pretty, lively, heavyset widow somewhere in her fifties, feared that if she knew Angelo was "a real Sicilian," she must know other things about him that there was no obvious reason for her to know. Including what he was like in bed.

I knew now. Just because of the extraordinary blush. I knew what he was like with women he was married to and women he wasn't married to. I also knew, or thought I knew, who my competition was. I was less upset than I might have been, maybe because Helena was maternal rather than glamorous, perhaps because my absorption in the grandparents-grandchild love affair was keeping this romance from penetrating deeply. Or maybe I was just in shock.

Helena didn't have a dishwasher and I'd intended to dry dishes as she washed, but she was so uncomfortable having me around that after a few minutes I "remembered" an errand and said good-bye. Then, as I reached the street, I had an idea. If my parents' suitcases were emptied, I could store them at home so they wouldn't clutter up the tiny room. I turned around and went back upstairs.

Since this was the hour when Livvy usually napped, and she'd become so comfortable with my parents, I thought she might have fallen asleep. I knocked very softly, then opened the unlocked door. Livvy was, indeed, curled up at one side of the bed, happily asleep. Back to back against my daughter was my mother, and then, facing my mother, his arms around her, was my father. They, too, appeared to be asleep. And of course they were dressed. But as I watched, they snuggled even closer to each other, and their faces touched, and they kissed lightly, then passionately.

When I could move, I closed the door and went downstairs, leaving the boarding house without saying good-bye to Helena. I didn't know where I was going, but it wouldn't be home.

It was the first time I'd actually understood that my life

rested on false assumptions. My parents, particularly my father, had always been visibly affectionate with each other; my brain had refused to connect their affection to sex. After all, they hugged and kissed us, too. Never mind that they'd had three children. Intercourse didn't have to be all that sexual. Then there was the converse cliché of peasant warmth and affection, the fantasy that had carried me, when I was no longer a kid, through pregnancy and marriage to someone whose brain was foreign to me. Once I'd asked Angelo why he never—I think it was why he never came up behind me to hold me, lift my hair and kiss my neck, as he'd done before. He'd looked at me as though I were crazy and said, "You are my *wife*." An answer so absurd that it had silenced me, although I now had to see the parallel between those words and my view of my parents' marriage.

I had never seriously considered leaving Angelo except for long enough to get some ingredient I couldn't find in our neighborhood. Now, as I walked, I tried briefly to let my mind roam among the possibilities for another life. It resisted. It could not contemplate either winning or losing a custody battle with Livvy's father.

What it could think about was dinner for my parents. They'd told Angelo they wanted to take us all out. But not only would shopping and cooking help me pass time, suddenly I was eager for them to see the way I lived, to take in what until now I'd wanted to conceal. I wanted them to register a horror that would make me *do* something. Or, alternatively, that would help me understand how to remain with Angelo, to believe our lives might be better in Rome.

It was all a fantasy, of course. They would have been horrified by any salvation fantasy that included trying to take Livvy from her father.

Their adoration of Livvy smoothed over spots that might have been rough during the visit. They were wonderful with Angelo, questioning him at length about the wine business and Italian wines, marveling at his expertise, nodding and clucking as he explained how Eleanora Steinpark had prevented her husband's vineyard from doing as well as it might have. He, in turn, nearly puffed with pride as they marveled over Olivia's beauty and brilliance, the extraordinary ease with which she was learning the English words they were teaching her, the quality of the questions she asked. If his face clouded over when Olivia asked me to make rice cakes like Helena's (he detested rice), this was quickly forgotten when my father said that soon she would be writing the recipes for them. And he appeared to be pleased when they said they would try to rent a summer house in one of the beach towns outside of Rome. By then we would have moved. They hoped Livvy would be able to spend lots of time with them.

Our only rough moment came during their last evening, as we sat in a restaurant Angelo had chosen because the friend who owned it was crazy for Livvy. My father began to describe an extraordinary meal they'd had with friends in Bologna. *Maiale al latte.* Pork loin braised in milk.

Angelo put down his glass. He looked nauseated.

"Is anything wrong?" my father asked.

Angelo picked up his glass, but didn't respond.

"I thought you knew already," I said with a laugh. "He can't stand butter, milk, any cow stuff but cheese, and he thinks they're really disgusting with meat."

My mother giggled. "And we thought he wasn't Jewish."

"It's nothing to do with Jewish," Angelo said, turning to her. "I don't like the *taste*."

"This pork loin might change your mind," my father said, so absorbed in his taste memory as to be insensitive to Angelo in a way that was unusual for him. "They use a little butter in the oil, and then, after the meat's browned, they add milk"—he'd closed his eyes and didn't see Angelo fighting with himself about leaving the table—"and later, uh, whipping cream. And Parmesan. Sometimes, not always." He smiled. "The Parmesan, I mean." He opened his eyes, was startled to see Angelo on his way to the men's room, glanced at my mother, then at me, smiled and shrugged.

The matter of dishes mixing meat and dairy products did not arise again, but shortly after we'd moved to Rome, my father sent me, with a note saying he was sure Angelo would enjoy it even more than I did, a book called *The Classic Cuisine of the Italian Jews*. I didn't even open it. If my father's impulse in sending it had been mischievous but benign, I knew Angelo better than I'd once been willing to and sensed the trouble it might cause. Life was complicated enough.

Complicated, but not really awful. In the last couple of months before our move, if Angelo wasn't home, I usually knew where he was. He had become thoroughly absorbed in dealing with contractors, buying equipment, and overseeing every aspect of the restaurant's renovation. Even Livvy saw little of him during this time—or during our early months in Rome. She did not appear to mind, although she usually ran to him at the end of the day with an eagerness suggesting she'd been waiting the whole time.

When I returned to the States, my friends who knew Rome would be sympathetic to hear I'd lived on Via dei Greci, one of the tiny alleys close to what they called the Spanish Steps. They remembered the noise, the commerciality of the area, the tourist hordes. I minded none of the above. In fact, my misery became even less dense within days of our move. I was enchanted with the blooming azaleas on the Steps, thrilled to hear English (not to speak of German, Japanese, and Swedish) being spoken, delighted to follow Livvy as she climbed toward the top, asking any tourist who greeted her if he or she was American. She loved steps but we'd seldom been near any in Florence recently except the steep, dark ones up to Anna's— our—apartment. There was no time of day or night when the Steps weren't covered with hundreds of people, many of them kids, quite a few of whom had managed to bring their guitars to Rome. These public places were a wonderful solution for a mother who didn't have the will to look for friends for herself or her kid but needed human life and noise around them.

I slept later than I'd have expected to, given the noise from the workmen below. In the morning, Livvy and Angelo shared an early breakfast, then he went downstairs and she climbed into bed with me, sometimes with a picture book. Often I awakened to find her nestled against my back in a way that reminded me of her with my parents in Florence. Once up, I'd make myself a *caffè latte* and have it with a chunk of bread and jam—when we had it, *bergamotto*—while Livvy had her second piece with the ghastly American grape jelly my parents sent her, which they'd explained that American kids loved. (When I was young they'd refused to buy "junk" like grape jelly and American cheese.)

Our apartment, which belonged to the syndicate that owned the building and the restaurant, was all brown leather, chrome, and glass. Not uncomfortable, but not a warming place to be. When we'd finished breakfast, I would dress and help Livvy, then we'd head downstairs with her collapsible stroller, also a gift from my parents. (We'd never had one in Florence, no doubt one of the reasons she was walking when she was eleven months. Angelo always picked her up the moment she got tired.) We'd wave to the workmen, stop to say hello if Angelo was around.

I remember Livvy's triumph the first time she made it to the top of the Steps on her own, how she ran around telling people she'd done it by herself. The first time she heard people speaking English, she asked if they knew her Nonno and Nanna. She loved the fountain near the base of the Steps, which she called the *fontana di barca*, the boat fountain. Once she'd seen older kids doing it, she insisted we walk the narrow path to the stone barge in the middle of its pool. She also liked the Fontana di Trevi, about fifteen minutes from home, and the one she called the *fontana di pesce*, the fish fountain, in front of the obelisk in the Piazza del Popolo.

As Rome grew familiar, we ventured farther and farther. On a happy day a month or two after we'd moved, we stumbled upon the wonderful *fontana della tartarughe*, the turtle fountain, which was responsible for Angelo's and my first serious fight in Rome. It stands at the center of a small courtyard in what is still known as the Jewish Ghetto. It is surrounded by very old stone and stucco buildings, at least one with a beautiful courtyard of its own. Around the fountain's pedestal, holding the big saucer with its water spout, are four naked, very beautiful boys. At first, you think they're sort of sitting, but as you examine them closely, you realize they're standing and leaning against the pedestal. Each rests one foot on a dolphin. Each lifts a turtle to the fountain's huge saucer, above his head. Water from that fountain and from a couple of spitting satyrs under it runs down the front of the boys' bodies. Setting off the pool from the surrounding square is a very low wrought-iron railing, easy to climb under or over.

On a morning not long after Livvy and I had discovered the turtle fountain, we came downstairs and walked through the dining room, looking for Angelo so we could say good-bye. He was in the kitchen next to the newly delivered stove, yelling at the guy who'd delivered it that it was *rugginoso*. Rusty.

He stopped yelling when he saw us, took Livvy from me, kissed her. She asked him what *rugginoso* was. He explained, his voice low and caressing, his anger gone, as it was always gone when he spoke to her, no matter what had happened before. A reality of which I continued to be jealous.

He showed her the rust spots on the stove, then he kissed her again and handed her to me with a signal to get her out fast. I obliged him. But before we'd even reached the Steps, Livvy announced that she wanted to go to the turtle fountain.

We made our way down the Via del Corso, around the Piazza Venezia, toward the courtyard with the fountain. Nobody was there, except a man sweeping in front of one of the buildings. Livvy climbed out of her stroller and, with one hand on the rail, began to circle the fountain, stopping at each boy to regard him seriously and at length. She showed no interest in the trickly water she usually wanted to put a hand in. Finally she settled in front of one of the boys. They're all so beautiful and graceful that their models might have starred in some ballet movie, but over the years, the streams of water have left rusty trails down their bodies, most particularly down the torso, the penis, and one leg of the boy in front of whom Livvy had stopped.

Suddenly I understood.

"The boy is rusty, just like the stove, isn't he," I said, smiling as she looked up at me.

She nodded seriously, sat down on the cobblestones of the courtyard, and stared at him for a long time, consenting to get into the stroller only when I told her we could search for rust in other places. As we walked home, I pointed out spots on car fenders (or she pointed them out to me) and explained why she mustn't touch them.

The following morning we came downstairs to find Angelo's rusty old Fiat parked in front of the restaurant.

Livvy pointed to the fender and said it was *rugginoso*.

"Do you believe this child?" Angelo asked proudly, looking around to see if anyone else had heard. "I tell her a word once and she—"

But Livvy had already turned to me to say, *"Voglio vedere il ragazzo con il pene rugginoso."*

I want to see the boy with the rusty penis.

"I meant to tell you yesterday, Angelo." I giggled. "We went to the fountain, you know, with the—"

He was furious. "I don't believe what you're teaching the child!"

"Wait a minute," I said. "She learned what a penis was because she had boy cousins who—"

"Stop!" he shouted, no longer concerned with whether workmen were listening.

I stopped. Waited. He had been about to hand over Livvy to me, but now he wasn't sure I could be trusted with her.

"Sweetheart, you want to come with me in the car?"

She nodded. She must have assumed that she would get to see her boy again. But that night her father informed me that I was never to take her back to that place. I didn't argue or point out that all over Rome there were statues of naked men and boys. The next time Livvy wanted to see the turtle statue, I told her to ask her father. She never did; she just kept asking why I wouldn't go there.

I wrote my parents, telling them the whole story. I said I hoped they wouldn't mind if I confided in them from time to time; I hadn't a friend in Rome to share jokes with or help me get things off my chest. They said that of course I should write, but they thought life would be better once I was working again. Maybe I should start planning the menu. Opening day wasn't that far away, after all. I took this excellent advice.

If you know even a little about Italian food, you know that Italy has many regions, each with its own favorite dishes and modes of preparation. Some dishes—omelets, sardines, salt cod, artichokes, eggplant, and lasagna come to mind—are prepared in many regions, albeit with variations. While Anna had always been willing to try any recipe and had a wide range of their dishes on her menu, she understood that men, in particular, tended to prefer those remembered from childhood and to resent deviation. One of the reasons she got along with Angelo was that she had a bias toward the Sicilian, but, when she experimented, never gave the result the name of a classic Sicilian dish. Walter and Anthony, raised in Rome by parents with more catholic tastes, were open to new dishes and had scorned Angelo's provinciality.

Our wedding feast, because there was no negotiation with Walter and Anthony (Angelo's problems were just with Anthony, but from the time of our ouster, we lumped them together), included *caponata*; *farsumagru*, the stuffed beef that was Angelo's favorite main course in the world, meat having been a precious commodity in the poor seaport where he was raised; *pasta con le sarde*, that is, with fresh sardines brought up from Sicily by our supplier the morning of the wedding; a wedding cake that was essentially a *cassata siciliana*, the extraordinary layered pound cake with almond paste, candied fruit, and unsweetened chocolate; and superb *cannoli*, another Sicilian classic.

The arguments about food when nobody was getting married were kept under control while Anna was alive but grew in number and intensity after her death. As much as any about money, quarrels over the menu between Angelo and Anthony had precipitated our ouster.

Friday dinners in Angelo's home, where the family fasted through breakfast and lunch, had consisted of *pasta con la mollica*, pasta with breadcrumbs and anchovies, fresh ones whenever possible. Anthony was accustomed to having the dish with Parmigiano-Reggiano and liked it that way. Angelo's family had used only breadcrumbs, an even more important staple in Sicily than elsewhere, and the idea of using cheese, or even a mixture of breadcrumbs and Parmesan, was repellent to him.

Angelo's mother didn't use rice, though many Sicilians do. Little filled rice croquettes, *arancini*, are sold like sandwiches at bars in Sicily. If they're not wonderful, they're awful, and Angelo had long since dismissed them and anything else made with rice as unfit for human consumption. Anna's sons had been raised eating as much rice as pasta, there had always been *risotti* on their menu, and Angelo wouldn't have dared to quarrel over them, even if they'd been less popular. But one of the first arguments in the spring after her death had been about *risi e bisi*, a rice dish with peas and pancetta that Anthony was crazy about and told me to put back on the menu after Angelo had ordered me to take it off.

Gnocchi and *polenta* were two other northern dishes Angelo disliked. Nobody in the family cared much about *polenta*, but *gnocchi* had always been on the menu. It occurred to me that it would be fun to play with *gnocchi*, which are usually made with potatoes, and with *canederli*, dumplings from the northern border territory of Trentino, but this time made with stale bread instead of mashed potato. I felt virtuous in my choices, all of these items being cheap to make at a time when we were concerned about keeping expenses down to please our investors.

Though it was spring and the dish was economical, I dismissed the possibility of putting *risi e bisi* on our new menu. Nor did I consider most of the Florentine or Milanese specialties (turkey and anything with spinach come to mind) that I knew Angelo detested. *Risotto*, a universal classic, was another matter and we'd always had its variations on the menu at Anna's including the classic *risotto alla milanese*, which is made with butter. He'd kept quiet about that. But one of his rare spats with Anna had occurred when he said something nasty because she'd put *arancini* on the menu. She'd informed him they were a Sicilian classic and he'd vehemently denied this, saying that the fact that you could find them at a lot of cheap bars and sandwich joints didn't make them a classic. (At other times he railed against the snobs who wouldn't give a cheap bar or sandwich house a chance.)

If Angelo had fallen in love with my *caponata*, praised my preparation of various dishes, asked me to learn others, and shown a continuing desire to eat the food I prepared, he had at some early point in our marriage begun to take my cooking for granted, as he took it for granted that my warm body would be waiting in bed when he chose to enter one or both. I'd assumed that even if he was too absorbed in the problems of renovating and reopening a restaurant before the tourist season to think about my misery, he understood, in his own way, that the loss of my adopted family, not to speak of my occupation, had been as painful to me as his quarrels and losses had been to him. Surely he would be pleased to learn that I'd turned my attention to our new menu, that I was already working hard to make the restaurant a success.

On this evening, once I'd cleared the dinner dishes, I proudly set before him the lists I'd made: pots and equipment we'd need; suppliers and cleaning help that still had to be found; and, finally, the menu. Three pages, headed *Antipasti, I Primi* and *I Secondi*.

Angelo remained at the table, with Olivia, three-quarters asleep, on his lap, as he looked at my lists. After a while, he stood up slowly so he wouldn't awaken her, and carried her to the bedroom. When he returned, he refilled his wineglass, sat down, looked at the menus again. Had he noticed the Sicilian classics Anna never made, most notably Emir of Catania's Chicken, in which the chicken is baked in a loaf of hollowed-out bread instead of with rice? I thought he would be particularly pleased with this dish because, though he didn't care for chicken himself, he didn't hate it, and it was economical.

Now he handed me back my pages and said, without looking up at me, "No *risotto.*"

"I don't understand." I warned myself to stay calm. "I mean, I know you don't eat it but—"

"This is a Sicilian restaurant," he said. "No *risotto.*"

"So many people order it," I began. "We always—" But before I could finish, he'd stood up and was folding his plans.

"Where are you going?" A question I didn't normally ask.

"What difference to you?"

"What difference is anything to me?" I asked. "We both want Trattoria Angelo to be a success, we both—"

"No Trattoria Angelo," he said. "It stays Lambino. Like before."

My tears were checked. It must have been the owners' insistence. Was he already having trouble with them? But why couldn't he even have told me?

"I'm sorry."

He shrugged. "It doesn't matter."

It did matter, but I knew better than to insist.

"Where're you going?" I asked again as he headed for the door.

"What difference to you?"

"If you're taking a walk," I said desperately, "I wouldn't mind going with you."

"Olivia is sleeping," he said as he opened the door. "Only one can go."

Lambino, seating forty comfortably, another six to ten in a pinch, and with a long bar, an extremely good collection of Italian wines, some unavailable elsewhere, a genial bartender, and a chef who apparently received a great deal of praise from the diners, though it was seldom relayed to her, opened on July first and did extremely well so quickly as to banish from the chef's mind all thoughts not connected to its kitchen.

I had no hired assistant, although one of the two waitresses, Benedetta, assisted me between lunch and dinner with the washing and slicing of vegetables and other prepping chores. The second waitress was Isabella, who was young and pretty and who'd come up from Naples to live with her aunt. Isabella did not stay in the restaurant between the time we finished serving lunch and six P.M., when she returned for dinner. The only men on the premises, aside from Angelo, were the dishwasher, a sad, elderly gentleman named Salvatore who was permanently hunched over from a life at the sink, and Tomaso, a small, wiry Neapolitan who came to Rome on Friday afternoons, worked at the bar with Angelo Friday and Saturday nights, and returned to Naples on Sunday. During the week, Angelo handled the bar by himself.

He also made the almost daily trips to the Mercato Generale for meat and produce, and to the small seaport beyond it, Fumicino, where the fish prices were better than Rome's. Other suppliers came to the restaurant. Once or twice I'd told Angelo I wanted to accompany him to the markets to get a better feeling for what they sold, but he'd always claimed I was too busy and there wasn't anything he hadn't told me about. Certainly the first part of this statement was true. Actually, it was only when he took Livvy with him that I could work without interruption. In fact, during those last, frantic days before we opened, and then in the crush of our first tourist season, I went from being a mother whose greatest pleasure lay in being with her daughter to one who was constantly trying to get her out of the way.

These are the days Livvy remembers when she talks about her childhood. When she recalls the fountains and statues of Rome, she remembers her father as having taken her to them. When she began to tell her tales about the mad monster of the kitchen, I could never say any particular story was a lie. Only that the whole picture was wrong. Nowhere in it was the mother who adored her, hugged and kissed her, read her stories, was easily patient when not cooking dinner for forty or fifty people at a time. That mother seemed to have vanished from her memory so thoroughly as not to have existed.

During the incredibly busy summer months, Angelo kept Livvy out of the kitchen altogether, carrying her meals to the dining room when we were closed, to the little room in back of the bar when we were open. It was a great relief not to have her underfoot downstairs, and the truth is that since it was midnight by the time I'd finished wrapping and storing or throwing away unused food and dragged myself upstairs to bed, I only dimly registered, for a while, that she was avoiding me. I first felt her distance in a more than momentary way when October had come and gone and the number of meals had diminished to a point where they could be prepared by a mortal. Isabella began working Friday to Sunday only. Benedetta could handle the Tuesday-to-Thursday crowd. I calmed down some. Livvy began occasionally to look at me when I spoke, allowed me to kiss her good night, though she never kissed me back. Given the choice of a walk for *gelato* with me or a ride with her father to the fish market, she invariably selected the latter, but that seemed natural when she was accustomed to being with him. It took time for me to become upset about the continuing gap between us. I've learned that most little girls go through a period of preferring their fathers, but even if I'd known it then, I doubt I could have separated her coolness from what happened in the kitchen. How can I separate them now, when they are still simple cause and effect in her mind?

As business slowed, I became friendly with the wife of the couple who ran a framing shop a few doors from us. Vera. They had two stores and her husband was normally at the other one. More important, they had a daughter, Bettina, who was only a little older than Livvy. Vera was happy to have the girls play together in the back of her shop and, later, at her home. I could reciprocate painlessly by making them welcome in the restaurant during all but peak hours. Often, when there were no customers, Vera would hang up her sign and bring over Bettina, who'd play with Livvy while the two of us had coffee and pastry, or a glass of wine.

Vera and I didn't complain about our husbands except in that general Aren't-Men-Impossible? way. But as the years passed and Livvy was in school all day, Angelo grew casual about using our apartment with whomever he was screwing. Even then, if they were careful and I didn't have to notice specifics, I could make believe it wasn't happening. But at some point I began to find hairpins on the floor and the bed remade in a careless fashion. And then I found an unfamiliar lipstick on the bathroom sink.

The following morning I left a note, written with the lipstick, on the mirror: *Attention Occupants—Please clean up this bathroom and leave the bed as you found it.*

My husband was furious.

"What if I didn't see it and Olivia came home?"

I stared at him, astounded, after so many years of living with him, by his ability to ignore the crucial aspects of any question.

"First of all, she can't read that well," I said, then cursed myself for entering the fray on his grounds even as he was leaving, slamming the door behind him. The door had become his standard last word to our arguments.

"I was very naive," I said to Vera the next afternoon. It was four o'clock, the restaurant was closed, we'd had lunch and were sitting inside with our espressos while the girls played on the narrow sidewalk outside. "When Angelo used to disappear, it never occurred to me that he was screwing around."

Vera shrugged. "They all do it."

I laughed. "They can't all do it. There have to be some who're happy with just . . ." She had three other children, ranging in age from eight to sixteen. "When did you . . . did you always assume it would be that way?"

"Each wife thinks she will be different," Vera said. "Each thinks she's the first to drive him wild. Vincente was crazy for me. I was sure he would never want anyone else."

"And what happened?"

Another shrug. "Nothing happens. The craziness passes, and then they want it back, and they look someplace else."

"So, what do you do?" I asked, feeling stupid, but it was the question on my mind. What do I do? How do I live?

"What is there to do? You tell yourself the Isabellas, too, will get married and have children and the same thing will happen to them."

"Isabella?" I was startled.

Now Vera was confused and upset. "I thought . . . Mother of God . . . I thought that was who you were talking about."

"Because you thought—or because you knew? And you thought I knew?"

She looked down at her lap for a long time.

"I didn't know," I said.

"I'm sorry," she said.

"You don't have anything to be sorry about," I assured her. "I'm not sure it matters who . . ." I let the words trail off. I was remembering how eager to please me Isabella had been until a month or two after she'd begun, when, I could say now, she'd ceased volunteering help, stopped speaking to me except when she had to, no longer met my eyes. I hadn't thought twice about what had been a not uncommon trajectory at Anna's, from new employee, eager to please, to old hand who didn't bother to look at you. Some came to understand and tolerate the kitchen's tempo, others never did. They stayed if they needed a job and there was nothing better around. Isabella lived with her aunt, which gave her the flexibility to accept part-time work when that was all we required, although it deprived her of a place to go with Angelo.

Oh, my God! The little room in back of the bar! There was a sofa bed in it, ostensibly because one of the owners might want our apartment occasionally for a night and we'd have to sleep downstairs. I'd heard nothing about the owners since we bought the sofa bed. Angelo, when I'd finally questioned him, had told me they'd decided to stay at the Hassler rather than disturb us. At the end of a night's work, when I dragged myself upstairs and had to force myself even to wash and brush my teeth before I fell into bed, Angelo could easily put Livvy into hers and go back downstairs.

Tears came to my eyes. Right in our real home. The *restaurant*. The part of our home where I lived.

I told my parents the next time they came. They advised me to keep silent on this matter. Pretend not to be aware, but keep track of what I knew. Just in case. It was excellent advice. Discussion was futile. Angelo wasn't going to change and he wasn't going to let me take my daughter with me if I left him, which meant I wasn't going to leave.

I dealt with Isabella by pretending not to hear her when she spoke to me. I thought she might feel too guilty to complain to Angelo. It was a calculated risk that worked. She left after being paid on a Sunday night and wouldn't come to the phone when Angelo called to find out why she hadn't shown up the following Friday. He feigned puzzlement but immediately replaced her with someone slightly older and somewhat less pretty. Someone I might have assumed he wasn't screwing if I hadn't begun to comprehend the range of his taste. Or lack of it.

Each year Angelo spent more time away from home. At some point I began to wage my rebellion through food. I bought my first chunk of sweet butter, storing it, like a fourteen-year-old hiding a diaphragm, in the back of the refrigerator bottom, bringing it out, when Angelo had left on one of his trips, to play with various *risotti* (a Venetian dish, *risotto di secole*, with leftover bits of roasted beef and veal, and then a

Milanese favorite, with beef marrow, another item that hadn't previously seen the inside of our kitchen). Eventually I began to experiment more broadly, making dishes like a northern-style *stoccafisso*, in which cod is layered with artichokes and potatoes and covered . . . with milk. This last I didn't dare leave in our refrigerator but gave to Benedetta to take home.

On a Friday when Angelo hadn't returned from the market by noon, and I was growing frantic about who would manage the bar at lunch, Tomaso, who usually came at four, appeared. He said he'd come up early on an errand and would just hang around. A few minutes later, Angelo called to say he was having car trouble and would be late. We were years past the time when I believed in such coincidences.

It was a holiday week. The girls had been at Vera's and she'd brought them back for lunch. As I stirred sauce on the stove, I suggested without thinking twice, an understudy who's been waiting for months to hear that the star had a cold, that they try something new I had in the refrigerator. It had *pancetta*. I reheated the *risotto* for all of them. Vera was amused but nervous. I'd long since told her about Angelo and *risotto*. Livvy wanted more but didn't care about the name of what she was eating. Her brain had no interest in food.

Angelo arrived home at four with the fish and vegetables. He was in a jocular mood as, in Tomaso's presence, he told a dramatic story of the car's stopping dead in the middle of the highway. When I failed to respond, he said he hadn't had lunch. I told him there was a meat-leftovers *risotto* he might care to try. He laughed as though I'd gone slightly mad. Nothing so serious it had to be tended to. He had a meatball and eggplant sandwich and a large glass of Cerasuolo, a Sicilian rosé of which there was half a bottle in the bar refrigerator. He asked where Livvy was and I said she was probably with Bettina but they might have gone to another friend's.

I sat down with him at the table closest to the kitchen, poured myself the remainder of the rosé, was reminded of how little I liked it, threw it away, and poured a glass of the Tuscan wine that was then our house white, although Angelo wouldn't touch it. He finished eating, stood, stretched, said he was sorry there'd be such a rush with the fish. I said that my sauces were done and I wanted to talk to him. He sat down.

"So?"

If I told him I just felt like talking, he'd think there was something wrong with me, a sort of *risotto* of the brain, so I reminded him that there was a time when we'd spoken of expanding the menu. We'd been so busy all the time since we'd opened that we had both sort of forgotten about it. But I'd been cooking almost the same dishes, year after year, and I needed to try something new. Not necessarily *risotto*, though I was making some terribly good ones these days. But *something*. I was bored.

He nodded, doubtless because his brain wasn't engaged yet. He stood up.

"I thought we were going to talk for a couple of minutes."

"So? We talked."

"We didn't settle anything. I mean, not in my mind, and I'm the one who's bored with the cooking."

He looked at the ceiling, went to the bar, came back with a bottle of Chianti, sat down. He filled his glass.

"So? What do you want from me?"

I'd accomplished something; his good mood was gone.

"I mean ... ." It wasn't the way I'd meant to say it, but there was something so aggressive about his boredom, he had so little interest in whether my life was reasonable. "I'm used to the fact that you never say anything good about the food, tell me you couldn't have a restaurant without me. But if I want to put a *risotto* on the menu, the least you can do is discuss it with me."

"*Risotto?*" For the first time he realized it was serious. "Are you crazy?"

"No, I'm not crazy, but I'm crazy about *risotto* and I know people ask for it and I'm the chef and I want to make it sometimes."

"You're crazy about it, you make it. You make it, you eat it."

"Livvy's crazy about it, too." It had been there, waiting, from the beginning. "She had it for lunch today. She likes rice."

He stared at me. He sipped at the wine in his glass without ceasing to stare.

"So," he said after an interminable time—a stranger hearing him would have thought I'd just sold Olivia to someone who liked little girls—"I'm away, you give my daughter *risotto*."

(I knew at the time this was funny, but it took me years to laugh over it.)

"She loved it."

"You don't know that. You only know she ate it. I was away."

"Exactly. You weren't there, telling her it was terrible."

"So, now I tell her."

"Oh, Jesus, don't you see what you're doing, Angelo?"

He stared at me, hatred unlike anything I'd ever seen in his eyes. "Jesus? Jesus? Don't *you* call for Jesus!"

Someone closed the door from the kitchen side.

Remarkably, the matter hadn't arisen in our nine or ten years together. Well, not so remarkably. A reasonable delicacy had always prevented me from invoking Jesus in Anna's presence, and I'd lost the habit, having acquired acceptably profane substitutes along the way. Now that I'd gotten what I was looking for, I grew calm.

"I wasn't calling for him. I was cursing."

"You stay away from Jesus when you curse!"

"Listen to him, the big churchgoer! Once a year on Christmas Eve he goes to—"

"That's nothing to do with it, *Ebrea!* Just stay away from him! He's not yours!"

I sank back into my seat, beaten in the first round. The only fight we'd ever had that carried a weight much heavier than the weight of the moment, and instantly I'd turned into *Ebrea*.

"And stay away from the fucking *risotto!* You want a *risotto*, make it in the apartment, not in my restaurant!"

"*Your* restaurant?" I managed to choke out. "The restaurant is yours?"

"You bet it is. Look at the lease. Look at the contract. Look at anything you want to look at."

"How about the kitchen?"

A pause, then a shrug. "The kitchen is whoever cooks in it."

"Whoever cooks in it. It doesn't matter who it is."

"Sure it matters. But there's plenty of good cooks around. I have a list of cooks who want to work for me."

"Mmm. Women."

"You bet," Angelo said emphatically. "That's who works in my kitchen. Women."

I'd gone my limit, and I gave up. But the conversation played over and over in my brain, full of themes I'd avoided hearing until now. *Ebrea*. He'd shrugged off my being a Jew when it had to have meant *something*. Maybe it was so important that when he found himself wanting me, the only way to deal with it at all was to dismiss it. The alternative, after all, would have been to lose me and the child he was delighted that I was bearing. Maybe Angelo hadn't been in love with me any more than I'd been with him. Maybe in his mind I'd been no more than a carrier womb, like the woman I'd read about in one of the magazines my parents sent me from the States. All of which might have been tolerable . . . I had, after all, married him as much because I wanted a baby as for any other reason . . . except that it was turning out that Angelo had a daughter and I did not. Livvy, perhaps encouraged by him, maintained a cool indifference to me. Our estrangement was so keen as to make me feel I'd exaggerated her distance during the time when she'd just loved to be around her father. She'd become averse to so much as a hug and a kiss from me when she left for school in the morning, and always arranged to go to her friends after school when her father was away.

At nine years Livvy was not the ravishingly beautiful child she'd been, but she was a skinny, pretty little girl with big, dark eyes, shiny, wavy, black hair, and a lovely deep skin tone (kissed by the sun, as Angelo had it). When I claim she was less than ravishingly beautiful, I am saying something I couldn't have said in front of Angelo, who was fond of telling her that he had talked to God before she was born, describing how she should look, and God had followed his specifications.

In fact, Angelo's references to God expanded geometrically in the weeks and months following our fight. *Per amor di Dio!* became his favorite exclamation and there was often a sort of righteous-holy aura to him, like a priest who's been forced to hide his own clothes and dress like the cannibals but can no longer conceal his connections to heaven. He began taking Livvy to church Sunday mornings, traditionally the only time the three of us spent together in our apartment. She lost interest in the English she'd been learning, was less eager to answer my parents' letters, told them she was very busy with her schoolwork, and asked that they write to her in Italian from now on, if they still wanted to write.

I tried to think of it as a stage she was passing through. I advised myself to get absorbed in something interesting enough so I wouldn't be brooding over her every moment I wasn't working. But the only something that engaged me at all was food.

On a Sunday evening when Livvy had gone to her room to study, Angelo had left the house after kissing her good night, and I was exhausted but too tense to sleep. I roamed around our steel and leather living room looking for something to divert me. Finally I picked up *The Classic Cuisine of the Italian Jews*.

> *"Vesti da turco e mangia da ebreo"* is a well-known, ancient Italian adage which advises one to "dress like a Turk and eat like a Jew." We are thus exhorted by the Italians—who created a cuisine that is the delight of gourmets the world over—to become acquainted with the cuisine of the Italian Jews if we really would like to eat well. . . . Jews modified traditional Italian dishes to make them kosher, often creating delicate and delicious new ones (see *Lasagne Verdi;* made with tomato sauce instead of meat sauce, it became a dish of great delicacy) . . . eggplant and finocchio (fennel), the quintessence of Italian cooking, were originally used only by Jews. . . . The world-famous *carciofi alla giudia* . . . consists of very fresh artichokes trimmed in the manner that was devised by the Roman Jews. . . . Many dishes which are traditionally and uniquely Italian-Jewish are seldom, if ever, found in Italian cookbooks. When they are, no mention is made of their Jewish origin except for a very few such as *cuscussu all ebraica* (Couscous in the Jewish style), *carciofi alla giudia* (artichokes in the style of the Jews)—which was originally called *Carciofi Arrosto* by Roman Jews and was changed to *alla giudia* some fifty years ago . . . original Jewish recipes . . . Concia, Baccala Mantecato, Maritucci Bread, Torzelli and Sfratti come immediately to mind.

It was fascinating, really. They read like a list of dishes Angelo loved. He adored artichokes. *Carciofi alla giudia* had been on the menu at Anna's whenever artichokes were in season. That they were not on our menu I'd attributed to Angelo's passion for the Sicilian. But there was no dish among the others listed that we mightn't have served. There were instructions for cooking cardoons, cauliflower, chicory, and other eggplant dishes, as well as escarole and fennel, every one of which

Angelo's mother had made and he adored. The one for *torzelli*, fried chicory, began with the note that it went well with anything and was reminiscent of *carciofi alla giudia*, but much less costly and easier to prepare. The recipes for *maritucci*, a bread lightly sweetened with anise, and for *sfratti*, a honey- and orange-sweetened pastry, called for numerous ingredients guaranteed to please the Sicilian tastebud.

Artichokes hadn't quite come into season, but in a burst of deluded defiance (see if he can get another cook so fast!) I put *torzelli alla giudia* on the blackboard lunch menu one day that week. Angelo probably wouldn't show up for lunch, I told myself, and if he did, he probably wouldn't notice.

A few people ordered the dish and there were no compliments or complaints, so that I'd forgotten about it, nor had I thought to erase the blackboard, when, as I was preparing the *mustica* for the dinner antipasto, Angelo stormed into the kitchen, clutching the board with one hand, hitting it with the other.

"What the hell do you think you're doing?" he shouted, loudly enough so that Benedetta, who had just arrived to help me, froze in her spot.

The lie I'd prepared in case he complained didn't come to mind.

"If you are referring to the chicory dish on the lunch menu, I can't understand what you're so excited about. I didn't have time and there were no nice artichokes."

"Since when do you start changing the menu?" he yelled, his face redder than I'd ever seen it. "Since when do you—"

"I've been adding new things here and there for ages," I lied, my exterior growing calmer as his grew wild. I knew I was passing the point of no return. "I thought you didn't mind, or at least you didn't care enough to notice. Anyway, what is it you mind, that it's new or that it's Jewish? I mean, your chef's Jewish, in case you've forgotten."

Benedetta walked out of the kitchen and wasn't seen again until dinner. Livvy had stopped in briefly after school, but I hadn't seen her since. Perhaps thinking of her, Angelo stopped shouting, walked over to me, and grabbed my arm so hard that it was black and blue for a couple of weeks.

"Are you telling me you've been putting Jew stuff on my menu?"

"I'm telling you," I said, remembering more of what I'd

read than was healthy, cranking it out in spite of a voice telling me above my pain to shut up, "that there's been Jew stuff on your menu all along. Not just artichokes. The Jews ate fennel before anyone else in Italy did. And *eggplant* . . ."

His eyes widened, his grip on me tightened.

"I have news for you, Angelo, your precious fucking eggplant was discovered, it was the Jews who first—"

With his free hand he hit me so hard that I crashed out of his other hand to the floor. I was crying but I couldn't shut up.

"What I don't understand is why you wanted to marry me if you hate the Jews so much!"

"I didn't want to marry you," he said, standing over me with clenched teeth. "You were pregnant. Whore."

It silenced me. It even dammed up my tears. Its cruelty, its absurdity, its implicit and explicit lies, set it beyond response. Later my brain would go over the words, trying to find a place where I might have heard something he hadn't actually said. In the meantime, he helped me to my feet, walked me to a chair where I sat down, and left me alone in the kitchen.

Although life wasn't lovely, there were few episodes so horrendous as that one, and I held on until Livvy was ten. My parents had bought a summer home in Westport. Not only were they tired of traveling, but Beatrice and Larry now had a son, Max, whom his grandparents adored as they'd once thought they could only adore Livvy, in whom they found those qualities of brilliance and beauty they'd thought unique to her. They still visited us, but the visits were shorter and less frequent, and each time they urged us to come to the States next time. This was not something Angelo was about to do, or permit Livvy to do with me. They would have given me the money to come without her, but I was afraid. At some point I'd come to feel that not only did Angelo face the possibility of my leaving him (and, of course, his daughter) with equanimity, but that once I touched American soil—pavement—I might not be able to make myself leave again. My parents sent me American magazines, from their new subscriptions— *Architectural Digest* and *Better Homes and Gardens*—to the old standbys—*The New Yorker*, *The Nation*, and various arts magazines. I read about everything American with the fervor I'd once reserved for M.F.K. Fisher's adventures in Paris or Elizabeth David on southern France.

I told Angelo that I would love to visit my parents. He said that was fine, he'd buy a ticket for me, one-way or round-trip, but I shouldn't think for a minute that I was taking Olivia. I just nodded. I had, after all, known it all along.

That Easter my father, who was speaking at a conference in Frankfurt, took the occasion to visit for a few days. Livvy was unavailable most of the time, uneasy when she did see him. He tried hard to convey to Angelo the sense that they loved their grandchild and would not hold against him what happened between us as husband and wife, that is, they would not side with me in a manner visible to Olivia. When Angelo didn't even pretend to be interested, my father gave me the name of a good lawyer in Rome, "should the time come" when I required one.

Angelo worked increasingly hard to make me believe the time had, indeed, come. Whether with his encouragement, or simply because she had become uncomfortable with me, I could never find Livvy when he wasn't around. When he was, they spoke in a muted, exclusionary way that turned me into an uninvited guest. A light (ha) query as to what they were talking about was always met with *"Niente."* Nothing. When I complained once that I might as well not be there, neither protested. Still, I couldn't let go. My parents would pay for my divorce if Angelo wouldn't, but they warned that their funds were more limited than they'd been before they bought the house, and they couldn't promise me money for frequent visits to Rome. I mustn't leave Livvy until I was ready.

Whether it had always been in Angelo's mind (back of or forward) that a civil marriage to a Jew did not have to be taken seriously, or whether he'd decided this only when I became an insufficiently docile wife, he now took steps to ensure that I would leave. He allowed, or, more likely, instructed, Livvy to refer casually to Mirella, the woman in Sicily who'd been his mistress for years, and whom Livvy had apparently come to think of as The Person who was Most Like a Real Mother to her. Mirella began to give me her real name when she called. It was made obvious to me that when Angelo took Livvy to Sicily, they stayed with the other woman.

For some years I had been extremely careful about birth control, inserting a diaphragm at night as automatically as I washed my face and brushed my teeth. Now the part of me that couldn't bear to lose my daughter, no matter what, made me careless. It was after a night when Angelo had rolled over on me at around three in the morning and made sex to me, and I'd realized afterward that I hadn't worn my diaphragm, then lay awake until morning in cold terror at the possibility of becoming pregnant by a man I'd never loved and couldn't live with anymore, that I understood that, ready or not, I had to proceed. I went to see the lawyer. I became extremely polite to Angelo, a sign he understood for what it was and reacted to in kind.

It had become my custom, as depression cost me much of my energy, to have a double espresso with my early-evening meal, just before the dinner rush began. Early one evening, as I sat sipping the coffee and looking at an Italian women's magazine, Angelo entered the trattoria with an extremely attractive girl who might have had on a neon headband reading *American*. She had long blond hair, worn in a single braid, bright blue eyes, and freckles. Tall and slender, at least when you didn't see her rear end, she wore a black sweater, blue jeans, and sneakers.

Angelo introduced her as Polly Smith, told me she had recently finished cooking school with Marcella Hazan and was looking for work as a *sous*-chef. He thought we should hire her. Right away. Under normal circumstances I might have argued for temperance and trial, but as things were, I readily consented. Whatever vague feelings I had against wanting to be easily replaced were outweighed by the knowledge that if the divorce was to go smoothly, and Olivia was to remain available to me for visits, I had to be helpful.

This turned out to be easy because Polly was wonderful. Angelo had discovered her working in one of his "friends'" restaurants. Now he found it within himself to be flexible in the matter of the menu; the first couple of days she was working with me, Polly cooked only the dishes she'd done with Ms. Hazan. She was a quick learner and amiable, in that way of certain girls who're rich and pretty and have never come to think of new people as the enemy. The only vengeful thoughts I'd entertained had been of taking my cookbooks and index cards without copying them or giving Angelo the opportunity to do so. Let him find out how unimportant I'd been! But in my last weeks at the restaurant, I instead encouraged Polly to copy all my notes, showed her some of my tricks to make kitchen life easier.

More painful, of course, were my conversations with Livvy. I told her that I was going home to the United States because her father and I had grown too much apart to live together, and, after her, everyone I felt closest to was there.

She nodded.

I told her that if I thought she cared, that she really wanted me to stay, I would remain, no matter how miserable I was. She was silent.

"Have you ever thought," I asked hesitantly, "about the possibility . . . that someday you might want to come to the States? If not now, maybe a little later?"

She appeared startled.

"I know you wouldn't want to leave your father. Your Italian life." Her whole life, except for me. "It's just that it's hard for me to imagine not seeing you for . . . for . . ." I couldn't say it. Weeks? Months? She'd never been away from home for more than three days, and then it was with her father. She seldom slept at another girl's house. She was *there*. *Here*. With me. It wasn't just my throat that hurt; my jaw felt as though it were trying to pull away from the rest of my face. My daughter hadn't seemed to be masking feeling but to lack it. Now she appeared alarmed, doubtless at the prospect of my crying. "Your father and I have agreed . . . I hope you'll visit me. And want me to visit you."

She shrugged, as though I'd suggested something a little bizarre, not worth arguing about. She had Angelo and she had Mirella. Why would she even notice that I was gone?

The dam burst. I didn't begin by weeping gently. A howl of anguish escaped me, then was broken by the first tears. She stared at me for a moment, then turned and ran from the room.

She was ten years old. Maybe she didn't know what to make of it; I was doing something I wanted to do, why was I so upset? To this day I don't know when she'd shut down on me, but this was not the time when she was going to open up, and I suppose that if she wasn't going to do that, running was her only recourse. During my remaining time in Rome she avoided me more strenuously than she had before.

With the help of a couple of competent lawyers, the end came quietly and easily, as was appropriate to a marriage that didn't precisely exist. Angelo gave me a lump sum in lira that came to about five thousand dollars in American money in exchange for my promise not to attempt to get custody of Olivia. (My lawyer

went for ten thousand, but Angelo was able to convince him he
didn't have it.) My parents and I would not be prevented from
visiting Livvy, and when she wished to come to New York,
Angelo would allow her to do so and pay her airfare, up to
twice a year. I visited the few friends we had whom I thought
of as both of ours, told them what appeared to be news to no
one except myself. When it was time for Angelo to take me to
the airport, Livvy was nowhere to be found. Angelo said she
was too upset to come with us. I gave him a letter for her in
which I told her that I would write to her every week, call her
once a month. For now, she could call me collect at my parents'
anytime she wanted to. Angelo took me to the airport, where,
dry-eyed, I kissed him good-bye, boarded the plane, and sat like
a zombie for the next eight hours, unresponsive to stewardesses'
questions except about what I wanted to eat (anything; I didn't
notice the taste) or drink (gin with lemon), unwilling to exchange the most basic pleasantries with the nice American busi-
nessman sitting next to me.

I didn't cry until I laid eyes on my father in the waiting area
at Kennedy. Then it took me some weeks to stop.

In the meantime, I received a note from Polly that began by
pointing out her new address in Florence. She had quit the first
time Angelo yelled at her, and now that she'd come to understand what I had put up with, she thought I might like to know
that she had taken all the notebooks and card files with her.

I hadn't expected to be happy but I'd expected to feel relief. My head had been in a vise controlled by Angelo and the vise would be gone. So it was, but along with pain, any sense of purpose had evaporated. My parents had said I must stay with them until I'd "recovered." The word had sounded strange at the time, but now I understood that not only was it apt, but accomplishing it would be more difficult than I'd dreamed. I'd assured myself I wouldn't miss Livvy much more than I had when we lived in the same house and she barely spoke to me. I'd lied. At first, I called every Sunday. Angelo always checked, then said she wasn't there. He sounded strangely sympathetic, and I felt he was really trying to get her to the phone. One day he insisted but she was so cold and abrupt that it was worse than not speaking with her and I didn't call again.

I could get accustomed to being miserable, what I couldn't get used to was feeling weird. *Disembodied.* It wasn't just missing my daughter, I missed *myself.* It was as though I'd had surgery to remove Italy from my brain and everything else had been taken instead.

I hadn't been in Manhattan for eleven years. I walked around it more than I did anything except sleep. I recognized everything old, could differentiate it from the new if my father, say, was walking with me and asked. But without someone's asking, nothing registered. Certainly none of it interested me. The buildings under construction that he deplored, I could only shrug at. In my absence, the mental hospitals had been emptied and the homeless had begun to appear on the streets. My father, a good liberal, spoke of the various horrors attendant

59

upon the situation for people who should be hospitalized or "put up someplace," as well as for those of us who loved the city. But when he divided the two groups, I was briefly confused; my brain had set me with the homeless. I looked at girls Livvy's age so intently that a couple of times one of them grabbed the hand of the person she was walking with; I'd made her nervous.

My parents had told me to prepare our meals only when I felt like it. I'd assumed I would cook all the time, but I didn't. I wasn't even at ease in their kitchen. I couldn't find things. The stove was too small. And I had no desire to adapt to it. Or to anything else. Or to eat, for that matter. The only thing—person—in New York who interested me was Beatrice and Larry's son, Max, now an adorable two-year-old.

My sister had never shown me a simple, competitive hostility but had been, rather, bossy-friendly, condescending, overly concerned for my health and welfare. When I was really young, a splinter in my finger had been enough to cause her concern for my very survival, while the briefest attention paid me by our parents had caused her concern for her own. Like Gus, she was academically accomplished. If Gus's physicist's brain was usually out to a not-so-solid-state lunch, Beatrice lived in a real world that extended as far as the dining room, but not the kitchen. She had always treated me as though I were sweet but dumb, smiling condescendingly when anyone praised my cooking. As though, in the absence of any reasonable skills, I were weaving baskets or selling pencils on the street. Now she was a psychologist, married to another who taught at NYU, and she was more content with the world, friendlier to me. Particularly when it turned out that I was crazy about her son and was available to take care of him any day or night.

I had left Rome at the end of October, right after Livvy's birthday. I wasn't making my futile phone calls anymore, but I wrote once or twice a week. She didn't write back. At Christmastime, I called. She said she was too busy to talk, they couldn't even go down to Sicily, so Mirella was coming up to Rome. I told her I'd call in January and she asked if that wasn't a little too soon. Maybe I could just keep writing.

That day I baked cookies with Max for the first time. It was the pleasure he took in helping roll out the dough and press down the forms—I was able to find a Christmas tree, a "gingerbread" man, and a star—that led me back to cooking, in a modest way, both at Beatrice's and at my parents'. But I couldn't yet imagine cooking in a professional kitchen, nor did I have any idea how I'd go about finding such work, if I wanted it. It was 1984. If there was a professional female chef in Manhattan, I wasn't aware of her. My parents thought I ought to use this "period of adjustment" to begin working toward a degree, but when I thought about school, I could only see myself with my head on a desk, fast asleep, dreaming about my daughter. On the other hand, I had to think about earning a living. My parents had made it possible for me to keep nearly intact the money I had from Angelo, but I couldn't live on (or off) them indefinitely.

On a Sunday morning in January or February, when I'd slept at Beatrice and Larry's after baby-sitting, I opened the *Times* help wanted section.

Accountant. Administrative Assistant. Advertising. Auto Sales.

Auto Sales?

I stopped, looked back, looked forward, and saw what I hadn't noticed before, that the ads were no longer divided by sex. I was utterly thrown by this radical change in a world I was sure I'd intended to enter sooner or later. How was I to look for a job if I didn't know whether they wanted a man or a woman?

The whole idea, idiot, is that they're supposed to be looking for someone who can do the job, not for a man or a woman.

Yes, but everyone knew they were looking for a man *or* a woman most of the time, even if there was plenty of work either one could do. Like chef. Problem was, everyone who was looking for a chef was looking for a man *or* a woman. Well, maybe not everyone, but almost. Look at Angelo! Look at a lot of other Italians who weren't even thinking about having an employee they could screw, and they still wanted a woman . . . *or* a man.

I picked up the paper again. *Bank. Bilingual.* The bilingual ads were for Spanish- or French- or Japanese-English-speaking secretaries. Or administrative assistants, as they were now apparently called. Sometime during the decade I'd been away garbage collectors had begun to believe that if you called them sanitation engineers they weren't collecting garbage anymore. *Cabinet Maker. Cashier. Chef.*

It was ridiculous not to read the chef ads, even if I couldn't imagine myself going to work in a strange kitchen.

Kaiseki Chef—Experienced Japanese food specialist.

Sous Chef—Min. 2 yrs. sous-chef experience.

Did chef experience count as *sous*-chef experience? Probably not. Anyway, they doubtless wanted someone who knew French food better than I did. Besides, *did they want a male or a female?* Chefs usually had strong feelings on the subject.

Chef Executive. Head Chef. Pastry Person.

Pastry person. Shit. Lingual revolutionaries never understood the comforts of the status quo, in which I tended to wallow. The one old friend I'd been mildly pleased to run into was Evelyn Fox, a history major now deeply involved in and teaching about the women's movement. A capsule description of my life in Italy had filled her with sympathetic horror—"Oh, my God! Chained to a stove!" was the line I remembered. I'd started to tell her that you couldn't appreciate being chained to a stove until you'd come unchained, but the look of horror on her face had stopped me. We'd exchanged numbers but neither of us had called.

Chemist. Clerical. College Grad.

Maybe clerical wasn't such a bad idea. I could stand at a file and stick papers into it like the zombie I was.

Construction. Dental Asst. Dental Hygienist.

I pictured a burly construction worker with hands like prosciuttos and short, blackened nails applying for a dental hygienist's job and being told they'd be perfectly happy to hire him, if only he had experience.

Driver. Editor. Engineer.

Driver didn't actually sound like such a terrible thing for a woman to do. At some point I'd have to learn how to drive; it had never seemed important in Florence or Rome. But driving reminded me of the last time Angelo, Livvy, and I had driven to Delfina and Walter's for one of their kids' birthday parties, and I put it out of my thoughts.

Executive Secretary. So secretaries of a sort still existed, even if they had to be called executives to admit it. *Finance. Food Buyer. Food Manager. Food Service.* When you read the rest of the ad, the job never seemed to have anything to do with food. This was all very well except I couldn't imagine anything I was qualified to do that wasn't about food. Well, maybe with one exception. Next year Max would be in nursery school half a day and I was already panicky about his being unavailable during those hours. If there were some way to teach nursery school without going back for a lot of awful classes that would turn out to have very little to do with teaching young children . . .

When spring came and I'd still made no serious move to find a job, my parents suggested I spend the summer with them in Westport. Several of their friends had said it was the best time of year for them to take cooking lessons. Perhaps I could conduct classes out of the house up there, which had a full kitchen, and see how teaching felt.

There was no way for me to refuse even to try.

It was part of the reluctance with which I came to the idea of teaching that my classes, on and off television, were conceived of more as conversation than instruction. If I'd thought of myself as a teacher, I doubt I'd have been so comfortable with an audience that was encouraged to interrupt me at will, and that was to be an important factor in the show's success. Of course, this casual geniality that drew people to my classes and, later, to the show, infuriated Livvy, who claimed that my benign personality was manufactured for the occasion. What her deep quarrel with me kept her from seeing was that no manufacture was required. I'd grown up with parents who treated my cooking as though it gave me an understandable but inappropriate pleasure, like a loud fart at a formal dinner party. I'd left home for Angelo Ferrante, who valued my culinary skills above any other, at least once we were married, but apparently thought that a pat on the head would cause me (or him) to lose all control. Only with my classes would I discover that I was a show-off, an entertainer, much cleverer in my stage kitchen than in everyday life. More rather than less likely to find the *bon mot* when many ears were waiting.

The classes and the work they involved helped me to keep thoughts of Livvy at bay. One of the women in the first group wrote a glowing column about it for the *Westport News*, and in the autumn I set up classes in Manhattan, which several of the Westport women came in to take during the rest of the year. Through the friend of a friend of my parents, I'd found a mildly dilapidated loft in a more than mildly dilapidated block of West Fifteenth Street. The neighborhood was grungy but said to be getting better, and, most important, there was a full (unwalled) kitchen along one end that was ideal for cooking classes. My parents' housewarming present was a coat of white paint over the whole place, and with various hand-me-downs and junk-shop purchases, I made the place cheerful if not elegant. I supplemented what I earned with the (barely touched) money from Angelo.

By the second year I was doing three daytime classes in pasta and sauces, each with six students. The suburban women managed complicated lives and were mostly delighted to sit back and let me run the class. My evening students were a more varied lot.

My six o'clock Tuesday class, Fish and Their Sauces, was all male, none heterosexual. There were a couple of mannered fairies who described themselves as housewives; a charming English professor who'd just come out and felt, for the first time, that it would be all right to cook; Perry Marcus, the kind and sharp advertising man who was the first link in the chain that led me to television; and Lance Garfunkel, a coat buyer for Macy's who, it became clear during the pre-course "coffee," would be my most difficult pupil.

I'd baked two chocolate cakes and I asked the group to sample each. All confessed to preferring the moister of the two. Then I revealed that I'd used the same recipe for both but had taken one out of the oven earlier than the recipe specified. This had become my standard gambit to persuade students that religious awe interfered with cooking's pleasures as thoroughly as it did with life's other offerings, with the obvious exception of religion.

Lance was upset.

"Surely," he said, in a tone both fatuous and aggrieved, "there are rules that must be followed. I mean, Hollandaise comes to mind, but there are plenty of others. . . ." He fanned himself with the mimeographed outline for the course.

"Indeed," I replied, "in almost everything there are rules that are proven to work, and that are very helpful. And there's a lot to be said for letting people learn from experience. But you can probably try over and over and never find out that the Hollandaise is separating because you're adding the butter too fast . . . or the *risotto* is soggy because you added the broth all at once . . . or whatever. What I have a problem with is thinking you can't play with it. Or you have to throw it away because you made a mistake. I think you should try to fix it.

Change it. Maybe you'll end up with something interesting. And don't fail to try out some combination that appeals to you because the book doesn't promise it'll work."

Lance was silent for a while, but he began again when I asked for their ideas and reactions to my outline. The first session listed was a visit to my fish market in the Village, with a discussion of what was available seasonally, what to look for and to avoid, and how to have the vendor prepare fish for you.

"Oh, God," Lance said with a fatuous sigh, his eyes closed, his nose covered by one hand. "Right into the mouth of the whale!"

"It's not a whale market we're going to," I said, "although these days you can find a re—"

"That's what I'm afraid of!" Lance interrupted. "What we can find. I mean, the *smell* of what we can find. I mean, *fish markets*!"

"Ah, yes," I said. "Well, smell is always an important issue in choosing which fish to buy, and that's one of the reasons—"

"What about to *eat*? I mean, is there any hope I'll get to like something besides shrimp and lobster?"

I paused. It was the kind of moment I might have backed away from in my first year, but I now knew it was best to meet head on. Lance's boyfriend, Chris, sitting beside him, looked miserable. The others looked uneasy. As though they shared Lance's sentiment but knew it was unacceptable.

I took a deep breath. "Fish are like women," I said. "You have to begin by acknowledging their variety before you can start to think about which ones you might like."

Lance's eyes opened. The class was quieter than quiet as it waited to gauge the extent of my hostility.

I smiled. "Also, live ones smell better than dead."

Everyone else smiled. The tension was gone.

"She has a sense of humor!" Lance exclaimed, feeling that the class was now with me and not wanting to be left alone at the Anti-Female side of the road. He pressed his wrist to his forehead in a manner he might have thought of as Garboesque. "Everything's going to be all right. I'm going to learn to cook fish. I'm going to like to *eat* fish. After all, anyone who can make a superb Beef Wellington should be able to handle a piece of goddamned fish!"

Simple frying and broiling would be my next lessons, and then we would move on to fish stew. I pointed out that among the virtues of the various stews, whether it was the one-*d* *burrida* of northern Italy, the two-*d*'s *burridda*, a French *bouillabaisse* or a San Francisco *cioppino*, was that if they were less than perfect, there were many easy ways, beginning with *aioli* and *rouille*, to improve them.

I was having fun with my classes, but over the next year my life improved in other ways as well.

Beatrice and I remained close. Partly because I spent so much time with Max, she and Larry were able to do more writing connected to their work, and they'd invested in their first computer. On the morning when the computer was to be delivered, both had appointments, and I stayed with Max at the apartment to supervise the young man, Jim Whatney, who came to install it.

Jim was from a small town in Mississippi. A math whiz whose family had been too poor to send him to college, he'd come to New York, where his first job was as a repairman for Con Edison. Then he'd gotten into computers and found a home. He'd repaired IBMs for a couple of years after breaking up with a girlfriend who'd gotten him the first job. (When I asked why they'd broken up, he shrugged and said there was no particular reason, an important clue to who Jim was, if only because from his point of view, it was true.) Then he'd gone to work for Fastrack, the company that had sold Larry the computer. Jim seldom went home to Mississippi and said the only thing he missed about it was the food.

He had, of course, come to the right place.

With my old index cards from Suallen, as well as the wonderful Evan Jones book, *American Food*, and Princess Ida's *Soul Food*, I made Southern fried chicken, beaten biscuits, and collard and beet greens, then went on, though Jim claimed he could eat that chicken every night for the rest of his life, to Creole shrimp, Charleston shrimp pie, seafood gumbo, and a good jambalaya. Unlike Angelo, Jim enjoyed any dish said to be from the right territory. No authentication was required, no dish rejected because he was unfamiliar with it, though he loved best the fatty, highly seasoned foods he remembered from his childhood.

Jim was a very tall, very skinny paleface type whose intelligence was substantial but even narrower than his taste in food. It was, in fact, limited to those functions that might have been performed by one of the computers he installed, repaired, and talked to when he thought they were alone.

"You sound as though computers are people," I'd teased him after his instruction session with Larry.

He'd stared at me in that way people have when they don't see what's funny about what you thought was a joke. Why wouldn't he think so? his expression asked. And he failed to comprehend my amusement upon discovering that in computerese, a table of contents, for example, was called a menu.

"Maybe that's why I learned it so easily," I said.

He nodded.

Nor did he chuckle when, having polished off a bottle of wine between us, we rolled into bed for the first time and, finding me moist and open, he slipped right into me and I murmured that I seemed to be user-friendly.

Occasionally, Jim and I slept over when I baby-sat for Max. At first I thought he was not simply tolerant of but shared my pleasure in my nephew. If the sensible section of my brain knew that Jim and I shouldn't even live together, the longing part occasionally fantasized about marrying him and having babies. A good lover, a low-keyed but physically affectionate human being who routinely placed an arm around my shoulders when we walked, necked with me in the movies, and held me in bed even when neither of us was interested in sex, surely he would be a good, steady father, if not a maniacally devoted one.

"Do you ever wish you had your own kids?" I asked one night when he'd brought my thrilled nephew an inoperative keyboard and was showing him the keys while I cooked dinner.

"Nope," he said with a short laugh. "I only want 'em if I can leave when I feel like it."

"You'd feel different if they were your own," I assured him. "Anyway, men can usually get out of the house when they want to."

Silence.

"If I ever remarried," I said, "I'd want two or three kids."

"In that case," Jim drawled, chucking me under the chin with his free hand, "we better make sure we don't get married."

"I can understand," I said later that night, when Max was

asleep, and we'd made love on the sofa with particular satisfaction, "not wanting kids right away. But . . ."

He drew me back down on the sofa, covered us with the afghan we kept close in case anyone should walk in before they were expected. He had another erection in what was an unusually short time since the first.

"No buts about it," he said.

End of conversation.

Beginning of period when Jim ceases always to show up at my place when he's told me he'd be there and, finally, disappears altogether.

I would have been devastated had not something more important been going on in my life.

I'd continued writing to Livvy and a few weeks earlier, I'd sent her a thirteenth-birthday present, a gold heart-shaped locket. She'd written me back for the first time, thanking me, telling me she wore it all the time. I'd answered and soon had another letter in which she apologized for not having written earlier, said she would like to correspond with me now—in English, which she'd been studying in school. Her teacher said she had a talent for it. But she didn't just have a talent, she wrote, she had the books Nonno and Nanna had given her years ago, and she studied them all the time. She would appreciate my correcting her errors. I said I would be happy to do this and asked her to tell me what was going on in her life. She wrote that school was pretty much the same as ever, she got the best grades in everything, Benedetta said hello. She, Livvy, had become friendly with an American girl named Sally who lived in Boston, did I know where that was? There was no mention of her father or of Mirella. I wondered whether she felt uncomfortable about referring to them and assured her, in my next letter, that it would be fine to talk about anyone who was part of her life, including Mirella. I asked whether she would like me to try to visit her sometime, or whether, since her English was getting so good, she might like to come to New York. In her response, she spoke a great deal about her English class, asked me various questions about New York, including how far it was from Boston, and, in a postscript, wrote, "We do not know Mirella anymore." She didn't answer my query about visiting, but asked increasingly pointed questions about my apartment, my parents, and New York, which we were now calling Manhattan. The next time I asked if she would like to visit, she said she would love to.

It took me a full day to calm down to a point where I didn't fear putting her off, another day to get over my apprehension that my apartment, my whole neighborhood, weren't nice enough for a young girl who lived in the middle of Rome. Then I called.

She answered the phone. Her voice was exactly the same.

I told her, the tremble in my voice so slight I thought she might not hear it long distance, how happy I was that I was going to see her, asked if she'd like to come at Easter.

She said she couldn't because of the wedding. (*Il matrimonio.* No previous or further reference.) She would come when school ended, if I wanted her to.

If I wanted her to! Having to wait two additional months was more than made up for by the fact that she could be with me for much longer. If she wanted to be. And if her father didn't toss in some last-minute monkey wrench.

I asked if she'd discussed this with her father. She said she hadn't, and requested that I talk to him. Anticipating difficulty, I wrote to Angelo, advising him of our plans and reminding him of the agreement we had that he would pay for her transportation. When I wrote to Livvy again I asked whether Angelo was remarrying.

"The answer to your question regarding my father," she wrote in her next letter, "is yes."

When Beatrice, with one of her knowing looks, said there was likely some relation between Angelo's marriage and Livvy's desire to come to the States, I shrugged and said, "Who cares?" A couple of times I got angry when Beatrice tried to tell me something about adolescents I didn't want to hear. The line I often thought of later was "Fourteen-year-olds are difficult even when they don't have a lot of things going on in their lives."

I replied, huffily, that a lot was going on in Livvy's father's life, but not necessarily in hers. I felt that most of me had been in suspension since the day I left Rome; why should I not believe that after I'd left, Livvy had felt the same way? Maybe my sister was annoyed because my devotion to Max was a little less overwhelming than it had once been.

"You're not listening!" Max shouted at me one day. "I'm telling you about my truck, and you're not listening!"

When I confessed that I'd been thinking about something I had to do before my daughter's visit, he got even angrier, said he wasn't going to let her visit if I didn't listen to him.

I was considering asking my landlord to let me make two bedrooms at the opposite end of the loft from the kitchen, where only my (open-space) bedroom had been. Having gotten the feeling that Livvy might want to stay for longer than a week or two, and having received a polite note from Angelo saying she could stay as long as she liked, I finally asked for and received the landlord's permission. Now I had to figure out how to achieve the greatest possible degree of privacy for the smallest amount of money.

With the help of two friends and a few hundred dollars from my bank account (my parents offered to chip in but I wanted to pay for it myself), I put up eight-foot-high plasterboard walls (the ceilings were around sixteen feet high) that left us with adjacent, reasonably private rooms, each with a door opening on what could now be called the living room. I furnished hers with a double bed like mine so we could use the same linens, as well as a chest, a night table, and an ancient but bright cloth rug, all bought at Connecticut tag sales, then decorated the walls with posters I found around the city. When it was finished, I told myself that if Livvy liked it as much as I, she might not want to leave. Then I cautioned myself about getting my hopes up and being miserable later. After her father's wedding, Livvy had a new address, in the fanciest residential neighborhood in Rome, although she never mentioned having moved. I looked at my apartment with sadder, wiser eyes, told myself to enjoy what I could have of my daughter and not long for the impossible.

She would arrive at the close of her school year in Rome, when my spring classes would also be finished. I would conduct summer sessions in Westport, but aside from those, we'd be free to be in either place, as the weather and our wishes dictated. I could think about nothing else. I slept much less than usual but I was never tired. We continued to correspond, but I started a series of parallel letters to her in a notebook; I was flooded by so many intense memories that I was afraid she would think I'd gone crazy if I sent them to her. There would be plenty of time when she arrived, if she wanted to hear such things, to tell her about the Turtle Fountain and the time she

and Delfina's second son tried to make a house for themselves
under the fig tree in Delfina's backyard.

The waiting area outside Customs, at Kennedy. I stood in
the crowd behind the thick rope, straining to scan each face as
though the person inside that six-foot-tall redheaded model or
the old Italian farmer in black might turn out to be my daughter. My parents had driven me to the airport, but we'd agreed
they should wait in the parking lot so Livvy and I could have
a few minutes alone. When she finally appeared, I stopped
breathing altogether.

She was utterly recognizable and entirely different. The girl
coming toward me, wearing a backpack and pulling a suitcase
on wheels, had Livvy's huge, dark eyes and silky-curly, pitch-
black hair, but her face had bones, most particularly strong
cheekbones and a sharp little chin, that hadn't been so visible
when I left. She was close to my height and her body was no
longer a child's. She wore a cotton-print dress that didn't conceal full breasts, a small waist, strong legs. She hadn't seen me
yet, and I tried to call out to her, but my voice choked in my
throat as I remembered how I'd cleared a shelf for her in the
wicker cabinet that held shampoo and Tampax, wondering
whether she had her period yet. The girl walking toward me
might almost have had her first child. She would be fourteen
in October.

In the absence of a voice, I'd been waving to her. Now she
saw me and came around the rope barrier in my direction. She
smiled at me in a shy, tentative manner. I felt a nearly unbearable excitement as she moved along one side of the rope
toward the exit, and I moved along the other. At the end, I
threw my arms around her and burst into tears. She hugged
me, waited patiently, and, when I didn't move or stop crying,
took my hand as though I were the child and led me through
the first corridor. When she refused my offer to pull her suitcase, I placed my hand on top of hers on the handle.

"I just want to hug you and kiss you." I'd said it, without
thinking, in Italian.

She smiled patiently. "Please let us use only English,
Mother."

I smiled back. "I speak it all the time here, of course, but
when I saw you . . . All right. Mama's the same in English, by
the way. Mother is sort of formal."

(She continued to call me Mother, even during those early good months. I see it now as a signal that no matter how loving she might sometimes have seemed, she didn't mean to trust me with the name of Mama.)

Finally we reached the outside.

"Are Nonno and Nanna here?"

My parents. Their names hadn't changed. Jealousy clutched at me. I wished I'd taken the bus.

"They waited in the car so we could have a little time alone."

She looked around us. "Alone?"

I laughed. "*Solo.* With nobody we know around."

"They are where?"

"Come. I'll show you." I mustn't be ridiculous. There would be enough of my precious daughter to go around.

But I forgot the row where they'd parked, though I was fairly certain I had the right lot. And before I saw my parents, who were standing outside their car, a joyful voice exclaimed, "Nonno! Nanna!" and Livvy let go of her suitcase and made a beeline toward them.

As the three happily hugged and kissed, I began to cry again. They didn't notice, but a woman passing by called to me that I shouldn't leave my luggage like that, anyone could grab it. I picked up the handle, walked to a few feet from where the three of them were hugging and kissing, and stood silent as they babbled in a joyful mix of English and Italian, nobody worrying about who used which. Finally we put her baggage in the trunk and got into the car, Livvy in the front with my father, my mother and I in the back. I sat on the left-hand side because that way I could at least see part of Livvy's profile, more when she turned to watch my father. They quickly figured out without her telling them that she wanted everyone to speak English. They couldn't believe how good hers already was. (I'll make no attempt to duplicate errors and uncertainties; everything she said was comprehensible, from the beginning.) She giggled when my father told her this, claimed he was just saying it to make her feel good.

Finally, I had my daughter back, and I didn't have her at all, my parents had her. It was just as it had been the first time they came to Rome, only then they were the ones I'd wanted more of. Now Livvy begged them to come to the apartment with us, rather than drop us there, as they'd planned. Of course I said they would be welcome to stay with us for dinner.

They'd already moved to Westport for the summer but had come in to meet Livvy with me. They intended to drive back later in the evening. We'd be welcome to go with them, but they assumed Livvy would want to see the city first. I tried to figure out what might convince her that she wanted to remain with me in Manhattan for a few days. But then, as soon as I did that, my brain began to compare their lovely white-frame house with my loft. How could the loft, as bright and pretty as I'd tried to make it, compare with that house, never mind Angelo's elegant new home? How would Livvy react to the gray and grungy street where I lived? I'd be lucky if she wanted to stay long enough to have dinner!

As I sank into self-loathing misery, each small event—or nonevent—solidified my despair. If Livvy, as we parked the car a block away and walked to my loft, appeared oblivious to the filthy street, that was because she was too absorbed in my parents to see anything else and would notice the garbage in the street only when they left us. (If she let them leave. She might insist on going to Westport with them immediately.) If she barely looked around before settling between my parents on one of the two navy-blue Bon Marché sofas, telling them they really had to correct her English, that wasn't because I was already fussing in the kitchen, but because she wasn't even certain my English was good enough to help!

On the ancient wood-and-Formica counter that divided me from the main room (from my daughter! from the world!) I set out a bottle of Chianti, glasses, and an antipasto that would hold—or would it?—anyone who was hungry until dinner. Changed my mind. Brought everything over to the coffee table. Asked if there were any special requests for dinner.

I'd been prepared to give them a list of possibilities. They looked at me blankly. Then both my parents consulted their watches. It was about twenty minutes past five and nobody in the room was accustomed to eating before eight.

I felt myself blush.

My father laughed. "I think your mother can't wait to get us out of here, Livvy."

"No, no!" Livvy protested. "That cannot be true."

"Sure it could," my father said. "And it would be perfectly natural. She wants you to herself."

Livvy looked puzzled, whether because she hadn't understood the phrase or didn't believe the sentiment, I couldn't tell.

"Don't be silly," I said brusquely, "I was just confused by time. Her time, our time. I thought she might be hungry, I didn't know—"

"I am not hungry," Livvy said. "They feed you all the time on the plane."

"Fine," I said, "then I'll forget about dinner. There's plenty to eat right here, anyway."

I poured myself a glass of Chianti, sat alone (Always alone! Always the extra person!) on the second sofa, listened to the conversation for a moment before my mind wandered off. Was the whole summer going to be like this? Me wanting to be with Livvy, look at Livvy, listen to Livvy, and Livvy wanting only to be with my parents?

They were telling her about the house in Westport, how they remained there once the school term ended. My father said that he and I had become gardeners, had a real vegetable garden this year for the first time. And we were only a few blocks from the beach. My mother explained that once my classes began up in Westport, I would spend as much time as I could up there, since summer was not a wonderful time in Manhattan. It got really hot. Livvy, thoroughly absorbed in this joint narrative, stopped them only to ask that they slow down a bit or define a word.

My father said that they'd begun to think about adding on a couple of rooms, now that the family was growing.

Livvy smiled, thinking, I suppose, that they were talking about her.

"Do you realize," my father asked my mother, "that Livvy and Max don't know each other yet?"

My mother was momentarily bewildered. "Good heavens," she finally exclaimed. "It's true."

Livvy looked bewildered.

"Well," my father said, "you both have a treat in store for you."

"Both?" she asked.

"You and Max," he replied solemnly.

"Max?" Livvy asked. "What is Max? Who is Max?"

"Max is your cousin," my father said. "Your mother must have told you that you have a cousin. Soon you'll have two."

Livvy still looked puzzled. No lights flashing yet.

"Cousin."

My father nodded. "Your mother's sister, Beatrice, whom you don't know, but they'll be in Westport, so when you come up. . . ." He smiled. "It's hard to realize you've never even met Beatrice and Larry. They've never been to Italy, and of course you haven't . . . Anyway, we now have two wonderful grandchildren and a third on the way! We've told Max about Nonno and Nanna in honor of your coming."

(Never mind that Max normally refused to use either.)

My father stood, clapped his hands exuberantly, picked up the bottle to pour some wine.

Livvy looked as though something had been dropped on her head. She had no questions about Max's age (he was six now) or anything else. She was off someplace. My mother went to the bathroom. My mother, I remembered for the first time since my return, had the world's most suggestible bladder; the hint of trouble had always been enough to send it to the bathroom. Livvy still looked stunned, but I wasn't sure what it was that had affected her—or even how. I'd referred to Beatrice and Larry once or twice in my letters, but I hadn't discussed them. I wasn't sure whether I'd mentioned Max. Maybe not. Max hadn't had any place in the long and complex list of subjects we might write each other about. Anyway, it was hard to see why the news that two people she didn't know had a child should affect her. I'd heard about sibling rivalry from Beatrice; was there such a thing as grandsibling rivalry?

My father made an antipasto plate, offered it to Livvy, who took it and ate so quickly that she was almost finished by the time he sat down with one for himself. My mother came out of the bathroom, tested the emotional waters, tried to determine whether it was safe to jump in.

"So," she said brightly, "have we decided when everyone's going to Westport?"

Silence. Livvy looked at me.

"What I think," I said, "is that Livvy's the one who should decide, and it's too soon for her to decide anything. She just got here, for heaven's sake. She might want to see some of Manhattan before she gets whisked away."

Livvy smiled at me.

Something had changed.

I made an early dinner. My parents would go to Westport as planned. Livvy and I would join them when we (she) wished, a week from the coming Monday being our deadline, since my summer classes would begin the following day. She kissed them back when they kissed her good-bye, but there was none of the loving urgency I'd seen earlier. She was content to remain with me, amenable to being hugged and kissed, interested in Manhattan.

I was very happy, quite unconcerned with her reasons.

We remained in the city that weekend. I took her down to the Village, shopped with her there, explained that it was the only real Italian neighborhood left in Manhattan, the area called Little Italy being just restaurants, cafés, and bakeries. But she was interested in what was American, not what was Italian: the Statue of Liberty; the Staten Island Ferry; the Empire State Building. All of which we visited in those two days. I bought a map of Manhattan, which she clipped over the Klee poster I'd hung in her room and ran to consult when I mentioned a new place. She was mastering place names with the same ease as she'd mastered English grammar, daily improving in both, never forgetting anything she'd learned. The only meal she wanted when we were out was hot dogs and papaya, though she ate anything I served her at home. She hadn't mentioned her father or his wife, but a couple of times she'd referred to being at Mirella's.

The second time, I said, "It must have been difficult for you when your father stopped seeing Mirella."

Tears came to her eyes.

"I wanted to go down there without him. She didn't want me."

"How awful."

She searched my face to see if I was taking it as seriously as I seemed to be. When she saw that I meant it, she allowed herself to cry a little, me to hold her.

"Poor Livvy," I murmured. (I admit to duplicity here.) "I hope at least your father's wife is nice."

Abruptly, she sat up. The tears were still there, but now her face was contorted with scornful rage.

"Nice? Queen Annunciata? She does not have to be nice. She is The Queen. She does what she wants. Tells everyone else what to do."

I smiled. "Not your father. Nobody—"

"You think so? She does not have to tell him. He does what she wants before she tells him!"

Behind my smile, I was in shock. The earth had moved. Angelo had been brought to heel. Was it possible I could have done it and saved myself a lot of anguish?

"Are we talking about your father?"

"No. It is not my father. It is another person."

"People don't really become someone else."

"He goes to church every Sunday with her."

I was impressed. On the other hand, he'd gone to church for a while after our big *Ebrea* fight.

"Well," I said, "it probably won't last."

"To marry her, he had to promise. To go to church, I mean."
Careful now, Caroline.

"How do you know that?"

"He told me! Everything she makes him do, he promises. He *likes* this. It makes him laugh."

As I gaped at her, she grew more intense.

"He thinks she is beautiful. He calls her his madonna. She is ugly. The most ugly . . . He thinks, I cannot tell you, everything she does, he—her baby will be the most beautiful baby that is ever born!"

"Her baby? You mean she's pregnant already?"

Livvy nodded. "She is *una maiale*." (A pig.)

"When is the baby due?" For the first time I was seeing a glimmer of hope that Livvy would stay with me past summer's end. I warned myself not to bring it up before she did.

She shrugged. "I do not know. In January. January nineteenth, perhaps."

I couldn't be certain who had arrived at this date, but it was almost precisely nine months from the day Angelo and Annunciata had married.

The city grew extremely hot and humid. I was able to persuade Livvy to go to Westport that Friday by telling her that we'd spend only as much time as we wished with "the others." We would ask my father to drive us anyplace we wanted to go when we didn't feel like being with those nameless others. And we could easily walk to the beach by ourselves, as someone with a young child, for instance, could not.

When, on Friday morning, I said we could ride up in the car with my sister and Larry and Max or, if Livvy preferred, we could take the train, she made a show of being puzzled about why she wouldn't want to go in the car. But then she suddenly remembered having promised her best friend in Rome that before the end of her first week in New York she would write a letter about Bloomingdale's. So we spent two or three hours in Bloomingdale's, Livvy with her backpack, me with my usual airline bag, more ingredients than clothes. Then we had a leisurely late lunch and went directly to Grand Central Station.

During the ride up I was preoccupied with food matters—what I'd cook over the weekend that we could shop for on the way to the house; what I should make on Saturday night, when friends of Larry and Beatrice who had a daughter Olivia's age were coming for dinner; what I'd do for my first class on Monday. Occasionally Livvy asked the name of someplace we were passing, but there were no queries about the family or the weekend. If there had been, it might have occurred to me to prepare her for the likelihood that Max would be at the station with my father. Not that anything I said could have altered the hostile course each was on by virtue of the other's very existence.

Seeing us, Max broke free from my father and ran to me, holding out his arms for me to pick him up, which I hadn't done in a couple of years. I laughed, bent over to kiss him, whispered that he was too big for me to carry, now, especially with my suitcase.

I took his hand, said, "Sweetheart, this is my daughter, Livvy."

"You expect me to believe she's yours?" he asked indignantly. "She's way too big!"

Laughing, my father turned to lead us to the car.

Not laughing, Livvy muttered under her breath, in Italian, "And you're too little to have such a big mouth."

I promised he'd get used to her and simmer down.

But as the weekend progressed, it became clear that *she* wasn't going to get used to *him*. At the house, there was an instant and nearly total coldness between my very pregnant sister and Livvy, each of whom claimed, as we used to say when we were kids, that the *other* had *started*. Livvy acted as though Max didn't exist. Larry attempted peacemaking and succeeded to the extent that Livvy found him a delightful person, was willing to go to town with him on errands, and so on—as long as Max or Beatrice didn't happen to be going. Alone with

Beatrice, I told her what I'd discovered about Angelo's new wife having gotten pregnant immediately, and so on.

The response of my sister Beatrice, the psychologist, was, "Fine. But that doesn't mean she can't be decent to Max. He's got enough problems with my pregnancy."

I nodded, but I was still on uncertain ground with Livvy, afraid that any suggestion about her behavior might put her off *me*, as well. I didn't want her to feel that I, like my parents, was unfaithful.

We ate most of our meals on the lovely screened porch that ran the width of the house's rear. There were cushioned rattan chairs at one end, while the other held the big, round table where we ate. A window over the kitchen work counter opened on the porch just above where the table was and made it possible to pass dishes back and forth without walking around through the living room.

On Saturday night I made a *brodetto* in the style of the Marches, or I should say, in one of the styles, for the region has more and better fish than almost any in Italy and this was a time of year when I could easily find the eight or more varieties a *brodetto* should contain. In the mood *marchigiano*, I did the potatoes that were a regional favorite, the spuds sautéed and then baked with a lot of rosemary and garlic. The salad combined store lettuce and cucumber with the arugula and lettuce that were coming up in our garden.

Livvy and Marsha, the friends' daughter, quickly became friends, perhaps because as I was passing the big, flat bowl of fish stew through the opening to the table, and the adults were murmuring appreciatively, Marsha whispered audibly to Livvy that hamburgers were her favorite food, Livvy whispered that they were hers, too, and both dissolved into giggles. Marsha spoke very quickly and Livvy couldn't bear to keep asking her to slow down, but after that, Marsha began to do it on her own.

Now I was in front of the window on the kitchen side, whipping egg yolks for the *zabaglione* that was a company treat. Water was heating for decaffeinated espresso. (I'd barely heard of decaf until my return from Italy.) As I rested my arm from its beating work, I heard various jokes about how these kids suffered, having to eat the glorious food I prepared. Larry offered to take them to the ice-cream parlor after dinner if they couldn't bear *zabaglione*.

"More for us," he said, laughing.

"I don't think so," Livvy said. "My mother will be angry at me."

Through the kitchen window, I called, "Good grief, I can't imagine that I'd get angry, but what would happen if I did?"

"Oh, well," Livvy said, turning to look at me, "you know how you used to yell at me."

My hands stopped beating the yolks—as though I'd been accused of egg abuse.

Certainly I'd yelled at her once in a while, always when I was working in the kitchen under intense pressure and she'd gotten in my way. I was about to point out, jokingly, that I'd never given her so much as a light smack on the backside because my hands were always occupied during such moments, when an incident I hadn't thought of in years flashed through my brain.

The kitchen of the trattoria. Our last autumn in Florence. Livvy was two. Angelo had bought a basket of truffles. There had already been fights about money with Anthony. As Angelo set the truffles on the worktable, he lectured me on their price, and on the necessity of wasting none and making certain none was stolen by the help. The lecture made me so nervous that I decided, as I wrapped the truffles in the usual damp cloths within the basket, to put exactly three in each packet. Should anyone see the carefully wrapped packets—maybe I'd even make a sign saying there were three in each packet except the started one—surely they'd think twice before stealing any.

Livvy had been napping in her little room in back of the bar. She awakened to Angelo's voice, ran into the kitchen and was scooped up in his arms. After a couple of minutes of kisses and Papa's-girl talk, he set her on the worktable, not far from the truffles. I gave them tartini with prosciutto and olives, their current favorite snack. (Neither had a great taste for sweets then, though Livvy seemed to have developed one recently.) It was a joke among us that Livvy's fuori tavolo, literally a snack eaten away from the table, was often eaten right on it.

The phone rang. I was in the middle of sautéing in two different pans the soffritto, the mixture of onion, carrot, and herbs with garlic in one pan, that serves as a base for many dishes, and which it's important not to cook for so long that the onions

*and garlic brown. Angelo left Livvy on the table, telling her
not to move until he got back, then went to the phone, which
was on the bar wall near the kitchen door. After a moment, he
took the phone through the doorway to the bar, doubtless because one of his girlfriends was on the other end. As I moved
the first pan to a cold burner, a loud shout from Angelo made
my heart leap and my hand drop the pan. I turned to see what
was happening.*

*Livvy had pulled the truffle basket closer to herself and was
opening the cloth containers, in the process spilling most of
their contents onto the table and the floor. With Angelo's shout,
she'd burst into tears. Now he rushed to her, scooped her up
in his arms, and continued to yell—at me. What did I think I
was doing, leaving such things around a child? What kind of
an imbecile thought you could leave millions of lira worth of
truffles on a table—*

*"Why are you yelling at me?" I'd screamed back. "You were
the one who left her with them, you were the one who didn't
tell her to stay away while you . . . Livvy, you know you're not
supposed to touch the stuff on the table. You know you—"*

*But as I turned my wrath on her to stop myself from scream-
ing about his girlfriends' calls, he scooped her up and stalked
out of the kitchen and the restaurant. I didn't see either of them
again until five minutes before we opened for dinner. Angelo
brought her to the little room; she wouldn't come into the
kitchen.*

Now I felt as though I'd been watching a filthy movie I'd
starred in—and that everyone on the porch had also seen. By
the time I brought out the *zabaglione*, they were talking about
the weather, but I felt too defensive to let it go.

"Well, here it is," I said, light as a ten-ton truck on a corru-
gated (my voice was shaky) road, "no fuss, no muss, no
screamings, beatings, nothing."

I looked at Livvy. I was fighting tears, but she smiled. Plac-
idly.

"You are different now, Mother."

I (fake) smiled back.

"I'm not cooking for fifty people at a time now."

"Just hearing that number, I can't imagine . . ." Marsha's
mother said. "I mean, I can't cook like you do for *two* people,
but . . ."

I shut up and let them move on to a discussion of which

foods they could cook for how many people at what time of year, which led me further into self-pity. Felt like cooking, indeed. What I felt like had never been an issue in our restaurants. In our *lives*. My daughter had no sense of what my life had been like. Maybe she didn't even understand why I'd had to leave. Maybe she had no idea of the extent of her father's screwing around, or how I'd suffered from it. Maybe she thought he'd just grown attached to a Sicilian woman who was a more appropriate mate for him. Maybe she'd never understood why I left. I wasn't ready to tell her, even without consideration of the other people present, but for the first time it occurred to me that someday I might.

Livvy appeared to have forgotten our first bad moment, or, at least, to have thought of it simply as a moment when she reminded me of something I'd forgotten. Nor did I live with it in any way that might have prepared me for what was to come. If I'd lost her to Marsha instead of to my parents, that was because she was a normal teenager and normal teenagers wanted to be with their friends, not their parents. Someday, it might be years from now, I'd make clear to her the pressure I'd been under, see if she couldn't understand that there was no way to be even-tempered in such a situation. Tell her that placid chefs were few and far between. In the meantime, she was content to be in Westport for the summer because her best friend, Marsha, was in Westport, and introduced her to a couple of kids whose parents had summer homes there and who attended Hunter High School, along with Marsha. They spent more time at Marsha's house than at ours. Marsha had a younger sister, but hers was a bigger house with fewer people in it, and escape was easier. Marsha wouldn't correct Livvy's speech, she loved the way Livvy talked, although she taught her some of the current slang with the eagerness of a kid who isn't one of the first to know it. And she did immediately correct Livvy's taste in food. Or, to be more accurate, she nudged Livvy along a path my daughter was already interested in treading: Fish was yucky. Sauces were yucky, except ketchup, the sauce of choice for almost everything. All Italian food except pizza (and an occasional spaghetti with meatballs) was yucky. The foods of choice for two meals a day (three, if you were away from home) were hamburgers, hot dogs, and French fries. Marsha's mother must have told her to behave at our first dinner, but once the two were a team, all bets were off. If I wanted to see Livvy, I'd have to see (and hear) Marsha, and if I wanted them there for dinner, I knew what to cook. Actually, Larry was happy to grill meat for the kids over the weekend, if I was occupied. Hostilities between Beatrice and Livvy never came to a head that first summer because Livvy spent all her time with Marsha. Larry was more than pleased to do what he could to help keep the friendship going. It was Larry who assured me that if my daughter barely talked to me anymore, that was because she was turning into a typical American teenager at a precocious rate. And, indeed, she was losing her Italian accent with remarkable speed. There were moments when I almost wanted it back, when I felt that more than twelve years of my life had disappeared, after all.

At the end of July, I went into the city for a day to pay my bills and do errands. While I was home, I went to the loft's one long closet, which had ended up in Livvy's room when we put in walls. (For now I had the room that was slightly larger and closer to the bathroom.) I'd left for Westport with just some white pants and shirts, thinking I'd be returning to New York before long, and now I wanted to get some of the clothes I'd left behind. As I edged toward the back of the closet, I kicked Livvy's suitcase. Which did not move.

I got my dresses and left the room, but the suitcase nagged at my mind because it was cloth, with vinyl sides. Lightweight. Theoretically, Livvy's clothes had been unpacked and put in the bureau or hung on the left of the closet's two rods. I'd observed but not thought twice about its being not much clothing, considering the size of her suitcase.

Cautiously, as though she might walk in at any moment, I returned to the room. The closet was dark. I pulled out the suitcase, set it down, opened the zipper that went around three sides, lifted the flap. It was more than half full of fall and winter clothing—sweaters, skirts, tights, shoes, a pair of boots, a parka.

I sat down on the closet floor. Livvy had wanted all along not just to visit, but to come to live with me. Or she'd thought she might want to. All right. It made a kind of sense. I'd been so eager. She might have been concerned about how disappointed I'd be if she said she might stay, then decided against it. It crossed my mind that maybe she'd wanted to see whether I was still the ogre she remembered, someone worse than her father's wife, but I told myself not to get carried away. When things went well, I got scared because it couldn't last; when they went badly, I was afraid she'd take off. Our first week alone had been wonderful, the succeeding ones good to all right, more like real life (or what I still thought might be real life). At some point jealousy over Marsha had mixed with theoretical relief; it was clear that she was having a better time than a fourteen-year-old could have with just her mother. Now I wouldn't need to be at all jealous. On the other hand, if she really wanted to stay, there was a great deal to be done. It had occurred to me that Angelo might not stand in our way, but I'd need financial help from him. I couldn't imagine plunking her into one of the ordinary, rotten Manhattan public high schools, and it was too late to test for one of the special schools, even if she could have gotten in. Once upon a time, I might have asked my parents to help me pay private-school tuition. But they were already complaining about the money required to keep up the house, even as they talked about adding rooms because Beatrice and Larry's family was growing. If Livvy stayed, they would be more interested than ever in adding bedrooms; two of the four they had were small and now that Beatrice and Larry were there for August, I was sharing a room with Max. It was out of the question for Livvy to do so.

I zipped the suitcase, pushed it back to where it had been, shut the closet door, and left the room. I was in turmoil. Not at all the way I'd have expected to be upon discovering Livvy might stay. Maybe it would have been different if she'd said something to me. Or maybe . . . If I had someone who helped me with Livvy the way Larry helped Beatrice with Max. Shortly before Livvy's arrival, a pleasant man at a Westport cocktail party had invited me to dinner and I'd told him I had to get back to New York. I'd been afraid to get involved with someone when Livvy was coming. By the next time I'd seen him, he had a girlfriend. Now I felt I'd been foolish. A nice, mature man who knew what teenagers were like was just what I needed. To advise me, to keep me sexual and other company, to give me the affection that, whatever my brain told me about adolescents or anything else, had been part of the fantasy of Livvy's return. I needed to be very close to someone who didn't address me as Mother. Beatrice and I hadn't regained our closeness. If I complained about Livvy to my parents, I was interrupted with assurances of how purely happy and grateful for her presence I should be. I needed to be very close to someone who liked Livvy but understood. Someone who was like a husband but like a father as well.

I returned to a hot afternoon in Westport. Everyone had been to the beach and come home. I changed into shorts and a T-shirt, let my father grill halibut for dinner (hamburgers for Marsha, Livvy, and Max, who'd begun to want hamburgers when "the big kids" were having them, which drove Beatrice wild), and we enjoyed the first local corn of the season. Beatrice couldn't stand anything about Marsha, and when it appeared that the girls were settling on the porch with us, she told Larry she wanted to go to a movie after Max went to bed. She'd entered her seventh month and she was huge. Much larger, she said, than she'd ever been with Max. My parents considered going to the movies, too, but Livvy said there was something she and Marsha needed to talk to them about, that was, to me and to them, and my mother said it was just as well, she wasn't really in the mood for a movie. When Larry and Beatrice had left, I brought out ice cream for the girls, cold drinks for the rest of us. I felt a drowsiness it was hard to understand since I'd barely done anything all day.

Marsha began to giggle.

"Go on, butthead," she said to Livvy. "The world is waiting."

Livvy was disconcerted by her use of the name. She told Marsha to wait for her in the front, then, as soon as the other girl had left, she said, looking at my parents, never at me, "I don't want to go home!" And burst into tears.

"Sweetheart!" my father said, holding out his arms. "That's wonderful!"

Livvy rose from the table, came across the terrace to settle within the warm, grandfatherly crook of his arm.

My father saw my expression and asked quickly, "What has your mother said about it?"

Livvy sat up, wiped her eyes and nose, waited for me.

I smiled sweetly. "I haven't said anything because this is the first I've heard of it."

It wasn't fair. I should have been able to be happy now.

"Oh, dear," my mother said, then put her hand over her mouth lest she say anything else that would convey even the mildest disapproval of her granddaughter's behavior.

I sipped at my iced coffee, although I was already telling myself it should have been decaf, I was going to have enough trouble sleeping.

Livvy looked at me, nervous-expectant, as though she really believed there was some way in the world I was going to not want her to stay.

I said, holding my voice as steady as I could, "You must know that I want you to stay. I just don't understand ..." I trailed off, not knowing how to finish the sentence.

"I think your mother's a little hurt," Livvy's grandfather said, "that you didn't talk to her about it first."

"I was afraid," Livvy said.

There we were again.

"Oh?" I said. "What were you afraid of this time? That I'd scream at you again? Beat you?"

"Caroline," my father said, gently reproving.

"I was afraid you'd say no."

"Why would you be afraid of that?"

She shrugged. "I don't think you mind if you don't see me."

The first in a series of bitter laughs issued from my mouth.

"Oh? Would you like me to keep you from seeing Marsha to prove that I want you around?"

My father, certain I'd hoisted a line that would yield useless matter, said, "Let me ask you something, Livvy. How will your father feel about your staying here?"

She shrugged. "He'll be just as happy."

"Come on," I said. "Your father never wanted you out of his sight for a day and a half."

She looked at me levelly, said, "He never wants me around now."

Of course, she thought I didn't want her around, either.

"Oh, Livvy," I said, "just because he has a new wife ... and she's having a baby ... doesn't mean he doesn't love you just as much."

"He beats me."

We all gaped at her. This was before accusations of abuse had become standard fodder for the six o'clock news, and any-one's doing such a thing was shocking, never mind that we were talking about a man who had adored his daughter more than any living creature. Later, I would find it more believable. Later, there would be times when the possibility of slamming her crossed my mind, when I was convinced she'd go as far as required to provoke such a reaction. But at this time I was barely aware of the possibilities.

My mother murmured, "No."

My father held her more tightly.

"I can't believe it, Livvy," I said. "Your father got mad if I even yelled at you!"

"That was before Annunciata," she said pathetically.

"Do you understand," I asked after thinking for a while, "that I *want* you to stay here? That I love the idea? That your father doesn't have to do anything terrible for me to want you to stay? For all of us to want you to?"

She nodded. "But he still beats me. If the house isn't quiet enough. If I don't do what she tells me to do."

"So," I asked after a long time, "you think that if we, if I, ask him, he'll say it's okay for you to stay with us." *Dammit.* "With *me*."

"He'll be glad to be rid of me." She began to cry again. My father held her, stroked her, told her he was sure it wasn't true, but in any event, we all wanted her with us. And I sat there, feeling just as I had in the old days. Out of the loop. The Angelo-Livvy loop. The grandfather-Livvy loop. It barely mattered.

Marsha shouted to ask Livvy what was going on.

"Can she come back?" Livvy asked me.

I smiled. "I didn't ask her to leave." I sounded defensive, even to myself. Was I going to be defensive for the rest of our lives?

Livvy called to Marsha to join us.

"School," my mother said. "That's the first thing we have to figure out."

"I want to go to Marsha's school," Livvy proclaimed as Marsha came around to the porch.

My parents and I smiled uneasily. Marsha went to Hunter, which, for those who don't know it, is a school in Manhattan for academically gifted students. We knew, just from the way Livvy's English, good when she arrived, was getting better in spectacular fashion, that she was academically gifted, but we didn't know whether she was nearly as good in math or science as she was in language. And even if she was, the exam for fall entry was held in the spring.

My father began to explain all this to her, but Marsha interrupted.

"My mother knows the assemblyman."

We stared at her blankly, three adult, voting Americans who had never understood that knowing one's elected representatives might yield as many benefits as a thorough reading of *Gadney's Guide to Contests, Festivals & Grants*, and we repeated, as one, "Assemblyman?"

Marsha nodded. "She wouldn't talk to him unless we asked you first, but she'll call him, and—"

"Hold on for a second, Marsha," I said. *Never mind that Marsha's mother knew before I did that Livvy wanted to stay in New York. Stick to the operational realities.* "It's a very nice thought, but the test for next year was given in the spring."

She shrugged. "My mother said he can get her the test, if he wants."

He wanted. Marsha's parents had thrown two fund-raisers before his election, and Marsha's mother volunteered in his office. Livvy was given a date to take the test. Angelo readily consented, in an English far better than I remembered his as being, to her remaining. When I asked whether he'd want her to visit, he said it was too early to worry about that. He would ship over her clothes. His surprise, when I said that she already had most of them, was transatlantically transparent. I began to wonder if she'd ever had a return ticket. She spent most of the remaining August days going over old exams with Marsha and on her own with an intensity that made me nervous when I wasn't admiring. I quietly investigated the other school possibilities, then wrote to ask Angelo whether he'd pay for a good private school if she didn't pass the Hunter test. It seemed to me that whatever was going on between father and daughter, I'd best have his response in writing. I received a letter from a man named Joseph Giulini who explained that he was the accountant for the Pirelli family, and now, of course, the Angelo Ferrantes as well. He wondered if I would be so kind as to outline for him the tuition for each school, as well as any other costs I anticipated for Signorina Ferrante in the coming four years. With my father's help, I detailed tuition costs at Fieldston and the U.N. school but said I did not, as yet, have a good idea of what it would cost to have Livvy with me. Perhaps they would think about some sort of modest allowance until I did. Also, I needed various papers she hadn't required for her passport, most particularly her school transcripts.

Signor Giulini obtained those with remarkable dispatch and sent them with a letter saying Signor and Signora Ferrante could promise to pay her tuition and four thousand lira a month, then the equivalent of about two hundred dollars, to cover her allowance and other expenses. I told Livvy that her father was being generous. She made a comment to the effect that he would do anything to get rid of her. I said I didn't think that was fair, that she was a real student and he knew as well as we did that if she didn't get into Hunter, we'd have to take a shot at one of the good private schools.

Her response, uttered in as plaintive a voice as the little matchstick girl ever possessed, was, "I don't want to go to a private school. Marsha says all those kids are buttheads!"

I laughed. "What's a butthead? Someone who doesn't like Marsha?"

She looked at me suspiciously. "Maybe you just don't want me to go to Hunter."

"All I want," I told her, "is for you to realize they only take a tiny fraction of the kids who apply, and it won't be the end of the world if you have to go someplace else."

She wasn't interested. I was with 'er or I was agin 'er. And, in fact, when she received word a short time later that she had not been admitted (she'd made excellent scores in math and science but hadn't been able to handle the extremely difficult section on English usage), she turned on me, or perhaps I should say, away from me, with a coldness suggesting that if I hadn't talked about other possibilities, she might have gotten into the school of her choice.

It was our first really bad period together. I need not detail our initial attempts to get her into Dalton or the U.N. school. She refused even to interview for either. A couple of kids she knew from the beach who lived in the Village were going to the High School for the Humanities, a new public school on West Eighteenth Street, and that was where she wanted to go. When my parents urged her to reconsider, she told them that she couldn't bear to have her father take money from Annunciata to send *her* to school. (She never objected to any other reason for taking Annunciata's money.) When I urged her to reconsider, she said that maybe I thought the High School for the Humanities was no good because the kids weren't all Jewish. (This was the first sign that the anti-Semitism she'd come by through her father hadn't dissolved along with their attachment.) Or maybe I didn't like the idea that she'd be so close to home? Why was I making such a fuss, anyway? It wasn't as though she was such a great student that she had to go to the best school in the world. If she were that good, she'd have gotten into Hunter.

Indeed, the only person she appeared to dislike more than me these days was herself.

My parents checked out the High School for the Humanities for me. It was the reincarnation of an old school called Charles Evans Hughes, which had once had a good academic reputation. Now, with its new name and a small student body, the Board of Education had restored it to academic health. I was relieved not to have to fight her on the issue, and pleased that she'd have to walk just a few blocks to get to school. I remembered a ridiculous amount of my high-school time as having been spent on trains.

Even before we returned to the city to enroll her, she refused to see Marsha or take the other girl's calls. When I told her that Marsha's mother had called to say that Marsha was very upset, she shrugged, said that once school began, they wouldn't be able to see each other, anyway.

Before the test results had come in, Marsha had taken Livvy on a first, exploratory shopping trip in Westport, explained what was cool, if not essential, in the way of clothing for a New York City high-school girl: Levi's or army pants (a pair for every day of the week; this generation washed its clothes almost as fanatically as it washed its bodies. Early on, Livvy had giggled about this with me, but she was already spending so much time in the shower that I'd asked her to warn me when she was going to take one, just in case I had to use the bathroom during the next hour); Lacoste T-shirts, Brooks Brothers men's shirts; sneakers—their brand names less rigidly ordained than they would be a couple of years later, when anything worth putting on their feet cost more than dinner at Lutèce.

I couldn't tell what was reasonable in the way of allowance. The first monthly check from Angelo for two hundred dollars had come in. After checking with a couple of parents who gave me wildly different figures, I told Livvy I would give her twenty dollars a week for basic expenses (she'd have no carfare) and I'd pay for her clothes, within reason. It seemed best not to raise the possibility of my getting more from her father until I had a better feeling for what she really needed. But when I told her that I could afford Levi's, if not a pair for every day of the week, and that we could find nice substitutes for Lacoste and Brooks Brothers shirts, she stared at me as though I were trying to thwart her entry to the new world, then immediately tried to call Angelo. By the time she reached him, she was frantic about beginning school "looking wrong." I'd said she could ask whether he would reimburse me if I allowed her to put a few things she absolutely had to have on my American Express charge. I sat in the living room, trying not to look as though I was listening as she spoke from the wall phone in the kitchen, the only one I had. Then Angelo apparently insisted that she put me on. She called me to the phone and stormed into her room in the manner that would become her standard exit after a conversation she found unsatisfactory.

I picked up the dangling phone, cautiously said, "Ciao," and waited.

"Ciao, Cara," Angelo said jovially. "How are you?"

"I'm okay, thank you," I replied. "I feel as though we can't always talk to the lawyer when she . . . You know."

"Already she gives you a bad time?" he purred, the old, seductive Angelo.

"Well," I said cautiously, "she needs clothes and stuff for school, and I was trying to figure out what I could afford, and what I should ask you for."

"Ah, yes," Angelo said. "I told her, I will send you money. I will not send it to her. Ask her what she did with the money from the return ticket. From the time she sees my wife's family has money . . . If I send it to her, she will spend it and want more. This way, you give her what she should have."

"Well," I said as my brain tried to absorb all that was going on, "it's nice that you're going to send it." I didn't know how to negotiate with this kinder and richer Angelo, whose only suspicions were of his daughter. "Did you have any sum in mind?"

I had a feeling I would never see any money from a return ticket. So did he. He asked me a few questions about what things cost in New York. I explained about kids and clothes, and he said he would wire me a thousand dollars for everything she needed, aside from the monthly sum. I would give her what she needed from this. When it was used up, I would tell him and he'd send me more.

"Oh, Angelo, that's wonderful!" I breathed into the phone. "That will make everything—"

"I suggest," he said, "you do not tell her what you get from me. Whatever you tell her you have, she will want."

I was silent. It was so mean. Gratuitous. On the other hand, he hadn't required pressure to be generous.

I thanked him, told him I was glad he was so comfortable. I understood Annunciata was pregnant and hoped she was doing well.

"She is a saint," Angelo said.

The suggestion being, I suppose, that saints always did well, rather than just doing good.

"Well," I said lamely, "that's wonderful. I'm really glad you're so . . ." Comfortable? Happy? "I'm really glad."

Livvy had come back out of her room and I felt vaguely guilty at being so friendly with her father. I told him I would let him know how we were doing, then motioned to ask if Livvy wished to speak to him again.

She shook her head.

I smiled as I hung up. "Well, your father's going to send us money so you can get some of the clothes you want. He was very nice about it."

"How much will he send me?"

"He'll send it to me, love." Why was I uneasy? "You know, I'll deposit it in my account. And in the meantime, if you need to use my American Express card . . ."

"How much?" she repeated.

"Five hundred, for now." The lie came as though I'd prepared it. "That's in addition to, you know, your allowance."

Her lip curled in a way I'd not previously seen.

I smiled. "That's a lot of money, Liv. Remember, you won't even need carfare to get to school. I think you'll be able to buy everything you need."

No matter how good a school Humanities was, it wasn't going to be full of kids with seven pair of Levi's. I had to hope she would make some new friends who didn't think the sun rose and set over Brooks Brothers. I'd never been particularly taken with Marsha, a large, lumpy sort of a girl, slow in body if fast in wit, neither pretty nor pleasant. I couldn't tell how much of my reaction to her could be blamed on jealousy that she'd taken Liv away so thoroughly and so fast. But Livvy had been happier when she did have a good friend, and for all I knew, at her new school she'd have friends and be friendly to me as well. At least once the financial negotiations were finished. (They're never finished.)

School began. My queries about it were met with shrugs, "All rights," and lists of what was still needed. But she did appear to be doing a lot of homework. I had a full load of classes that fall and she made no move to help with any household chores. Larry and Beatrice suggested I write down everything that needed to be done and discuss the division of labor with her. I told her that she could change her clothes as often as she wished, but I'd need help with the washing *and* ironing. This was before the time when the torn and bedraggled look had become *de rigueur*, and she'd begun to change her clothes every time she left the house. She reluctantly agreed that the chores should be divided between us. She would do the laundry, which had to be taken to a laundromat a couple of blocks away, once a week. She would be responsible for her own room. I would be responsible for the rest of the apartment as well as the kitchen chores, including, of course, the massive job of cleaning and straightening after each class.

I gave her a schedule of my classes: one each evening at six, Monday to Thursday, two on weekday mornings at ten, which wouldn't affect her, and three in the afternoon, between two and five. During those times, she'd have to be quiet in her comings and goings, couldn't have friends around or use the kitchen or living room, and so on. She made no comment. I don't know what she did with the schedule, but for a while we had no problems with it.

What I had a problem with was never seeing her for more than ten or twenty minutes at a time and feeling, then, an unbreachable distance between us. If we shared dinner (that is to say, if we sat at the same table; she seldom ate anything but chops or cheeseburgers with Coke), she usually brought a book to the table. If I tried to talk, she said she was studying. I told myself she was really terribly busy learning the city, starting a new school, making friends, and so on, but I still felt deprived. Beatrice and Larry said that very few fourteen-year-olds were even civil to their parents, and probably the less I saw of her the better, but surely I should have a grace period to make up for the four years when I hadn't seen her at all. A longing remark to this effect one day—I think I said I didn't see her much more now than I had when she was in Rome—brought forth such an extraordinary response, "Are you saying you wish I'd never come?" that I was afraid to complain anymore.

Fortunately, I became absorbed in my classes, in getting to know the new people, reacquainting myself with the old. The class with Lance and Perry had reconstituted itself. Lance had informed me that I should be flattered; they'd all applied elsewhere last year and only come to me when the other classes were full. This year, they'd decided to stay with me. We were going to work on some fairly elaborate sauces. The Westport group had asked for a course in bread-baking. I'd consented with the understanding that I would be learning much of it along with them. They'd loved the idea.

The weather was still warm, but when I asked Livvy about going to Westport for the last weekend of September, she said there was no way. She was picking up American lingo as though it were sold at Brooks Brothers. "Dweebs" remained a favorite, although when I mentioned a couple of kids who occasionally spent a fall or winter weekend in Connecticut, the response was, "They suck."

"It's going to be gorgeous weather," I said cautiously.

"I have a lot of homework," she replied.

"Can't you do it up there?" I asked.

"Not with the kids screaming."

I didn't respond. There was only Max. Beatrice's baby was due in a month. Occasionally Max's friend came from down the street to play in the backyard.

"Anyway, I have to do some shopping. Nothing fits me."

I remained silent.

"Can I please just have the rest of the money?"

I was startled. "All of it?"

She shrugged. "Why not? It's mine, isn't it?"

"Well, yes," I said, "but your father gave it to me because, well, he wanted it to last for—"

"He doesn't trust me and you don't, either."

"Of course I trust you," I said. "But it's a lot of money, and I'm not sure you should carry it around all at once. I mean . . ." I smiled. "What if Brooks Brothers goes out of style next week and you've spent it all?"

She'd begun to grumble about her weight, but the one suggestion I'd made, that she switch from Coke to Diet Coke, had been met with the irritated response that Diet Coke tasted disgusting. When I said maybe she could get used to it, she walked out of the room. Now it took her a moment to understand that I'd made a sort of joke, then she was angry. Anything resembling a joke had begun to irritate her, while humor was the only way I could cope with many situations that were arising.

She'd made at least one friend at school, a girl who asked if she wanted to go on a tour of the Times Square pinball machines. Pinball machines were this girl's passion and she intended to write her first essay for English class about them.

I said I didn't think it was such a good idea, Times Square was pretty awful.

"I'm talking about the daytime!" she'd argued. "Nobody wants to go at night."

"It's pretty ugly, even in the daytime," I said. And as she mustered her forces for all-out war, I added, with a smile, "I'm afraid you'd rape somebody."

It took her a moment to get my feeble joke and then she exclaimed, "You're always making fun of me!" and headed out of the apartment. "You're always—" She couldn't think of anything else I was always doing, but she decided she didn't have to, she was already at the door and was able to open it and run without finishing her sentence. I made a mental note: No more jokes. Funny or un.

When I finally met a new friend of Livvy's, Mayumi Sakai, it was because Mayumi called one day when I was in the middle of a class and I apologized for being abrupt, said the class was just taking something off the stove, I'd have Livvy call when she came in. I don't know what Livvy had told her, but Mayumi thought it was exciting to have a mother who did something besides shopping. Furthermore, Mayumi adored Italian food. Not only did she adore Italian food, but when she finally persuaded Livvy to let her come home and have me cook a meal for the two of them, Mayumi walked into the apartment, looked around, and said, "This is awesome! It's like an artist's loft in Soho!"

Not only was I pleased, but it earned me a respite. If Livvy hadn't been able to find anything good about me except that I was in America, Mayumi's appreciation of my cooking skills, not to speak of my "artistic" home decoration, gave my daughter pause. There was no question in Mayumi's mind that, given the choice, she would prefer our loft to her parents' apartment in London Terrace, on Twenty-third Street. I did not ask myself why a Japanese girl who lived in London Terrace and went back to Japan every summer with her family was attending a fair-to-good public high school rather than one of the special public schools or a good private school, along with every other Japanese kid in Manhattan. I couldn't afford to consider such matters. Mayumi told Livvy she'd swap her apartment for ours any day, and was delighted to be invited for dinner and even to sleep over. This had an excellent effect on my daughter, who consented to my having a phone conversation with Mrs. Sakai during which it became clear to each of us that it would be acceptable for her daughter to stay over at the other's. Livvy began to show me tests on which she'd gotten *A*'s, occasionally to consult me when she was writing a paper.

I had been bought a respite in the soap opera called "The Gathering Storm," and it was a while before I would have to notice further warnings.

Our first crisis in this new period came because Livvy had gained weight and the jeans she'd bought at the beginning of the term didn't fit her anymore. Three pair was the absolute minimum she needed unless I wanted her "to spend the rest of my life in the laundromat." She settled for two, having spent every penny of the initial big lump, as Angelo had predicted she would. (By now I'd become expert in carrying out his advice to conceal what he was sending me.) I gave her the money for the two pair, but then she began obsessing about her weight, American style. With Italian-operatic variations. If she'd gained weight in New York, this was because she couldn't stand the food I had in the house and "had to" eat the junk food that she'd gone for as though it were water in the desert. If I offered to stock whatever dietetic food she requested, she said it wouldn't do any good because all the other stuff would still be around. That other stuff being the food I ate, served, and used in my classes and that she claimed to despise. Except that frequently one or another of the despised foods, the chunk of Reggiano I was never without, or leftovers from various dishes she'd professed not to care for, or ingredients like the Italian sausages and hams I used bits of in various dishes, disappeared from the refrigerator, so that I'd go to get one of them for a class and find that it wasn't there. I took to hiding things among the greens in the vegetable bin so I'd have them when I needed them.

Mayumi was about a size one-and-a-half. This was because her parents served mostly fish and rice and other healthy things. But if I broiled some fish for dinner and served it with rice, Livvy would barely touch it, then later she'd go out and return with a grocery store's paper bag full of Fritos and other junk she'd ordered me not to stock. If our eyes met, she'd say she couldn't help it if dinner was inedible. At all times when my kitchen wasn't responsible for her difficulties, my refusing her enough money to buy clothes that fit was. She was so convinced and so convincing with each new argument that I'm sure if Angelo hadn't warned me, his checks would have been gone within minutes of coming in each month. Once or twice I almost called him to talk about her, see if he could say something as helpful as that had been, but then, I would hear her saying, "He beats me," and decide against it. As it was, I just noted what he sent and what I gave her, so the record would be there when she was certain she hadn't spent that much money.

In December we had the first of these battles that was more than a skirmish. In January she informed me that she had gotten a baby-sitting job through the school's employment office. The children's father was a doctor at Beth Israel Hospital. She would baby-sit one evening during the week, and then most Saturday nights, with an occasional switch to Friday or Sunday. The family lived nearby and she would be walked home or put in a cab. There was a housekeeper who remained with the children until six each night but was no longer willing to stay later. Livvy had had to promise to be available those nights when they wanted her.

I was startled and asked the wrong question.

"Do you like children enough to do that sort of thing?"

She flushed, but held her ground.

"They're older, they're eight and nine. And they're not brats!"

No need to go into who *was* a brat.

She would be earning five dollars an hour, she proudly informed me, and would be able to buy what she needed for herself.

Indeed. I whistled. "That's wonderful, Livvy. I'm proud of you."

She watched my face as though there might be some hedge to what I was saying, but could identify nothing.

And the arrangement seemed to work. Not just because she was earning money for what she wanted, but because when she was home, she wasn't always straining to get something from me she couldn't have. The children were well-behaved, not at all the kind of kid who was raised in my family. The doctor was swell. (She never talked about Mrs. Klein unless I asked. Mrs. Klein had some kind of big job uptown; Livvy wasn't sure what it was but thought she made a lot of money. She didn't seem to pay much attention to the kids.)

I had their number on the bulletin board, along with unpaid bills and recipes I hadn't filed yet, but it was understood I would call Livvy only in an emergency. I didn't have emergencies, but I still missed her, at least I missed the daughter I'd left in Italy. Or *someone*.

There were tenants on the five other floors in my building, some with children. I'd never exchanged more than a hello with any of them, the exception being a little boy I'd helped when he couldn't fasten the air pump to his bicycle tire. The mother was a pretty blonde, the father a slightly shaggy New York Jew. There also were two girls. The one time the younger and friendlier girl had volunteered shyly that my apartment smelled wonderful, and I'd asked if she and her sister would like some of the cookies I'd just baked, they'd chorused, "No, thank you," in a way that reminded me: In the New York I'd returned to, children were trained to reject all offers from strangers.

Like it or not, I was a stranger.

Shortly after the time I'd helped the little boy with his tire pump, his father came down the steps as I was opening the top lock to my apartment. We exchanged nods. I turned back to the second lock.

He said, "I appreciate your helping my kid. I'm Leon Klein."

I said, "Caroline Ferrante. It was a pleasure. Ciao."

I was late preparing for a class and I went in and closed the door behind me, a move which turned out to be fortuitous in terms of Leon's loosening up even enough to allow his children to talk to me.

The next time we spoke it was because my apartment smelled especially wonderful. Most particularly, it smelled of chicken soup. I'd had a request from Evelyn Fox, whom I'd been seeing occasionally, to make a soup from Escoffier I'd done for her once before, Consommé Favori, which began with chicken soup and went on to artichoke bottoms and hazelnuts, among other things. It was Saturday morning at about eleven, the broth was finished, and I was going out to do what remained of my shopping. As I closed the door behind me, Leon and the two younger kids had unchained their bikes from the well under the staircase and were heading for the front door. He held the door for them, then I held it for him. He apologized for holding me up. I said it was no problem. He thanked me, then asked why my apartment smelled wonderful.

I smiled. "Chicken soup."

"You mean you're always cooking chicken soup?" he asked, apparently serious.

"No," I said. "I mean, I teach cooking, and I'm usually cooking when I'm home."

He moved out his bike and I came out after him.

"I don't suppose you make matzo balls," he said.

"Well," I said, smiling, "if matzo balls by any other name . . ."

He looked puzzled.

"I mean," I said, "the closest thing was *gnocchi* where I did most of my cooking, but I . . ." The children were getting impatient and he still looked as though I were speaking Chinese. "I'll tell you what. Sometime I'll make real matzo balls and I'll invite you all down."

"You will?" He sounded as though I'd offered him conclusive proof of Santa Claus. A Santa Claus with matzo balls. Well, almost conclusive. He'd believe it when he tasted them.

"Sure," I said. Then, when he didn't move, probably because he was going through one of his frequent Fear of Giving Hope to Single Woman moments, I added, "How about lunch next Saturday?"

"What time?" he finally asked.

"As late as the kids can handle it."

"One o'clock?"

"Fine. See you then."

* * *

The week passed. I waited for a call from the children's mother, explaining that she'd made family plans for Saturday afternoon. No such call came. On Friday night Livvy slept at Mayumi's. The girls were going to spend Saturday together. I had a fantasy: It turned out that everyone in the building except me knew everybody else. They'd thought I was standoffish. Aloof. Now they were thrilled to learn that not only was I friendly, but I loved to cook for friends. We became like one big, happy family. In Italy I'd been closed off from people by a kitchen door. Here nothing closed me off except the size of the city, the nature of my work, and having returned in a period where you could no longer imagine striking up an acquaintance with a man who talked to you in the park, or to you and your girlfriend in a bar. Maybe some member of my new family would introduce me to a nice man. Surely many married couples in New York had single male friends who wanted to meet a woman who cooked.

By a quarter to one on Saturday the table was set, the soup had been skimmed and was heating on a low flame, the matzoball mixture (I'd used the recipe on the back of the matzo-meal box, as had my one grandmother who cooked) had been chilled and molded into dumplings I'd drop into the soup. At two minutes to one, I dropped them into the boiling broth. At one I welcomed the Kleins, minus Mother Klein. Nobody offered an explanation for her absence.

The children were wide-eyed but demure—as though they'd found themselves inside a diorama at the Museum of Natural History. They were Rennie (Bernadetta), Annie (Anastasia), and my friend Ovvy, whose proper name was Ovid. I asked whether their mother would be joining us. I was greeted by silence. Leon was dumbfounded because, while he hadn't had any difficulty getting laid since his wife had left him, it hadn't occurred to him that a single woman in New York might make a meal for someone with a wife.

"The kids' mother lives in California," he said. "I'm sorry. I thought you . . ."

"Well," I said, "I'm sorry, too. I mean, I thought that blonde woman I see you with . . ."

"She's my girlfriend," he said, giving Rennie a warning look as she pantomimed throwing up and the other two giggled.

"Well," I said, "uh . . . Why don't you come sit at the table and we can talk while I finish up."

It was a dark, rainy day and I'd turned on all the lights so the place would look cheerful. I'd set six places. I removed one. There was Zito's bread on the table and butter, along with chunks of Reggiano and an aged Gouda I thought kids might like. Salad waited on the work counter. The matzo balls would be ready in another ten or fifteen minutes. I finished the dressing for the salad, using the real balsamic vinegar and Mostoli Venturelli olive oil that were my steady, guilty extravagances. Every time I looked up I found the Kleins staring at me or at the pot of soup with a raptness that at some point struck me as extraordinary.

"You can talk, you know, if you feel like it," I said. "If you're wondering how come I do this so easily, it's because I was a professional chef. I lived in Italy for eleven years."

"You mean you're not Italian?" Leon was astounded. "I thought you just had terrific English."

I laughed. "Ferrante's my married name. I'm a Jewish girl. New York. I see you're like me, you can't tell who's Jewish. Jews from outside of New York can, you know. Anyway, I was married to an Italian. We had a restaurant. I have a daughter. . . . She's fourteen. She's—"

"Yes, of course," Leon said. "Olivia's our baby-sitter. I just thought you were Italian."

The children giggled but I was, of course, dumbstruck.

Leon realized that something peculiar was going on, apologized.

"I assumed you knew. I thought that was why . . . She's been wonderful, and of course it's so convenient for me, having a sitter I don't need to take home."

I went to the kitchen bulletin board, lifted up a couple of recipes from the *Times*. There it was. Dr. Klein, with the phone number. No address. I read aloud the number, asked him if it was his. It was.

"Well, there you are," I mumbled, horribly embarrassed.

"Teenagers," Leon said. "I've heard a lot of stories about what I have waiting for me."

"I just thought . . . I just thought . . ." I *hadn't* thought. Certainly it hadn't occurred to me . . . Certainly Livvy had conveyed the impression that there was a Mrs. Blonde Klein. And they lived nearby; I'd never actually asked how nearby.

"Are you a doctor?" I asked, returning to the table.

He nodded.

"Beth Israel. I don't put M.D. on the doorbell because I don't want someone thinking there are drugs up there. Anyway, I don't practice at home."

Fortunately, lunch was ready. The Kleins were rapt as I ladled matzo balls and chicken soup into their bowls. At one point Rennie asked if anyone remembered when Mrs. Borelli used to cook, before her back got bad, but the other children didn't. Leon explained that Mrs. Borelli was the housekeeper, who'd once cooked for the children. He knew I was in shock and he was being particularly careful.

"Does anyone want some juice?" I asked, then wondered if I should offer them soda.

Annie solemnly shook her head. "We have that all the time."

I perceived for the first time the sadness of the child, who was then eight. (Ovvy was six, Rennie, eleven.) I said it was nice to be doing something special and told them that Livvy also liked things different than I did them at home.

"You mean," Annie asked, her eyes widening as though I'd been reading from Ripley's "Believe It or Not," "Livvy doesn't like chicken soup with matzo balls?" (She hadn't tasted them yet, but due to Leon's fond descriptions, matzo balls had achieved mythic proportions on the family's dream menu.)

"Well," I said, putting down the last bowl, then sitting with them, "what Livvy likes is a long story, and I'll tell it to you sometime, but first let's see if you like the soup."

To say that their (and my) first chicken soup with matzo balls was a raging success would be to understate the case. They only stopped when the big stockpot was empty of soup as well as dumplings, Leon as eager and childlike as his children, all of them making the most gratifying noises and paying me the most heartwarming compliments throughout the meal.

For my part, I talked. I told them how I'd always liked to cook and how I'd gone off to Italy for Christmas and ended up married to someone, cooking in restaurants there. I told them how Livvy had grown up in restaurants and had never had any interest in food, and how, coming to live with me, she'd wanted only hot dogs and anything else American. I said that even if matzo balls were more Jewish than American, I was glad that, thanks to them, I'd finally made some.

"You're not trying to tell me you've never made them before," Leon said.

"Not with matzo meal." I laughed. "You know, it's not one of the world's most difficult dishes."

He shook his head disbelievingly. Leon was one of those men who still believed there was a sex-determined gene for cooking, and no number of stories about the great male chefs who didn't think women could prepare *haute cuisine* would dissuade him. He pointed out, on a later occasion when I made an issue of it, that there was a disproportionate amount of homosexuality among male chefs. But when I asked what it meant, he wouldn't answer except with something vague about genes. He placed a nearly unbounded faith in the notion of genes, the corollary of this being that Rennie, the Difficult Daughter, had her mother's genes, while Annie the Easy possessed his own. He tended to worry less about such issues with his son. In fact, it would be fair to say that he tended not to worry about Ovvy because he was a boy, or to see his son's idiosyncrasies in the same light as he saw his daughters'. If neurosis was born in the womb, it remained there, seldom choosing to resettle in the less hospitable climate of the male body.

Of course, I knew none of this on the Saturday afternoon when the Klein family lingered so happily over chicken soup and salad that I suddenly worried because I had nothing for dessert, and asked the kids if they'd like to bake cookies. Leon, whose wife had run off to California with another woman when Ovvy was two, and who thought of himself as an available male, didn't yet realize I did not yet view him in that light. I think he would have insisted they all leave had he not understood that I was in shock about Livvy. As it was, he said he really had too many errands to do, the shopping for the week, and so on, but, if they liked, the kids could stay and bake cookies with me. The two younger ones liked. At the door, he thanked me again, said he'd just go along with Livvy as though nothing had happened and leave it to me . . . He trailed off because he didn't know any more than I did what "it" was going to be. On the other hand, there were three children involved, and even if it had been my inclination to let the matter go, I couldn't take the chance that one of them would mention our lunch before I did.

"Can I ask you one question? Did you—did Livvy find the job through her school?"

He shook his head. "We'd pass her in the hall, or on the street. She was always nice to the kids, and one day I asked if she did any baby-sitting. She said she had cousins she baby-sat for."

I went uptown to talk to Beatrice, whose baby, Rebecca, was now a couple of months old. Max greeted me happily as he always did when Livvy wasn't with me. I, in turn, made it a point not to pay too much attention to Rebecca, whom he still found intolerable. When he and his father left the house to go to the park (he wanted me to take him but I explained that I had to talk to his mother), I could happily hold Rebecca, change her, kiss her soft tush.

Beatrice was less smug and sure about Livvy these days. If she didn't like my daughter any more than she had before, she was less certain she could have handled Livvy better than I. With Rebecca's birth, Max had turned from a lively, adorable little genius into a maniacal brat who couldn't be managed by anyone but his father, who was at once firmer and more phlegmatic than Beatrice. This, in turn, made it possible for me to consult her about what was happening with Livvy.

She went into her psychological mode, gave me a long story about Livvy's recreating a family for herself, a more bearable family with no infants in it. Doubtless, Livvy had formed an Oedipal attachment to Leon, which was why she'd had to keep the family secret from me, lest I compete with her for the attention of . . . and so on . . .

At first I was interested, then I was patient. But as she continued, I got more and more upset. Everything she was saying seemed to suggest that I mustn't talk to Livvy, mustn't interfere in this new family she'd found for herself, but I could see no way to maintain such a charade. I left more confused than I'd been when I arrived, even less certain of how I would handle my daughter.

Fortunately, or unfortunately, the matter was already out of my hands. Leon had suggested to the kids that they not talk about our lunch until I'd had a chance to do so. Ovvy had interpreted this literally, to mean that they shouldn't talk about The Lunch, so that when Livvy passed them on the street as they were coming home from their late-afternoon bike ride, he had called out, "Guess what, Livia?" (She'd always used Olivia with them, though she didn't insist upon it at home until later.) "We made cookies with your mama!"

Leon told me later that she'd stopped short on the street, stared at them for a moment as though she didn't know who they were or where she was, and then run into the house ahead of them. He'd been uncertain of what to do about his plans for the evening, and had given her some time to cool off, then called. No answer.

But she was home, and stormed out of her room when I came in, wanting to know how I managed to ruin everything in her life.

I stared at her, open-mouthed. Where was the embarrassment I'd thought would make it difficult for her to face me? Where were the shame-faced explanations, true or false, of why she'd been lying to me all these weeks or months, since she'd gotten the job?

I asked her what she was talking about.

"You know exactly what I'm talking about!" she shouted. "I'm talking about the way you poke into everything. You think I couldn't tell you poked into my suitcase? You think I don't know why you weren't surprised when I stayed?"

I should have been relieved that at least there was a shred of sanity there, but I wasn't, of course. I was trembling.

"And I suppose I knew," I said after a long time, "that the people you were baby-sitting for lived upstairs."

"Of course you did. It was right there on the bulletin board! All you had to do was look in the phone book!"

The trick was to act calm. "It never occurred to me."

"I don't believe you."

"I see. You've been lying to me all along, so I must have been lying to you. Is that it?"

She let out a wordless scream, but then the words came.

"Can't you just stay out of my life?"

"No. I can't. If you want me to stay out of your life, the place for you to be is with your father. You're only fourteen years old and someone has to watch out for you and—"

I stopped because I could tell, from her expression, that I'd said something terrible.

She burst into tears.

"I know that's what you want!" she cried, heading for her room. "You think I don't know it?"

"Oh, my God, Livvy, that's not true!" I called. "All I'm trying to—" But the door had closed behind her and no begging of mine could make her open it, no tears of my own could convince her that she was wrong.

Leon called again.

Livvy wouldn't come out of her room.

I told him that I wasn't doing anything that night and if she didn't come up, I would. He was embarrassed but he had no choice but to accept; he and Christina had theater tickets, couldn't find another baby-sitter at this hour (five-thirty P.M.), he hadn't been able to get Mrs. Borelli, and it was out of the question to leave the younger kids with Rennie; I must have noticed that she and the other two didn't get along.

I baby-sat. Rennie stayed in her room. I played all the card games I had thought I'd forgotten with Annie and Ovvy. Then they watched television in their rooms and went to sleep. Leon was so grateful, I was embarrassed, asked him if he thought it would have been easier for me to stay in my own apartment with Livvy that night. We laughed together and he stayed away from both of us (Livvy refused to work for him anymore) for some time. In fact, it was only when the school year had passed, with the younger kids coming by to bake cookies and without his hearing from me either on pretext or with good reason, and we'd gone through another summer when he hadn't seen us, that Leon would become willing to think of me as a friend—or at least to let me cook for all of them again.

It would be difficult to exaggerate the difference the children's visits made in my life—and I, if I may say so, made in theirs. If the classes were pleasant work, Annie and Ovvy were my play. And I became the motherly person who delighted in them as their own mother had not. Mrs. Borelli was nice to them but had several grandchildren of her own and didn't have the feeling for them that I did.

If Livvy entered the apartment when the kids were there, she went to her room without acknowledging that she'd even seen them. Leon told me that if they passed her on the street she nodded, her eyes downcast. Life in my own apartment had become, and remained, an armed camp. When I suggested to Livvy that we could have an argument and be done with it, she asked if I had bought her return ticket, because she couldn't afford to, she had no job. But with all her unpleasantness, with all the arguments about any and every issue that arose, she had, until several weeks after our Leon debacle, stayed out of the way when my classes were in session.

The previous week's Tuesday-night group had done a Sicilian *ghiotta*, in which swordfish is fried in olive oil, then baked with a sauce consisting of the same oil, tomatoes, olives, raisins, capers, and pine nuts. *Ghiotta* means dripping pan, and we'd talked about differences and similarities between what the French and Italians did with sauces, how they utilized drippings. Two of the men were going to Maine, they were hipped on lobsters, and they'd offered to buy them for the whole class if we'd steam them and then do lobster butter, à la Julia Child. Now we had steamed and shelled the lobsters, then decided, giggling, to eat them with melted butter, rather than wait for our usual after-class dinner. The men were clustered at the burners, taking turns stirring the shells, along with a little meat and coral, in the butter. I was setting up strainers, large bowls of ice cubes and small bowls. I explained that the lobster butter would harden faster over the ice cubes.

"Just like the Duke of Windsor," Lance said.

The rest of the class cracked up. I smiled, trying to think of who could explain the joke to me.

The apartment door opened and Livvy's voice loudly exclaimed, "*Merda!* She's got one of her idiot classes!"

As everyone turned to see who was speaking, and I stood, struck dumb by anger and embarrassment, she disappeared for a moment, then came back in, closed the door. She smiled shyly, an adorable little girl.

"I'm sorry. I didn't mean to . . . I was so hungry, and I had no money, and I just wanted to get something to eat."

I didn't respond. The class looked back and forth between us, as though they were at a tennis match. Livvy grew smaller, her voice, lower.

"Could I just . . . Could I take a little something to eat?"
Please, sir, can I have s'more?

I couldn't speak.

She came toward us, head bowed, took a can of Coke from the refrigerator, then began rummaging in the cupboard, where she eventually located a bag of Fritos and a box of Oreos, both of which had been just above her eye level. Walking back toward her room, she told everyone in a tremulous voice how terribly sorry she was to have interrupted the class. Then she fled.

I felt everyone standing close by. My hand was still on the sponge I'd been using to clean the counter. It didn't want to move. I looked at the lobster shells in their butter. Even Lance held his tongue. I looked at the clock. It was seven-thirty already. After an incalculable amount of time, I took a deep breath, threw the sponge into the sink, and asked the men to take their seats.

"If nobody minds terribly, we're going to have a slight change in the menu—I mean, the *curriculum*—for tonight." As I spoke, I poured the lobster butter through the strainer into one of the two bowls set over ice. "Anyone who's interested can check in a little while to see that the lobster butter has really become solid enough to spread. Or to do a lot of other interesting things with. In the meantime . . ." I erased the recipes on the blackboard and wrote *PASTA*.

There wasn't a sound.

Under *PASTA*, I wrote: *Flour, eggs, salt, and water.*

"I know most of you live in the Village, and you can get fresh pasta whenever you want it, so probably the last thing on your minds is bothering with your own. But I'd like to make a case for doing it occasionally. Nothing to do with where you live, or what you can buy, or whether you have one of those machines that are all over the place. It's a case for making pasta because you happen to be in the mood."

The salt box and the flour canister were already on the counter. I got the eggs from the refrigerator.

"This isn't going to be our usual class M.O. If we have one. I'm just going to demonstrate. I'll be glad to repeat it as a regular lesson sometime, if you decide you want me to." I measured the flour onto the counter, made a well in it, broke in the eggs, added the water and salt. "Actually, enjoyment isn't precisely what's on my mind." I folded over the flour and began kneading it into the eggs. "Except to the extent that eating and breathing . . . or hitting a punching bag . . . are enjoyable because you need to do them. You need to knead, you might say." I held the ball of dough with one hand and, with the other, pushed it away, digging in deeply with the palm of that hand, then folding the dough back toward me and doing it again. "Bread can serve the same purpose. There's a recipe in the first *Times* cookbook for something they call Cuban bread.

All you need to have in the house is flour, salt, and yeast instead of eggs. I just happen to be in the mood to do something Italian right now. Five or ten minutes of dealing with something Italian, or with the whole world, in a ball of dough, and the world never knows." I continued kneading and folding the dough as I spoke. "There're people who use pasta machines, and bread machines, and the bread hook on the KitchenAid, but I don't know why you'd bother to make bread or pasta if you were going to use machines instead of knocking out, kneading—that is, K-N-E-A-D-I-N-G—your own dough." I divided the dough in half, rolled out one half, stretched it around the pin, sprinkled a little flour on it to keep it from sticking, and so on, until it was somewhat transparent and I could leave it stretched out over one end of the counter while I did the other half, then left both to rest for a while.

A little calmer now, I filled my big pasta pot with water, put it up to boil, then discussed a few possibilities for dressing the pasta, beginning with simple butter and Parmesan, going on to, say, lobster butter. Finally, I cooked the pasta and gave them a choice of dressings, warning them not to offer the buttered one to a Sicilian. "There're a lot of Sicilians who, if you offer them butter in any form, will act as though you left a dead cow on their plate."

They were all enchanted with the class that evening.

"It's been a pleasure," Lance said, with something between a bow and a curtsy, as he picked up his coat from the sofa near the door. "You should ask your daughter to come in more often. She really livens things up."

He threw me a kiss and followed Chris out, having jolted me back into my anger so that I didn't fall asleep until six in the morning.

Livvy was in school by the time I awakened. She came home while I was giving my afternoon class, went to her room. When the last of the women had left, I cleaned up, rehearsing in my mind what I wanted to say to her. Then I knocked at her door. There was no response. I knocked again.

"Livvy? I have to talk to you."

"I'm doing my homework."

"Well, stop for a minute."

There were sounds as of a heavy book being dropped, a chair being scraped back heavily, the button-lock knob turning.

(The door was never unlocked now when she was inside.) She opened it, stared at me angrily.

"We need to discuss what happened last night."

"What happened last night?" she repeated. "Oh, you mean . . . It was an accident. I was hungry. I thought we were eating at Mayumi's, but she thought we were coming here."

"Well," I said, "maybe you forgot I had a class, but you knew they were here when you said, 'Oh, shit, she must have one of her idiot classes.' "

"Okay. I won't do it again. Now can I go back to my homework?"

I hesitated. My heart was beating as wildly as though she had a knife in her hand, but I felt I had to talk to her.

"No," I said, trying to steady my quivering voice. "I . . . We . . . We really have to talk, Livvy."

"My name is Olivia!" she yelled. (It was the first time she'd objected to Livvy.) "And I have a biology test to study for!"

"All right, Olivia," I said. "Then we'll have our talk tomorrow. When you come home from school."

She turned around and slammed the door behind her.

"And until then," I shouted, rage bursting loose, "stop slamming the fucking door!"

"You know that you embarrassed me in front of the class, and I was very upset," I said the next day, having succeeded in cornering her before she could lock herself in her room.

Her eyes narrowed as though she were estimating whether it would be worth the enormous effort involved in saying she was sorry.

"I wasn't thinking," she said. "It just came out."

"It came out loud and insulting. Not just to me. To my students. It must never happen again. Either the insult or the coming into the kitchen. Except in an emergency."

She was bored. "You said that already."

"You're still going to have to sit down and listen to me." I beckoned to one sofa, sat on the other.

She waited.

I took a deep breath.

"I was very angry with you yesterday. Furious. But I didn't shout until you slammed the door in my face. It's not that I held back because of what you said about shouting, it just didn't happen. I was under pressure, but not the same kind as when you were young and I was cooking in the restaurant. Does that mean anything to you?"

"I slammed the door," she said after a long pause, "because I could tell what was going to happen."

I didn't know whether to laugh or go to the airline office and buy her a one-way ticket to Rome.

"I see," I finally said. "So, it's not that anything you do ever makes me mad, it's just that I'm mad all the time. How can you imagine living with someone like that?"

"Maybe," she said after barely a moment's pause, "I can live with Grandma and Grandpa."

You had to admire a kid who didn't fool around about sticking a knife into you. I don't know what my face registered, but she felt obliged to say something.

"At least," she said, voice quivering, "they like me."

"They love you," I told her. "But it's different from the way I love you. With grandparents it's much simpler, it's—"

"You never loved me," she said.

"What on earth are you talking about?" I asked, my headache back from its vacation. I'd had more headaches in the past year than in my entire life. "I adored you! I loved you more than I ever loved anybody! When you were a few months old and I had to go back to the restaurant, I kept you in a car bed in the kitchen so I could look at you. I couldn't stand to be twenty feet away from you. I was jealous when your father took you someplace."

"He told me he took care of me all the time."

"Oh. Is that what he told you." I instructed myself not to speak until I could keep my voice steady, but I couldn't obey my instructions. "Well, if he said that, he was lying. Not about taking care of you. He loved you and he took care of you a lot of the time. Especially once you were walking, and I couldn't keep you with me in the kitchen. And *I* loved you and *I* took care of you a lot of the time. I adored you. I used to go crazy because you said all these wonderful things, and I wanted to write them down so I'd remember them, but I was always in the kitchen with stuff in my hands."

"All I remember is the yelling."

I gave in, or something gave in, and I began to cry. It didn't matter anymore. As a matter of fact, I forgot about my headache. Or it forgot about me. I just kept crying.

"I can't help what I remember," she finally said.

"I guess you can't," I said when I was able to. "But you might listen to what I remember, too."

Her mouth twisted as though to suggest that my memories were no more than attempts to deny hers.

"Do you understand, at least, that I don't lie to you? I mean, I'm not a big liar in general, but I never lie about anything important."

Her expression remained skeptical. My smile was so bitter I could taste it.

"Or did your father tell you I was a liar, too?"

"He didn't have to tell me," she said before standing to go to her room. "I remembered."

We moved around the apartment as though a clothesline of white flags was strung between us. My father called me during school hours to say that Livvy had asked if she could live with them. He and my mother had explained why they didn't think this would work, aside from the matter of its hurting me, which Livvy claimed was ridiculous. I didn't tell my father that at the moment the idea was not without its appeal. Friday night, when we'd planned to go to my parents' for dinner, Livvy said she had too much studying to do and stayed home.

The following Monday, Perry Marcus called to ask if he could bring a visitor to Tuesday's class. Sheldon Halstead lived out of town but was moving to New York. He was interested in a sample session for which he would, of course, expect to pay. When I demurred, Perry pressed me, claiming that Halstead would want to enroll for next fall. Finally, I consented. A stranger's presence could be a welcome diversion from what had happened, might even assist me in regaining the assured self who'd been in easy control.

On Saturday I made brownies with Annie and Ovvy, joked with them about making no-cook cookies when it got hot out. I felt something resembling panic when they reminded me they would be in camp during July and August.

"Oh, no!" I said. "Where's your camp?"

It was in the Berkshires, but it might as well have been in California. I felt bereft. They saw, and rose from their seats to come around to hug me.

"I'm going to miss you so much," I said, my voice trembling.

"Maybe you can visit us," Annie said.

"Oh, dear, I don't think so." I hugged them tighter. "That's just for parents."

"You could come with Daddy on Visiting Day," Ovvy said.

It was tempting to ask Leon if I could, but I knew I wouldn't.

"We'll write," I said. "You give me your address and I'll give me mine in Connecticut. I'll write to you and you can write back as often as you like."

Beatrice's kids would be around. Somewhere nearby there would be kids, a kid, who loved me, enjoyed me, who would fail to recognize the picture of me my daughter drew.

Mayumi called after school on Tuesday to ask if it was okay for Livvy to stay at her house through dinner. They had to study for a test. Her father would bring Livvy home. I said that would be fine. For my class, I prepared the next scheduled lesson, on some of the wonderful main-course sauces Italians made with walnuts or hazelnuts as a base. The previous year, on my father's birthday, I'd invented in his honor one I called Academia Nut Sauce, but when I wrote it on the blackboard now, my old joke seemed dumb, so I erased it and left the standard stuff. I couldn't read or look at the television news or do any of the things I normally did before a class. Finally, at ten minutes to six, I erased the rest of the blackboard and wrote two recipes from a new favorite I'd found at Kitchen Arts and Letters, a wonderful store devoted to books about food and wine which, if it had existed when I was in school, I'd never have gotten as far as I did. This one was called *The Northern Cookbook*. The first recipe I wrote was for Squirrel en Casserole with Biscuit Topping and began, "Skin and clean squirrels. Remove scent glands from inside forelegs. Wash thoroughly and cut into serving pieces." The second was for Reindeer Pot Roast with Vegetables. I need not go into cooking details here.

Class members came in somewhat tentatively, as though uncertain, or so I felt, whether the class would be taught by Dr. Jekyll or Mrs. Hyde. As was their custom, they left their coats on the sofa, then joined me at the kitchen end of the room, where I'd lined up their folding chairs. When the first three looked at the blackboard—it was Chris Ganbarg and then Perry with his friend Sheldon—there was a moment of silence, and then hearty laughter.

"That's wonderful," Perry said. "Caroline, please let me introduce you to Sheldon Halstead."

When he reached to shake my hand, as men had come to feel they had to do or you'd sue them for sex bias, I sighed.

"Sheldon, if you're really interested in cooking lessons, you might have come to the wrong place."

He took my hand between his and said I shouldn't worry about it, that the recipes on the board were worth the price of admission.

Sheldon was a pleasant-looking man of average height, jogging-maintained weight, frizzy hair, and glasses. In those days he wore a black T-shirt, black sweatpants, and new-looking white sneakers so regularly that they might have been attached to his skin. If he caught anyone glancing at his feet he announced that you could take the boy out of California but ... I've come to suspect he would have preferred to wear Gucci except he then wouldn't have had a chance to tell everyone that no matter how he sounded (like a Brooklyn Jew with the awful speech everyone had in Brooklyn), he was from California.

The rest of the class had filtered in, laughed, settled in the chairs. I erased the blackboard, told them we were actually going on with the lesson we'd originally planned.

Lance asked, "Who's going to make her mad so we can have more fun?"

"There's no guarantee it works that way," I said, wondering what the newcomer must be thinking. "I can be a tough sombitch when I get mad."

Ask my daughter.

"Show us," he said.

"You and me. After class. Alone," I added with a wicked grin, as uncertainty about whether I was serious silenced him. "On the other hand, if you behave yourself, maybe I'll read you some more stuff from the place where I got the squirrel recipe. Like Moose Sukiyaki, Fried Woodchuck, Casserole of Seal. And one for Stuffed Muskrat that begins, if I remember correctly, 'Clean the rats well.' It's an interesting question, actually, why people are repelled, amused, whatever, by any meat they're not accustomed to eating. And then, of course, there's the matter of food that takes on some symbolic meaning, for one reason or another.

"This evening, we're going to talk about nuts. And nut sauces."

"I really appreciate your letting me come tonight," Sheldon said, when the class was over and he and Perry were the only ones remaining.

"Think nothing of it," I said with a yawn.

"I don't suppose there's any coffee left."

It served me right.

Perry laughed, shook his head.

"I wanna have a little talk with you," Sheldon said, ignoring him.

I was curious. He didn't sound like someone who was considering taking the class. In fact, he sounded like someone who, as the old expression went, couldn't boil an egg. And didn't want to learn.

"I can make some," I said, awake now.

Perry dropped the coat he'd picked up from the sofa and followed us to the kitchen, where I started some water as Sheldon delivered a disquisition on the jerks who thought coffee would keep you awake any longer than you wanted it to.

"First of all," he said, when I'd cleared the table of the remaining dishes and we were sitting, "let me tell you what a good time I had. You know, I was a kid in the sixties when I saw Julia for the first time. I never cooked a meal in my life, but from that time on, I was crazy about her. Never missed a show. Gave all my wives her books."

I nodded. "They're excellent. Especially the first one. When I came back from Italy, all I read were Julia and Escoffier and a wonderful book called *American Food*."

"I package shows for television."

Naturally, it took my breath away. Never mind my breath, it took my brains. I looked at Perry.

He said, "I didn't want to make you nervous."

I laughed. "I'm smarter when I'm nervous."

"See what I mean?" Sheldon asked Perry, as though he'd brought Perry, instead of vice versa. "She's a natural." He turned back to me. "There've been okay food shows, but nobody that held a candle to Julia. Nobody who had a personality to compare. As soon as Perry told me about the class last week, I knew I found her."

"The class last week?" I repeated.

Sheldon nodded happily. "So the first question is whether you can do it again."

"Do it again?" Still not understanding.

"You know, the whole *tzimmes* with the pasta."

Tzimmes, for those who don't know it, is a carrot and prune pudding eaten by Jews at holiday dinners, but it has come to mean a fuss, a big deal. It was just dawning on me that last week's *tzimmes* with Livvy was what had brought Sheldon to my class. With the realization, I became upset and angry.

"You mean, you want me to get hysterical so I can be on television?"

Sheldon nodded happily. It was called acting. People did it all the time.

Perry placed a hand on my arm.

"You mustn't be offended, Caroline. It's not about craziness, it's about spontaneity. I told Sheldon about you as soon as I began the class, because you were charming in a spontaneous way. Funny. Even last week, when you were so upset, you were funny. It was hearing about last week that convinced Sheldon to take a look."

"I didn't have time before," Sheldon said, afraid that the recorder of deeds was listening.

"It was a real test," Perry said, "and you passed it with flying colors."

In spite of myself, I was mollified. Flattered.

"I thought you worked for an ad agency," I said to Perry.

He smiled. "I do. Ad agencies and poll takers are what television's about."

Livvy came home, hesitated, as though in fear, asked whether it was okay to come in.

"Certainly," I said stiffly. I introduced her to the two men. She nodded and went to her bedroom as we sat in silence.

Sheldon said, "So, that's the kid."

"That's the kid," I repeated.

Perry spoke into the ensuing silence.

"There are a few things we, Sheldon, has to know, do, before he begins to think seriously about a show. Even if you're willing to fake getting mad again, he has to get a feeling for things you might be able to talk about, besides Italian food, which there's been a lot of."

"I don't know what's been done," I pointed out. "I've never

seen Julia or the others on TV." Nor did I really think of what I cooked as Italian Food, but just as food.

"Well, that could be an advantage. That you're fresh."

"In the meantime," Sheldon said, restless with no crisis to amuse him, "can you do it again? For a tape?"

I smiled. "Maybe you'll have to be the one to make me mad."

"You get mad pretty easily," he said. "You were mad at me, anyway, and you got madder when the kid walked in."

"That's not true!" I said, stung. "If I was in a bad mood it was bec—"

"Don't waste it on me, sweetheart," Sheldon said. "I have four of 'em."

"You mean everything that goes on with everyone's kids is the same?"

"The shit's the same."

Perry laughed. "He's been reading Dostoyevski."

"I never read Dusty Anything," Sheldon said. "I'm not like you guys. I was a dropout. I didn't learn what I know in school."

I was about to tell him he wasn't the only dropout in the room but stopped myself because it sounded competitive.

"All right," I said. "So she gets me mad. So, now what?"

"So now maybe you wanna do the pasta lesson for me?"

"Are you kidding?" It was almost ten o'clock.

He shrugged. "Only if you feel like it."

Perry laughed, got his coat from the end of the sofa.

"I'm going to say good night. I can tell that you two'll be able to carry on without me."

Sheldon barely nodded but I thanked Perry, said I'd love to talk to him during the week.

"You don't have to thank him for anything," Sheldon assured me. "Fate would've arranged for us to meet, one way or the other."

With an embarrassed laugh, I waved good night to Perry.

"I know we're supposed to be tolerant of fags now," were Sheldon's first words when the door had closed behind Perry. "But every time I think of what they're into, I wanna throw up."

I was silent, wondering how I would be able to deal with this man even if he could make something wonderful happen. Then I asked myself if I thought I was kidding me; Sheldon

Halstead might be pointing to a way out of almost everything that was difficult or inadequate in my life, while allowing me to keep the life, the cooking life, itself.

"All right," Sheldon said, pouring the last couple of ounces of coffee. "So here's what we'll do. I'll come back tomorrow afternoon with a cameraman, and you'll talk to us. Talk about yourself, talk about your life, how you got to Italy, and then you'll work up to, you know . . ."

"I have a class tomorrow afternoon."

I had to be careful not to throw away my real life while daydreaming about a better one.

"You can't cancel it?"

I shook my head. "I'm sorry. I could do tomorrow morning. Or the foll—"

"Oh, shit. All right. I'll wake up in the morning. Ten A.M. That's my final offer."

Perry would tell me later on that Sheldon's Julia Child story had been fabricated, there'd never been any mention of a cooking show until Perry dragged him to my class. If I didn't know that, and if I was much too excited by the prospect Sheldon offered to dwell on his objectionable personality, that didn't prevent me from being leery of the man, the aggressive gloss on his deficiencies, his awful speech, his prejudices, so much less understandable than my own.

I would do bread instead of pasta. One of my Westport ladies had called me in tears because just as she'd mastered the pasta machine, a store selling fresh pasta had opened a block from her husband's office. They were all over the place now. Soon pasta machines would join espresso makers and the various other items that people used two or three times, then set on a high shelf for display (Cuisinarts being the known exception). Bread dough had at least as many possibilities as pasta, more interesting variations. And you could tell people about the wonderful smells they'd be missing if they never baked their own bread. I'd do bread.

Settled. But I wasn't satisfied.

If Sheldon had perceived that I was an entertainer, my subject food as another's might be sex, race, or his mother-in-law, if my spontaneity had been my attraction, then surely he was going to have to allow me to get happy instead of mad. Surely one could attract people with humor. Surely . . . No. I stopped myself. Something in the way I sounded reminded me of the old days, when, as soon as my parents had an idea for something I should do, a reason for doing something different had presented itself. I hadn't wanted to be in school then, but I would most certainly love to find fame and fortune as a TV chef now.

I was going to have to get mad again.

I could. I did. I made bread, instead of pasta, having promised Sheldon that bread dough required the same kind of pounding as pasta dough did. And when it was time, I worked myself into another mad frenzy by thinking of how, if I didn't put on a good show, I was going to spend a lot of my life teaching cooking to six or eight people at a time and fighting with my daughter about money. When it was over, I collapsed in the chair facing Sheldon's. He was staring at me in a way I couldn't interpret. Selena, his attractive young Chinese-American camerawoman, was folding up her equipment to prepare for takeoff. But Sheldon wasn't going anyplace.

"I can't believe you," he said, having already made it clear that he'd gone through life until this day not understanding that anyone actually baked bread. "I have found a new star in the cuisinary firmament."

"Culinary firmament," Selena said as she joined us at the table.

"The culinary firmament," Sheldon repeated, unfazed. "We're going all the way, kiddies. Take my word for it."

By a month later, my contracts with Sheldon were signed, I had inherited Larry's computer (they'd bought a laptop they could move between Westport and New York), and I'd begun entering my class outlines as well as anything else I thought might be interesting for a TV program. I never wanted to leave the apartment for fear I'd miss Sheldon's call. He didn't call. The summer was approaching, and not only had his initial enthusiasm diminished, but another show of his, "Joy Beach," had been picked up as a summer replacement by one of the networks and required a lot of attention. He assured me (for the first time) that nothing was going to happen so fast, anyway, it was too late for the coming season. But when I told him I would be teaching in Westport all summer, he became concerned about being able to reach me at all times. I told him we had a telephone. He wasn't offended—or amused.

It was as I was telling myself to come down to earth and

start outlining Westport's and next fall's classes that Leon
called to invite me out for a quiet dinner so we could talk
without the kids around "before we all disappear for the summer."

I was so excited that I phoned Beatrice at her office. She decided to tease me about the kosher chickens coming home to
roost. I was annoyed. She'd been dubious that anything would
happen with Sheldon, she knew too much about the way the
TV world worked, and now ... Why couldn't she just be
happy for me? Leon was a pleasant and intelligent man I liked,
and to whose children I was already attached. A nice-looking
man of average height and build, with brown hair, lovely eyes,
and, under a small, trim mustache, full lips that one could
think of as being sensual, particularly if one was already having se(x)nsual fantasies about him. Until now I had curbed
such fantasies because of Christina, and surely I still had to
keep some rein on them. But to think of having a boyfriend
who lived upstairs, and had children who were already attached to me, was better than any dream I might have come up
with. I had to calm myself with a reminder that however impossible my daughter's behavior was now, a romance with this
man who'd been involved in her humiliation might make it
worse.

We were seated in the Tiger's Eye, a comfortable Village
bistro Leon liked because it wasn't frequented by anyone from
the hospital. We'd had more than half a bottle of wine and I'd
explained how I had been able to leave Livvy in Rome, thinking that she'd never miss me because of her attachment to
Mirella. But whether or not she'd missed me, it appeared she
couldn't forgive me for going.

"I guess you know," he said, "Rennie's pretty difficult."

"I couldn't tell for sure. She doesn't come down with the
other two"—I shrugged, smiled—"but that could just mean
she doesn't like me." One day that week I'd heard Annie and
Ovvy talk about a fight between Rennie and Mrs. Borelli. They
hadn't begun to confide in me yet, but they'd become less cautious about what they said to each other in my presence.

"She's impossible. With everyone. Including me. When
there's no reason, she finds one. They say that about first kids
in general, but she also ... She was the one who suffered the
most with her mother. She was the most attached to her, the

most jealous, the most . . ." He smiled. "The most everything. Including intelligent, probably."

I nodded. None of us had mentioned his wife since that first day.

He laughed. "There you go again, not asking the obvious questions. Joanna, she wasn't clinically crazy, but she gave neurosis a new meaning. She had no interest in men or sex, or in taking care of children once they were born, for that matter. She just liked being pregnant, having babies, naming them. She didn't tell me right away when she was pregnant with Ovvy, she was afraid I'd insist on an abortion. I would have, even if I'm glad I didn't get to. It's nice to have another male in the house. Anyway, a few months after Ovvy was born, she took a female lover. A year later, they moved to California. A year after that, she left the woman very briefly for a man, but if my information's correct, she's gone on to another woman since then."

"It would be almost funny, if it weren't for the kids," I finally said.

"It was pretty rough. I had a series of people. Mrs. Borelli came when Ovvy was two. She cooked in those days. Nothing like you, but . . . If she hadn't stayed, I couldn't have remained at the hospital. I'd be practicing out of an office in a real apartment someplace. We'd have had to move. Being in this neighborhood was tied up with Joanna's idea that if you lived in a loft, you became an artist. Once or twice I've talked to them about moving to a real neighborhood—the Village, Gramercy Park, whatever, someplace where I could have a practice—and the girls objected violently. Rennie's shrink said there was some very primitive notion that if we moved their mother wouldn't be able to find them if she ever decided to look." He smiled. "Anyway, Christina says I'd have gone nuts in about two weeks if I'd tried to practice out of an apartment. As it is, the girls were always calling me at the hospital with something they thought they were dying from."

Christina says. Present tense. So much for my lovely romance with a man whose wife was permanently AWOL, and whose children were already filling a large part of the gaping hole Livvy had left in my heart.

Our dinners were served. They were pleasant. He asked if I minded eating in a place like this. I said it was just fine. He described his gruesome (hot dogs, potato chips, and so on) eating habits when he was working. I told him I didn't remember what kind of doctor he was.

"A pediatrician." He smiled. "What do you think of that?"

I shrugged. "I don't know yet."

"No wonder I like you," he said, laughing. "You're the first woman who ever didn't tell me how great it was." Then he grew embarrassed at what he said, tried to cover by telling me stories about various women he'd dated, including one who had treated him to a lengthy discourse on how much money a family could save with a doctor around.

I said, "I hardly ever go to doctors."

He said, "And you're trying to make me believe you're Jewish!"

"One of those half-assed Jews. No religion. No doctors."

"What about your parents?" he asked.

"Not religious. They're academics. They both teach at Columbia."

"You're kidding!" He appeared to be genuinely startled.

I shook my head. "My sister and brother're teachers, too."

"That's not the picture I had of you," he said.

"It's not the picture I have of myself," I assured him.

He fell silent.

"What about you?" I asked. "What do you come out of?"

"The Bronx," he said. "The Amalgamated. Do you know what that is?"

I confessed I didn't.

"Union housing. Amalgamated Clothing Workers Union. My father worked in the Garment Center, my mother was in the post office. My full name is Leon Nikolai Klein. Does that suggest anything to you?"

"Nikolai sounds Russian."

"You bet it sounds Russian. Leon is for Trotsky, Nikolai's for Lenin. I can't believe this. You now know a secret only my best friends know. I must trust you."

"Well," I said, at once pleased and discomfited, "I guess anyone who makes chicken soup can't be all bad."

"You betcha. I've never known a woman who could cook."

"Oh, c'mon," I said. "What about your mother?"

"My mother not only didn't cook, she disapproved of women who did. Said it was a form of slavery. She was the first woman in the Bronx to do takeout. I think she invented it. The only place I ever had a home-cooked meal was at my grandparents', her parents, and we didn't go there very often because they didn't get along. Politics. My grandparents were just these sweet old Jews who thought the United States was wonderful because it was better to the Jews than anyplace else'd ever been."

I said that my parents hadn't been hostile to religion but there hadn't been any in the household, either. By this time we'd each had a couple of glasses of Chianti and I found myself telling him about my belated discovery of Angelo's anti-Semitism. He said he wasn't surprised. On the rare occasion when he left New York, he was aware of being a Jew in a way that he never was when he was here.

The dinner proceeded pleasantly, and when we'd reached home, Leon said we'd have to do this more often, maybe some time he'd even take me for a decent meal. I told him he shouldn't worry about it, that, as he might have gathered, I enjoyed preparing food, even if it was fun to go out. He said good night and quickly went upstairs, leaving me to wonder whether my use of the suggestive phrase "go out" had left him concerned that I was, after all, trying to compete with his girlfriend.

Whether or not this was the case, the summer was almost upon us. I would be in Westport giving classes. At a time when Livvy was complaining about having to be there just because I was, my parents had saved the day by finding her a live-in baby-sitter's job that was an easy bike ride from our house. This was particularly helpful because the work on the house they'd talked about, turning a semi-finished basement into two more bedrooms and a bath, was finally being done and there was going to be chaos. In fact, I'd arranged with two women to alternate my classes between their large, well-equipped kitchens rather than doing them out of my parents'.

Leon and two friends from the hospital always rented a house in Southampton, to which he went whenever he had two days in a row when he wasn't working, and where the kids spent what they called their "real vacation" when camp ended. I wouldn't see any of them for more than two months. I had a new fantasy: A restless, sort-of divorced, heterosexual male doctor—you know he's heterosexual because he's engaged in the revolting male activity known as channel-surfing, scrolling through TV channels to glimpse what's playing—is doing same. His attention is caught by an attractive, youngish

woman, standing over a stove. She wears an apron and a peas-
anty sort of dress. Her hair is in a braided crown so it won't
get into her way. She is giggling over . . . over . . . He loves
this woman's laugh. Wait a minute! Isn't that the woman who
lives downstairs? How come he never noticed that laugh? Perhaps he hasn't been funny enough. He determines to find out
if this lovely creature giggles in bed the way she does on her
cooking show.

I'd been in Westport for a few weeks when the leading man
in my daydream called to ask whether I would by any chance
be in the city that weekend and, if so, whether I'd like to have
dinner with him on Saturday night. He was working Sunday
and had decided not to bother driving to the beach for one day.
I was even more startled than pleased. I didn't ask where
Christina was, but I hesitated for so long that he told me that
if this Saturday wasn't good, we could make it another time,
and I had to assure him that it was fine. In fact, weekends
were easier for me, because I had no classes.

My sister teased me about waiting "years" until this man decided to extend an invitation, and then running in to meet him
the moment he asked. Her teasing had gotten rougher since the
very possibility of a TV show had been raised. But Saturday
morning I took the train into a hot, stuffy city, and late Saturday afternoon I showered, washed and dried my hair, then took
a nap with the fan aimed at my naked body. For all the heat,
my apartment felt wonderful when I knew that a hostile Livvy
wasn't going to storm in at any moment.

I dreamed I was teaching a class that included Livvy and
Leon. I was showing them how to slice vegetables when Livvy
began to scream that it was her finger I was slicing, and as
Leon and I watched, helpless and horrified, the whole dream
picture filled with blood.

I awakened, crying. The phone was ringing. It was Leon,
telling me he'd made an eight o'clock reservation at the Coach
House, an elegant place in the Village. I had a headache so terrible that I couldn't imagine going to dinner with him or anyone. I got out of bed, took two super-aspirin, and wandered
around the apartment for a while with the kind of end-of-the-
world feelings I associated with New Year's Eve and the heavy
pressure to be jolly.

It was seven-twenty. Leon was supposed to pick me up at a

quarter to eight. The sane me kept the dream-crazed person of
the moment from calling to tell him I couldn't go to dinner.
From my closet I took one of two beautiful dresses I'd brought
from Rome, a blue and white silky-rayon print. I couldn't
imagine wearing anything with red. The dress was wrinkled.
Almost relieved to have something to do with my remaining
minutes, I set up the ironing board, heated the iron, brought
over the dress, and proceeded to iron my left thumb as it rested
on the cloth.

I screamed, but then I grew calm. I didn't do ice cubes or
butter right away because I had to iron the dress, which I did.
I'd never understood until then the relief pain could offer. I felt
no pain anyplace except in my thumb. Which wasn't why I delayed finding anything to relieve it; it would have been impossible to get dressed, put on makeup and earrings, and comb my
hair with a thumb wrapped in butter or ice. And I wanted to
be ready on time. In Italy nobody was ever prompt. I'd had to
become accustomed to people's being places approximately
when they said they would be (especially the shrinks who were
Beatrice and Larry's friends and who were never five minutes
late). Calmly, I did what I had to do. Carefully, I selected earrings, lovely silver hoops Beatrice had given me for my birthday, nearly cried out as I used my left thumb to close the right
hook, resisted so I wouldn't mess up my makeup. Artfully, I
coiled my hair on top of my head, letting one strand curl to my
shoulder.

"Wow," Leon said when I opened the door, "I never saw
anyone look so different when she gets dressed up!"

I held up my thumb and burst into tears.

"What happened?" he asked, coming in and closing the door
behind him. He told me later that in that moment when I burst
into tears and held up my thumb, which he couldn't see well
in the living room light, he'd wondered if he had been attracted to another lunatic.

"I burned it when I ironed my dress!"

"Oh, Jesus. Let me see."

Having ascertained that it was a real burn, he ran back upstairs to get a soothing ointment, then came down with it. I
stood where he'd left me at the door. He put on the ointment,
lightly wrapped a Band-Aid around it.

It still hurt. But I was calm again.

I said, "I feel like an idiot."

He grinned. "You're right to. Why didn't you come upstairs and tell me?"

I started to explain about the dream, and how I'd wanted my finger to hurt, but instead I just said I was worried about losing the reservation if we were late.

"Mmm," he said. "Well, that's not such . . . Maybe I'll call them right now and tell them we're delayed. You fix yourself up a little."

I went to the bathroom. Indeed, I was a wreck. With my right hand only, I washed and dried my face, put on fresh makeup, combed my hair again. No coil. My finger didn't feel better yet, nor were the aspirin working on my head.

"Maybe we should put off dinner," I said when I came out. "I feel so stupid."

He shrugged. "Stupid people get hungry. Anyway, we can talk."

I smiled, determined to stop being stupid, or at least to put on a good act, and we left for the Coach House. Slowly the pain in my finger and the ache in my head diminished to a point where I could forget about them for minutes at a time. At the Coach House we both ordered martinis, which neither of us was accustomed to drinking. I loved the taste but Leon didn't, and he asked me to select a wine. I picked a nice Italian white that was relatively reasonable. By the time I'd finished my martini and his, my pain was forgotten. We began with crab cakes. He asked me how the summer was working out with Olivia. I said very well, asked him if she'd always called herself Olivia with him. He said that she had.

"I always called her Livvy," I said. "I never thought about its not being Italian. Her father adored Olivia, and I liked it, too, but giving her a nickname was sort of the only American thing I did there. She's begun getting hysterical if I call her that."

Leon said, "I hear they're always hysterical about something at that age."

I smiled ruefully. "Everyone's heard those stories but me. Not that I would have believed they'd be about her."

I told him about Angelo's anger when I connected her name to the olives he loved, and then about the *risotto* that was my first real but sneaky step toward freedom, and about the boy with the rusty penis. He was reminded of a rare time when the girls weren't squabbling because they'd ganged up over the matter of wanting to take turns having Ovvy's penis. From the day they'd seen it, and Annie had asked for one, and he'd explained about girls and boys, both girls had found it unfair. He'd reminded them that men couldn't have babies, he'd promised them they'd have breasts when they were older, but they'd just wanted to know why Ovvy hadn't had to wait for *his* stuff. He told me how, after Annie's birth, anytime Rennie saw a sleeping child on the street, she'd asked why they couldn't exchange it for Annie. If she was playing with some kid she liked, she'd want that kid to come home with her and Annie could go to the other's house. This whole idea of interchangeability had persisted so that, for example, until recently, when he'd brought a female friend to the house, and he always went with someone for a long time before he let the kids meet her, or, he should say, exposed her to the kids ... Anyway, Rennie usually wanted to know why the woman couldn't be swapped for one of her teachers, or had to look the way she did or have that particular name. With Christina, she'd outgrown that one, then pulled something more outrageous; she'd claimed she could never get out of her head a picture of Christina nailed to a cross.

By the time our steak arrived, I was drunk and happy. The white wine was gone and Leon insisted that I choose a red. It wasn't as though he had to drive. I selected a Brolio Chianti, as much because it still came in a basket as because it was reasonably priced, and then Leon and I talked about having Chianti candle holders when we were in school, and Leon said he was going to keep this one if it would fit in my bag, which it did.

Even in my drunken state, in the part of my mind people refer to as the back, but that I picture as on top, like the heavy pot you set on top of the eggplant slices to help them lose their water, I cautioned myself not to invest too much in this dinner. Maybe someone in Christina's family had died and she'd gone home for the funeral. On the other hand, something terrible could have happened to her. Maybe Leon had spoken so much about my cooking that she'd tried to make a meal and had gone up in flames! I told myself to stop it, but I couldn't.

"You know what I was thinking?" Leon asked as we left the restaurant and I began wobbling heavily down the street. "It's a perfect night for a ride on the Staten Island ferry."

I stopped in my tracks, which was considerably easier than walking at this point.

"That is the best idea I ever heard in my whole life."

Leon hailed a cab because it was clear that I was too drunk to walk even a couple of blocks, and half an hour later, we were standing on the ferry deck, talking about what a brilliant idea he'd had. Halfway across the Hudson we moved inside because, even with his arm, then his jacket, around me, I was cold. I was telling him how the only times I ever wanted certain foods were in specific places. Hog dogs were for Coney Island, popcorn was for the movies, as long as they didn't put any coconut oil on it. The cold had made me chatter, but the warmth didn't stop me. What stopped me was that when we were perhaps three-quarters of the way across the harbor, Leon, whose arm was now around me under his jacket, turned my face to his and kissed me lightly on the mouth.

"Oh, dear," I said, "I was afraid of this." I was a little less drunk, and my hand was hurting again. Nor had I really understood until now that I was afraid of something.

He smiled. "Afraid of what?"

"What happened to Christina?" I asked, unable to answer his question.

"What made you think of Christina now?"

"Not just now," I said. "I thought of her as soon as you asked me to have dinner on a Saturday night."

"Well," he said after a long time, "Christina and I have reached . . . what you might call an impasse."

I giggled. "And we've reached a pass?"

He kissed me warmly. I succumbed.

But by the time we'd reached home, I understood what was bothering me, and when I put the key in the lock and he embraced me, kissing the top of my head and waiting for me to raise my face, I gently pushed him away instead. The couple who lived on the third floor came in, were briefly taken aback, nodded, and went up the stairs.

"I don't think this is a good idea."

"Why not?" he asked, moving back up against me, his manner still seductive. "You're not going to start in about AIDS, are you? Christina's the only woman I've been to bed with in three years and she was a virgin when I met her."

I shook my head.

Leon said, "Why don't we go upstairs? The air conditioner's on, and we can talk and be comfortable."

I shook my head. I knew what would happen if we were comfortable.

"I just ... I just ... don't want to ruin a beautiful friendship!" I burst into tears.

He, of course, didn't have the foggiest notion of what I was talking about.

"Listen," he said after a moment. "Let's go upstairs, or in here, if you prefer—I just realized Olivia isn't here, either—and we can talk about it. I promise not to, you know, to push. We'll talk."

I took out my keys, gave him his Chianti bottle, opened the door. The apartment was dark and uncomfortably warm. I turned on some lights, but decided not to get the fan from my bedroom. He took off his jacket, set the Chianti bottle on the coffee table, sat on one of the sofas. I chose the one catty-corner to his.

"Now," he said, "do you want to tell me what you're worried about?"

"It's really very simple," I said. *It's one thing to have fantasies about a romance with you, another to risk my love affair with your kids.* "My own kid hates me, and"—I held up a hand to keep him from protesting—"and yours, I love them, and they're fond of me. At least Annie and Ovvy are, and I keep hoping Rennie'll come around. I'm afraid if I have a—whatever—with you, and it doesn't work, and I don't see you anymore, I won't see them, either. And I couldn't stand that."

But it was Livvy's face I was seeing as I began to cry again.

Leon came over, sat down next to me, put an arm around me, which made me cry more. How long had it been since I'd felt the warm, hairy skin of a man's arm?

"So," he said when I'd finally stopped and I was looking at him, waiting to see if he was angry or just disgusted, "you're not afraid I won't be able to get it up, or anything like that. You just don't want my kids to know that we crossed the line."

"*If* we crossed the line," I corrected, unsmiling.

"If," he corrected, smiling.

I was silent. My finger was hurting terribly, but it would be awful to ask him for ointment now. At least my headache seemed to have vanished.

"I'll tell you what," Leon said. "I'm going to give you a peck on the forehead and go upstairs to the air conditioning. You can come with me or not. But I'll make you a promise. If we go to bed—tonight, next year, whenever—I promise not to let my kids know until you say it's all right. I'll be as secretive as if we were, you know, illicit lovers."

"Well," I pointed out, "you *are* married."

"Sure," he said. "So are the nuns."

"Yes, but your wife exists. She's alive."

"Don't start with that stuff," he said sharply. "I had enough of it with Christina. The first year I wasn't really married because my wife was a lesbian in California, and then the second year comes, and suddenly I have to get a divorce because I'm really married."

Fortunately, it wasn't the problem on my mind.

"Do you mean it?" I asked. "About not letting the kids know?"

"Yours *or* mine," he said.

"Livvy couldn't care less," I assured him.

"It seems to me she's more likely to mind than they are. I don't think you can do any wrong where my kids are concerned."

"I'll try to get my brain turned around," I said when he made no motion to leave. "But right now, my finger hurts, and I think I'm about to have a hangover, and I just want to take some aspirin and go to sleep."

He handed me the tube of ointment from his pocket, kissed my forehead, and left quietly. As the door closed behind him, I noticed that the Chianti bottle was still on the table. It was a long time since I'd had a Chianti bottle with a candle in it.

As the summer passed and I failed to meet another man I could imagine sitting through a movie with, much less enjoying in bed, I managed to convince myself that Leon and I could have a lovely, secret affair that went on for so long that it sort of seeped into all of our lives, and the kids got accustomed to it without even thinking about it. Having settled which, I dreamed that I looked out of my loft window to see Leon entering the house with a beautiful, deeply tanned, eighteen-year-old blonde wearing a white bikini and a wedding veil with a long train.

In the only other dream I remember from that summer, I

made *boeuf bourguignonne* for Leon and Elizabeth David, using her recipe. She tasted it, put down her fork, and spoke the words she'd used in her book to introduce the dish. "This is a favorite among those carefully composed, slowly cooked dishes which are the domain of French housewives and owner-cooks of modest restaurants rather than of professional chefs. . . . Such dishes do not, of course, have a rigid formula, each cook interpreting it according to her taste. . . ." She smiled at Leon. "Unfortunately, this is not according to my taste."

Everyone (except Beatrice) continued to assure me that my daughter had made a beautiful transition to being an American teen. Furthermore, it had become clear, though Livvy never acknowledged it, that she was steadily losing her extra weight. By the middle of August it was gone, though she'd become so American that, when complimented, she complained that her legs were still too fat. No amount of reassurance about body type or comments on how lovely she looked had any effect. On the occasion when she shared a meal with us, she ate like a horse, said that she was lucky, the food where she was employed was so awful, she never wanted to eat. One day Beatrice and I passed her in town at an ice-cream parlor, sitting over the kind of sundae one couldn't imagine tackling after turning voting age.

On a rainy weekend morning in August, when her charges were at camp, she did come by (on her employer's bike; the boys had taught her to ride). Beatrice and Larry were upstairs, my parents were out hunting for furniture for the new rooms. I was reading on the porch, Max and Rebecca in my charge. Livvy came around back, seemed positively startled to find me there.

I said, "Hi, it's nice to see you."

She said, "Where're Nonno and Nanna?"

I said, "In town."

She hesitated.

I said, "C'mon in. They'll probably be here soon."

Having decided that nothing major was at stake, she entered the porch. Not quite fifteen, she could have passed for a few years older, and was really looking lovely, slender and deeply tanned, with her wonderful, dark complexion that was meant to survive the sun. She flopped down on the other rattan settee, picked up a couple of magazines lying on it, thumbed through one, then the other, as though she were just exercising her thumb.

Max was seven years old by this time, Rebecca close to a year. Her playpen was a permanent porch fixture and she would remain in it happily for long periods of time, playing with the measuring spoons I'd given her or some other favorite toy, watching the activity around her, more recently, standing with the help of the mesh playpen sides. Most particularly she liked to watch Max, who since her birth had been willing to go to other kids' houses, but wanted none at his, though he created so much noise and movement that there might have been two or three. When Max talked to Rebecca he smiled, clowned, and grimaced in a way that made his hostility clear to everyone but the baby, who adored every minute of it. She held out to him each toy or piece of food that came into her possession. Often he took it only for long enough to set it somewhere outside of the playpen, beyond her reach. Some of his more aggressive tactics—like the grimace with his face stuck up against Rebecca's through the mesh—drove my sister crazy. After a couple of drinks one night Beatrice had announced she was glad they'd had a second child, it was the first one they shouldn't have had.

The phone rang; Livvy ran to answer it as though she was expecting a call there, then irritably summoned me. I went in, she returned to the porch and picked up her magazine as I took the call. One of the women in my class wanted to know whether her houseguest could attend the class that week. I was saying it would be okay when Rebecca yelped and began to cry.

I ran out to the porch and scooped her up from the playpen. Max sat on the floor, absorbed in a book, a child's caricature of an adult's pose of disinterest. A bunch of her alphabet blocks were in the playpen, suspiciously close to the corner where Rebecca had been lying. Livvy hadn't so much as glanced up from her magazine. I went back to the phone. A moment later, Beatrice, who could see the playpen from her bedroom corner window, dashed through the dining room onto the porch, took the still bawling baby from me.

"Thanks a lot, Livvy," she said.

Livvy looked up, returned to her magazine without answering.

In the house, Beatrice said it seemed to her that not responding to an infant's getting hurt went over some line. And then Livvy's absolute refusal to acknowledge that anything had happened!

I just nodded.

Beatrice had gained a considerable amount of weight and perhaps for that reason, among others, tended to be in a bad mood at all times when she was not actually caring for Rebecca. Bad moods always find their reasons and after this time, Livvy, when she was around, was Beatrice's reason. The following week, when Livvy had an evening off, she joined us for dinner. Whether because of Livvy's presence or just because she felt like it, Beatrice had more wine than usual with the grilled fish, corn, and salad I'd served, and became relaxed and very happy. As Livvy polished off her second burger on a bun with ketchup, mayonnaise, mustard, and sliced sweet pickle, Beatrice said, "Only a teenager can eat like that and lose weight."

Livvy didn't look up.

"Come to think of it," Beatrice said, "how *can* a teenager eat like that and lose weight?"

Livvy didn't bother to reply. My father pointed out that Livvy was working hard.

"So'm I," Beatrice said. "Seriously, Livvy, I mean, I'm jealous of the weight loss. I'd just like to know—"

Livvy stood up, said in a small, pained voice, "Please excuse me. I'm not feeling well." And left the porch.

We were silent. The kids were in bed. Beatrice had told my parents what had happened with the baby, and they'd not thought it important. I had mixed feelings. In recent days Beatrice had brought back to my mind the days when we were growing up, Gus was already in college, she was in high school, and she'd been on my case all the time, with comments on my behavior and jokes about my nonacademic proclivities. (She called me Dumbo when my parents weren't around.)

"You really mustn't keep thinking about that business, dear," my mother said. "She might just have been absorbed in her own, her own . . ."

"Her own selfish, adolescent thoughts," Larry finished. "You should be able to make some allowances. You see enough teenagers, God knows."

"Yes," Beatrice said, "but I wasn't being a psychologist. I was being a mother. And I was absorbed in my own motherly thoughts. I was also being a female, and I was wondering how a kid who eats like that could have lost so much weight. I was jealous. I mean, she's probably throwing it up, but I didn't want—"

My father and mother put down their forks.

My father said, "Stop it," in his no-fooling voice.

She stopped.

My father asked which movies were playing in town that one or another of us was interested in seeing, but the mood around the table had changed radically.

My mind went to the sight of Livvy, sitting in the ice-cream parlor with what had to have been the largest sundae they made. Then it went to one of the young women's magazines Livvy had left in the bathroom for a long time.

Bulimia had been sighted, identified, and discussed almost endlessly on television until AIDS came along and the media could wallow in an even more threatening and more obviously sexual disease. But occasionally some compelling personal tale of salvation from puking still got to float in the magazine mainstream, and this magazine had run the story of a young girl who called herself Scarlett, who wrote that she couldn't control herself when faced with ice cream. The first time she'd thrown up it was because she'd eaten so much, she was nauseated. But the next morning, when she'd weighed herself and she wasn't any heavier than she'd been the day before, she'd decided it was her solution. Her mother was one of those people who thought you couldn't be too thin, and she herself had dodged checkups because the doctors suddenly all knew about anorexia and bulimia. A friend of hers had suddenly been caught by the doctor. But finally, she'd come to understand, with the help of that very doctor, that her problems couldn't be solved by doing something so dangerous.

Beatrice said, "I think my sister thinks I hit on something."

My father said, "I'm afraid Olivia is who you hit on, dear."

Beatrice was furious. "I don't believe this. How come, whatever that little bitch does is okay, no matter how long she's here, and the slightest—"

"Come, come, Beatrice," my mother said. "It's easy to forget that she's still far from an adult. She needs understanding."

"Ah, yes! Just like Gus needed it when he locked me out of the apartment," Beatrice flashed out, astonishing me more than she did my parents, who were familiar with her old complaints.

"And you said he just wanted to be alone with you for a while!"

"Oh, dear," my mother said. "Why do children only remember the foolish things one did?"

I smiled sympathetically. "Better foolish than evil. Livvy thinks I'm evil because I yelled at her when she got in my way in the kitchen."

"Now, you have to admit, dear," my mother said to Beatrice, "I never yelled at you in the kitchen."

"You were never *in* the kitchen," Beatrice responded instantly, then relaxed slightly because her response had come so quickly and so well. "There was Caitlin and Caroline, then Suallen and Caroline, then Anna and Caroline."

By this time we were all laughing and the bad spell was broken. Later, I discussed the possibilities with Beatrice and we agreed that if her suspicion was substantiated, I would have to seek treatment for Livvy. But I knew that I had to be very careful, and I asked Beatrice please to stay away from the subject entirely. It was clear that the slightest verbal maneuver of hers would be read by Livvy as a declaration of war.

In the meantime, the summer was coming to a close, and I had the phone call from Sheldon asking if I could fill in on "Johnny Wishbone."

I'd watched "Joy Beach" all summer so that I'd be able to converse about it with Sheldon. The hero was a real-estate broker who looked like a TV detective and had amorous-mysterious adventures while seeking out Caribbean properties to develop into a series of singles resorts not unlike Club Med. The show's running joke had to do with whether the resorts would be called Sea for Two, Island-Uland, or one of many other possibilities that arose. I'd actually thought of one or two names for islands to tell Sheldon when we spoke. But the summons to "Johnny Wishbone" was his first call all summer, and it came in late August, during the Thursday-morning class I gave at Esther Steinberg's. She had a huge kitchen with a long counter running the length of one side.

We had devoted all eight classes to fish stew in its infinite variety, beginning with the (two *r*'s, one *d*) *burrida* of Sardinia, with its sweet-and-sour sauce, going through that morning's Ligurian *buridda* (one *r*, two *d*'s), for which an earthenware pot and the ripest tomatoes in the world were required. The *buridda* was ready; we would eat it for lunch.

The phone rang. Esther answered and said it was for me. It had to be some sort of emergency or nobody from my house would have called.

I said hello.

Sheldon's voice said, "Where the hell are you?" as though he'd been trying to reach me for weeks.

I said, "I'm teaching a class. In someone else's kitchen."

He said, "Oh, shit. Can you be ready for cameras in twenty minutes?"

I asked, "What are you talking about?"

He said, "Some cookbooker was supposed to do a segment on 'Johnny Wishbone.' "

He'd told me he was trying to get me on a program that showed housewives various fascinating jobs other women did away from home, then told them how wonderful it also was to be in the kitchen. It had been one of a long list of things he was trying to get for me or that were about to happen.

"The cooking segment," Sheldon said. "The one who's supposed to cook today is sick. Can you do it?"

"Yes."

At least I didn't doubt for a moment that I was going to try. He began to argue with me, then realized I hadn't said no.

"Where are you?"

"Westport." Oh, Jesus, maybe they wouldn't be able to get me where I needed to be on time.

"*Where* are you?"

I gave him the address. "Are they going to come and get me?"

"No," he said, "they'll do it right there."

"Who will?"

"The local station. Hold on a minute."

I asked Esther if it would be all right; she assured me it would. The women started to clear out, but I told them I'd feel better if they stayed. They were delighted. A couple of them ran to the bathroom to put on makeup. The others helped Esther clean up the kitchen. I'm not sure who forgot to put the blade in the Cuisinart.

Sheldon got back on the phone and said that someone from the station would be there in ten minutes.

"Be good, kid," he said. "This could be It. I'm taping you."

I combed my hair. I was wearing a white T-shirt and white pants, as I normally did for classes because food stains could be bleached out. There just wasn't time to worry about clothes. If Johnny Wishbone (or Leon) wanted a well-dressed, twenty-year-old gorgeous blonde to teach cooking, he was going to have to find her in the next ten minutes.

Sheldon was thrilled with the show, convinced the networks would be all over us in a nanosecond, but apparently the networks didn't know what a nanosecond was, because it was weeks before anyone expressed interest, months before anyone was ready to think about a show—for the following year.

In the meantime, Labor Day weekend arrived, Livvy's job ended, and on Sunday night we all had dinner together, an unexceptional meal because I couldn't focus on the food, all I could think about was Leon, who had very likely found a woman he adored among the millions of beautiful and accomplished females who spent their summers at the tip of Long Island. I would never see him again, except on the staircase. The only question in my mind was whether the woman he'd fallen in love with, in addition to being a superb cook, was a gorgeous actress, a gorgeous famous writer, or a gorgeous nuclear physicist.

At dinner, when someone teased Olivia about what she was going to do with all the money she'd earned, she said that first of all, she was going to get her own telephone so she could have some *privacy*.

"That's great, Liv—Olivia," I said sincerely. "You'll be able to talk in your room." This wasn't the time to say I hoped she'd be prepared to pay the bill. (She was.)

Silence. It was difficult, even for my parents, to ignore the suggestion that she was hounded and eavesdropped upon when she shared a phone with me.

"Well," Beatrice said brightly, "end of vacation, why don't I serve dessert. Who wants coffee? Iced coffee? Iced tea?" She took everyone's orders and she and Larry disappeared into the kitchen. She reappeared a while later with a bowl of fruit and a plate of *rugelach* from the local Jewish bakery. "That's what a month in Westport'll do," she announced, "make you ready to try *rugelach* that aren't from the Royale."

The plate was passed around, my father offering it to Livvy, telling her the name and, when she looked puzzled, saying he thought she'd love them. She obligingly ate one, told him it was delicious, took another, asked him to say the name again.

"Rugelach," he said. "It means little roll. It's not English, as you can probably tell. It's Yiddish." He paused, then asked, "Do you know what Yiddish is?"

She shook her head, nibbled more slowly than she had on the first one.

"Basically," he said, "it's Jewish German. That is to say, the German language as it was spiced up and made homier, more expressive, by the Jews." He then paraphrased what he'd said to make it more comprehensible to her, using *Ebreo* to define Jewish when she seemed to be failing to get his most basic meaning. "We're going to have some fun," he promised, "teaching you Yiddish as soon as you're bored with English."

Her face was a study in cautious confusion. It was as though she'd failed to understand, until now, that if I was a Jew, I'd gotten it from someplace. Here was this man she adored, telling her he had the same loathsome disease as the woman her father had taught her to despise. What could she do? Where could she go? I watched her looking around the table at our various faces as though trying to figure out how she might have known we were Jews if my father hadn't told her. Her eyes rested on Larry, who had the worst nose in the family, but then they weren't content to remain there because she liked Larry and she was looking for someone she *didn't* like. Finally reaching me, they were vaguely accusatory—as though I had figured out a way to ruin Labor Day by making everyone Jewish.

"Ah, well," I said, meaning to ease us all past a difficult moment, "I don't know if this is the time. Liv— Olivia and I haven't really discussed . . . the fact that she's half Jewish."

"I'm not half anything," she said angrily. "I'm a Roman Catholic."

"Okay," I said after a while, "you consider yourself a Roman Catholic. But your mother's Jewish, and you're surrounded by Jews in New York . . . here. . . . It seems like a good idea . . ." A good idea to what? Everyone else at the table remained cautious. Silent. "I mean, I don't know what your father told you, but the Jews are as different from each other as the Catholics are. There are Jews who are very religious, follow a lot of ritual, and ones like us who don't do very much about it but still feel we're Jews. Ones who believe in God and ones who don't."

"Don't what?" she asked.

"Don't believe in God," I repeated. "In some all-powerful creature who controls our destiny."

She looked at me incredulously, asked if I was trying to make her believe that there were people who didn't know about God. The silence at the table grew heavier.

"Indeed, there are," I finally managed. "But maybe we'd better talk about them some other time."

"There's nothing to talk about," she said. "I don't know any of them."

As she stood up and excused herself from the table, saying

she had to make a call, something that had tried unsuccessfully to enter my mind came to me, full blown: Of the various names of her friends that I'd heard since my daughter had begun school in New York, there wasn't one that was likely to belong to anyone Jewish. This was extraordinary in a city where Gentiles made jokes about finally meeting someone else who wasn't a Jew. If I'd known anti-Semites, I'd never had to be aware they were that, though my parents had referred to the days when Columbia had quotas on Jewish students and hadn't hired any Jews to teach. It had never occurred to me that this wasn't the truth, but the truth had changed. I'd always known that I was a Jew, but when a Jewish Columbia student from Detroit had asked me whether someone else was one, I hadn't been able to tell her. At first she'd thought I was just trying to prove something.

If I'd had any earlier experience of anti-Semitism, perhaps Angelo's would have surprised me less, left a deeper mark in my mind. As it was, I'd assumed that in leaving Rome, I'd left such nastiness behind. Then I'd had little snatches of Livvy's prejudice. During her first months at Humanities there'd been some comment about how only the Jews could get the schools closed down for every little holiday. I'd pointed out that they were the big holidays, and that, for a long time, most of the teachers had been Jewish, but she hadn't been interested. Anyway, it had seemed so clear that her anti-Semitism was about me. She'd once adored my parents; surely she'd known they were Jewish, even if she'd chosen not to think about it. I had agreed with them that it was probably only a matter of time until reality set in, until she noticed that the kids she was making friends with were Jewish. . . .

I waited until Beatrice and Larry weren't around, then told my parents I thought that of all the girlfriends' names I'd heard that year, none was likely to be Jewish.

They agreed that we might have to try to deal with the matter at some point. But they pointed out that being at Humanities and not having Jewish friends wasn't like being at the Bronx High School of Science and not having Jewish friends. Livvy had adapted so beautifully to life in New York. It seemed unlikely that she would hold on for any length of time to what seemed like such an anachronism in late twentieth-century New York.

* * *

We returned to New York early Monday, hoping to get around the Labor Day weekend traffic. On Tuesday morning, Annie and Ovvy came by on the way to school to hug and kiss me, explain that they hadn't reached home until almost midnight. We agreed they'd have dinner with me that night, but I didn't hear from Leon. By late Tuesday afternoon, I was angry. A simple call would have sufficed. A message on the machine. *Caroline, I have lost even minimal interest in you, so please don't bother to change your mind about going to bed with me.*

I did some shopping, returned home. The first message was from Sheldon, telling me to keep Friday morning open for a meeting. The second was from Leon, who said they'd all missed me and looked forward to seeing me. He would drop by on the way home. *Ciao.* My anger wouldn't go away just because it had lost its reason, so I homed in on the word *ciao*, telling myself he must have knocked himself out to find something that didn't sound too personal.

The closest I can come to understanding this nonsense is that I couldn't believe things were going to turn out all right, and I wanted to be in control of my misery when they didn't. It was too much to hope that Leon and I might peacefully come together, have a lovely, long affair, raise his children. Something or everything was going to get fucked up, and I needed to be able to cut my losses when that happened.

Even Rennie was feeling friendly after a summer of eating camp food, and consented to come to dinner with the others. The girls were looking at a magazine Livvy had left on the coffee table, and Ovvy was standing on a stool to stir the gorgonzola sauce for the fettuccine, the only sauce with no tomatoes in it that they all adored, when Olivia walked in. For a moment, she stood at the door as though she were going to leave again, but then she came in and closed it behind her. She didn't run to her room. Nor did she appear to notice the girls. She walked toward Ovvy and me almost as though she were hypnotized.

I said, "Hi, Liv— Olivia, I'm doing fettuccine with one of your old favorites. Gorgonzola sauce. Will you join us?"

Ovvy giggled. "You always sound like her name's Livolivia."

Livvy said, "Thank you. She doesn't believe me when I tell her that." But she was looking between Ovvy and the stove.

Ovvy attended more closely to the sauce.

Olivia didn't move.

Leon knocked at the door. Livvy fled to her room, mumbled something about having too much homework to think about dinner. Annie opened the door and Leon came in, waved to me.

I said, "Hi. I'm going to make dinner for the kids. And you, of course. If you're free."

Leon was puzzled, because he was sane.

He came past where Ovvy was stirring, to the place at the other end of the counter where I was assembling the salad.

"What's going on?" he asked me in a low voice.

"How could anything be going on?" I asked back. "I haven't even seen you."

He laughed. "That's what I mean."

I couldn't laugh with him, but stopped making pretend motions at the counter.

"You're acting as if you're mad at me," he said, still *sotto voce*.

"I don't know how I could be mad at you," I whispered back. "I don't even know what you've been doing since I last saw you."

He laughed again. "You see? There it is again. Wait a minute. I know what you sound like. You sound like you're jealous!"

I said, "Don't be ridiculous," but I turned away from him because my face was hot and its color would give me away.

"But I haven't seen you all summer," he said. "What else could I have done besides . . . besides . . ."

Now that he was pfumfering around, I grew calmer.

"Listen," he said. "After dinner, we'll send the kids upstairs and then we'll talk. Okay?"

A nice signal, but I was not about to be tricked into reading signals instead of realities.

"Unless you just want me to go upstairs and stay there," he said, forcing me to shake my head, to acknowledge that even at nine o'clock in the evening, there might be some reason I wanted to see him.

We had a pleasant What-I-Did-This-Summer dinner, after which I brought Olivia a tray with a plate of fettuccine and, on impulse, a glass of seltzer with about a tablespoon of wine in it, as her father had always done. To my surprise, she opened the door and accepted it with a thank-you. The kids were very quiet. A little while later, Leon took them upstairs, whispering that he'd be back soon. I cleaned up the kitchen, then paced the floor, trying to decide what I'd do if he returned too late, without defining what too late would be.

"Now," he said, when he'd finally come down and I'd brought some espresso to the table, simply because it was farther from Livvy's room than the sofas, "tell me what I've done besides being a nice Jewish doctor in a place where that's what every single female Jew and Gentile is looking for."

The truth made me relax slightly. My hands rested on the table, around the little cup. He placed a hand around the one closer to him. It might have been my breast, for the thrill that went through me.

"So," I said, though it wasn't easy, "did one find you?"

He shrugged. "I'm here, aren't I?"

That didn't mean a thing. I moved my hand out from under his hand.

He said, "You're pretty possessive for a woman who wouldn't even go to bed with me."

"I'm not being possessive," I lied, because I felt ridiculous. "I'm being careful the way you're supposed to be in this day and age."

"Well," he said, "I haven't been near anyone's rectum all summer. Or anyone who's been near anyone else's."

I said, "There are other things to be careful about."

"Like what?"

I said nothing.

"Anyway," he whispered, "for the past two years I've carried condoms around with me all the time. In case I meet the girl of my dreams and she's not prepared for me."

"And you haven't met her?" I asked sweetly.

He shook his head.

"Who will she be when you do?" I asked.

"I'm not sure yet," he said. "But I decided it would be better if she was Jewish. And if she could cook."

I stood up. "Am I supposed to be applying for some kind of job?"

"Oh, for Christ's sake." He stood up. "I don't know what's going on, but . . . Look, Caroline, I spent a lot of years trying to pacify a woman who basically just didn't want me. I was always trying to figure out what I'd done to put her in her moods. I'm not doing it anymore. You're not my wife. You're not even my girlfriend. You wouldn't go to bed with me, for

Christ's sake. And you're acting as if . . . as if . . . Maybe I'd just better say good night."

I got sane. And scared.

"You're right. I'm sorry." I went over to the sofa that was farther from Livvy's wall, sat down.

He thought about it.

I said, "I missed you."

He came over to sit next to me, let his arm rest on the sofa in back of me. I twisted around to embrace him, kiss him. We held each other and kissed for a long time. It felt unbelievably good. I was almost unbearably excited. How long had it been that I'd been deprived of this most basic of pleasures? I might have stopped to feel sorry for myself in retrospect if some better reason for stopping hadn't come up: Livvy called over the wall to ask if she could make a phone call.

"Sure," I called back, artificially natural. I pushed away from him, wiping my mouth although neither of us had been wearing lipstick. "I'm not on the phone."

Leon whispered, "Shit. Just when I thought I was finally getting to seduce you."

I smiled. "Remember, they're not even real walls."

Cautiously, Livvy came out of her room, tiptoed across the living room in back of us, her every motion telling us that she knew something was going on. She dialed, asked for Mayumi, thanked the person, hung up and dialed again, began talking to someone.

"Oh, well," Leon whispered, "it's time for my kids to spend a weekend with their grandparents."

"Oh? Your parents take them?" Nothing he'd said about them at that first dinner had suggested . . .

"Nope," Leon said, "my wife's parents. My kids are their only grandchildren. They have a beautiful place in Connecticut. Greenwich." He winked. "That's why I vacation on Long Island."

Livvy had returned to her room, making it a particular point, or so I'd felt, not to look toward the sofa. Leon was as much with me as though he hadn't gone upstairs. There was no way I was going to sleep. I felt as though I could run a few miles, but the prospects for even a walk were poor. The apartment was comfortable, but outside it was warm and muggy, and Fifteenth Street was empty and uninviting, although there would be some activity on Eighth Avenue. I undressed, put on a long T-shirt, washed, brushed my teeth, and turned on the computer. On Friday I would be seeing Sheldon and a man named Bob Kupferman, the only cable executive who'd expressed interest in talking to me after seeing the tape. I was supposed to come up with some ideas that "were just as much fun" as the pasta murder, and the blender fusillade. I kept trying to explain to Sheldon that the fun had come from the spontaneity, and that other good things might happen if I was allowed to just swing with . . . That was it, I'd said. Maybe there could be a small audience that asked questions and made comments and set me off. He'd dismissed the idea out of hand. Said it sounded too much like school. And who was I to argue that one with him?

Most of the subjects that interested me, he'd already informed me, were "boring for TV." When I asked what that meant, he said there was "nothing to look at." I'd told him the visual part came in the doing, but he'd dismissed the notion. Sheldon had readily believed I was two professors' daughter. But the stuff that struck me as interesting wasn't academic, it was just . . . well . . . interesting.

I had notes about purity as opposed to inventiveness, about breaking down the mental barriers that existed where cooking was concerned. Some people wouldn't marinate anything in soy sauce, ginger, and garlic because the combination was Japanese, others would never try the wonderful Italian hams and salamis they saw in Bleecker Street windows, or the exotic fruits and vegetables you could find now at Oriental markets around the city. I'd put kiwi slices on a lovely marinated-shrimp dish from *Food & Wine*, and my father had teased me about becoming one of the kiwi people, but the combination was superb. On the other hand, there was the real possibility of losing variety, not to speak of history, if everyone's national ingredients got married. On the third hand, it was possible to argue that when you played this way, still another species was born. Homeless foods?

Sheldon was certain that nobody was interested in the line between being a meat-eater and being a cannibal, though he'd been fascinated when I showed him the wonderful Escoffier recipe for turtle soup, especially parts of the section called "Particulars of the Operation," which began, "For soup, take a turtle weighing from 120 to 180 lbs., and let it be very fleshy and full of life," and, having given detailed slaughtering instructions, goes on to describe the dismemberment: "To begin with, thrust a strong knife between the carapace or upper shell and the plastron or lower shell, exactly where the two meet, and separate the one from the other. The turtle being on its back, cut all the adhering flesh from the plastron, and put the latter aside. Now cut off the flippers; remove the intestines, throw them away, and carefully collect all the green fat."

"Holy shit!" Sheldon had said. "A hundred and eighty pounds." But then, as though he'd been caught peeping in the ladies' lounge, he cast aside my notes, said there was no way we were dealing with a hundred and eighty pounds of turtle. When I pointed out that the same issues were involved with a chicken or a lamb chop, he shouted that I was to drop the whole thing, "Right now!"

Nor had he seen as a possibility the differences between men and women in tastes or in cooking ability, his definitive statement on the issue being, "The whole women's movement gets a hard-on if you tell them there's a difference between men and women."

I said, "Listen, Sheldon, there's stuff in here women'll love." I'd proceeded to read him some of the quotes I'd collected. Nietzsche: "Woman does not understand what food means, and yet she insists upon being a cook!" Samuel Johnson: "Women cannot make a good book of cookery." And others. I was curious to know if any of the bias against women as serious chefs had to do with the fact that, until modern times, we had been so burdened with arduous kitchen labors as to be kept from adventure. Sheldon was not curious.

There were economic issues. It was safe to guess that women who worked in their own kitchens had dealt with more financial limitations than had chefs like Escoffier and Christoforo di Messisbugo, who'd come to cooking purely by choice. In trying to check out this issue, I'd discovered that the classic chef's toque was a white version of the black hat worn by orthodox priests, and had probably originated in Greek monasteries, where famous cooks had fled to escape persecution. I'd love to compare women's being kept out of the priestly orders and out of the important kitchens. No mastery of food, no direct line to God.

Sheldon couldn't have cared less. Nor did the matter of whether there were legitimate distinctions to be made in the matter of male-female tastes interest him. I'd never met a het-

erosexual North American male of my generation or older who
adored fruit, or a woman who didn't. Although the young men
now, often of less determined sexuality, seemed to eat seeds,
nuts, and raisins, even fresh fruit, with pleasure.

Sheldon thought diets would grab a lot of people. My response had been to read him a passage from Brillat-Savarin:
"Gourmandism is far from unbecoming to the ladies: it agrees
with the delicacy of their organs, and acts as compensation for
certain pleasures which they must deny themselves, and certain
ills to which nature seems to have condemned them. . . . A
married couple who enjoy the pleasures of the table have, at
least once a day, a pleasant opportunity to be together; for even
those who do not sleep in the same bed (and there are many
such) at least eat at the same table; they have a subject of conversation which is ever new; they can talk not only of what
they are eating, but also of what they have eaten, what they
will eat, and what they have noticed at other tables."

This cooled him off on diets, at least briefly, and I'd tried to
get him interested in the subject of drinking. I had many good
quotations, beginning with the old Italian proverb "Beware of
the man who doesn't drink," going through a rhyme from *She
Stoops to Conquer*:

> *When Methodist preachers come down*
> *A-preaching that drinking is sinful,*
> *I'll wager the rascals a crown,*
> *They always preach best with a skinful.*

"Where're the visuals?" he'd wanted to know. "You gonna
stand there and get drunk while you cook?"

I'd recently started a file on Jewish food, that is to say, on
Jewish-Italian, Jewish-German, Jewish-Arab, and Jewish-
Jewish food, and had entered some anecdotes and recipes on
the computer. I'd begun with my childhood discovery that
Jewish bakeries' corn bread, which has no corn in it, was
called that because *korn* was the German word for wheat, gone
on to a mythical Italian who was furious to hear that the Jews
were the first to use artichokes.

Sheldon had been irritated that I didn't understand the difference between an Idea and a Concept. Now, sitting at the computer, I tried going for something that would be recognizable
as a Concept, came up with two ideas I thought might pass for

same. First, there was Basics for Brides, in which young
women would be taught some rules about cooking and kitchens throughout the world. Second, there was the one I called
Cucina Casalinga. Literally, the language of the kitchen. Of the
home. The language of food that was passed on from mother
to child. It would be easier for me to do if we confined ourselves to various regions of Italy, but not impossible, as long
as I had time for research, to extend to other countries. I made
a few preliminary notes for Cucina Casalinga, thinking of basics Anna had taught me when she first came to us. Finally,
tired as well as exhausted, I turned off the computer and went
to bed.

Leon was on my mind as I fell asleep, but he wasn't in my
dreams, which at first were jumbled, chaotic. Then I dreamed
that I was on television, doing a show called "Cucina
Casalinga," and Livvy appeared in front of the camera and
said, "Mother-daughter, hah! She never let me in the kitchen!
She hit me when I asked how to make *farsumagru!*"

I awakened distraught and in tears. It hadn't happened, of
course, but that didn't matter. It felt true.

Maybe what Livvy had been looking at when she walked in
today was just Ovvy and me, working happily in the kitchen.
As she and I never had. As we mostly couldn't. Certainly we
couldn't have worked—played—in the kitchen when the restaurant was open. And it had never occurred to me to offer to,
say, bake cookies with her when we weren't. We'd normally
purchased our cookies, and cookies were what kids loved most
to make, if Max and Annie and Ovvy were any indication.
What else might I have asked her to do with me in the
kitchen? The answer came back, simple and painful: Anything.
When I'd had time for her, it was time to get out of the
kitchen. Walk. Talk to people. Get a *gelato*. She came into the
kitchen like a trespasser. No wonder she wanted nothing to do
with me or my cooking. No wonder . . . Maybe I could talk
about this with her sometime, see if she was interested in
learning to cook any particular kind of food. It didn't have to
be Italian. There was a wonderful Japanese cookbook I'd been
drawn to because M.F.K. Fisher had done the introduction.
Livvy might get a kick out of making a Japanese dinner for
Mayumi. Livvy and Mayumi had become part of a group that
included three other girls, Juno, Sumara, and Shevaun. This
was the group that had made me realize none of her friends

was Jewish, which might or might not have happened naturally at the High School for the Humanities.

The one besides Mayumi who sometimes came home with her was Shevaun, a tall, slender black girl who'd been extremely reserved until one night I served her and Livvy a roast with the walnut sauce I'd been working on for my class. Shevaun was crazy about it. I remember wishing Sheldon were there as this girl, who hadn't spoken ten words to me in all her visits to the apartment, began to talk about her grandmother, a wonderful cook who'd used nuts, mostly peanuts but some walnuts, in lots of interesting ways, not just the peanut soup "everyone" knew about now. When she saw that I was interested, she told me a story that made me wonder if I could do a program on soul food.

Her mother and grandmother had moved to New York from South Carolina in the early sixties. One day, they were standing on a crowded street corner not far from the United Nations, when her grandmother got very excited because right in back of them were men talking in the precise accents of their hometown. She turned to see who the men were, and found herself looking at two Africans in dashikis. Only at this point did she realize that the words the men spoke were foreign; it was the accents that were identical to her hometown's.

Shevaun had been pleased by my fascination with this story, had begun to talk about learning from her grandmother that the great Southern dishes like chitlins and sweet-potato pie had mostly been taught to Southerners by African slaves, rather than vice versa. I told Shevaun I'd love to talk to her grandmother or her mother sometime, that I was trying to put together a television program about food, but Livvy had grown restive as Shevaun and I spoke, and now she said they'd better go and study. Maybe Livvy would like to surprise Shevaun someday with a Southern meal cooked by the two of us.

The next day, Thursday, she consented to have dinner with me. I casually raised the question of whether she was interested in cooking. Her first reaction was incredulity. I told her what I had been thinking, at least a sort of watered-down version. She shrugged, smiled, said she didn't think it was my fault, she'd always wanted to be with her father, anyway. But her manner was less hostile than usual, and, after some hesitation, she said it was possible she'd like to learn sometime, but did I want to know what she needed right now? The phone company was going to install her wiring the next afternoon, between one and five. She'd asked them to make it as late as possible, but if the guy should happen to arrive before she got home from school, would I let him in and show him the spot?

As it worked out, she was home at three-twenty and I left to do my shopping for the weekend, so she dealt with the phone company man when he came. After work, Leon would drive his kids to Greenwich, and then he'd return to the city, and then he and I would be . . . where we would be.

Thus did our friendship progress to a lovely affair. He kept his old promise of secrecy, which created difficulties, but nothing we couldn't handle. In fact, I would say in retrospect that we thrived on them. Everyone's dimly aware that discarding the old rules about sex in the sixties and seventies was followed by some loss of interest in same during the eighties. Perhaps what was lost was the excitement in the forbidden that had once carried people who weren't certain they wanted sex or marriage through one or both. If it was still nearly impossible to find the flatly forbidden, Leon and I at least had the juicy pleasure of waiting until nobody was around, the childish thrill of locking doors and lowering voices, the fun of being able to forget about how much noise we were making on the rare occasion when there was nobody on the other side of a wall. Mostly we made love in his apartment, because the walls were real. I crept downstairs later if the kids were home, as they usually were. But during those giddy first months it was hard for us to keep our hands off each other, and occasionally, if the key turned in my lock when we had just laid them on, we scampered guiltily into my room, whispering and shushing each other, burying ourselves under the heavy quilt for as long as we could bear to.

At some point Leon made it clear to me that he wasn't seeing anybody else. And, of course, I had grown deeply and firmly attached to him. In fact, I had fallen in love, and thus come to understand, for the first time, the meaning of the phrase.

It was the beginning of winter, one of those all too rare weekends when each of his kids was invited away someplace. This weekend provided a first-time delight in that Olivia had been invited by Mayumi's parents to a weekend of ski instruction in the Berkshires, so we had both apartments to ourselves.

We sneaked up and down the stairs between them, pretending it was important that the neighbors not see us. We slept in his bedroom, ate in my kitchen, lounged in both living rooms. At Saturday breakfast I attempted to duplicate an apple pancake he remembered having years earlier at a Vermont inn. He claimed mine was much better. Then we settled into separate sofas, he with some professional journals, me with the pile of books and magazines I needed to plunder for my next talk with Sheldon and Bob Kupferman.

I looked up. He was reading. It happened. I understand why people, in the absence of anything better, use the phrase *falling in love*. But I didn't so much fall as something in me dissolved at the center. The outside did what I had to do, but I lost sway over some inner part of me. Nor did I appear to need it. It was only the part that had told me that I was I, and he was he, and what happened to him was less important than what happened to me. Instead of my being at my own center, he was there. I was off to one side someplace. Watching him. Taking him in. How could I not have realized how extraordinarily beautiful he was? (My outsides still knew that he was not beautiful, just an ordinarily pleasant-looking man.) How could I have failed to notice the way his eyes played with what they saw?

"Jesus," he said, "listen to this." He looked up, was thrown by the intensity of my gaze. He'd been in love, but wasn't with me. He grew uneasy even as he prepared to bask in it. He read me something from one of his journals characterizing children who were ill and under stress. He thought it was brilliant. I thought it was dumb, went against what I remembered of Livvy and Max, not to say his own kids, but I had no need to argue. It appears to be a characteristic of the state of being in love, as opposed to the latter (if you're lucky) stage of just loving, that nothing the loved one does can alter it. Acts that earlier and later are deemed dumb, hostile, repellent, might be understood to have any of those qualities, yet do not repel. The understanding goes no farther than the part of the brain that perceives; it can't touch feeling.

He had me. If he was my faithful lover, I did not yet "have" him. That would happen in a later and more comical way.

The conference was held in Bob Kupferman's office and included Perry and a woman who took notes but was not identified. Bob Kupferman mostly just nodded and shook his head, but his eyes were keen and he was always listening. It was time, Sheldon announced, to get going if we wanted to have something ready for the following autumn. He showed the tape of me he'd made way back when my traveling bread show was supposed to zoom past Julia into the stars. When the tape was finished, he gave an idiotic speech about how ridiculous it was that "we" (sic, although Kupferman had made no commitment as yet) had "a major talent" (sic) on our hands and weren't doing anything with her. We needed "a concept."

"I don't actually understand what the problem is," Perry said in his soft, rather hesitant, manner. "It's clear that it turns her on just standing up in front of a class and teaching people about food. She's sort of quiet the rest of the time, but as soon as she gets up there, she has everyone. They listen. They laugh when she means to be funny. They want to try what she wants them to try."

"Teacher," Sheldon said, making a face. "School." It was the first time his reaction to anything had been the same as mine. "Anyway, a class would cost money."

Perry shrugged. "Use the audience."

"You know," Kupferman said after a moment, "I think we might have something there. I mean, if the classroom is what turns her on, why shouldn't part of the audience be her class?"

Sheldon said to Kupferman, you couldn't even hear his gears shift. "You know, I think you might have something there."

"The beginning of something, anyway," Kupferman said. "And we don't have to call it a class. It's just this big, warm kitchen a few people gather in to learn something about food. 'Caroline's Kitchen.' "

"Some people call me Cara," I volunteered.

He nodded. "That's even better. 'Cara's Kitchen.' "

I remained an interested observer during the months in which Kupferman finally contracted for thirteen weeks of a show to be called "Cara's Kitchen," worked out with the people in Sheldon's small company the details of a show called, at that point, "The Melting Pot," and with me as something resembling a consultant, put the final touches on what was now called, and would remain, "Pot Luck."

We'd pick eight to ten people from the studio audience. They would sit on the stage in an "almost semicircle." My

kitchen would be "large but cozy, modern but old-fashioned."
I insisted that I needed some shelves for cookbooks I could refer to. Sheldon was concerned about advertising the competition, a conceit that left me speechless. The matter was settled
when someone said they'd fix the books so none of the titles
was conspicuous. I didn't bother to mention that I might want
to read from some of them. They always got nervous if I mentioned doing something that wasn't active. *Visual.* Anyway, the
books were more talismanic than practical for me. I could remember most of the lines I'd want to quote, but the books
meant I wouldn't be up there alone if I forgot something. The
issue that most concerned everyone was who could be trusted
to select my stage pupils, and on what basis they would do it.
Some should be good-looking, young-bride types, while you
didn't want too many of those because you might turn off . . .
etc. I suggested they find people who looked difficult, because
they'd make it livelier, but nobody was prepared to listen to
that one yet. They wanted people who'd give me the opportunity to be funny, but got nervous at the suggestion that such
people might themselves be out of control. So be it. At least
for the time.

In fact, it worked very well, my life's proceeding without all
of me in it. Bob and the agency's sporadic opacity, Sheldon's
dumb cunning, Livvy's rages and rudenesses, all mattered, but
not as they might have if I weren't in love. The show took me
away from the apartment, and from my daughter, which was
useful. At home, I was still too much controlled by her moods,
tended to worry from the beginning of my afternoon class
about her coming home after school and, if so, whether the
person who came through the door would be my worst enemy,
or an indifferent-to-reasonably-friendly human.

As the spring term of her sophomore year progressed, she
began to talk about going to Harvard. I heard Mayumi tease
her when she mentioned it, but apparently Shevaun shared the
dream, and Livvy's good marks. That was all to the good, but
what worried me, and should have more than it did, was that
Livvy talked about Harvard as though it were the only school
in the United States worth going to. Even as she acknowledged
that some good students went to other schools, a shrug of the
shoulders, a bored expression, dismissed the possibility that
she'd be one of them. I kept thinking she was doing what
she'd done once before, refusing to acknowledge the possibil-

ity of not getting into the Chosen School. But my parents and I agreed that if we'd known more about the specifics of that exam, we'd have tried harder to discourage her. While the guidance counselor at Humanities thought that between her close-to-perfect grades and her unusual background, not to speak of the fact that she was coming from a new experimental school rather than one where every senior applied, she had a good shot at Harvard. Anyway, we didn't have to think about all that before her junior year. Her friends came home with her less often, she was spending far more time on the phone. When her words were audible, they were usually about homework. Apparently she lowered her voice for the good stuff. Once in a while, I eavesdropped on the theory that if there were things she didn't want me to hear, it was possible that I should hear them. I'd sit with a book or magazine on the sofa that backed up on her bedroom wall. I began to be uncomfortable on that sofa even when I wasn't trying to eavesdrop.

Everyone except my sister thought I worried too much about my daughter; I was afraid that between my classes, my love affair, my scrambling for a TV show, and my upstairs children, I worried too little, and only when it was convenient. That is, when Leon wasn't around.

Late on a Friday afternoon, when he'd announced that tonight he was going to take out "just my kids," his girls were feeling neglected, I sat on the sofa, feeling neglected myself. There was nothing I wanted to do that didn't involve him. Or him and them. Livvy's phone rang and, when she'd answered, her voice lowered in the way I'd become accustomed to. But for the first time, I had the impression that she was speaking flirtatiously to a male. I was uneasy, whether because there was a sexual tone to the conversation, which made it different for me to be listening, or because— The girl was fifteen years old, for heaven's sake. There was no reason she shouldn't be flirting with a boy, though there was every reason to make sure that she knew how to protect herself before she got anywhere near a bed with him. Surely nobody in Rome had ever told pre-high-school girls about condoms. My ruminations were cut short when, apparently in response to some question, Olivia said, "Oh, you know. It's better than the ones that are full of Jews."

I felt as though I'd been privy to plans for an assassination. Someone I knew well. Probably me. I stood, went to get a jacket and my handbag. I was no longer concerned about Livvy's knowing I'd heard her. I *wanted* her to know. I tried to figure out something I could say to her, but when I left the house, she was still on the phone.

I walked toward the Village, my usual destination, but when I got there, I didn't turn toward the Italian markets on Bleecker where I normally shopped. Instead I continued south toward Houston Street, then east. It was in the back of my mind that I might cross the Manhattan Bridge, as they say, when I came to it. But it was nearly dark by the time I got there, so I just continued walking, toward the Bowery and the Lower East Side.

All four of my grandparents had come to the Lower East Side from Russia (my mother's parents) and Lithuania (my father's), had joined the neighborhood associations of immigrants, sent their children to the public schools, eventually moved on to Chicago (my mother's parents) or Newark (my father's). My parents had met at the University of Chicago, then come east together to do their graduate work, marry, and earn their Ph.D.'s. (My brother and sister both were born before my mother had hers.)

Beatrice and Gus had memories of early-childhood holidays celebrated with our paternal grandparents before they left New York, but I had none. At first, we'd gone to New Jersey to celebrate Passover with them in the spring, Rosh Hashanah in the fall, but then, as we grew older, and my parents became increasingly drawn to Europe, increasingly capable of getting grants to subsidize their travels, they'd sometimes been abroad during the most important holidays, in the spring or fall, and formal celebration had often fallen by the wayside.

I'd never been to Jewish landmarks like Ratner's restaurant and Katz's Delicatessen until I went to them with friends, the former after an evening at the Fillmore, the latter with a group of Columbia students who'd heard from their suburban parents about Katz's pastrami and corned beef. After moving to the Village, and at my parents' suggestion, I'd shopped on Grand Street for bed linens and wallpaper, Orchard Street for clothing. But aside from those specifics, nothing had drawn me.

Was it Jewish anti-Semitism that had prevented me from relishing the neighborhood? Probably not. There wasn't much there anymore. I'd spent more time in a couple of Chinese food markets on Mott Street than in all the Jewish stores combined. They were more inviting. Even if good cheap Chinese food was so readily available as to make it the first you thought of for a cheap meal out, the last you were likely to cook at home, many ingredients—roast pork, Szechuan peppers, dried mushrooms, ginger, and a variety of fresh vegetables—had found their way into my cooking.

So had matzo meal. Not that cooking matzo balls made me Jewish any more than making roast pork egg foo yong made me Chinese. Of course, nobody had to make me Jewish, I was that already. On the other hand, even if one were willing to have her entire cultural identity reside in the mouth, good Jewish food had fed and been fed by a wider culture, which made for a somewhat more confused identity than I was willing to grapple with at the moment.

To the extent that Jewish identity required false subordination and real exclusion, it had been dealt lethal blows by our diverse, loosely embracing American culture. Actually, when you thought about it, American culture was so diverse as not to exist. That was why we had all suffered a loss under the awful regulations that moved every American holiday except Thanksgiving to a nearby weekend that became three days. Those holidays had formed a fragile link between us and the past; now Thanksgiving and the Fourth of July were the only ones you still felt like celebrating.

I thought of an evening during my childhood. A Sunday with my father's parents, who would only come to dinner that night if we'd listen to their radio lineup, then Jack Benny, Phil Harris and Alice Faye, Fred Allen, Edgar Bergen and Charlie McCarthy. On this evening, my father's father would not be swayed from the notion that Fred Allen was Jewish.

My father, with a wicked grin, finally asked, "Okay, and what about Charlie McCarthy? Is he Jewish, too?"

"What difference?" my grandmother had replied with a shrug. "He's only a puppet."

What difference if he hadn't been a puppet? Why was it so important to my grandparents that these comedians be Jewish? Well, immigrants needed to feel a foothold in this country. The pride of identification. Myself and others. Ourselves and others. A logical extension. The world was too big not to be broken down into some kind of groups. Maybe you needed customs because, without them, groups' identities would lie only in their competitive and hostile feelings, their impulse to war. No. There was something else. Ways were needed to mark time. To give a shape to life. And perhaps, in so doing, to pay tribute to whoever you were, as well as whoever, whatever, you weren't. The parts that it wasn't for you to decide. Maybe if Livvy had naturally taken part in some Jewish holidays with us, from the time of her arrival in New York, or better yet, when she and I were in Italy, she would have had some sense of being Jewish, part Jewish, that provided an internal counterweight to her father's anti-Semitism. Well, there was no sense flaying myself over that now, when nothing else I'd said or done appeared to have weighed in the balance.

Approaching Grand Street, I remembered my eagerness to tell Angelo that some of his favorite dishes (his likes and dishlikes, as I just found myself writing) were very Jewish. Recently, in researching for interesting programs, I'd found a variety of other wonderful foods that had been brought by the Jews to countries other than Italy and adopted as national dishes. But even if one were willing to have one's entire cultural identity reside in the mouth, the good Jewish food had all been adapted and neutralized, and could no longer provide that identity.

Grand Street was dark and depressing. Filthy sidewalks and rundown stores, many permanently closed, evidently deserted by Jews for places that were more Jewish or less so, or simply more comfortable. No community appeared to have replaced them.

I walked back to Katz's, ordered a pastrami on rye and a bottle of beer, although the first boy who took me to Katz's had tried to convince me that Dr. Brown's Celery Tonic was de rigueur with pastrami. When I told my father I'd been there, he remembered that during the war Katz's had a sign up that said, SEND A SALAMI TO YOUR BOY IN THE ARMY. (It was still there.) The people eating around me now, black and white, did not look Jewish. I put down my sandwich. I had always laughed when I heard my parents say that someone in the newspaper looked, or didn't look, Jewish. This was the first time in my life I'd found myself doing it. I decided I'd have to talk to my father about Livvy's anti-Semitism, preferably sometime when my mother wasn't around. My mother would just sit there, never saying anything objectionable, but just getting an I-told-you-so expression, without specifying what it was she'd told me. While my father had the ability to tackle problems in a practical way, free of sighs and glances and little remarks about what might have been, free of the weight of the past.

My mother's mother had been a terrible cook. She'd been the family's free-thinker, the reader, the socialist, the atheist, the active antiracist who'd joined the NAACP and laughed at the thought of joining the UJA. A *mamzer* (roughly translated as bastard), her husband would say, shaking his head in anger and admiration. She had sneered at the dietary laws, made it a point, when she was at our house for a meat dinner with the other grandparents, who were kosher, to ask where the milk was for her coffee. We'd stopped having it in the house when all four visited, to avoid doing the unacceptable. (In a kosher household, dairy products aren't served with a meat meal.) Was it only difficult people who discarded tradition?

Beatrice said after one of those visits that Grandma Rose should have been a doctor or lawyer and never married or had children. My mother laughingly thanked Beatrice, but her ability to laugh might have come from the fact that her father, who, by the time she was born, had a grocery in the same building as their apartment, gave the children much of the affection they did not receive from their mother.

My father's mother was an excellent cook. She made a pot roast I don't feel I've ever equaled; maybe my mind's tastebuds imbue it with a quality only childhood can lend. She prepared her own herring, and it had actually been from her, early on, not from Anna, that I'd learned to make a good chicken soup. Her borscht and stuffed cabbage were to die for, and until she was well into her seventies, she was putting up her own pickles, tomatoes, and fruit compotes. She was a docile, unintellectual woman who practiced Judaism and Jewish custom as it had been practiced by her family in the ghetto for generations. She might still have been living in a ghetto, for all the times she ventured to walk outside her own neighborhood, or to meet people she didn't know from the temple or the building where she lived. She'd been an infinitely more peaceful person than my mother's mother, and there was no question in my mind that her peacefulness was framed by, and rested upon, tradition.

How long did it take to create a tradition, and of what might that tradition consist in an age when tradition had become nearly synonymous with constriction, when people were forbidden the pleasures as well as the limitations of even sexual stereotype? And how would I ever persuade my daughter that we needed to share something in the way of custom, when it was often more than she could bear to share a two-bedroom apartment with me?

The next day I broached this question to Leon, who sympathized over my difficulties with Livvy but was unwilling to turn his mind for a moment to the matter of custom. For my benefit, he ran through a typical day, then week, in his life, beginning with six A.M., when he woke to the alarm, going on to the time he was expected at his hospital office, which times he was due at the clinic, when his kids expected him home, and so on. He said that if there were one more job, obligation, ritual—whatever you wanted to call it—to think about, he might go out of his mind. Furthermore, Leon said, I had no reason to assume my grandmother was peaceful *because* she was traditional; she might have followed tradition because she was peaceful and unadventurous.

I could not, of course, demand anything of him in this regard. It wasn't as though we were married. Or he had any ties to Livvy. Or our own relationship was growing more complex in any way.

I consulted my parents, who thought a family conference might be useful. We debated whether they should tell Livvy there were matters we needed to talk about, or simply invite us to dinner, but it turned out not to matter. When I told her my parents wanted us to come up one Friday evening, they'd hardly seen us since the summer, she informed me that she'd found a job for Friday and Saturday nights, she was almost through her summer money. Her allowance barely covered lunches and phone bills were astronomical. I was floored. Aside from any other issue, she wasn't yet sixteen years old. When I asked what kind of job she'd been hired for, she said she was going to be a waitress at Moffetta's Restaurant, on Mulberry Street in Little Italy. She would be paid off the books.

"Wait a minute," I said. "It's a little more complicated than that."

She didn't explode, as she would have if she hadn't known I could stop her.

I asked how this was going to affect her homework, and she said that if her schoolwork was affected, she would quit.

I asked how she would get home at night.

She said, "Mr. Moffetta's son is going to bring me. Tony. He has three cabs and he promised to drive me or put me in one of the cabs."

"My goodness!" I said. "They must like you a great deal."

"His daughter doesn't speak Italian."

"I see. And how old is Tony Moffetta?"

"I wouldn't know." She was dripping sarcasm. "He has three children."

And doubtless a wife, which of course made him safe. As safe as Angelo. Olivia was a sexy, full-bosomed, good-looking girl I'd have assumed was becoming more attractive to males even had I not overheard any conversations that were probably with same. She'd regained some of her lost weight, then gone down again and up again in a pattern I assumed was more about America than any eating disorder. At least I'd seen no sign of the latter.

"Do they know how old you are?"

She hesitated.

"You probably told them you were sixteen."

A reluctant nod.

"I don't know that that's so important," I told her. "I worked off the books when I was in school. It's not my idea of a serious issue."

"They'll pay me twenty dollars a night and I'll make fifty or more in tips."

"That's wonderful." Not only could she make endless phone calls, but she'd be able to buy various items central to life, like Justin boots and audio component parts, for which she'd otherwise have to wait until her birthday.

"Well, then, I guess . . . I'm going to have to check them out, and then—"

"You don't think you're going over there!" she shouted.

It hadn't actually occurred to me, but it was the simplest way.

"That's exactly what I think," I told her. "Furthermore, any Italian father will find it quite natural that a mother wants to check out her daughter's employer. Even if she's sixteen years old."

"You sound as though every Italian's the same," she flashed out. "You wouldn't think that if you were a real Italian instead of a fake one."

I smiled. "Touché. I guess any group's more varied from the

inside. The Jews certainly are. That's what I am actually. A real Jew who likes Italy and Italian food. Not a fake Italian."

She turned away, paced for a moment, came back to face me. "We'll eat there. Mr. Moffetta's usually at the register. We'll go on a Sunday or Monday. When it's slow. I'll introduce you to him . . . You'll probably have to pay. Can I go now?"

"Okay," I said. "Except, I'd just like to know how you heard about the job. It wasn't advertised, was it?"

She hesitated, decided that even if the question was absurd, she'd best answer it.

"Billy Moffetta, the other son, he has a *salumeria* on Bleecker Street. I go there sometimes with my friends."

I probably knew the place; there weren't so many. Anyway, this was the first I'd heard of her going to the Village since I'd tried to interest her in it during the weeks after her arrival.

"Oh? And you started talking?"

My questions were so incredibly stupid that she grew calm, as though she were talking to a child.

"Usually they know people who come into the store who pronounce everything right. Billy didn't know me, so he asked where I was from."

"And he told you about the job."

She shook her head. "That was last year, when I first went down there. We talk whenever I go with my friends to get a sandwich. He knew I was looking for a job. *Now* can I go do my homework?"

I nodded. I was thinking that her abandonment of everything Italian had been less thorough than it seemed. And indeed, as she started toward her room, she turned back to me.

"When we go, please speak Italian. I told them we mostly speak it at home. They think . . . They don't know . . . you're . . . American."

Ralph Moffetta was a tall, sad-eyed gentleman who told Livvy that now that he saw how her mother watched out for her, he understood why she was such a good girl. He joined us briefly for an espresso, promised me that one of his sons would drive her home or put her in one of Tony's cabs. Whoever drove would make sure she was in the house with the door locked behind her. It would never be later than eleven.

He said, "My girls don't want to speak Italian or work in my restaurant."

I smiled back. "Livvy was lucky to find you."

"My mother calls me Livvy sometimes," my daughter said with the sweet smile I'd seen frequently since we entered Moffetta's. "I don't know if I told you, she was born here."

On an evening not long after that, while I was teaching, a male voice called on my phone. He said he was Pablo, he'd been trying Olivia's number for almost an hour, and he had to leave work now. Would I be so kind as to tell her he needed to talk to her? I went to her door and told her to call Pablo, then returned to my class, certain that it wasn't a boy's voice, but a man's, that I'd heard.

Later, I told her I hoped she'd feel free to have her boyfriend, if Pablo was that, come to the apartment.

She said he wasn't her boyfriend, just a friend, so I shouldn't worry about it.

I asked if Pablo went to her school. She said no and waited to see if I was going to push it.

I said he sounded a little older, like a man, not a boy.

She said he was twenty. (He was twenty-seven.) I asked where she'd met him. After a struggle with herself, she decided to tell me. He was a friend of the guy who'd installed her phone, who'd taken her to a party where she'd met Pablo.

"Oh? When was that?" I asked, hoping I could pass for casual.

I couldn't.

"What do you mean, *when*?" she asked. "What night of the week? It was a Saturday night, right after the phone was installed." She smiled nastily. "You were upstairs."

I nodded. "With Leon." I wasn't going to get aced on this one. "Is there anything you'd like to ask me about that?"

She shrugged.

"I've known Leon for a couple of years, and I began sleeping with him this past September."

Unless I was mistaken, her lip was curling in disdain. It seemed like a good idea to continue.

"I'm thirty-five years old, divorced, delighted to have a nice lover, and I use a diaphragm all the time to make sure I won't get pregnant. I hope that when the time comes when you go to bed with someone, you'll protect yourself with—"

"You don't think . . ." She appeared to be genuinely

shocked, but recovered sufficiently to retrieve disdain. "I'm a Catholic. We don't believe in sex when we're not married."

I shrugged. "A lot of people get pregnant who don't believe in it."

She said, lofty again, "Pablo's a Catholic. I go to church with him."

"Oh?" I asked, not even meaning to catch her, but just trying to let the conversation move where she wanted it to. "Which church is that?"

She couldn't answer, struggled for a moment, finally said she didn't know what difference it should make to me. She was poised for flight again.

"Look, Livvy. Olivia. I'm out of the house more than I used to be, and even if I were here, it wouldn't mean . . . All I'm trying to tell you . . . For now, let's just say, a young girl who wants to go to Harvard shouldn't do anything to complicate her life."

I'd done it. Harvard, the promised land you got to go to if you were good enough, might make her protect herself as I could not.

I asked what Pablo's last name was.

Another struggle before she said, "Cruz."

"Ah," I said. "Is he Puerto Rican?"

"He's an American."

"Puerto Ricans are Americans," I pointed out.

"Then why did you ask?"

"I guess I was trying to get some kind of handle on him. I mean, I hope I'll meet him sometime soon, if he's just a friend, but meanwhile . . ."

"He was born and raised in New York City."

I smiled. "So was I. But that doesn't mean I'm not a Jew." It wasn't a precise parallel, but maybe she wouldn't notice. She grew more alert.

"Where does he work?" I asked quickly.

She struggled with herself for a while, finally practically gagged on, "For the phone company, too." She paused, finally spat out, "And *he's* not married."

"Oh? Does it disturb you that Leon's married? His wife has lived in California for seven years. But it's true, technically, he's married. On the other hand, you might not think it was a real wedding, since his wife's family are all Protestants, and he's a Jew."

Her head snapped up. There was no question that she was startled.

"You didn't know he was Jewish?"

She wanted to deny it, but she couldn't get it out.

"It's funny, a lot of people who don't like the Jews don't exactly know who they are. Anyway, that's not what we need to talk about now. I just wanted you to know . . . that if the time comes when you need advice about making sure you don't get pregnant, or have any of the other complications, diseases that people get these days, I'll be happy to help."

Maybe under other circumstances, she could have resisted, but not now. She smiled at me, sardonic if not triumphant as she got up to go to her room.

"I don't really need that kind of advice. Maybe you should talk to a couple of the Jewish girls at school. They're the ones who're the whores."

But the impression that I had something to worry about was reinforced when I met Pablo, a nice-looking, shy but well-spoken, clearly hetero and distinctly sexual man, who appeared to be crazy about my daughter. If he was restraining himself for any or many reasons, or if Livvy was holding him back from sex, I couldn't believe such restraint would last. At some point, preferably before she went to bed with him (or with anyone, for that matter), I was going to have to figure out how a Jewish whore who believed in contraception could talk to her snotty Roman Catholic kid about the necessity to use it. Leon had said that the women who came to the hospital who were more or less Roman Catholic had often turned out to be more when it came to contraception, less when it came to admitting it. Pressed, they would say that their husbands didn't like it.

Leon agreed that I had to impress upon Livvy the need for condoms if she had sex. Aside from AIDS, there was still pregnancy to worry about. She was a teenager. Teenagers were all impossible. The Jewish stuff, too, he shrugged off.

"So maybe she's a little anti-Semitic. Who'm I to be critical? I was more than a little. You think it was an accident that my first wife was a WASP?"

"So what are you saying, Leon? Did you know you were anti-Semitic? Or did you just think you went for WASP types?"

"Female WASPs. Males, it didn't matter." He laughed. "I didn't know what was good, I just knew what I liked."

"Maybe it's still what you like." I was getting more and more upset.

He didn't notice, shook his head playfully. "I was converted by my first matzo ball."

I was not amused.

"Well," he said, "I was converted by *something*. First of all, I didn't do so well with my fancy Gentile, did I. Then . . . being around the hospital, you sort of lose your sense of— Jesus, I don't know how the hell you've managed to put me on the defensive. You didn't exactly marry a Yeshivah *bocher*."

"But it was an accident, in a way. I mean, I don't think I would've married him if I weren't pregnant."

"Did you date Jewish guys?"

I nodded. "Both."

"You could've had an abortion."

"But I didn't want an abortion, I wanted a baby."

"Ah, yes. I see them bringing in their kids all the time. Women who wanted babies but had no idea of what it meant to take care of them."

"But I *did* want to take care of her." I was angrier than I'd been with him since I'd osmosed into love. "I loved the whole *idea* of taking care of her. Hugging her. Kissing her."

He nodded. "The idea and the reality are different. The reality is it can be pleasant having a baby if you're a sane person with full-time help."

"I don't know what you're saying." I was on the verge of tears. "I never needed full-time help. I just needed to have someone *there*, especially when Angelo was away. At first I didn't even need someone there, I needed to feel there was someone around who cared about me. Anyway, I don't know why we're having this conversation."

He knew. He said that he hadn't been in love with Christina but he'd been ready to settle down. Sooner or later he might have thought about marrying her if he hadn't been certain that sooner or later she'd want children. He'd seen it happen over and over with men who already had kids and women who didn't. He needed me to know, before we went much further, that he'd finished being the father of babies.

In fact, he didn't seem to be going further, but, rather, retreating. Annie came down less frequently than she once had, and if she was sometimes the old affectionate Annie, I'd worried, since the day she joined Rennie in specifying dinner without me, that she was moving toward total rejection. Anyway, Leon was arguing a point I hadn't reached. I hadn't been in love for that long; I still wanted to *be* his baby, not have another, even his. Life was complete, if not simple. As Livvy settled into her job and felt less dependent on me, she'd begun sometimes to do homework in the living room. Occasionally she was so friendly as to ask me how to spell a word, rather than look for her dictionary.

One evening she asked me to read an essay she'd written for school. Her assignment was to contrast the place where a grandparent—*or* a parent—had been raised with the place where she now lived. Predictably, Livvy had chosen to contrast Sicily with Manhattan to the detriment of the latter. Less predictably, she was uncertain about some of her memories, and asked me to check them out. The piece was called, "My Father's Sicily, My New York," and began by contrasting the filthy water of the Hudson with the clean and beautiful water you could swim in off the northern coast of Sicily, where her father had been raised. At first I thought I was mixed up; I could remember only filthy seaport water within any distance of Palermo. But as I read, I became certain something else was wrong; she was describing a town very much smaller than Palermo, or even Castellemare or Trapani.

I looked up. She was watching me. I smiled.

"It's written so nicely, but I'm a little mixed up. The place you talk about visiting—the villa with the courtyard, the mosaics of animals—I don't remember a place like that. Not that I remember everything, I wasn't there as often as you, but somehow . . . it sounds like a much smaller town, even than Trapani . . . It sounds . . ."

I stopped talking because her expression had changed from patient-snotty, as in, *Why did I ever ask her in the first place?* to puzzled, and then to dismayed. She took the paper from me, looked at it for a moment, looked up at me. She was close to tears.

"What is it, Liv? I'm sure you can fix whatever's wrong, no big deal."

"It's Mirella's town." She dropped the paper. "I mixed it up. It's not Trapani. It's Patti, where Mirella lives."

She began to cry. I didn't know what to say. I started to move from the chair where I was sitting to the sofa next to her, but she put up a hand, signaling me not to. I sat back down, waited. After a little while, she wiped her eyes, said that the paper was due tomorrow, and she had a lot of other homework, and a math test, and she didn't see how she was going to fix the paper in time. As she spoke, her panic increased.

"You don't think the teacher'll give you an extension?"

She shook her head. "No way. She's a real . . ."

"Well, let's see. Maybe it doesn't have to be rewritten entirely. Maybe there's a way to salvage it. I mean, in the part of the paper I read, there was nothing about Mirella. Do you talk about her later on?"

"No."

"Well, then, maybe you can sort of . . . uh . . . cheat a little. Like . . . well . . . The teacher's never going to know the difference between a town in Sicily where your grandparents live and a town where your father's mistress lives."

She stood up abruptly.

"What are you talking about?"

I stared at her, confused by what my brain was telling me she meant.

Then she continued. "Italy isn't New York, you know. Everybody isn't always . . . always screwing everybody else, just because— I should've known better than to show you anything." She was working herself into hysteria now. "I shouldn't've showed you— Just because you put out for anyone who—"

"All right, Livvy," I said sharply. "That's enough. I can't tell if you know you're being ridiculous, but—"

"Don't tell me I'm ridiculous! I was there all the time and you were never there! You don't know anything about my father, or Mirella, or what they were doing! You don't know—"

"I know that I left your father because he was screwing anyone who'd have him from the day we got married!"

She stared at me, her face contorted by rage and disbelief.

"It's the reason I left, Livvy, it's the only thing that could have made me go. I didn't want to leave you, but I couldn't bear it anymore, and you seemed—"

I stopped because she appeared actually to be gasping for breath.

"Livvy? Livvy, I'm sorry, I get very angry and I didn't realize . . ."

What hadn't I realized? I'd known I might someday want to

explain why I'd left, but I hadn't understood the nature of the task.

"Are you all right?"

She wasn't all right. She was like someone who's swallowed a piece of chicken bone and is just realizing it's jammed in her throat. But when I took a step forward, she gestured at me to keep back. Finally, she brushed past me and went toward the bathroom, closing the door behind her. It didn't lock. I went up to the door and listened. Water was running. I heard choking, then coughing. Then it was quiet.

"Livvy?" I called after a bit. "Olivia, just let me know you're all right and I won't bother you."

She opened the door. I stepped back. She walked past me without looking at me, and went to her room.

She barely spoke to me in the days that followed.

I'd written Angelo an occasional brief note, but now I called him for the first time since asking him for money. I said that Livvy had been with me for a long time and I needed a vacation. Also, I thought she needed to know that he hadn't forgotten her. Furthermore, while she was over there he might try to undo some of the damage he'd done to her view of me. He might want to tell her that however temperamental I'd been, I'd loved her and taken care of her much of the time—good, low-voiced care—when we weren't in the kitchen. I said it was important to get her out of this notion she had of her mother as the devil, her father, the angel who never went astray, was always there to care for her. When he pretended not to know what I was talking about, I said that if he told Olivia some of the truth, like that Mirella wasn't the Virgin Mary, it might be easier for me to live with her until she graduated from high school. He caught the implied threat, said he would speak to Annunciata, see if they could bring Olivia to Rome for Easter week. Olivia would have to behave, though; Easter week was very important to Annunciata. Annunciata, how could he tell me? This was no *"porca madonna."* This was a true saint.

"Yes, of course," I said as I tried to concentrate on the business at hand. "That's very nice. Now, one of the things Livvy has to learn is . . . I mean, you might talk to her about her boyfriend. It would be a good idea for her to know that if she's not a true saint, if she ever goes to bed with him, no matter how Catholic she is, she should protect herself."

"Protect herself?" It was nearly a whisper. "Of course, she protects herself. She isn't sixteen yet! She must not, she must not . . . Who is the *fijo de 'na mignotta* (son of a bitch) who tries to—"

"I'm not sure he's trying anything," I said. "But she's spending a lot of time with him, and sooner or later—"

"You must not allow it!"

I smiled into the phone receiver.

"Indeed. Why don't you fly over for a few weeks, and then *you* can not allow it."

A lengthy silence.

I said, "It'll be better if she doesn't know the visit idea came from me."

He said, "No problem, I talk to her all the time."

"You do?" I was astounded. "You mean, you call her?"

"No," he said. "She calls me. Through her friend who works for the phone company."

A few days later Livvy informed me, obviously very pleased, that her father wanted her to come to Rome so she could spend the Easter holiday with him.

"How nice," I said. "Did he call you?"

"I called him."

"I hope you did it on Sunday. Those calls cost a fortune."

"It doesn't cost anything," she said.

"Oh? Pablo?"

She laughed. "Pablo wouldn't . . . He's such a straight arrow."

"So who's the other guy?" I risked asking, since she was in a civil mode.

"Nobody," she said. "The guy who came to install my phone. The one who . . . He's how I met Pablo."

I nodded. "Does the company know about all these calls?"

She shrugged. "It's one of the reasons they work for the phone company," she said. "They can call all their relatives."

I asked no more questions. Actually, I was relieved to hear that Pablo was a straight arrow. That was the impression I'd had during my one brief conversation with him.

It was the best of Easter vacations, it was the worst of Easter vacations. Mrs. Borelli was retiring. It had been decided that, particularly since I never gave classes Easter week, no sitter would be needed for Leon's kids. I gave Annie and Ovvy

keys to my bottom lock, the only one I kept on during the day.
(Rennie refused the offer.) I'd thought of doing this before, but
since Livvy often seemed irritated by the kids' presence, I'd
held off. In fact, it was during this week, when life seemed so
easy, when Annie and Ovvy wanted to see if *Parenthood* was
around any place that I admitted to myself for the first time
that I wished Livvy had never come to the States. I knew how
I would feel if I hadn't been allowed to see her at all. But if
she'd continued to live with her father and had visited me, or
allowed me to visit her ... It was a rainy afternoon and we
told Rennie we were going and took off, no need for me to
worry about what kind of hostility I'd face when I brought
them back for dinner.

Rennie, at thirteen, was no fonder of me than she'd ever
been, but she had grown more involved in life away from the
home, had friends, went to sleepovers, and so on. Annie was
almost ten now, Ovvy seven and a half. When they had dates
that required an escort (Ovvy, primarily; Annie could go to
many of the places she wanted to go on her own), I happily
walked or rode with them. Sometimes I wanted to go even if
I wasn't needed. On another rainy day toward the end of the
week, a friend of Ovvy's who'd thought he wasn't interested in
making cookies was visiting. Tears of contentment came to my
eyes when I heard Ovvy tell him I'd bake any kind of cookies
they wanted. It was as though my pleasure in cooking with and
for him had become a badge of worth. Leon thought it was
funny that I insisted on maintaining the charade of not sharing
his bed, but I was afraid of change. Life was sweeter than it
had ever been, and I was terrified to upset some balance we'd
reached without knowing its precise weights and ingredients.

The kids had announced that they didn't want to go to camp
that summer. Leon said, "All this seems to be working so well,
I thought maybe you'd want to spend the summer with us in
Southampton."

He laughed at my happy, hopeful expression.

"Of course, if you're determined to maintain the separate-
beds nonsense ..."

I was silent. Of course, the charade would be over. It was
probably time for the charade to be over, but it still scared me.
A lot of things scared me. The show scared me. It was scheduled to begin in September. Sheldon had informed me that I
must be available for "last-minute stuff" he wouldn't specify,

and it would surely be more convenient if I was in the Hamptons, since that was where everyone else connected to the show would be. I promised Leon I'd stop running downstairs in the middle of the night, but then I woke up at three in the morning and couldn't go back to sleep upstairs, so I did. I left him a note saying I apparently needed to wake up in my own bed. On Friday, the same thing happened, except I didn't even fall asleep.

On Saturday night, with just one day of Easter vacation left, we took the kids to some dreadful movie they adored, then picked up the Sunday *Times* on the way home. When they were in their rooms for the night, we brought the paper into Leon's room to read. While I was still looking at it, Leon pulled me toward him, making nice around the edges, kissing my close ear, then the back of my neck. When I'd put aside the paper, he made love to me with exceptional tenderness and vigor.

Afterward, he said, "No downstairs, Cara. It's way past time, even without the summer factor."

I drifted off to sleep, but awakened at a later time, crying over the loss of someone I couldn't even identify. I snuggled up to Leon, then grew afraid of awakening him. But when I tried to get up, he rolled over on top of me and made love to me again. Then, still lying on top of me, in me, he realized I was crying.

"Jesus," he said tenderly, "you really are . . . Listen to me. In the morning, you stay in bed, and I'll go out and tell them you're here. Okay? So it won't be a surprise?"

There were all kinds of jokes I might have made if I'd been awake enough so the joking part of my brain was assembled. Like: And if they don't like it, we'll take it all back. As it was, I simply allowed my eyes to close again, dry this time, and when he got off me, I curled up away from him and drifted into sleep.

I awakened, though not enough to know where I was, to someone's knocking at the door.

"You see?" I heard a child's voice I couldn't immediately identify ask. "I told you she wasn't there!"

It was Annie.

Rennie said, "She could be sleeping."

Now I knew where I was. But where the hell was Leon? I looked at the clock. It was ten past nine.

"Phone call, Caroline!" Rennie called loudly.

Oh, Jesus. The only person it could be was Livvy.

"Okay," I called back. "I'll take it in here."

The door burst open. It was Annie, distraught. She looked at me as though there were an axe in my hand and a bloody baby on the bed. Then, before I could speak, she closed the door.

Oh, Jesus, where on earth was Leon?

I picked up the phone and got a dial tone. I hung it up. My head hurt for the first time in a while. I went into the bathroom, where a legal-pad page was taped to the mirror over the sink.

Sweetheart: The girls are still sleeping, Ovvy and I are getting some bagels and lox. If you wake up before I get back, just wait in the bedroom so I have a chance to tell them you're here. Love and kisses, L.

Terrific. I got dressed and went back to bed, lying there until I heard the front door open and close. Silence. Voices. I thought of Livvy's outrage when I'd referred to her father's mistress, told myself I should have fought Leon harder. But we couldn't have gone on indefinitely as we were. A couple of minutes later, Leon opened the door, smiled ruefully.

"I seem to have screwed up."

"Mmm."

"It's Annie, not Rennie, who's upset. Rennie seems to have been telling her for a while, and Annie was denying it."

I told him I wanted to go downstairs.

He said that he was really sorry, he shouldn't have gone out, but now, here we were, and my running out wasn't the way to make it pass.

I didn't believe it would make any real difference, any more than his being there would have made a big difference, so I stayed.

It didn't pass.

Breakfast was very quiet. Afterward, Leon said he thought we needed a sort of family conference, and Rennie pointed out, in the snotty fashion to which guessing correctly had entitled her, that we couldn't do that because we weren't a family. Ovvy, with no strong sense of a line we'd just crossed, was purely bewildered by what was going on.

"What I don't understand," Leon said, "is that you were

Cara's friend before I was. She was crazy about you before she ever met me. She cares about you more—" He stopped himself. "She didn't want to sleep up here, because she was afraid you wouldn't like it."

Annie shrugged. It didn't matter what I hadn't wanted to do. It mattered what I had done.

"Of course we don't like it," Rennie said. "We don't like anyone else in Mommy's bed."

Annie began to cry.

Leon put his arm around the back of her chair, caressed her arm.

"But it hasn't been your mommy's bed in many years. Your mommy and I . . . It's just as though we're divorced."

"You're not!" Annie said fiercely, Rennie only slightly less so. "You're not divorced."

"I think I'd better go downstairs," I said. "I have a lot of work to do."

If Annie wasn't the kind of kid to keep carrying on over our sleeping arrangements, neither did her love affair with me resume. She hadn't liked any woman who shared her father's bed, and she wasn't going to make an exception in my case. Ovvy was puzzled by the fact that she passed up even afternoon cookies and milk at my apartment, not to speak of any other meeting with me that didn't include Leon, and some that did.

Leon wasn't hurt, as I was, but he felt circumscribed by the children in a different way than before. For the first time he talked about divorce. I told him I was afraid they'd be even angrier with me. He said he couldn't be controlled in this matter by what would make his children angry. In fact, the angrier it would make them, the more he knew he had to do it. They had to understand that the split was real and permanent. He hadn't told me many horror stories about his marriage, but there were plenty to be told, and if I ever entertained the thought that he might go back to Joanna, I could forget about it right now. That was not one of the thoughts I'd entertained. On the other hand, the children, particularly Rennie, apparently had daydreamed about it in some serious fashion.

I've come to believe that the world our children carry around behind their eyes is vastly different from the one we see, that even as adults, we trust our memories over what reality tries to convince us happened. I told Leon about Livvy's shock when I referred to Mirella as her father's mistress. He joked that you could take the girl out of Rome more easily than Rome out of the girl. It was too true to amuse me. And, predictably, no matter how much he "made it clear" to his children that this divorce was "for himself," and "just makes legal something that's been true for years," the girls blamed it on me. Ovvy, who had no memory of his mother and had long since deposited his lovely Oedipal baggage with me, was unaffected by the news. But Annie began going to substantial lengths to avoid me. And Rennie, who'd been less upset than Annie about my sleeping with Leon, reacted violently.

Rennie remembered her mother in ways she assumed were specific and accurate. She remembered sitting on her mother's lap, hugging and kissing, being dressed and undressed, listening to her mother explain the contents of the shop windows they passed as they walked. She remembered her mother, very pregnant, letting her crawl between her legs and rest her ear on the huge mound of belly to hear Annie kicking in the womb. But now she began to have nightmares related to "memories" of events that hadn't happened. She remembered being carried onto a plane by her mother, and then, for some reason, having to get off. She remembered awakening in the middle of the night after a specific school event to find her mother, who'd left a year or so earlier, sitting at her bedside. Her mother had never come back but Rennie still felt she might. Nor would she buy Leon's insistence that her parents had been, to all intents and purposes, divorced for years. There was no such thing as a marriage that didn't exist. If there was a piece of paper that said you were married, then you were.

"There's something to that, you know," Leon said. "There's some final step, whether it's a piece of paper or a ring or just holding hands with people watching. If you take the final step, you're married. If you don't undo it, you're not divorced. It's time for me to undo it."

Olivia returned from Easter vacation and settled into school and her job. She'd dieted before going to Rome, gained weight while she was there, was frantic to take it off again. She said Pablo was still around, but I never saw him at the house, nor did her girlfriends visit. Mr. Moffetta had offered her full-time work for the summer. A major problem if I was going to be in

Southampton with Leon's kids, full time. She didn't see what the problem was. Didn't I trust her to walk, talk, and brush her teeth, just the way she did when I was there? I said that trust wasn't precisely the issue, and maybe she could find a waitressing job in the Hamptons. She said that was pretty funny, my thinking she would live with Leon's brats for two months. I said she hadn't thought they were brats when she baby-sat for them. It was my first reference to that time, and it was a terrible mistake. She left the room and called her father, who called me. He said he understood why I'd been so concerned about Olivia, she was turning into quite a young woman.

"I'd like her to be happy," I said, "but I'm worried—"

"*Non mi frega un cazzo* she's happy," he said. "Just make her behave. Sometimes the mother doesn't see this. But the girl needs protection."

"Oh? Are we talking about her getting pregnant, or just about getting laid?"

"Caroline," he said stiffly, "you are speaking of my daughter."

"Well, since she's your daughter," I said instantly, "maybe she should go back to Rome and live with you and *you* can protect her."

He heard me. His voice softened instantly.

"You know this is not possible. She loves New York. Her school. Her friends."

"How interesting. She never told me any of that."

A pause, then: "I am not trying to make trouble."

"But what *are* you trying to do, Angelo? Or, maybe I should ask, what do you expect me to do? She doesn't talk to me at all. Whatever she's told you, she hasn't told me."

Silence.

"Has she told you she's sleeping with somebody?"

"No," he said. "She tells me that *you* are sleeping with somebody."

"Oh, shit. You're not going to dare to bawl me out for having an affair, are you? You're not going to do some macho routine about how it's okay for men but a woman who's been divorced for years can't—"

"Please, Cara mia, calm yourself."

"What did she tell you, for God's sake? I thought you were finally going to tell her the truth about how I loved her."

"I did, I told her the truth. She says I was the only one to love her, so I told her. She begged me to see Mirella, so I took her down there. But Mirella would not see her. She was, you know, embarrassed."

Of course. Mirella needed to be embarrassed. Mirella was a female.

"Then she tells me, Mirella's house is very old, you know, with stone walls. She tells me you do not have real walls. Sometimes she cannot concentrate on her schoolwork."

I wanted to scream, but I held myself in until I could speak, then told him it was true the walls were not thick, but my lover and I were extremely careful when Livvy or his children were around, that Livvy concentrated very well on her schoolwork, got excellent grades, and was talking about going to Harvard College when she graduated from high school. As a matter of fact, she talked about it so much that I worried about what would happen if she didn't get in. It was the hardest school in the United States to get into.

There was a lengthy silence. Finally Angelo, with a sigh, said, "I am sorry, Cara. I am truly sorry. I see she is not so different with you as I think. Let us be friends now."

I took a deep breath and told him that would be good. We agreed to speak more frequently and to let her know we were doing so. I called her Livvy, then laughed.

"You heard me call her Livvy? That's a crime. She yells at me every time I don't call her Olivia."

"Are you kidding me?" Angelo replied. "If we say Olivia, she tells us in America she is called only Livvy."

"Oh, my God." But it made me feel a little better. "Angelo? She didn't tell you anything about her boyfriend, did she?"

"She spoke of nothing but school and her girlfriends."

"Well, she has a boyfriend. Or she had one. I'm not sure if he's still around. I'm not sure if . . . But sooner or later . . ."

Angelo sighed. "I don't know what I can do about this, Cara. She will know . . . from what I tell her . . . if it's from you or from me."

What he was able to do was to instruct his daughter in the terrible things that can happen when a man beds a young woman to whom he is not married. So that on one of those rare evenings when my daughter and I sat quietly in the living room, and she initiated a conversation about her stupid hygiene class, where nobody ever wanted to talk about anything but

AIDS, and I said that in the concern about AIDS, everyone had forgotten the first reason for condoms, which was to avoid pregnancy, she said, "There you go again. I'm not the same person you are and I don't behave the same way."

I sighed. After almost two years in a New York City high school she was still talking as though I were the first unmarried woman in history to get laid.

"Are we back to Leon, Olivia? You know, Leon really isn't your problem."

"No, we're not back to Leon," she said, very slowly and deliberately. "We're back to my father telling me why he had to marry you."

It took my breath away. I'd have to remember not to ask Angelo for help anymore.

I smiled. "Not a very good lesson, since you gave us both more pleasure than anything else in our lives."

"Oh, sure," she said. "That's why . . ." But she trailed off, for once unable to come up with a suitably devastating reply.

"The point is," I finally said, "I think you're a real student, which I never was. And if you want to go to college, as you seem to, then it would be better if you didn't get pregnant. I'm not saying you shouldn't go to bed with Pablo if you feel like it, only that—"

She stood up abruptly.

"I'm not going to bed with Pablo or anyone. I'm not even talking to Pablo anymore. All right? We're finished. Are you happy?"

"I'm sorry," I said. "I mean, if you are."

"Don't worry," she said. "If I was sorry, I'd see him."

My whole life was holding its breath. The P.R. people were trying to get coverage of my fall show, but they hadn't found a hook, and nobody was interested. We were going to look at summer rentals as soon as Leon had a Saturday and Sunday off, but he hadn't yet, and he seemed to have stopped talking about renting. I'd been seeing less of him, anyway. Rennie's shrink had suggested it would be helpful if he could spend more time than he had been with the kids. Rennie had complained that he was downstairs with me whenever he was free.

"Maybe it'd be a good idea for a while . . . I don't mean weekends, but maybe during the week, you should stay downstairs, and I'll stay upstairs."

Gee, Leon, I think it's really great that you're getting a piece of paper that proves you're divorced so you and I can sleep apart.

But I didn't say it and he didn't press to find out how I was feeling about what he'd said. At that point, he didn't really want to know.

I refused to allow myself to think a great deal about Leon or his children. Ovvy was still very much my son-pal. Life being what it was, maybe I was lucky to have lost only another daughter.

On this night I was reading *The African Heritage Cookbook*, the only one I'd found that tied African food by its region into the specifics of soul food cooked in this country, when Leon called to ask if I felt like taking a walk. We hadn't spoken in a couple of days. I said all right, left the door ajar and went back to my book, feigning such concentration as barely to notice when he entered. Then, almost reluctantly, I set aside my book and left the house with him.

It was a beautiful night in May, comfortable for a jacket, though he was just in shirtsleeves. I'd put on a sweater. We walked in silence for a block or two.

"You mad at me?" Leon asked.

"Mad? No, I'm not mad at you."

"You seem very cool," Leon said.

"Well, that sounds right," I said. "I'm cool at you."

"Why?"

It was a trap. Anything I told him, he could say was necessary for his kids.

"I don't know. Does there have to be a reason?"

He laughed shortly.

We were at Twenty-third Street. By common consent, we headed east. There would be more people on the street in that direction.

"How's Madame Olivia these days?"

A clear bid to change me-against-him into us-against-her. He would be utterly sympathetic. There'd be none of those suggestions I occasionally heard that I must have done something worse than getting mad in the kitchen to make her hate me so much. He could, after all, trace any problems *his* kids had. To their mother.

"She's okay. She seems to have broken off with Pablo."

"How come?"

"I don't know. But when I tried to talk about birth control, she said she wasn't seeing him."

"She should learn about it, anyway."

"Ah, yes," I said. "Should. We all know about our children and Should."

He thought he might as well steer away from that one, too.

We turned off at Lexington Avenue, walked down to Gramercy Park. It was close to ten and dark out, but the park was lighted and beautiful.

"Maybe," I said, "if I get rich and famous, I'll move to someplace where I can see a park. Central Park. Riverside. It'd be nice to have a view. And real walls."

And to be someplace where you'd have to put a little more effort into finding me. Of course, the kids would, too. Ovvy.

He put his arm around me as though we'd returned to the old days, walked so springily fast that I had trouble keeping up with him. At Union Square he asked if I'd like to find a cup of cappuccino someplace. I said I'd just as soon make it at home. But at home I poured wine for both of us and we settled on the sofa that wasn't against Olivia's wall. The lights were off in her room. We hadn't been in bed together in a week. I felt like a mouse near a trap baited with room-temperature *bleu de bresse.* I moved away from him.

He said, "So you *are* mad at me."

I shrugged.

We both sipped at our wine.

"It hasn't been very easy for me, either, you know," he said seductively.

I shrugged again.

"They feel as though I put one over on them. They thought you were *their* friend and then it turns out—"

Given the choice at that moment, I would have gone back to being their friend rather than remain his.

"Then it turns out that you're not just my friend but my . . ."

Cook? Fuck? I kept my mouth shut.

"I'll tell you what I've been thinking," he continued suavely. "I think I'll be free next weekend. It's getting past time to find a place. Maybe . . . you're working hard on the show, anyway. . . . Maybe the kids and I should go out there and look at some houses. Then, if we see something we like, you can go with me and check it out."

So, there it was. I'm not sure precisely what he saw on my

face that made him stop talking, but I felt like a sack of potatoes that's been deposited in the mudroom until someone has use for it. Tied up in knots so I could be left behind more easily while he and his children went off to find the house where I would take care of them that summer.

"I think that might work very well for you and the kids," I finally managed. "I think I'll go up to Westport. Maybe I'll rent a cottage there. I can get into the city more easily if the TV people need me. And it's closer to my family."

The only family I have in the world.

I was too steeped in self-pity for my tears not to spill out, but I wasn't going to let Leon see them. I went to the kitchen for the wine bottle.

Leon sighed. "I can't say I didn't expect this, but I don't see why it has to be such a big deal."

That took care of the tears, though I still couldn't look at him.

"No big deal."

He sighed. "All right. I get it. We'll all go."

"I'm busy."

"Are you really or are you just getting back at me?"

"I'm just getting back at you."

A short laugh rode out on a sigh. This man was sorely tried.

"No," I said. "Not just. I'm trying to tell you something."

"Okay. So tell me."

I didn't want to begin the way I did, but it was what had entered my mind, and until it left, I wasn't going to be able to deal with the present in any simple way.

"When I was little . . . Sunday was the housekeeper's day off, and my parents always wanted to do something with the older kids, a museum or some movie that I wouldn't enjoy, and I'd get so restless, I'd make them all miserable. They had to find someone to take me on a day when every other kid in the world was with her family. Or so it seemed. I know better now, of course. But that doesn't leave me in an entirely different place. I still feel like, you wanted me in your bed, I was there. Your kids want me out, I'm out. Like some big stuffed animal that was taking up too much space."

"You were the one who didn't want them to know we were sleeping together," he said. "You were the one who knew how they'd feel. I had no idea. Maybe if they'd known all along . . ."

I shook my head.

"I just would have had them for less time."

And they were the best thing in my life.

I wasn't even sure it was true anymore. I'd thought it in the past tense. If falling in love with Leon hadn't diminished my affection for them, it had altered my priorities. At some point, I'd needed to see him even more than I'd needed to see them.

Leon came over to me and held me, kissing the top of my head, smoothing back my disheveled hair.

"Poor baby," he said. "It's not me you're upset about, it's them."

"It's everything," I said. "Everything is too goddamned difficult."

"Come," he said. "Let's go to bed and try to figure things out."

I inclined my head in the direction of Olivia's room. I was even more self-conscious than I'd once been since my conversation with Angelo.

"We'll go upstairs," Leon said. "My little sweethearts are all tucked away."

We didn't figure out much that night, but in the next few days, whether for reasons of affection or something more practical, Leon made a serious effort to improve matters, and, of course, he succeeded. He told his girls (Ovvy would just have been puzzled by the conversation) that I had to look at houses with them because the plan they'd had, of spending the summer at the beach instead of going to camp, would work only if I stayed with them. They didn't have to love me, but they had to be nice. If they made me feel unwanted, they were going to end up in camp.

The recession had already hit the Hamptons, and we found a reasonably priced renovated Bridgehampton farmhouse whose owner had put in a pool, then decided he couldn't afford any of it. Nobody was crazy about the furnishings, but there were five bedrooms, and the fifth was downstairs, with its own bathroom, as I told Livvy when I was trying to persuade her to look for a job out there.

I could not. (Probably because she knew, as I did not, that she was seeing Pablo again, had begun to sleep with him, and was keeping him invisible so I'd feel less uncomfortable about leaving her "alone.") Her line ending that phase of the discussion was something to the effect that I treated her like a three-year-old who got dragged wherever Mommy had to go. Just close enough to my own sack-of-potatoes line to stop me. On the other hand, I couldn't leave her unsupervised all summer. Our compromise (the name I gave her triumph) was that I'd give Leon a set of our keys and he would "check the apartment" frequently. I told her, though I wasn't sure it was true, that I would also be coming into the city regularly, and wouldn't feel I needed to give her notice. As she began to protest, I said, quickly, "And of course I hope you'll come out whenever you have a couple of days off. With any friend you want to bring. There's plenty of room."

I had a yen to do a couple of summer classes in Bridge-hampton. I needed to believe I'd have work if the show flopped. I'd explained to my regular groups why I wasn't doing fall sessions. They'd been excited for me but I'd been uneasy ever since. Summer groups seemed like a good compromise, but Sheldon dismissed the idea. Sheldon's house was in Southampton, less than a ten-minute drive from ours. If I was becoming anxious about the show, he was borderline-hysterical. As the summer passed he took to coming by the house without notice to discuss something that was never important. The kids thought he was funny, "a dweeb" (Annie), "an asshole" (Rennie; she wasn't allowed to say this in her father's presence, but she and I had developed an understanding). Ovvy looked at me slyly and laughed. Leon's attitude, when I complained about Sheldon, was close to the way it had been when I worried about Livvy: I should lighten up and get a kick out of the guy the way his kids did. Maybe my problem was that the summer was going too well; the kids had begun by behaving themselves and gone on to forget, a good portion of the time, that they didn't like me anymore. Did I know that I was very Jewish in at least one way? I found it impossible to relax when too many good things were happening to me. Then Sheldon showed up without warning at nine o'clock on a Sunday morning in the middle of August because he'd been playing tennis nearby and there was something he had to tell me instantly if not sooner.

All three kids had slept elsewhere. Leon and I had been in bed until a short while earlier. I'd come downstairs in my bathing suit to put up coffee and make breakfast. Sundays I always made something special in the pancake or waffle department. I had some good local peaches and I'd already cut them up, mixed a pancake batter, and brought in the *Times*, in its blue-plastic bag, from the doorstep, when Leon came down and settled at the table. I gave him his coffee.

There was a knock, the kitchen door opened before either of us said a word, and Sheldon appeared, all sweat and white tennis clothes, pleased with himself for having had the foresight to know where I'd be.

"Well," I said, "look who's here."

Leon stared at him. I dumped the peaches into the batter, turned on the heat under the big frying pan.

"I need to talk to you," Sheldon said. "Mind if I take a cup of coffee?"

"Oh, sure, please," Leon said after a moment as I poured the batter into the pan. "I'm sorry. I didn't realize you'd called."

"I was two blocks away," Sheldon said, meaning that he hadn't called.

I grinned.

Sheldon sat down with Leon. Sniffed the cooking pancake. "That for the show?"

"Of course," I said. "We never eat except to rehearse for the show."

He was not amused. Sometimes I couldn't tell whether Sheldon really didn't get a joke or was making it a point not to be amused. Or the reverse. That is, when he laughed because he knew a joke was funny, he was sort of showing that he knew it was funny rather than enjoying it. Kupferman and I often exchanged glances when Sheldon did his I-get-the-joke routine. Anyway, now he wasn't even bothering to Get It.

"Would you like a piece?" I asked as I took three dishes instead of two from the cabinet.

"Yeah. Sure."

It was only when he'd polished off his pancake and gone for the last coffee in the pot that he settled back at the table and made his announcement.

"We have to go into the city."

"We?"

"You."

It was gratifying to watch Leon, who for months had been arguing with me on Sheldon's behalf, reacting to this real-life invasion of the body snatcher.

"What for?" I asked.

"To see how we can fix you up for the show."

Under the napkin Leon had left on the table, his middle finger was signaling "Fuck you."

I smiled radiantly at Sheldon. I had long since stopped trying to figure out whether he deliberately couched his thoughts in the most insulting possible manner.

"I know they'll want me to wear makeup. And I'll put up my hair, and wear these nice cotton prints that look *hamisch*, and—"

"Never mind *hamisch*. Kupferman thinks you could be good-looking."

Leon stood up to get the paper.

"It's not me, Leon," I said. "It's occidental females."

Sheldon shook his head. "Bob doesn't wanna go for the Julia look. You're not fat enough. They decided to go for a little glamour. We're taking a shot at the first glamorous female chef."

I laughed.

If finding my own way in an academic family had left me with no strong sense of myself that didn't reside in the kitchen, a fringe benefit of having grown up in that family was never to have developed the pervasive anxiety about appearance that many women had always had, and that seems to oppress male and female of all ages now. Recently, whether because men's eyes were full of television females or their brains were full of women who'd threatened to sue for ocular rape when they were eyed on the street, I was more likely to have my existence noted by strangers if I wore makeup and dressed up a little. I could tell Livvy had grown more and more anxious about her appearance, not just her weight. She was spending a huge amount of money on cosmetics and products guaranteed to remove hair from one place, make it silkier in another. But a few fast looks around me told me she was no worse than her friends and others I saw on the streets, in places called nail parlors (the first time I'd seen a sign for one, I'd thought I was reading it wrong), and in department stores, where you got the impression that cosmetics, perfumes, and powders were doing more for capitalism than the clothing and furniture industries put together. Walking into the elevator of Sheldon's office building, I'd be bowled over by the scent worn by some young woman who'd been promised it would lure a man and had decided to use enough to lure ten.

If they tried to make me wear perfume on the show, I'd tell them it interfered with the smell of the food.

Anyway, I knew I was lucky that I didn't obsess over the way I looked. On the other hand, it would have been too much to hope that they'd be the same way. Or to anticipate what they had in mind.

Or the results.

Daphne Kupferman brought me to her hairdresser, Gilbert. Pronounced Zheelbear. Who had an accent that was either false French or real French-Canadian, and who never spoke directly to me. He talked to Daphne, a young and glamorous second wife who avoided meeting my eyes in the mirror as she listened to him.

First he described, for our benefit and not without pain to himself, how I would appear on the screen if I were so foolish as to go on the air with "zis." Zis being my hair, a lock of which he raised with an expression I'd have reserved for a dead waterbug.

"She weel fade into za woodworrrk."

Then he described the various possibilities, beginning with Jane Pauley blonde, going on to Vanna White blonde, Madonna blonde, and several other blondes I hadn't heard of. I asked uneasily whether maybe we could start with just a little henna rinse. He ignored me but Daphne smiled sympathetically, patted my shoulder.

To make an afternoon-long's story short, I left Zheelbear with my hair shoulder-length, curly instead of wavy, and Sarah Jessica Parker blonde. I had been heavily made up under Daphne's supervision. She needed, she said, to get a feeling for the possibilities. I'd kept my eyes closed, refused to look in the mirror, and when I accidentally did so, was uncertain for a second or two whom I was looking at. They kept telling me I'd get used to wearing makeup and appeared not to believe my claim that I always had. (Of course, I'd worn it to look better when I got dressed up, not to be someone I couldn't recognize.) Now I felt more self-conscious than I had the first time I wore a brassiere, as embarrassed as the first time I got my period—in school. Daphne brought me to Bob's office for approval, and approve he did, but all I wanted was to sneak home before anyone saw me. I felt like one of those women you saw sauntering along Fifth Avenue on weekdays who really wouldn't know what to do with the afternoon if the stores closed.

It was Monday. I was scheduled for a Tuesday-morning clothes conference with Daphne's Personal Shopper, after which I'd take the train back to Bridgehampton. Leon had hired a local high-school boy the kids liked to stay at the house and supervise them, particularly with regard to the pool. They didn't really need anyone to take care of them, especially if Rennie was being nice because she liked the young man; Annie was capable of preparing the simple meals they ate in our absence. I had no idea of how Leon's kids would react to my ghastly transformation, but I knew I wasn't ready to face their father.

I hailed a cab, changed my mind, let it go. If I got back to my apartment too quickly, I might jump into the shower instead of trying to get accustomed to the way I looked. From a street phone, I left a message for Leon that I wouldn't be home for dinner. Then I began walking down Fifth Avenue. It was only when I was somewhere below Thirty-fourth Street that I started trying to remember Olivia's working hours. Having her see me, if she was in one of her nasty moods, could be worse than facing Leon.

By the time I reached home, I was in a less extreme state, though still too fragile to let Leon see me. By now he'd be curled up in his icy-cold bedroom with some awful food he'd brought home with him. Maybe when I walked in his whole digestive system would go haywire. I'd walk over to Sixth Avenue and pick up a bread and some cheese in the doubtful event that I'd get hungry later. I took off my clothes, showered with a shower cap on, dressed in a T-shirt and shorts, combed my hair without looking in the mirror, cursing because the front ends weren't even long enough to pull back away from my face. Why couldn't they have waited until the end of the goddamned summer to do this to me? I put on a little makeup because my old face just didn't look right with my new hair.

As I pushed open the building's front door, someone pulled it from the outside, so that I fell forward slightly, reached out for the wrought-iron railing at the steps' side.

"Whoops, sorry," Leon's voice said. Then, as I turned

around, it added in a somewhat more seductive tone, "Are you okay?"

I looked up at him. We were inches away from each other, but it was several seconds before he realized that it was me. Then it was his turn to start. After which his face turned bright red under his Hamptons tan.

"Oh, my God!" he exclaimed.

"It was His hairdresser, actually," I said, tartly defensive.

"You look gorgeous!" He set down the shopping bag he'd been carrying.

Now it was my turn to be stunned. Maybe he was being sarcastic. No. Looking at him, it was impossible to believe this. My mind went to the first time I'd gotten dressed up to go to the Coach House and he'd made his first pass. But this was on another scale entirely. His eyes took me in as though I'd managed, in his absence, to find and occupy Marilyn Monroe's undamaged earthly remains.

"Let me look at you!" His hands were on my arms. "I can't believe—" His arms came around me and he tried to kiss me but a car horn honked nearby, startling us both.

"Leon, this is—"

Again, he tried to kiss me, but I could feel passersby looking at us and I pushed him away. I said I wanted to go to the store. He said there was something he had to show me first. Inside, he led me upstairs to his apartment, and then to his bedroom, where he made love to me with a vigor that was particularly noteworthy because he'd been working since eight that morning, and later, when we'd had dinner out, and come home to bed, he made love to me again. I didn't understand yet what had happened, but I liked it enough to forget everything else for a while.

In the morning, I got back into my T-shirt and shorts, had a glass of what Leon called "fresh-squoze orange juice" with him, resisted his efforts to go back to bed for a quickie, went down to my apartment when he left for work. I was under orders to stick around for dinner even if I finished early with Daphne Kupferman.

I turned the key in my top lock, which wasn't on. I'd have to speak to Livvy about doing it automatically at night. I turned the key in the bottom lock, opened the door to face Pablo, just coming out of the bathroom, wearing his pants, but no shirt, socks, or shoes. If I was thrown for a loop, he was thrown further by this strange blonde with a key to the apartment. When he realized it was Olivia's mother under the hair, he was stunned, then terribly upset.

I said, "Hi," came in, closed the door behind me. "It's me. They made me do my hair for the TV show."

He nodded, but he couldn't speak. He might not even have heard yet about the show.

"I slept upstairs."

Nothing.

"Olivia sleeping?"

Another nod.

I smiled. "Maybe it's just as well. Do you have time for a cup of coffee and a little talk?" He hesitated. "I think it's really a good idea, Pablo." I smiled. "The talk, anyway."

He whispered, "She won't like that."

I nodded. "I know she won't. But she's fifteen years old and I'm concerned about her."

He looked at the floor. "I wouldn't hurt her."

"You don't have to want to hurt her to get her pregnant, you just—"

"I'm very careful," he said earnestly, looking at me now. "I'm not the one to take chances. I try to tell her—"

Later I would think about the phrasing, but at that moment Olivia opened her door and walked into the living room. She'd wrapped a cotton blanket around herself. She'd heard my voice and decided to tough it out, but of course she hadn't been prepared for the hair. She did a double take. Her lip curled. She looked away from me to Pablo, sitting at the kitchen table.

"I hope you're comfortable," she said to him, in a tone of voice I'd thought she reserved for me.

"Your mama," he said after a moment, "wants to talk to us, O. She's worried, you know. . . ."

It was the "us" in "wants to talk to us" that made me decide I could trust him.

I put up water for coffee.

She said, "Since you and my mother agree about everything, why don't you two talk, and I'll go back to bed!"

But she went to the bathroom, and when she came out a moment later, she was wearing one of the twin towel robes my parents had bought us. I'd been setting up coffee cups, afraid to speak lest she think it was behind her back. As she sat down, I looked for a way to open a conversation without adding to the tension at the table.

"I'm glad you two've made up, and I hope you'll spend some time with us at the beach. I told Livvy, there's a downstairs bedroom with its own bath for you this year."

"That's very kind of you," Pablo said.

Olivia gave him a dirty look. He looked back—imploringly. He hadn't arranged all this. What was he supposed to do?

"Look," I said, having poured coffee for each of us and sat down with them, "I don't want to make a big deal out of this. It's very simple. L— Olivia's not quite sixteen years old. She wants to go to college. She shouldn't get pregnant."

"Mother of God!" she exploded. "Don't you have anything else in the whole world to worry about, beside me having a baby?" She stood up, with her coffee. She looked at Pablo meaningfully. "You must be late for work by now." She turned to me. "If you think of something else you care about, please knock at my door and tell me. In the meantime, I'm going back to sleep."

With an apologetic shrug, Pablo finished the last of his coffee, went to finish dressing, came out again. At the front door, he turned back.

He said, "I wouldn't do anything to hurt her, Mrs. Ferrante. I love her. I . . ." Words failed him.

I smiled. "I can tell you're a good man, Pablo," I said, to cover the acute uneasiness his words caused me. You could take care of a young man who wanted to get laid; a young man in love might be much more difficult.

I walked upstairs to Leon's apartment and called him at the hospital. He could only talk to me for a moment, but he ordered me not to go back to Bridgehampton after doing my clothes shopping. I should wait for him at his apartment or mine. He would call the sitter and his kids and explain that I'd been delayed. That way, we could drive out together on Friday.

I told Livvy I'd be in Leon's apartment until Friday, that I'd ring first if I had to come down for anything in the early morning or the evening. My computer was out at the beach, but I brought up some books and notes. I'd told my father, before we all separated for the summer, that I was afraid my ability to be, as they say, quick with the snappy answer wouldn't be up to par for television. He had suggested that I do what he did in teaching, compile a list of answers that I'd be able to adapt to whatever questions were asked. I'd laughed at the idea, but now I was going to try to do just that.

The clothing trip was relatively painless, if only because Daphne agreed that I had to wear clothes I could really prepare food in, skirts not so tight I couldn't pick up something that fell, et cetera. I ended up with slightly more glamorous cottons than I already owned, and the low heels that were, fortunately, in style.

I prepared dinners for Leon and me at home, upstairs. Main-course salads and other dishes appropriate to the hot weather and a kitchen with only a fan to make it bearable. On hotter nights, I served them in the bedroom. And as I moved back and forth between the hot kitchen and the cool bedroom, look-ing for the salt and pepper or something else I'd forgotten, and then, later, brought back the dishes, or went to find one of the books I was scouring for ad libs, Leon, more often than not, followed me. Sometimes he'd just thought of something he wanted to tell me. At other times he was sure he'd had a rea-son to leave the other room, but now he couldn't remember it. Often it was just a sudden urge to kiss me. Or hug me. Or make love. I made jokes about how it was true blondes had more fun, but he really seemed not to get them. Nor did I catch on immediately. It was too absurd.

I'd told the kids over the phone that I'd been turned into a blonde and they mustn't tease me too much about it. Their re-actions, when we reached the house Friday night, varied from Rennie's enthusiasm to Annie's polite "You look very nice, Caroline" with Ovvy's appearing not to notice. He came run-ning out of the house when we parked the car to show me a huge and particularly wonderful shell he'd found intact on the beach, allowed me to kiss his cheek though he was becoming shy about hugs and kisses, then ran off to find the sitter, who was inside watching MTV.

Leon continued to follow me from room to room. If I asked what was going on, because the girls were around and I was self-conscious, he was disconcerted. He hadn't thought about it, he'd just done it. The girls grew uneasy. On Saturday morn-ing, when they usually hung around until he or we were ready for the beach, they went with friends and remained out with them. Their father was in no hurry to get to the beach, unless I was. If he had been grateful for my attentions to his children, had come to like me, to enjoy me and my assorted hospitalities, and had, finally, grown deeply attached to me, the blonde he'd bumped into on the steps had caused Leon to fall over that peculiar line. He was, as they say, madly in love.

On Sunday morning, when I'd separated the eggs for pancakes and was beating the whites in the big, tin-lined copper bowl that had been my first post-contract purchase, he came into the kitchen, kissed the back of my neck, and asked what I was doing. I told him.

"Can I try it?" he asked.

I turned around, laughing, but he was serious. I handed him the whisk, showed him how to hold the bowl, and guided his hand as he began to beat.

"Whew," he said, when a minute or more had gone by and I was occupied elsewhere. "It hurts."

I smiled, came back to his side. "You're not used to it."

"Why am I doing this?" he asked.

"You're beating air into the eggs," I said. "They're getting stiff, see?" He turned to see if I'd intended a double entendre—in those weeks almost everything had some sexual meaning attached to it—but I ignored him. "It's what you do to make the meringue on a lemon meringue pie. You whip air into it and you bake and it hardens that way."

"You're kidding!"

It was more extraordinary than anything he'd learned in medical school.

"Except they won't be sweet unless we put in some sugar."

His eyes gleamed. "Let's do it!"

He was having an enormous amount of fun as we beat the yolks in their little bowl, combined them with the flour mixture, added the whites and finally the cut-up peaches. It's one of cooking's pleasures that understanding how it works doesn't rob it of its magical quality, and he was unbelievably excited when I showed him how to use the spatula to lift the part of the pancake that was trying to stick to the pan, thrilled when I said that yes, we could serve it directly from the pan, an act he'd seen me perform many times.

The kids came into the kitchen, stopped at the sight of their father with a spatula in his hand.

"Look what we're making for you!" he announced proudly. "Are these the most beautiful pancakes you ever saw?"

First, they all gaped. It was a joke. It had to be. They couldn't believe it. Then my adorable Ovvy angrily informed me that I wasn't supposed to be teaching his *father* how to cook and he wasn't hungry, anyway. Rennie said Ovvy was an idiot and anyone who wanted to cook could, that was what the women's movement was about. Annie said it was the fluffiest pancake she'd ever seen, far fluffier than any I'd made with them, and at breakfast she said that it tasted the best, too. I asked Ovvy to come sit on my lap, "the way you did when you were little." He'd gotten too old to let himself do that, but he did consent to move his chair close to mine, and I whispered to him that I didn't think his father was really interested in cooking, it was just this one little thing that had grabbed him. But when Leon suggested that the kids walk to the beach without waiting for us, and we'd drive over when we'd loaded the dishwasher (a machine I hadn't known he understood to exist), Ovvy joined the girls without protest. They all wanted to get away. There was an intensity in the very air of the house that they needed to escape. That was when I understood that finally my feelings were well met.

Leon said he loved me.

I told him that if I'd only known, I'd have bleached my hair earlier.

He didn't know what I was talking about.

I asked if he realized that if the show wasn't a success, it would cost me a fortune to keep my hair blonde and curly.

I wanted him to say he'd love me with my old, wavy brown hair, but he told me not to worry about it, he would pay for the beauty parlor.

That night, as I prepared for bed, I had to force myself to insert my diaphragm. I hated it as I never had. If Leon hadn't given me his speech about being finished having children, I think I might have managed to forget it. As it was, I lay in the much-denigrated supine position that had always been my absolute favorite, the only one that was no work and all play, except the play wasn't quite as wonderful as usual, because I couldn't get Olivia out of my mind, even as Leon sucked my nipples, played with me, then came into me like a sixteen-year-old hitting a home run. Olivia, asking me whether I didn't have anything in the world to think about besides her getting pregnant.

Maybe she was right. At least partly. Maybe I should concentrate on my own temptations instead of worrying so much about hers. In any event, she knew what was necessary, as did Pablo. They would have to take care of themselves.

* * *

They came out with Leon for a couple of weekends. She was gaining so much weight that if I hadn't seen how much she was eating, if I hadn't made my own connection, I'd have worried that she was already pregnant.

I was grateful for Pablo's presence. He was a sweetly reasonable man who served as a sort of interpreter between me and my daughter, essential because since I'd come upon him in the apartment, she assumed a malevolent curiosity that turned the simplest question about, say, whether they'd join us for dinner, into an attempt to pry. Pablo explained to her patiently.

"No, sweetheart," he would say. "That's not what your mom asked. She just wants to know if she should make supper for us before she goes out."

Livvy, certain that the motive she'd imputed to me was correct but unwilling to relinquish her victim's role, would subside.

Late Saturday night of that first weekend they were with us, as we returned from a party, we passed their room and heard the sounds of lovemaking.

"They do know all the possibilities," Leon said, when we'd reached our own bedroom. Until now, he'd been inclined to think I worried too much. They were clearly sane, clearly . . .

I shrugged. "I've done what I can. He seems responsible. She always acts as though she's safe because she was raised half a mile from the Vatican."

"Does she think every pregnant teenager is the daughter of liberal West Side Jews? She should spend a little time at the clinic. See how many of them are nice little Catholic girls."

"I think that's a very good idea," I said. "I hope you'll invite her to do it."

He became contrite, as he wouldn't have before.

"I will talk to her. If you want me to."

"I don't know what to say, Leon. When I do it, she acts as though I'm trying to take away some kind of prize. She knows what's involved."

If Leon remained at the center of my existence, even he was displaced from my thoughts in the days between our return to the city and the first "Pot Luck." I would tape on Thursdays at five; the show would air at seven. Ovvy would be responsible for our home tape, whether or not Leon was there. We agreed, giggling, that during the first airing, we'd not only all be there, but we would send out for pizza.

The weekend before the show began, I had a call from Mrs. Sakai. I hadn't heard her daughter's name all summer and I was pleasantly surprised. She said they'd been in Japan and now were driving to Boston to visit their "American relations." While they were there, Mayumi wanted to just take a look at Harvard. They would stay in a hotel in the city and would like Olivia to join them. I said that would be lovely, thanked her. When I asked Livvy why she hadn't mentioned the trip, she said I got nervous whenever she mentioned Harvard. When I tried to explain that it wasn't Harvard that made me nervous, but that in her sophomore high-school year she had already decided there was only one school in the world where she could be happy, she ignored me. As though what I'd said had nothing to do with anything we'd been talking about or that had happened before.

The first few shows went well, but not well enough. There was no press coverage of what was just one more food show on a lesser cable channel, so nobody became interested who hadn't just happened to turn it on.

"Hi, I'm Caroline Ferrante and this is Pot Luck. The expression 'taking pot luck,' as you probably know, means turning stuff you find in the cupboard or the refrigerator into a meal. Here, the pot will be my brain, full of odds and ends about food that I hope will interest you. Some of the food I'll just talk about, some I'll cook. Sometimes I might dance because the producer keeps telling me television's a visual medium and I'll bore you if I stand still and talk. Sometimes I might just complain about the producer, report our arguments—with funny gestures that'll make them *visual*. His trouble is, he's not really interested in food.

"People's brains are like magnets; what they're attracted to is more likely to stick. From the time when I was very young, anything about food stuck to my brain. As an adult, well, sort of an adult, I went to Italy and cooked in restaurants there for years before returning to the States. I should mention that one reason I could do this was that women were accepted as chefs in Italian restaurants when the cooking establishment here was still acting as though females were structurally unequipped to prepare food away from home.

"When I came back to the States, I brought hundreds of recipes from Italy. Then I found myself playing with ingredients I'd never seen there, like ginger and wonderful Oriental vegetables that hadn't been in many stores here when I left. Incidentally, the way I keep ginger is, I buy a root, peel and grate it, then make little bundles in plastic wrap and freeze them so they're there when I want them. They defrost in about thirty seconds in the microwave, and don't take much longer on the counter. Ginger and reheating coffee are the only things I really love the microwave for. Whatever its virtues, a microwave isn't lovable. It provides heat without warmth.

"Today I'm going to play with something very lovable, an Italian dessert called *tiramisù* I learned to make when I was growing up. I recently put a little ginger juice in a *tiramisù* when I didn't have any of the liqueurs people customarily use, but most Italians would probably consider that beyond the pale."

"Who'd you learn from?" a woman in the stage audience asked.

"A wonderful lady named Anna Cherubini. She was our housekeeper. The keeper of our home and our kitchen. My mother worked."

"It's easy to like cooking if you don't have to do it!" the woman said.

I shrugged. "Sure. But some people—Anna was one—love it even if they do. Anyway, how come nobody ever says that about sex?"

The audience laughed. In the wings, Sheldon nodded violently, clapped silently, I should Do More of Same. Sheldon never laughed if I said something funny, he just wanted more of same. He never believed it wouldn't be as funny the second time.

"As you can see, I've listed different ingredients for *tiramisù*. Tourists have a good one at a restaurant in Venice, and they order it in Rome, expecting the same dessert. But a Roman's idea of *tiramisù* is quite different from a Venetian's. Which is not a Florentine's. There's a wonderful dictionary-encyclopedia-cookbook called *Gastronomy of Italy*, in which the author, Anna Del Conte, tells us that the cake was created by a chef near Treviso in the late sixties and is most often made with ladyfingers or sponge cake, soaked in rum or brandy, then layered with mascarpone, a sweet, creamy, soft cheese. As you can see, I'm beginning to put together a version based on Ms. Del Conte's comments. But as I do this, I want you to look at the other recipe on the blackboard, for something called Mascarpone Cheese Cake. This comes from a book called *The Classic Cuisine of the Italian Jews*, whose author, Edda Servi Machlin, says the cake is a classic of Italian-Jewish cuisine. The ingredients, the basic concept, if you will, of this cake is clearly very close to that of the cake that was ostensibly born in the late sixties. This happens over and over again."

I'd been prepared to be pressed on the matter of who was stealing what from whom, and had ready a few lines about simultaneous invention, and Isn't It Surprising That This Sort of Thing Doesn't Happen All the Time—It Probably Does! But the next question came from a huge woman in a pink dress, who asked, in a little girl's voice, "What about salmonella?"

"I wanted to mention that," I lied. "When the Machlin book was published, we weren't worried about raw eggs the way we are now. You might want to try various solutions. The first is to find a chicken farm near you where you're sure the eggs aren't carrying salmonella. Or a small store where you trust the people, and they know the farm. Or you might want to experiment with some of those new fake eggs. As far as I could discover, they're all homogenized. My own preference would be to play with eggless versions if I couldn't find eggs I knew were all right. But, you know, if there's one thing I'd like to do here, beside getting rich and famous, it's to make people stop treating food as though it were atomic waste. Honestly, there aren't that many things you can die from in the kitchen. And when there's something really unhealthy, often there are substitutes."

On the stage, another hand went up. It belonged to a chubby blonde who had been playing with her hair until I called on her.

"Why did you come back from Italy?" she asked in a tiny, timid voice.

I hesitated, smiled in what I hoped was a friendly fashion. "Let's just say it had nothing to do with the food, and this show is about food."

"Are you interested in health food?" someone else asked.

"You mean, health with a capital *H*? Somehow, when you call it that, it's not too interesting. But if you read, say, Elizabeth David's wonderful book about Provence, there are moments when you think you're reading about Southern Italy. They're both healthy cuisines, they both use olive oil, not butter, one of the main points anyone's going to make about eating right, and of course it's easy to eat healthily when you live in a warm place where fruit and vegetables have a long growing season. Anyway, there are a million health-food cookbooks for anyone who wants them, but I hardly ever have bean sprouts on the brain. Which isn't to say that I won't be happy to hear about what's on yours. Especially if you happen to be curious about any of the subjects that interest me. I'm interested in food customs, in what you eat on holidays, religious or national. I'm fascinated by forbidden foods, beginning with Adam's apple." (Sheldon had warned me that I was not to bring up cannibalism, under any circumstances.) "And in the matter of how we can maintain any sense of continuity in a country where the politicians are so stupid they think you can just change the dates of holidays because the date of a date doesn't matter. So, let me hear from you. In the meantime, let's see what's going on with our first *tiramisù*."

Sheldon said I had to stop giving authors' names—as though the second it took to say Del Conte or Machlin slowed up the show beyond repair. He wanted more about food and sex, but the closest I could come was with a program on wine. I quoted Horace—"No poems can please for long or live that are written by water drinkers"—and pointed out, at Bob's insistence, that the alcohol in wine evaporates when you heat it, and only the lovely flavors remain. (There were still protests from a number of Muslims, all at the same address, who said I was encouraging the use of liquor.) I quoted an explanation I'd read for the Jewish history of moderate drinking: Around 500 B.C. the Babylonians had brought the Hebrews to their country as slaves. The Babylonian enemy was the Persians, who knew the former loved the darkness, and drank too much when they had parties. The Persians attacked and destroyed the Babylonian empire very late on a party night. They also freed the Jews, who might have learned a lesson in the value of not drinking too much. A couple of the letter writers objected to my "holding up" as an example any group except the Muslims, who lived well and ate wonderful food without touching pork or liquor.

"What's with you and the Jews?" Sheldon wanted to know. "I want you to leave the Jews off the goddamned show for a while." When I asked how I could do that when I was a Jew, he said he only meant the "Jewish *stuff*." The Jews didn't know how to cook, anyway. He kept pressing for an arranged disaster. When I pointed out that he was the one who'd called me a natural, he said there was natural enough for cable, and then there was natural enough for network.

I was startled. I'd only been on cable for a few weeks. He'd never referred to network before. I said I didn't understand. He said he was trying to get network people to pay attention, then made some slighting remark about Bob Kupferman and his penny-ante cable programs.

I asked if Bob knew that.

Sheldon shrugged. "If he's got a brain in his head, he knows it."

It appeared that nobody with a sense of humor ever wrote a letter or asked a question. By the fourth week, Bob was beginning to consider Sheldon's very strong opinion that we needed to "arrange" the questions. But they agreed to give me one shot at picking questioners who didn't look reasonable. Who might give me a hard time. Which might be entertaining. That was the week I did A Sicilian Wedding Feast.

I'd decided it was prudent to keep in touch with Angelo, in spite of my vow.

"I tell you, Cara mia," he'd said recently, when I told him I was cooking on television, "I didn't appreciate you enough. How I long for your *farsumagru!*"

"Poor Angelo," I'd replied. "I hope you get to eat out sometimes. I can't bear to think of you sitting in front of a bowl of rice every night."

He hadn't liked the note of pity in my voice.

"Well, you know, Cara, when I go out, there are more important things on my mind."

I'd been vaguely relieved to learn that the trait that had made it impossible for me to stay married hadn't vanished with the advent of a new and better wife.

"I hope," I'd lied, "you are not making Annunciata suffer too much."

"No, no, Cara," Angelo had said. "She does not suffer at all. She takes no notice of ... She is beyond all this. She is a saint."

Finally, a definition of sainthood for the twentieth century.

"Mmm," I'd said. *"Farsumagru."* It had a certain appeal, if only because it was one of the five or ten unhealthiest dishes in the world and I was already sick of the health questions. Nobody ever put food in her mouth anymore without estimating the number of years it would take from her life. "I'll tell you what, Angelo. If I do it, I'll send you a tape."

Sheldon's response to *farsumagru* was, "Oi vei, Cholesterol City," but Bob thought controversy about cholesterol was better than no controversy at all.

"Unless Sicilians are horrendously poor, their wedding feasts are extraordinary in both the quantity and variety of food. The dish of dishes at many such feasts, which I'll do with you today, is *farsumagru*, a rolled steak stuffed with ground pork, spicy sausage, eggs, prosciutto, and a couple of kinds of cheese. *Farsumagru* is intended to reinforce the laws against divorce. If everyone in the family gets married once, you'll only eat it ten or twenty times, which will be enough cholesterol for a lifetime." I displayed the meat, pounded it to the proper thickness and into something resembling a rectangle, sliced the hard-boiled eggs, and prepared the stuffing.

I'd stored up a couple of jokes about forbidden foods. If worst came to worst, I'd be serious: "Well, you know, the trick is to balance your diet and save dishes like this for special occasions." But the question, when it came, wasn't a question and had nothing to do with diets or cholesterol. It was screeched at me by a tiny woman with pitch-black hair, tiny black eyes, and a chin so pointy it could have been a finger. As I began to spread the first layer of stuffing on the meat, she waved her hand frantically in the air. I signaled the cameraman to focus on her. An assistant hastened over with the microphone. When he reached her, she leaped to her feet and hoisted up a black-bordered poster that'd been rolled up in her bag. On it was a blown-up photo of a cow with its new-born calf, the calf pleading: MOMMY, SAVE ME FROM THE MURDERERS!

"You're a murderer!" she screeched at me. "Killing babies! Telling the others to do it!"

"Oh, well," I said after a long moment, my voice, I am told, smacking of resignation, "Hitler was a vegetarian, you know."

Because it caused such hilarity, because someone did a piece about the show for the *Times*, because of the letters and phone calls we received (I was recognized on the street for the first time since we'd begun), because it was the beginning of our real success, I've been asked hundreds of times when I'd actually learned that Hitler was a vegetarian, whether the question had been planted, and so on. But I'd learned it years earlier from my father. In high school I'd asked a history teacher if I could fulfill an essay requirement by writing on the mass murderer as vegetarian. He'd assumed I was being a wiseass, but I wasn't. (I ran into that teacher at some point after the Hitler program. He claimed always to have regretted not encouraging me to write that paper. Whether you believe him is related to how much you know about the way some people behave before and after you're a little famous.)

As the audience laughed and the man with the mike moved away from her, the little, screechy lady stalked off the stage and out of the auditorium. When the laughter had subsided, someone else, without waiting for the microphone, called out, "How about Mussolini?" Before answering, I held up my spatula, demonstrated how I was spreading the stuffing mixture on the flattened-out steak, leaving some room around the edges.

"My memory is that Mussolini had tendencies in that direction," I finally said, tasting the prosciutto I was about to layer on the stuffing, rolling my eyes in pleasure. "But he was a pol, you know. The opposite of a real fanatic. They hardly believe anything, it's not that they get some fixed idea and can't shake it. I don't think he ever went all the way. He was from a little town in the Romagna, the family wasn't rich, and they must've eaten more fish than meat. On the other hand, they used a lot of lard ... and some sausage. ... Anyway, the man changed his mind radically about Jews and birth control, or at least changed what he said about them, so we can't assume he felt the same way about meat all his life."

I'd added the slices of hard-boiled egg and Provolone. Now I held up my basting needle, showed the camera and studio audience how I threaded it, rolled the filled steak and sewed it up. But not everyone was ready to let fascist-vegetarians go, and, as I worked, I nodded at someone who asked if I was saying that all vegetarians were nuts.

I cut up the onions to sauté in the pot where I would brown the meat, explaining what I was doing and how, then repeated, "Nuts? Gee, I don't think so, but there's something ... I mean, some of my best friends are meat eaters. Come to think of it, *all* of my best friends are meat eaters." I poured some oil into the pot, threw in the onions, explained that they shouldn't get brown or they'd burn when I put in the meat. "Even the phrase 'meat eater' is peculiar, because it makes it sound as though you don't eat anything else. Like lions and tigers. And the fact is, most meat eaters who're people eat mostly other things. I don't eat meat a lot of the time, sometimes a week or two'll go by and I don't have any, but I know how I'd react if someone told me I could never again have *osso buco*. Or a BLT Down. Does that make me a Meat Eater, capital *M*, capital *E*? If it does . . . well, *ad aspira cum carne*, as they say in . . . They must say it someplace."

We were overwhelmed by (mostly) admiring calls and letters from viewers, requests for interviews by various newspaper and magazine people who'd been uninterested in my existence, piles of unsolicited cookbooks from publishers who hadn't previously noted or cared that I referred to books on the show, calls from people I hadn't heard from in months or years, and, most important, by potential sponsors and a couple of networks that had been certain there was no interest in one more cooking show, surely not one without a celebrity chef. There was a change, sometimes subtle, sometimes obvious, in the way everyone connected to the show treated me, from technicians who'd been pleasant but became friendly, to executives for whom I'd become a valuable commodity to be taken to fancy lunches, instead of just another trick they might be able to turn. There was a change, I should say, in everyone except Sheldon.

I'd assumed he would relax a little, be happy with what he had wrought. But he became more rather than less anxious about the show's future, harassed me more than ever about the specifics. Now he had a level, the level of "the Hitler show," that we had to maintain if we were going to "get a network." The viewers we'd hooked onto our line with such difficulty would run away if they were bored in the first two seconds of my next show. Suddenly the qualities Sheldon had perceived in me from the first were qualities he had to make sure I retained. The next show, I quote him precisely, should be "the same, only different." He'd love it if I could find a way to bring up Hitler. I reminded him that surprise spun my wheels and many other people's. He said I should "break it down" and repeat only some of the elements. (He needn't have worried; for weeks someone always found a way to bring up Hitler.) He was concerned that I might say something to drive away new viewers. He was terrified that I would refer to network conversations in front of Bob. He insisted I put off a discussion of the differences in men's and women's food tastes because "We have to be careful about getting the lunatics mad while they're hooking into you."

I laughed. "That's pretty funny, considering I needed to get mad at a piece of bread to—"

"This is different." He waved it away, spilling his coffee in the process.

"So who's going to get mad at the men-women stuff? Feminists?"

He nodded. "They go crazy if you tell 'em you have a dick."

(This was before the Bobbitt case had made it clear that there were a large number of women with reasonable I.Q.s who actually thought it was all right to cut off an abusive husband's penis. I treated it as I treated most of Sheldon's inanities.)

"I promise not to," I said. "On the other hand, I could have some fun with tails. I have a wonderful Chinese recipe for ox-tail from Craig Claiborne. Kangaroo tail's supposed to be good. Can't say I've ever eaten it. And I read someplace, there's this deer, I think it's called black deer, the Chinese cook something with its tail that's supposed to cure impotence."

He was not amused, although Bob Kupferman was. He and I had liked each other even before Hitler—B.H., as I had begun to call it. A little, skinny guy who'd once looked into the distance when Sheldon got too ridiculous to be answered, Bob now met my eyes at such times instead.

"We could call it Tails," I said, "that's T-A-I-L-S, from the Kitchen."

"What else you got? Anything from history?"

I stared at him.

"History?"

He nodded. "History. No current events. If you date the show, we won't be able to sell it for reruns."

I asked my father if there were any more good food-history stories.

"Hmm," he said. "The only thing that comes to mind is Harding's daughter. He was quite a philanderer, you know, and his daughter said it was good he hadn't been born a woman because he'd have been pregnant all the time. Come to think of it, that's not about food, is it."

Of course, they weren't so easy to separate in the brain, a fact I might be able to have fun with sometime.

"It would require some research," my father said, "but George Washington refused a salary as President. He just wanted his expenses covered. They say it came to much more than a salary would've. A lot of that has to have been about food and wine."

Nobody sympathized with my Sheldon difficulties. Leon said Sheldon was right, I was being too Jewish, turning triumph into tragedy. A couple of nurses at the hospital had been talking about the show and he'd been proud to claim me as his girlfriend. He said he knew I was too busy to ask about the progress of his divorce, but, whether I cared or not, it was final. I said that I cared about everything connected to him. But my brain wasn't ready to absorb the fact that the divorce had anything to do with me. It was about him and his children.

Ovvy, at eight, couldn't stand to be kissed, but he was delighted that I no longer had afternoon classes and he could drop by any day with a friend to have milk and cookies before they went upstairs to Nintendo. He was less aware than the girls of my new fame; none of his friends knew about "Pot Luck." When we watched it together on TV, it was like seeing a home movie. Someone in Annie's social-studies class mentioned the show when they were talking about the Second World War and Hitler. Annie volunteered a tape, explaining that I was a family friend. The class viewed the tape the next day and talked at length about Hitler. Annie said the teacher had told them that while my joke had seemed funny to a lot of people, there was nothing funny about Hitler. Annie wanted to know what I thought about this.

I nodded, glanced at Leon, who was looking at the ceiling. "I think she's absolutely right," I assured Annie.

She had remained pleasant since the summer, and Leon repeatedly assured me our problems were a thing of the past. But it was clear to me that if her behavior was almost as friendly as it had once been, I'd forfeited real affection. Leon was convinced that she'd just come out of herself, was making friends at school, needed me less, but Ovvy needed me less, too, and loved me no less. The difference was clear to me, if not to Leon.

Rennie was almost fourteen and trying to become a more typical teenager than she'd ever be. Her standard response to almost any question was either "Fine. Really fine. Awesome" or, alternatively, "He [or She or It] sucks," an expression that irritated her father, puzzled her brother until he heard the kids in school using it, and made Annie smile because she knew how Leon felt about it. Rennie sort of imitated Annie's attitude toward me; I couldn't tell what was really there, but suspected that her sister's coolness made her less hostile to me than she'd once been.

And then there was Olivia. My daughter had never confessed to seeing the show, but civility had become her baseline with me, and once in a while she relayed a question from Pablo's mother. Mrs. Cruz worked from seven A.M. until three o'clock as a cashier in a neighborhood luncheonette and apparently rushed through any shopping she had to do in order to be home for "Pot Luck." Olivia was thoroughly absorbed in her own life, which was fine, except that the two parts of her life in which she was absorbed were Pablo and Harvard. Harvard and Pablo. The intensity about Harvard had increased since her weekend up there, when she'd come home talking about how wonderful it was, how the students looked great, how much nicer than New York Boston was. She had phoned Sally, the girl she'd met in Rome but hadn't, to the best of my knowledge, spoken to since. I couldn't tell if she was remaining in contact, but she spoke of Sally as though the girl were a close friend, Harvard as though she were expecting a call from the admissions office that week.

"When you think about Harvard," I said one evening, "I mean, maybe it's too far away to worry about, but do you figure you won't be seeing Pablo anymore?"

"Why would I figure that?" she asked, more puzzled than hostile.

"Well, because it's hard to imagine, I mean, I know it's a long time away, but ... Aside from your age, you have very different interests. You're talking about maybe going on to law school. You really love school. Pablo may be very intelligent, but he's not an academic." I'd never heard the two of them talk about anything but which movie they wanted to see, music they wanted to hear, restaurant they wanted to try. "I don't think the two of you're going to have many interests in common, once the first, you know ... as you grow older."

She looked up. "You don't know anything about Pablo's interests. Or mine."

I was going to have to be even more careful. No use trying to tell my daughter that her father and I had probably had more in common than she and Pablo did, and it still wasn't enough to carry us through a real life. From what I'd seen, Livvy was not only an academic of sorts, but a much bigger snob than I'd ever been. As a matter of fact, once or twice when she'd complained about some course and Pablo had asked what the problem was, she'd just said, "Ohhhh, you wouldn't understand," and gone to phone a friend about it.

"All I know is that whatever your interests are now, you need to have a chance to develop them. Or let them change. You're a bright, young girl, and maybe you should be seeing some boys, not a man, however lovely he is, certainly not a man who's a lineman for the phone company."

"He's not a lineman," she said with a superior little smile. "He works with the Secret Service. They check out hacker fraud."

"Hacker fraud?"

I was mortified that I'd never asked Pablo about his work, had to remind myself of how seldom we'd sat around and talked. The reminder didn't quite pull me through.

"Computer nuts." She stood, yawned. "You might want to ask him sometime. Meanwhile, I really have to do my homework."

I talked to Leon, who was convinced that it was my old Anything-But-Relax syndrome. Here my daughter was, finally growing up, acting human, making responsible choices, and I was, what? Worried! But it was, of course, her refusing to acknowledge that choice would be involved that worried me. I talked to my sister, who responded with a nasty comment about Livvy's delusions of grandeur. I told her it wasn't a delusion for a young girl with a ninety-five average to think she might get into Harvard, but it was clear that I couldn't talk to her about Livvy. Actually, the number of subjects we could discuss had diminished radically, since the success of "Pot Luck." My brother, Gus, was bringing his family in for Thanksgiving, as he hadn't in years, and my father said that on the phone Gus had talked about little but how they all loved the show. Beatrice's reaction to Gus's call was a snotty line about how it was good someone in the family had gotten on 'television or we'd never have seen Gus again. Apparently a couple of her friends who'd not seen the Hitler show had asked if she had a tape, and this had aroused her sibling bitchery. (The first time someone asked my mother for a tape, she'd asked what was broken.)

"Hello, everybody. The Italians have the phrase *cucina casalinga. Casalinga* homemade, and *cucina*, of course, means cuisine. For a long time the phrase simply meant mother-daughter cuisine. More recently it has come to mean peasant cooking. Maybe there's a natural association—peasants are less likely than others to leave their hometown, more likely to pass on ways of doing things, including cooking. But passing on methods and recipes can also be a way of allowing the past to contribute to the future, so that if you move from one province of Italy, say, to another, or even from Italy to a new country, you don't lose your old life but incorporate it into your new one."

On the blackboard I'd listed some recipes that changed from province to province, beginning with a soup (minestrone, made with pumpkin in Naples, etc.), going on to lasagna (which Neapolitans made with tiny fried loin of pork patties), and ending with a chocolate-truffle recipe that had nothing to do with Italy, but would allow me to do a chocolate riff when my imaginary peasant daughter moved to France. Everyone loved a chocolate riff.

"Why only mother-daughter?" a woman asked. "My son loves to cook."

I nodded. "Good point. Actually, in my experience, young boys and girls are equally interested in cooking. But their interest is not in learning how much water to boil green vegetables in. What they want is to cook something they like to *eat*. Most often this means baking. As they grow up, if they retain any interest in the preparation, as opposed to just the eating, they branch out some. Not that they beg to make vegetables. But the ones who stay are the ones who're interested in the process."

Someone asked why I thought it was that so many males lost interest in cooking. I said I gathered little boys didn't like sleepovers, either, and I didn't know the reason but could probably get into trouble speculating. In fact, the only thing I couldn't get into trouble with today was chocolate, which, as far as I could tell, was beloved by male and female alike.

"Did Hitler like chocolate?" someone called out.

I shrugged. "Who knows? He had to fill up on something. Vegetarians are always hungry. Before anyone asks, Mussolini was probably never offered any, except maybe when he went to Vienna. The Italians aren't that big on chocolate; it's used more as a flavoring than a major ingredient, although there're a couple of good desserts that use chocolate bits. And there's a rabbit dish they make in Milan that has grated chocolate in the sauce. Closer to home, many of us have heard of the Mexican turkey *molé*."

There were loud groans from the audience.

I smiled. "It's largely a question of what you're accustomed to. I once cooked for a Sicilian who'd have had me arrested if I made a turkey, never mind with chocolate sauce. He'd grown up in Sicily, never seeing a turkey. He thought of them as chickens gone haywire. Unfit for human consumption."

Someone called out, "No! It couldn't be true!"

"But, you see, years later, I was reading something about wild turkey in the *Audubon Field Guide*, and here's what I read: 'Although well known to the American Indians and widely used by them as food, certain tribes considered these birds stupid and cowardly and did not eat them for fear of acquiring these characteristics.' "

"Boo!" a couple of people called out. "Turkey is wonderful!"

I nodded.

"It also says that turkeys are polygamous, and the male gobbles and struts with fanned tail to attract and hold his harem." I grinned, put away the book. "Oh, well, maybe this guy identified with turkeys too closely to want to eat them." I waited for the laughter to die down, wondered uneasily how a program that had begun with my wanting to reach out, as they say, to my daughter had turned into something I'd be afraid for her to hear.

"Anyway, I have to believe that this last recipe on the board, for Michael Batterberry's Chocolate Truffles, would, if I'd known it then, have converted my Sicilian, uh, friend and anyone else I wanted to convert. As far as I'm concerned, it makes all other chocolate recipes unessential if not obsolete."

I began creaming the butter and sugar, set up the saucepan with the chocolate and other ingredients to melt.

Someone asked if it was true that chocolate had a chemical in it that made you happy.

I laughed. "I remember reading that one of those chemical-psychology guys had found such a chemical. He claimed that was why everyone loved it. There're people who can find a chemical to explain anything and everything about human nature. I'm just as happy to stick with the simple idea that people feel good when they eat something delicious.

"Chocolate isn't a universal food, actually. I don't know how many things are, aside from salt. I read that in the thirties, the Chinese Communists were occupying some area near the Yangtze River, and they had to get out because there was a blockade by the government and they couldn't get salt. I don't think there's anything else like that. Incidentally, the way the word *salary* got its name is that Roman soldiers were given an allowance to buy salt. The s-a-l in *salary* is from salt."

"Do you think there's a difference between men and women, in how they feel about chocolate?"

"Oh, dear. I'm not sure about chocolate, but I'm extremely interested in the differences in food tastes between men and women. I'd love to hear from any of you who have something to say on the subject."

"Are you going to do a program on it?"

I hesitated, finally said, "If they let me." I winked conspiratorially. "I mean, if . . . uh . . . Seymour lets me." Since the first show I'd not referred to my producer, but now it came naturally, though it also came naturally to give him a pseudonym. "That's pronounced See-more, always in a sort of singsong. Seymour's in charge of differences. I mean, he's in charge of me. Making sure I don't offend more than a couple of people per show. Any time I get into the matter of differences, I have to check with See-more."

My mythical character Seymour infuriated the unbelievable real person Sheldon, but drew more mail than Hitler had, so that he was permitted to take on a life of his own, and got me through shows that would have been slow without him. Within days he began to receive fan mail, including proposals of marriage from women who said that it was clear he was not appreciated at "home." When Sheldon grumbled, Bob Kupferman always pointed out that See-more had become one of our best hooks on the viewer line. It probably would have been no use, anyway, trying to get rid of the Seymour fantasy; my mail, often containing favorite recipes, sometimes with one "Seymour might like," others asking about his favorites, still others having nothing to do with food, had convinced me that when you adapted a public persona, a number of faithful viewers would grab hold of it and run where they'd wanted to go anyway, usually on some field that failed to resemble, except coincidentally, the one where your real life was played.

For a while, it seemed that the field had become level. I was working very hard on the show, which seemed to be maintaining its level of success, if not raising it. Sheldon continued to shop for a network as Bob Kupferman and I developed better and better rapport. Bob had taken to winking when Sheldon made suggestions that clearly had to do with his desire to interest a network rather than with improving the show.

I made Thanksgiving dinner at my apartment for Leon and my family, who'd never met. Livvy and Pablo went to his family's; Leon's kids went to their grandparents. Gus and his wife and his wife's children came in for the first time in years. His wife had always been pleasant, but it was wild to have Gus, usually a caricature of the disengaged scientist, asking me detailed questions about TV procedure, commenting in an intense manner on one or another show.

I had been given to understand that on top of the other problems she was enduring with a kid sister having her five minutes of fame, Beatrice was hurt that I never called her anymore. I'd done thumbnail sketches of family members for Leon, who proceeded to convince my sister that almost everyone in the world was mad at me because I never called anyone anymore. He charmed her out of her pique so that her comment, delivered as they all left in a fashion that would allow her to claim it was Just a Joke, was that I'd finally found a guy and he was too good for me. I'd barely mentioned Leon to my parents, though I'd talked about the kids a great deal, and my father and mother were astonished and pleased to find me tied in to an Unmarried Professional Jewish Male with a Pleasing Personality.

"Can I make love to you?" he asked, coming up behind me when they'd left and I was loading the dishwasher for the second time. "To the only Jewish girl in New York who doesn't tell her parents when she's got a doctor in hand?"

"In hand?" I repeated. I think I was suspicious. They'd all been almost too crazy about one another. "What does 'in hand' mean? That we're screwing? I don't think every girl in the world tells her parents when she's screwing a doctor." I was determined to get the dishes out of the way before I went to bed.

"They do when he gets a divorce."

"Your divorce was about feeling free to have your kids know you're screwing someone."

"Oh," he said. "So that's what it was about."

I didn't know what it was about. I was thinking of Gus's children. They'd had such a good time, been fascinated by everything I did in the kitchen. But I didn't feel it was the same as it had been with Annie and Ovvy. It was more that they'd seen me as their own private celebrity chef, doing for them a special demonstration of the sort of thing I did on television. Whatever the reason, I probably wouldn't see them again for a long time, and I was sorry. My relations with Leon's kids were, as they say on the news, normalized. No highs, no lows. Steady affection varying in degree from child to child. I was still in love with their father, but I wasn't *insanely* in love anymore. I could tell that I was sane because I wasn't happy all the time. When I was worried about something, I could *feel* the worry, not just know it was there. I was worried now, though I didn't know why. Maybe it was about Leon. This was about as long as he'd been with Christina; who was to say he wasn't going to find someone better for him than I was? Maybe he'd meet a woman doctor, an anesthesiologist with regular hours whom his kids liked! Maybe I'd end up in a soup kitchen, cooking Thanksgiving dinner for people who had no place else to go. Not because I was a good person, but because I had no place to go either.

I eased away from Leon's embrace.

"I just want to get the dishes into the dishwasher."

"What's going on?" Leon asked. "Wasn't I supposed to get along with your parents?"

"Don't be ridiculous."

But I was upset. Apparently the question wasn't as preposterous as it sounded.

"I'll help you with the dishes later, Cara. Just come with me for a while. Here, let's take the rest of the wine."

The eight adults had polished off nine bottles of wine—six good Chiantis, and three, my entire stock, of the lovely Vernaccia di San Gimignano that was one of my favorite whites in the world.

"Hmm, there's hardly any in here. We'll share it."

"I think what I really need is some aspirin."

He brought me aspirin and a glass of water, suggested we lie down for a while.

I shook my head vehemently. "Then we'll be making love, and then Pablo and Livvy'll come home, and we'll have to be quiet, and the dishes'll still be here."

He took a deep breath. "Then let's go upstairs. My kids won't be there till tomorrow afternoon."

I resisted but he urged me, teased me, got me excited so that I followed him upstairs.

"Maybe I am jealous," I said as we undressed and lay down on his bed. "I just remembered the first time a boy really was crazy about me. It was only after he came to the apartment. He was a real academic type, and he was entranced by everything in the apartment, my parents' apartment, all the books, you know, the . . . I decided not to see him anymore, that it wasn't me he liked. Only my parents and the books."

"Mmm," Leon said, "I rest my case." He turned me over so that I was on my side, facing away from him. "You know, it's really your mother's neck I want to kiss. But since she's not here . . ." He nuzzled the back of my neck, began to play with my breasts.

I was excited but not ready to throw it all away yet.

"I'm always self-conscious downstairs," I said. "It's just too close. Whether they can hear us or not."

"Maybe," Leon said, "you can get the landlord to let you make real walls. Or maybe you should just move up to my apartment."

"No good," I said. "You're forgetting about Livvy. Not to speak of your kids."

But I was pleased that he'd said it, and we made love, and it was spectacular, and I fell into a deep and lovely sleep. As we half-awakened in the early morning, we made love again. Then we slept until after eleven, when Annie phoned, lest our idyll be uninterrupted. When we finally got out of bed, we showered together in the nice big stall (my bathroom just had a tub with a showerhead), pushing each other in and out of the spray, scrubbing each other's backs, singing songs that were comical mostly because we were singing them right then. It was as Leon sang, "I am the captain of the *Pinafore*," sponging my buttocks and delivering the line about never being sick at sea, that he bent down to take a mock bite out of one of them and it hit me: I had never put in my diaphragm.

I sat down on the shower floor.

Leon laughed. "Did I take your breath away?"

"My diaphragm."

"I took away your diaphragm?"

"I didn't put it in last night."

"Aha!" He sat down, squinting at me as the hot water bombarded us from above. "So that's why you were so sexy!"

"That isn't funny," I said. "Or maybe you didn't mean it to be."

He shrugged. "You're always sexy. But last night . . . I guess we were both on." He took my hands. "When was your last period?"

I thought about it. "Two weeks ago."

He whistled. "Well, if you're pregnant—I mean, we have no reason to think you're pregnant, but if you are, we can take care of it." Under the spray, he kissed my cheek. "I mean, you came to the right place. Or I came in the right place."

"You're not angry with me?" I asked, but in fact, I was a little angry with *him*. This man who claimed to love me and then made jokes about how easy it would be to abort my baby!

"If I'm going to be angry with anyone, it should be myself," Leon said. "I'm the one who practically dragged you upstairs. And if I think about it, I can tell whether it's in. I wasn't thinking about it any more than you were."

My anger disappeared, then, in another rush of love. I got on my knees to embrace him and we fooled around, hugging, kissing, soaping each other, and giggling, until finally he turned off the water and we got out of the stall and dried each other off.

He asked me once when my period was due, and I told him, but as the day neared, I thought a great deal about how lovely it would be to have another baby. Leon's baby. A tiny, cuddly baby who loved me. Who'd know from the beginning that I slept with her father. And with whom, needless to say, I'd never make the mistakes I'd made with Olivia. Certainly I'd never scream at this baby in the kitchen. I wouldn't need to. I'd just be cooking for the family, not for forty or fifty hungry strangers. I hadn't forgotten what he'd said to me about not wanting more children, but he hadn't been in love with me when he said that. I smiled to myself: If he complained about my being pregnant, I could promise that the baby would be blonde.

Then, on Sunday night of the day before my period was due, we were sitting around the coffee table in his living room, playing Scrabble with the kids, and when it was his turn, he put down the word *ABORT*.

I stared at him, stunned, remembering the moment years ago when I'd heard Jim Whatney use it in connection with the computer.

Leon laughed, falsely hearty. "Computer language. You know, Abort, Retry."

Rennie giggled. "She looks as though she thinks you mean the other kind, Dad."

"Now, we'll have none of that stuff," he said.

"It'd be fun," Rennie said, "to play a whole game with just words that have two meanings."

Ovvy stared at her uncomprehendingly and then blushed; he'd heard of abortions—because of TV they all had—but until that moment, only the computer meaning had occurred to him.

Suddenly Leon was as uneasy with his little joke as he should have been all along.

"All right. Whose turn is it?"

The kids said it was mine, but the only word I could see was *IT*, using my letter *I* and the *T* from *ABORT*. Then I heard the two words together, *ABORT IT*, and I couldn't make myself set it down.

"I don't seem to see anything."

Rennie asked if she could help me. Nobody minded.

"You've got *loads* of stuff," she announced, leaning over. "You must not be concentrating. Here . . ." Happily she used the *A* from *ABORT* to make *AGAIN* and pointed out three or four other possibilities.

"I think I'm just not in a Scrabble mood," I said. "Maybe you can take over for me."

"Oh, c'mon," Leon said. "What's the big deal? We don't have that far to go."

We don't have that far to go.

Suddenly everything had two meanings.

"I'm sorry. I don't feel good." I stood up.

"She's upset about something," Rennie said as I walked toward the front door.

"Don't worry about it," her father said heartily. "She'll be fine."

"This is crazy," he said to me when he came downstairs.

I was lying on the bed, still dressed, not reading or doing anything else. "We don't even know if you're pregnant and you're mad at me over ... When I thought of the word, I wasn't even thinking about—I just saw the computer screen with Abort and Retry on it. It only occurred to me after."

"I hope you're lying," I said, "because if you believe yourself, we're in real trouble."

"Oh, shit," he began angrily, but then, abruptly, he stopped. "All right. I'm sorry."

"Okay."

"Do you mean it?" he asked.

"I accept your apology," I said, and began to cry.

He closed the door and lay down beside me on the bed, holding me, kissing me, fondling me while I cried. A while later we got washed and undressed and returned to bed. But he couldn't make love. It was the first time he'd wanted to and couldn't get an erection.

He laughed ruefully. "I'm finally running scared."

I didn't reply. A short time later he was asleep and snoring. I don't think I'd ever heard him snore until that night. Maybe I just hadn't noticed. Maybe it was a warning. Like the nasty Scrabble word. Maybe he was telling me that life was going to be somewhat more difficult than it had seemed. Whether or not I was pregnant. Whether or not we married. Whether or not I got to keep my baby.

On Monday Leon called from the hospital to ask how I was.

"I'm going crazy," I said, knowing perfectly well why he was calling. I was normally regular, and I hadn't gotten my period. "This business of providing visual action for things I just want to talk about. Did you know Uncle Sam was a Hudson

Valley meatpacker? The original Uncle Sam, I mean. Sam Wilson. I'd love to do something about how he got to be Uncle Sam, but what'm I supposed to cook while I'm talking? Red, white, and blue hot dogs?"

Leon asked if anything else was doing. I said no, not really, except that we hadn't been through our Christmas lists to see who was getting what for the kids.

"It's just as well," Leon said, "that you're not thinking about, you know . . . I mean, there can be psychosomatic delays in the onset of menstruation."

"That's very interesting," I replied. "Would you like to know what you can do with it?"

He whistled. "I was just trying to prepare you for a disappointment."

"You've done very well in that area," I assured him, slamming down the phone.

For a few days I didn't hear from him. I knew I'd been nasty, understood that he was mad at me, but felt he didn't understand how frustrated I was by his refusal even to *consider* letting me have this baby. Not that he could stop me if I were determined to do it, but after all, one of the lessons of life with my daughter had been that children needed both parents to be there. Nothing I'd seen of single-motherhood had convinced me otherwise.

On Wednesday morning I woke up with my period.

For a while I was too upset even to get out of bed. Let the sheets and mattress pad and the mattress itself, for all I cared, get stained. What did I care, if I wasn't going to have a baby? Finally I got up, washed, changed the linens and had some breakfast, but I remained in a state. I didn't call Leon, though I knew I should. I told myself it was more important for me to come up with a reasonable show for the next day than to let Leon know what wasn't happening. If I wasn't going to be a mother again, I'd best attend to the work I would be doing.

The problem was, I was still too mad at Leon, at the entire male race, to settle into some reasonable program that Sheldon, noticeably a man, would like. I flipped through my notes, looking for something he'd hate that would bring in hundreds of phone calls so he'd have to live with it. I wanted to do a piece on winemaking in California, where women had made important and interesting contributions, but I'd barely begun research on it. The director of the Wine Society Service had observed, in my one conversation with her, that when you dealt with wine people, you got good food, but when you dealt with food people, you often got bad wine. Something interesting was there, but my brain was still too bound up with Leon and babies to wander along the path where it might be found.

"Seymour has a weight problem and he's been bugging me to do a show about diets. Since a lot of people still have left-over turkey in the refrigerator, today we're going to do Nancy Pike's world-famous turkey potpie. She says her secret is a bit of thyme, T-H-Y-M-E, in the filling, but I think there's more to it than that. While I'm preparing the pie, I'm going to talk a little about diets.

"In between the time I left this country and the time I moved back, a lot of people got hysterical about food. Either about eating it, or not eating it, or eating it and working it off with exercise. See-more has a weight problem, and I thought I'd found him an easier solution. He tends to go for teensy, skinny little girls who make him feel huge, not to say old. I told him he should try going out with a nice big chunk of woman so he'd feel thin, but he didn't buy it. So. Diet program. I went out and bought everything from the *Pritikin Diet* to the *McDougall Diet* to the *Scarsdale Diet*. That's the one by the doctor who fed a woman loads of amphetamines when he wanted her to be thin for his dinner parties, then, once he had another girlfriend and he didn't need her there, wouldn't give her more no matter how depressed she got, and she went off her rocker for long enough to kill him when she thought she meant to kill herself. In a lighter mode, there's *Prince Wen Hui's Cook Chinese Dietary Therapy*, which includes lovely items like Ginger Beef and Ginger Seitan Beef, which it says are, I quote, 'stomach/spleen tonics, but with the seitan the dish is also a treatment for Hyper Yang Liver,' and Apple Agar Dessert, 'specifically to cool Hot Lung Syndrome and disperse phlegm. The agar cools the lungs, the peaches tone the Qi.' And so on. Then there's *Never Satisfied, A Cultural History of Diets, Fantasies and Fat* by a guy who writes well, but every time he gets close to the food-sex connection, he arches away from it. When he talks about anorexia, one of the more obvious signposts at the food-sex crossroads, he compares a food-filled belly to a baby-filled belly without ever saying what the anorectic who gets pregnant with food and aborts it thinks she's doing. That is, he never draws the conclusion you're waiting for him to draw even if you don't exactly know what it is."

I was measuring the crust ingredients into the Cuisinart, but having to talk about diets while I was thinking about Leon and men who didn't want you to have babies left me unable to describe what I was doing to the viewers. I just babbled.

"Which brings me back to the neighborhood of my earlier observations. Everyone needs there to be something they want and can't have. For a lot of people that used to be sex. At some point sex became—I mean, it wasn't just permissible, it was mandatory. Maybe something had to replace it as, you know, the thing you longed for. And maybe food, its variations endless, its specifics often sublime, was the obvious choice. When I was young, we talked about who was doing what to whom. Now when I hear young girls on the street, they're comparing chocolates or fancy ice creams and complaining about their weight. The whole world's on a diet. Nobody's obsessed with sex, but everyone is getting weighed!"

To the accompaniment of a few titters from people who heard the pun, I took the dough from the refrigerator, rolled it out, dropped it into the pan, brushed it with a little oil, spoon-poured the filling, set it in the oven.

"Let's see. Where was I."

"You were talking about food and sex!" someone called out.

"Ah, yes. Well, what is there to say? Food is sort of sex above the neck. If only it would stay there."

I'd been preparing the turkey filling. Now I poured it into the baked shell.

"Or maybe what you're really interested in is food and gender? I once started lists of food men like—puddings and such—and women like—bones, seeds, and nuts. Crunchy things. Is that about sex or just about gender?"

"The bone's about sex," the same man called back as his wife—I'd now located the young, chubby couple in the row behind Sheldon—and everyone else giggled. "The rest is just about gender!"

I laughed. "My goodness, you're a lively one, aren't you. Maybe you'd like to write me a letter; we don't have too much time now, but I'd like to hear your opinions about who likes which kind of diet, since I promised Seymour that that's what this program would be about. Oh, yes, and I'd also like your opinions on the matter of whether biting your nails makes you a cannibal. Or biting someone else's.

"Now, here's my diet for you, Seymour." I pulled the prebaked pie out of the second oven, held it up, then sliced it into four parts, pointing out that each of them made a nice portion. "Or maybe I should address this to Lee-nora." Seymour's girlfriend, invented during a recent program. "When you cut Sheldon's—whoops, See-more's piece, just do this. . . ." I cut one of the quarters into halves. "And fill up the rest of the plate with green stuff. And there you have it, he's on a diet.

"I'm going to close with a quote from the great Brillat-Savarin: 'It is not a great disadvantage for men to be lean . . . but . . . thinness is a horrible calamity for women: beauty to them is more than life itself, and it consists above all of the roundness of their forms and the graceful curves of their outlines.' "

I winked and said good night.

Sheldon wanted to know if I was trying to make some kind of goddamned fool out of him. I thought he was upset about my slipping and using his real name, but it was my suggestion that he had a weight problem. Only someone's telling him the phones were ringing off the hook, far more calls than there'd been for Hitler (there were far more viewers now), caused him to stop haranguing me.

I didn't worry about it a great deal. I had too much else to think about. Leon and babies. Leon and no babies. I'd been pretty snotty to Leon. Maybe I'd end up without Leon *or* a baby. Maybe I'd been wrong in thinking Leon and I had reached a stage where I could say whatever I felt like saying. Maybe I would lose Leon. Maybe I'd lose everything. Sheldon and I were scheduled for a conference with Bob Kupferman. It sounded ominous, I wasn't sure why. Yes, I was. For all my battles with Sheldon and the cable people (it sounded like a science-fiction movie, actually, *Sheldon and the Cable People*), I'd been mostly in control of what I did on the program. Something he'd said made me think that wasn't going to be true much longer. Maybe they'd want something I couldn't do. Maybe they'd found someone who could do it. Maybe I'd have nothing left of my life except a couple of cooking classes. And someone had told me classes weren't doing as well as they had when the economy was better. Maybe I'd have to work in a restaurant. Maybe my TV celebrity would at least make it possible for me to get a chef's job. Oh, God! It was unimaginable that I should again work in a place where I had to take someone's orders all day. Even if he wasn't an Angelo. No. If I worked in a restaurant, it would have to be my own. If I hadn't been on TV long enough to earn the money myself, maybe I'd be able to raise it. People started restaurants all the time. A restaurant was much easier than a TV show. If you had a restaurant and you made a wonderful dish, people wanted you to make it again, not find something different but the same for next week.

I began a new file on the computer: CASACARA. Casa Cara would be a family-style place. No bar. Bars took up an enormous amount of space and were extremely expensive to install. Of course, they were also the place where Anna's, and then Angelo's trattoria had earned the most money. Well, I'd said no bar, not no drinks. I would have big round tables where people could drink together, eat together, whatever. Maybe people who'd thought they just wanted to drink would end up having a bite because they liked the way someone else's food looked. Just as they talked at bars when they'd thought they only wanted to drink. The kitchen would be open to the dining room so I wouldn't be cut off from everything. No matter how small the restaurant was, I would always have an assistant so I could get out of the kitchen and mingle with the guests as I'd need to, especially if Leon . . .

That was what I was doing with my fantasy restaurant. Creating a shelter against the loss of Leon. Anyway, I'd started with something that wasn't true; my quarrels with both Angelo and Sheldon were about serving the same fare week after week. Still, I could have fun with a restaurant. If I could stand to have fun right now. I was saved from considering the question when the phone rang. It was Ovvy. He had a cold and had stayed home from school. Mrs. Borelli no longer came every day but his father was going to check on him at lunch.

"It's so good to hear your voice, sweetheart," I said. "Even when you sound like that."

He began to cry. "Daddy said maybe you wouldn't have time for us anymore."

"WHAT?" I howled. "What on earth was he talking about? Ovvy, hang up the phone. I'm coming up."

I turned off my computer, got my keys, which now included

the ones for Leon's apartment (he hadn't felt he needed the ones to mine), and went upstairs. Ovvy had gotten back into bed. I hugged him, told him that whatever in the whole world happened, I would always have time for him. He said Daddy had told him not to get too close to anybody with that cold and I said I didn't care, if I got his cold I'd do a program about what to cook when you had a cold. He loved that. He relaxed against his pillow. I told him that I was going to go down and get some chicken soup for his cold, then I'd be right back up. I met Leon on the steps.

"Where do you get off telling your kid I don't want to see him?" I asked.

There was a long pause, then Leon said, in a voice even lower than mine, "I had the impression that you didn't want to talk to any of us."

"Neither did you want to talk to me," I said. "Not if I was pregnant, anyway."

If he'd noticed the past tense, he wasn't sure yet what to make of it.

"I told you that from the beginning," he said in a low, troubled voice. "I might get married, but I'm not having any more babies."

"Well," I said angrily, "you can talk to me. Because I'm not having a baby, either." I edged past him and down the stairs.

"Look," he said, following me down, "I want to talk to you, but I just have a few minutes and I promised Ovvy—"

"Then I think you should go talk to Ovvy. Don't worry about me. I'm just getting him some soup."

But he followed me into my apartment, where I took a container of soup from the freezer and put it in the microwave.

"How about we just sit for a minute and—"

"I don't think we should sit for a minute," I said. "We both promised Ovvy we'd be there. And Ovvy was the one who wasn't ready to wipe me off the slate altogether."

"Don't be an idiot," Leon said. "I wouldn't have gotten a divorce if I wanted to wipe you off the slate. *I'm* the one who thinks about getting married. I just don't want any more children."

"You're right, it's the opposite for me," I said. But my anger was gone. "Although I'd surely get married if I could have more kids."

"You haven't raised three of them already."

"No kidding. I barely got to raise one," I pointed out. "And she doesn't even remember that I was there."

"I understand all that," he said. "But it doesn't change the way I feel."

So. There we were. I got the chicken soup out of the microwave. He opened the door.

"Did you mean it? You're not pregnant?"

I nodded.

"And since you're not pregnant, there's no reason to get married?"

"Well, there certainly isn't the same kind of pressure," I said as the door closed behind us.

"Why do we need pressure?" he asked.

I couldn't think of an answer, so I started upstairs with the chicken soup.

"What're you afraid of?" he asked, following me. "That I'll turn into Angelo? Am I anything like Angelo? Am I going to have a brain transplant? Or is it just that all males are alike?"

He opened the door for me and we walked in.

"If you think we are," he whispered, "please don't tell Ovvy. He thinks you think he's going to be a terrific man."

I had a dream in which I'd turned gray and Leon passed me on the street without recognizing me. He was with Christina. I awakened clutching my hair, had to stop myself from running to the mirror to make sure I was still blonde.

I had a conference with Sheldon and Bob, who were pushing about the matter of arranged programs. Bob had suggested that I make notes of ideas I had for giving the show continuity beyond what it had from my "lovely personality," and I was trying to do this, although everything in me rebelled.

I had a dream about a Casa Cara with one big round table at its center, and an empty high chair. Sometimes I thought it was Livvy who was supposed to be in the empty high chair; other times I thought it was my baby with Leon. My nonbaby. I had a dream in which Livvy disappeared and I had no idea of where she was.

Livvy had taken and done beautifully on the PSAT's, the rehearsal, as it were, for the SAT's she would take in her senior year and that would be the single greatest determinant of whether she got into a good college. Her adviser thought she had a chance of getting into Harvard if her interview the following year went well.

I'd grown accustomed to the fact that Livvy's mood swings, the differences in the way she talked to me, were seldom about anything that had happened between us. Now it began to seem as though the same was true of Leon. We hadn't spoken in a couple of days because one or the other of us had always been on the phone. Now he called to ask, in a voice dripping with sarcasm, whether I could spare the time to have dinner with him that night. I said I'd love to cook something wonderful for everyone, and he told me he wanted to speak to me alone. He sounded so angry, it was as if I'd turned out to be pregnant and refused to have an abortion.

He was waiting for me at the Tiger's Eye at 7:02, looking as though I'd arrived an hour late instead of two minutes. I took off my parka, kissed the top of his head, said I felt as though I hadn't seen him in a year and a half. He didn't acknowledge my presence. I sat down facing him, said hello. He just nodded. I ordered a very dry martini.

"Maybe you should tell me what you're mad about, Leon. Instead of inviting me to dinner and acting as if you're sorry I came."

There was a long pause. He squinted at me as though he were trying to decide whether to take a chance on the vacuum cleaner I was peddling at his door. The waitress brought my martini, which was terrible. I'd forgotten that with gin you always had to specify the label. I sipped some more. We ordered cheeseburgers.

"So? What's up?"

"I practically ask you to marry me, and you've been dodging me since that day and you want to know what's up?"

I could only gape at him. Was it possible? Did love turn everyone into an asshole?

"Why are you looking at me like that?" he asked.

I smiled. "I seem to stand guilty of saying no when you haven't really asked me any questions."

"All right," he said after a long time. "So, what if I did ask?"

Love was the opposite of a card game, your advantages were irrelevant.

"I imagine I'd say yes to nearly anything you asked me."

It stopped him cold. Maybe it was the first time he'd had to think about what he actually did want, instead of worrying about what I didn't. I spoke again only when it was clear he wasn't going to.

"One thing I was thinking when you complained about the calls, not being able to find each other, if you and I were in the same apartment, you wouldn't be so upset if you couldn't get me on the phone. You'd just come home. We'd see each other in the natural course of events. Sleep in the same bed. Feel each other there. Be together for meals without arranging it. Have a hug and a kiss just in passing. This way, if we don't see each other, we really don't see each other."

Fear, temptation, and I don't know what else made tracks across his face.

The waitress delivered our cheeseburgers and asked if we wanted anything else. Leon stared at his plate in such a way that I was afraid to start eating. Suddenly he stood up, fished out his wallet, slapped a twenty-dollar bill and then, after a moment, a ten on the table, the latter, presumably, for the tip, and said, "C'mon. Get your coat."

It was clear that there was nothing to be gained by asking questions. I put on my coat and let him lead me out of the restaurant and to Sixth Avenue, where, still gripping my hand like a mother who really does, or doesn't, want her kid to get lost, he hailed a cab. A couple of minutes later we were at Beth Israel, where he showed the guard his identity card, took an elevator up to a floor I was pretty sure wasn't the one where he worked, and pulled me to a reception desk, where he appeared to be known by the nurse standing in front of the desk with some charts.

He said, grimly, "Letitia, we want blood tests."

I stared at him. She stared at him.

"Blood tests, Dr. Klein?"

He nodded. "We're getting married."

Letitia and the nurse behind the desk burst into laughter.

"Dr. Klein, you don't need blood tests no more to get married!"

Leon's grip on my hand loosened in his astonishment.

"You don't?"

She shook her head. "It's been years. You sure are giving away your age."

Now I was staring at him; he was still staring at her. "All you have to do is go home and get a good night's sleep. Or whatever you care to do. Then, in the morning, you go down to City Hall with your birth certificates and your divorce papers, and then you stand on line and get married."

"You're kidding!"

Later he would laugh. But not yet. He needed to do something before he could change his mind.

At the house, he pulled me upstairs to his apartment. It was almost ten. The kids were in their rooms. We tiptoed to his bedroom, where he found that week's unwrapped package of shirts from the laundry. He pulled off the cord, carefully undid the brown wrapping paper, smoothed it out on the dresser and wrote, in large Magic Marker letters, CARA AND I ARE GETTING MARRIED.

Then he tried to lead me outside to help him find a place to tape it.

"Leon," I said, "you're making me nervous."

"Aha!" he said. "I knew it!"

"Knew what? That you could act so crazy you'd make me nervous?"

"You're looking for an excuse to back out!" he shouted.

"Of what?" I asked as Rennie knocked at the door and asked if something was wrong. He said that nothing was wrong except we were having a fight, and she should go back to bed.

I laughed. "Well, if she wasn't scared of living with me before, she will be now."

"So," he said, sitting down at the edge of the bed, "I was right. You don't want to."

"I've been trying to figure out what I want," I said. "And I think I know. But I'll only tell you if you stop acting like a maniac."

He stood up, wrestled with himself for a moment, sat down again.

"I want to live with you and see if we can be comfortable. And then, after a while, if we are, get married. I'll move up here tomorrow, *tonight* if you want me to. At least I'll move up some of my clothes, and my best toothbrush."

After a struggle that seemed intense and lengthy for a man who claimed to be unconflicted, he said, "I want you to. But

I don't understand why you talk about moving up your clothes, as though you weren't exactly moving up with them."

"My kid's downstairs. And her boyfriend. And my kitchen. And my computer. There's no way to move everything. And it's not as though we have to do it."

"What's wrong with the kitchen up here?" he asked.

"Downstairs is roomier. Much more counter space. It's better for classes. I haven't even told you what's going on with Bob. I'm not sure I can do what they want for next year. For all I know, I'll be giving classes at home again."

"I have a perfect solution. Maybe you should marry a nice Jewish doctor and become a housewife and stay home and just cook for him. And his family."

And he should be open to the idea of more children, so that if the ones he had turned against me when they saw my toothbrush, and my own daughter kept her distance, or solidified it by moving to Boston or some other remote clime, he'd be eager to recapture with me the pleasures only children could provide.

On Saturday morning I moved my winter clothes to Leon's long bedroom closet.

Rennie whispered something to Annie and they both laughed.

"Okay, you two," Leon said. "Let's have it."

"We were just thinking," Rennie said, "that now there'll be equal toothpastes. Two different kinds in each bathroom."

After that, everyone was in a good mood, particularly me, and Leon decided we should go out for brunch to someplace special. I said I'd get my winter coat and jackets, and meanwhile I'd check with Livvy and Pablo to see if they were awake and wanted to come. Leon's surprise suggested that he thought "my" kids had no reason to be at a family celebration. Or maybe it was just that the mood would be different if they were with us. But he didn't say anything, and I went downstairs, knocked as was my custom, went in and got my coats from the living-room closet. I didn't see Livvy and Pablo, but as I was about to leave, she came out of the bedroom.

She looked startled and I suddenly realized I hadn't spoken with her, except in passing, in the three days since Leon and I had made our decision. Doubtless she would be delighted to have me out of her way.

I smiled. "I'm moving my stuff upstairs, try out, sort-of-living with Leon. I can't promise you total privacy, I'll still work down here, cook, but—"

She said, "I don't understand."

I said, "About what?"

"Why you're doing it."

I laughed. "Not just to make you happy, word of honor."

But she wasn't amused. "Have I been bugging you?"

"No, it has nothing to do with you."

She was silent, still looked puzzled.

"Leon and I were talking about maybe getting married," I explained. "And it seemed as though we ought to try living together for a while."

"What will happen to me?" she asked, so plaintive a little girl that I moved toward her to give her a hug.

She stepped back.

"Nothing, sweetheart," I said. "Absolutely nothing. I'm still going to be down here to work. Cook. If I give classes, they'll be here. My office'll be here. I'll be here whenever you want me. There's no room upstairs for everything, even if I wanted to move it there."

She nodded thoughtfully, turned away to go back to her room.

"What I really came downstairs for was to pick up a couple of coats, and tell you we're all going out to brunch, and we were hoping you guys'd come with us."

She smiled, but there was a sort of ironic twist to her smile. " 'We're all'?"

I smiled back. "The upstairs bunch."

She nodded slowly. "And 'you' guys is Pablo and me."

I shrugged. "Not if you don't like it."

"No," she said slowly. "It doesn't matter. But I think ... Pablo isn't even awake yet, or hardly, so I think we'll just ... have breakfast here."

I nodded. "Okay. See you later."

I didn't see them later. I checked in when we returned from our brunch, but they'd apparently gone out to eat.

I continued to make dinner downstairs most nights, and to prepare for the show down there, but I didn't see much of Livvy until an evening when Leon was working, I'd come back downstairs to look for some coats and books, and she was alone, reading, in the living room. She mentioned, yawning, that she was invited to a New Year's Eve party at Mayumi's. Mayumi had a brother who went to Yale and a lot of his friends would be there.

When I asked whether she'd invite Pablo, on the chance that she wanted to discuss it, I tipped the scales and she said that of course she was going with him.

On New Year's Day, when I asked how the party was, she shrugged and said, "Boring."

"Oh, dear." I smiled sympathetically. "I don't know why it's harder to have a good New Year's Eve party than any other kind."

She looked at me speculatively as she did on the rare occasion when she was considering having a conversation with me.

"Most of them were idiots. Yale, Brown-type idiots."

She waited for me to point out that there were idiots—what was it Rennie called them, dweebs?—at Harvard, too, and when I passed the test by keeping silent, she went on.

"There was one boy I liked."

"Oh?"

"Very tall, blond, handsome."

Very Not Jewish. Or Italian or Puerto Rican, for that matter.

"Let me guess. Yale."

She shook her head, smiled. "Berkeley. He's Mayumi's neighbor's nephew. His parents live in California."

I smiled. "Oh, well, there are nice boys on the East Coast, too."

She shrugged.

"Did Pablo have a good time?" I asked cautiously.

"Are you kidding?" she burst out; I'd touched a button. "With that bunch of—? They ask which school you go to, and you say you work for the phone company, and they are shocked out of their gourds! They don't want to know what you do, you're just there because you're not smart enough to sell junk bonds or something."

I nodded sympathetically. After I'd written to a couple of my friends about marrying Angelo, I'd never heard from them again.

"That's too bad," I said carefully. "I hope he wasn't upset."

She shrugged.

"He doesn't care. I'm the one who gets mad. They think they're not prejudiced, but they are. They make sure to have a black friend, a bunch of them were hanging around Shevaun as if they really wanted to be with her instead of the skinny blonde they brought, but a Nuyorican? Forget it."

I smiled. "You won't put up with any prejudice, except about the Jews."

She looked at me reflectively.

"Prejudice is what you think before you know people."

I held my smile, although it was getting more difficult.

"And you've always known one Jew, your mother, so . . . ?"

She shrugged. "So nothing. Maybe you just tried to push it on me when I was too young."

"Push what?" I asked, astounded in spite of myself. "It never came up until I was leaving Rome."

"Hah!" she said. "Never. Who do you think you're kidding, Mother?"

Her attachment to Pablo seemed to grow stronger. There was no talk of other boys. Nor did she mention Harvard; I couldn't tell if she'd simply put it away for the following year. It was remarkable how little difference my having more or less moved upstairs had made in our lives. In mine, anyway. If Livvy's reaction hadn't been what I would have expected, there didn't seem to be any continuing problems. As far as I could tell, Pablo was never sleeping anyplace else. One night in the spring Rennie, and then, some weeks later, Annie, had a pajama party. Leon and I slept downstairs to make room for their friends. Where I'd once fallen asleep faster down there, it now took me longer than usual on those nights. But aside from that, I didn't feel as though anything had changed. Leon was content with the new arrangement and never mentioned marriage.

In fact, it wasn't until another summer had passed, and we were well into the new school term, and my show had resumed, and Sheldon was making exactly the same comments as he had the previous year (Bob was friendlier than ever but less involved than he'd once been in the program's specifics) that I grew restive. Once or twice I hinted to Leon that "all the business with the locks" to the two apartments was beginning to feel like a nuisance, and when he didn't pick up on my hints, I asked whether it might be time to think about getting married. Each time he said that things were too good as they were, we shouldn't risk a change.

In December Livvy learned she'd been refused early admission to Harvard. She left the notice on the kitchen counter where I'd see it, but didn't want to discuss it with me. Her adviser said she was as keyed up as ever about Harvard but didn't appear to be working as hard in her classes, and the results of her senior-year SAT's were less sensational than the previous year's. The adviser thought I should try to talk to her about this. She understood Olivia had a part-time job; would it be possible for her to give it up for a while? It wasn't a good idea for Livvy to relax about grades this first half of her senior year. I talked to Livvy about it, anticipating at least a little argument. But before I'd even raised the job issue, she said she was going to quit, she was tired of work, anyway.

Bob invited me to a lunch that he'd "prefer you didn't mention to Sheldon." He wanted to tell me something that was a secret, though it wouldn't be for long. He was moving to ABC in January. He would be developing new shows for the network, and he hoped to take some version of "Pot Luck" with him.

I was speechless. It took me a long time even to realize it was funny, and giggle. How long had it been since Sheldon had begun talking as though Bob were the only thing between us and a network? Now Bob *was* the network. A network, anyway. My long-term contract was with Sheldon's company, not with the cable people, so he would be part of such a deal, no matter what.

"Pretty funny, huh?" Bob said. "I know he's been scrambling all over the place, trying to get something."

I nodded, but I felt obliged to say that if it weren't for Sheldon, none of this would have happened.

"It may be true in a different way than you mean it," Bob said. "The people at ABC are crazy about you, but they're even more concerned with the stuff I always talk about. A thread. A story."

"A story?" I repeated uneasily.

"They like Seymour."

I was silent.

"What would be a good idea," Bob said after a while, "with everybody watching the show for possibilities, is to be as funny as you can be in the next few weeks. Especially at the expense of See-more." He suggested I try a new version of the bread-murdering routine, with Seymour as the person I was mad at.

"I don't know how Sheldon's going to feel about that," I told him.

"Don't worry about Sheldon," Bob said. "He's going to be crazy for anything you do that gets you on network TV."

During the second week of January, he told Sheldon about going to ABC and Sheldon met me for lunch sounding for all the world as though he had engineered the switch. Just as Bob had said a couple of things to me that he wouldn't say to Sheldon, my lack of enthusiasm had caused him to walk with Sheldon along lines he'd been discouraged from treading with me. Story lines, to be precise. At least that was the phrase Sheldon kept using. Where Sheldon had once been angry about my "turning me into Seymour," now he was dying for me to move into a See-more-Cara mode.

That week I did the familiar bread routine, the bread I was mad at being a Seymour who was never content with anything I did, wanted more drama in the show, asked why I couldn't for God's sake get excited about vegetables. Bob and Seymour both loved it, but I had other things to worry about.

Livvy seemed to be sleeping more than ever, since quitting her job, and to be somewhat depressed. For a while I thought it was just the early-admissions rejection, but she sounded as though she expected to be admitted for September, so that didn't make sense. I told Leon I thought she might be realizing for the first time that going away to any of the colleges she'd applied to would mean leaving Pablo. He was around much less than he'd been. She said he was working very hard, but working hard hadn't prevented him from being there in the past. He turned up late one night when I was working downstairs, and I told him I'd like to have a talk, but he apologized, he was exhausted, and it was a while before I saw him again. Livvy was sleeping a lot but eating very little, as far as I could see. She looked thin and drawn. Once I came into the bathroom in the morning to find the seat up, and it crossed my mind that she was throwing up again, then I reminded myself that Pablo had been there and doubtless used the bathroom. I had to stop looking to old explanations for new events. My brain kept working at the matter of what else I might be picking up, but it was like an object in one of those hard plastic packages that lets you see the front clearly but doesn't let you open it to make sure the underside is all right.

Robert L. Kupferman's appointment as vice president of ABC with responsibility for developing new series was announced. Sheldon and I had lunch with him the following week. Sheldon warned me not to think we were home free just because we were being taken to the Four Seasons. On the contrary. We were being courted, but courted to do what they wanted "us" to do, not what "we'd" been doing all along. I was to be a good girl, listen carefully, be open to new ideas. "Just remember," he said in a tone suggesting I'd spent my TV time in purgatory, "if we're not flexible, we're gonna be on cable for the rest of our lives."

Bob was, or pretended to be, interested in my ideas. He ordered a bottle of fancy champagne to celebrate what he hoped would be my move with him, gently pushed me when I was more interested in reading the menu than in ordering. Once our food had been served, he got down to business. The viewers loved me and tended to be faithful once they got hooked in. The only thing they complained about over and over was that I didn't *do* enough while I was talking.

"Which viewers?" I asked.

It didn't matter. Bob's answer was always the same. The ones they polled or who wrote or called.

He shrugged. "You know, that's the only way we can judge."

If I referred to Julia Child, he'd say that she was a larger-than-life personality, while it was part of my charm that I was just like the viewer, only livelier, and she was a great chef, which I kept saying I really wasn't, nor was I the first of the species on television. Furthermore, that was PBS. If I wanted to work for minimum wages and take a chance on having a cookbook that made a fortune someday . . . He knew damned well I never wanted to do a cookbook. Almost all my ideas were other people's, and besides . . .

I reminded him of my long-ago "Cucina Casalinga" idea, described some of the dishes I might do for a mother-daughter program.

"Mmm," he said calmly. "That's interesting."

"It wouldn't even have to be just mother and child. You could do different mixes. Parents and kids. Grandparents and kids. All kinds of possibilities."

"Well," he said, "it's certainly something to think about."

I looked at Sheldon triumphantly. Sheldon was looking at his dessert. He understood what was going on better than I did.

"In the meantime," Bob said, "there's someone I want you to talk to."

"Talk to?" I was startled. My sister was always saying Livvy should talk to someone, and I thought Bob meant I should see a shrink.

"His name is Rick Landy, and he's saved more shows than you've watched." He smiled to assure me that this wasn't a criticism. "He's an idea person. You can't believe the guy until you see him in operation. When they told me about him, *I* didn't believe it. He's in California most of the time. He was just here for a couple of days, and he'll be back in a week or two. We'll have dinner, we'll talk, and we'll see what comes of it."

On a night in February I slept fitfully, awakened when it was not quite light out, couldn't fall asleep again. My meeting with Rick Landy was coming up and I hadn't had any new ideas. In fact, pressure from Sheldon on this score seemed to have caused my brain to shut as tight as a clam Landy would be able to scoop out and devour in a second. I seldom went down to my apartment in the morning these days until well after Livvy, and Pablo, if he'd slept over, were out of the house. But by seven on this morning I felt as though I'd been up for hours. I got into jeans and a sweater, put up coffee for Leon, and went downstairs, figuring I'd make a small pot for myself down there. Pablo bought his weekday coffee near work, and Livvy hadn't been drinking any lately. I opened the door as the sun was beginning to send a little light through the window over the kitchen sink, decided to settle at my desk before Livvy went to the bathroom so she could ignore me, if she chose. In the past few days she'd been moodier than ever, and morning wasn't the time to try to talk.

I washed out the remnants of last night's coffee, put up a fresh pot and went to my desk, then realized for the first time that there was a light on in the bathroom. As I moved closer, the sounds of retching became clear.

So much for old explanations and new events.

I sat at the desk, watched as Livvy opened the door, turned off the bathroom light, and went to her room without glancing at me or the coffee brewing. She didn't look like someone who'd decided to throw up. She looked miserable. Nauseated. I turned in my chair so that my eye fell on the coffee pot. Until recently, there'd never been coffee left in the morning, Livvy would always have finished it.

Since I'd had my first cup, the only time in my entire life when I hadn't wanted coffee was during the nine months of my pregnancy.

Girls who threw up to lose weight did it after they'd eaten, not after a night's sleep, when their food was digested. This hadn't even sounded like someone vomiting food; it was a convulsive, retching sound, no wetness to it.

The sky was really light now. It was morning. *Morning sickness* was the phrase that had eluded me.

I felt ill.

I told myself to stop it, but I didn't know what to stop.

Livvy left the house a few minutes later. I wanted to talk to Leon before I talked with her, but he was at the hospital already. I *needed* to talk to Leon, although I didn't know why.

Leon was the one who'd been telling me nothing was wrong. Leon was the one who found it easier to reassure me than to help me figure out what was going on in my daughter's life. I felt very angry with Leon ... or someone.

I went upstairs and lay in bed like a corpse someone hasn't fixed up yet, all stiff and cold and full of unfinished business. When I looked at the clock I was astonished to see that it was past noon. I wasn't sure what had happened in my last dream, but I knew from the way I was feeling—hostile, jealous, more worried about myself than about Livvy—that the pregnant woman in the dream had probably been me. Life was too crazy. The last thing in the world my self-absorbed adolescent daughter wanted was to care for a tiny, helpless baby, while I so longed for one that I'd been ready to risk all with Leon to have it. And she was pregnant. And I was not.

I got out of bed again, washed again, brushed my teeth again, made fresh upstairs coffee, returned some phone calls, barely aware of who was on the other end from one to the next.

It must be more than a month since she'd begun to suspect . . . Maybe she thought admission to Harvard carried an automatic abortion.

Stop it, Caroline.

I should be grateful her heart was still set on Harvard. If she hadn't been inside a church since she'd arrived in this country, she surely thought of herself as a Roman Catholic. Harvard might be the only institution with a weight great enough to off-set the Church's.

I told myself I was to stop anticipating trouble where there might not be any. She might simply close her eyes, her mind, whatever she had to close, and have the abortion. Except that if she was going to do that, why had she waited so long? I could only hope she'd be realistic enough to understand what she would be doing to her life if she didn't. I could only hope . . .

I went back downstairs, tried to work for a while, turned off the computer when, scrolling through notes for a program about favorite desserts from country to country, I read *baba au rhum* as *baby au rhum.* I was sitting at the dining table, my brain arguing with Livvy the matter of whether she should sac-rifice these crucial years of her life to a baby she didn't want and that wasn't even a baby yet, when she came into the apart-ment, dropped her backpack, and said, in the tiny, shamed, and shaky voice of a three-year-old confessing to having wet her pants, "I'm pregnant," and began to cry.

"Oh, sweetheart!" I stood, walked rapidly to her, held her in my arms, began to cry with her. "Oh, my poor baby!" All other concerns vanished. I walked her over to the sofa, sat with her, cried with her. "My poor Livvy. I didn't understand until this morning. . . ." For a long time I just held her and rocked her as she wept. Finally, I spoke to her again.

"Listen to me, Livvy." (From that day on, for a long time, she didn't object to the nickname.) "An abortion . . . in this country . . . It doesn't have to be terrible. I mean, of course you're upset, but it doesn't have to be a big deal. You go to a good clinic or hospital, and it's over in a couple of hours. I know people who've had them. . . . It just takes a few minutes. There are clinics that just do that, but also, you know, there're people in Leon's department—"

"I don't want Leon to know. Or Grandma and Grandpa."

"All right. We'll just go to my doctor. He's affiliated with a different hospital." There weren't family doctors anymore, just families of doctors. If your doctor knew the other doctor, he might treat you like an individual human with a medical problem.

She began to cry again.

"I understand that you're upset, love. And I'm not saying it's fun. It's just better than having your life ruined. Changed enormously in a way you don't want it changed. I'll go with you, do everything with you, if you want me to. I mean, you don't have to do any of it alone."

Of course, she wasn't alone.

Be careful now, Caroline. Don't ask the wrong questions.

I waited awhile. "Have you talked to Pablo?"

"He wants to get married."

Oh, Jesus. I should've known.

Pablo wanted to get married. Angelo had wanted to get married, too. Angelo had wanted a more comfortable base to screw around from. Pablo wasn't another Angelo, I was pretty sure, but he was another Catholic.

"You don't want to get married, do you?"

In my arms, she shrugged.

"It's difficult to see," I said carefully, "how you could be married to Pablo, and have a baby, and go to Harvard. To any college, but especially an out-of-town one."

She began to weep again.

"When do you think you got pregnant?"

"December."

"You haven't been to a doctor, have you? I mean, are you certain that . . . you know . . . ?"

"I do the test every couple of days," she sobbed. "It's always positive. And I didn't get my period at the end of December. Or January."

"Oh, dear."

She sat up abruptly.

"What?"

"Nothing. I mean, not nothing, we just want to do this as quickly as we can. It really doesn't have to be a big deal. I'm not saying it'll be pleasant. But the actual procedure's not a big deal. It takes a few minutes. You might feel sad. Upset. But then it'll pass. Children don't pass. Or marriages where the people got together just for the children."

Especially if the people are Catholic and they're stuck for life.

But I wasn't going to open that door if she didn't.

Silence.

"I guess the first thing we have to do is talk to a doctor, confirm that you're pregnant. The sooner we do it, the easier it'll be. You'll have to miss a day of school. Maybe two, at the most. And I think, it just occurs to me now, that when all this is over—I mean, this is why you haven't been concentrating in school. When it's over, I think you'll be able to focus on your schoolwork again. Think about college."

She'd slumped back in the sofa. Her eyes were closed. I smoothed the hair back from her forehead.

"My poor baby," I said. "I'm sorry you have to deal with this now. I'm so sorry."

She did not open her eyes or acknowledge my words in any other way, but tears began to stream down her cheeks again. I set my hand on hers. My other arm rested on the sofa back, just above her head.

"Do you know what Annunciata would say if she knew?" The words were whispered so that I barely caught them.

"The hell with Annunciata," I said. "She has nothing to do with your life."

She curled up against me, her head resting on my breast. I thought her eyes were closed. After a while, I was certain she was asleep.

I had to call my gynecologist for an appointment, verify the pregnancy, arrange for the abortion. Tomorrow, or as soon as possible. If it was going to be difficult for me not to tell Leon, I had to make every effort to slip her past Pablo. I also had to finish preparing my show for the day after tomorrow. It seemed absurd, at the moment, to think I could muster my forces to do the one I'd planned, on how to start a restaurant, beginning with the differences between cooking in quantity and cooking at home. My daydream had been that "Casa Cara" might lead into another program on "Cucina Casalinga" so wonderful that Bob would send Rick Landy back to California without even introducing us. Now I found myself leaning toward a program that might be easier to plan during a week when I was preoccupied with getting my daughter an abortion and minimizing the miseries attached to same—a show on mistakes and disasters in the kitchen. There were endless possibilities, beginning with eggs, where the potential for disaster was almost as great as for triumph. I could begin with the story of my own first major disaster, go on to anecdotes from other people. There was a book called *The Cook's Advisor* in which the author listed a wide range of problems and what could be done about them. I'd forage there, for starters.

Livvy stirred. I whispered that we should go to her room. She let me help her up, walked there with her head on my shoulder.

"Mama? Please don't tell Papa." Her voice was that of a very upset child, her language, Italian.

What a relief, not to have to deal with Angelo.

"I won't tell anyone, sweetheart," I said, also in Italian. "You tell anyone you want to know."

I helped her to her room, where she lay down on top of the covers and appeared to be asleep. I kissed her, murmured that I'd be nearby, folded the free part of the quilt over her, then returned to the living room, leaving her door ajar so I'd hear her if she called me. Then I made an appointment for ten o'clock the following morning with my gynecologist. If our luck was running, he could perform the abortion the same day. Before she saw Pablo again.

I made dinner downstairs, and afterward the kids were happy to go upstairs to their Häagen-Dazs, a new brand-name fetish. As Leon and I were drinking our espresso, Livvy's phone rang. On the fourth or fifth ring, I went to her room. She was sound asleep, scrunched up in a fetal position, a description I tried to push from my mind, particularly since what her curled-up, arms-wrapped-around-herself posture actually evoked was the sense of someone trying to protect herself from harm.

You don't even know how she usually sleeps! Maybe she's that way all the time!

I picked up the phone. "Hello?"

"Hello, Mrs. Ferrante." Pablo was uneasy. I never answered her phone. "Is Olivia there?"

I touched her very gently, whispered that Pablo was on the phone. She turned over in bed, muttering that she didn't want to talk to him. I returned to the phone, told Pablo she was sleeping. He said he would call again in an hour.

I said, "I don't think she wants to talk to you, Pablo." I paused. "She's told me."

"I make a good living," he said immediately. "I can take care of her."

"That's very nice, but . . ." I'd started to say it was nice but not enough reason to get married. "But she wants to go to college. She's not ready to be a mother. You don't seem to realize how young she is."

"*She* was the one who didn't care," he said, fiercely defensive. "*She* was the one who kept saying don't make a big deal, nothing'll happen. I was—" He cut himself off.

I closed my eyes.

"Pablo," I said after a while, "I think maybe, if we talk, it should be with Olivia."

And if we're lucky, it'll be after she has the abortion.

"Yes," he said. "All right. I'm at work, she can't get me. I'll call later."

"Maybe tomorrow," I said. "She's really out like a light." With a little luck, we'd be out of the apartment before he called.

When I returned to the living room, Leon asked what miracle had occurred that had allowed me to walk freely in and out of my daughter's room and answer her telephone.

I looked at him uneasily, started to frame a lie, realized I couldn't do it.

I said, "I'm not supposed to tell you."

He laughed. "She thinks she's pregnant? You think she's pregnant? Sooner or later someone's got to be pregnant, right?"

I stared at him. I felt my face grow hot.

"Keep your fucking voice down," I said, my own voice as low as before. "Her period is six or seven weeks late."

"Oh, Jesus," Leon said. "All right. I'm sorry."

There was a lengthy silence. Then he asked how he could be helpful. I told him I'd already gotten her an appointment with my gynecologist, whom I liked, and that she didn't want my parents to know. Or him, for that matter.

He nodded. "There's always someone they don't want to know."

Clinical-cynical. She could have been a patient seeing him for the first time.

I said, "When I'm talking about one of your kids, I don't say, 'they.' "

He said, "I don't understand."

I said, "It makes her sound like some kid who walked in off the street to the clinic. Someone you don't care about."

Maybe Livvy wouldn't have gotten pregnant if he'd been as much a father to her as I'd been a mother to his kids.

He shrugged. "She's kept a pretty good distance from me ever since . . . you know."

I knew. On the other hand, "That was a long time ago. Maybe now she's ready to . . ." To what? Have a father again?

He smiled, a little smugly, I thought. "It's hard to see how I could help her through this if I'm not even supposed to know about it."

I said, "Last year you wanted to marry me."

He laughed without amusement. "Am I supposed to understand the connection?"

I said, "That's the problem. This way nothing's connected to anything else." I thought of how he'd dragged me to the hospital for a blood test that night. Of course, there'd been an air of desperation to it, as though it was an ordeal he could only subject himself to if he didn't think about it too much. "I remember perfectly well, I was the one who suggested we try living together. But in my mind, that was what it was. A trial. And it's worked, at least as far as I'm concerned." I waited, but he didn't say anything. "We get along. As far as I know, we love each other." I waited a longer time. With something that looked like reluctance, he nodded. "At least if there's something wrong I don't know about it."

"No," he said, "there's nothing wrong. That's the reason I don't think we should make any changes."

"You mean there'd have to be something bad for us to get married?"

He smiled grimly. "I seem to be in a no-win argument."

I said, "If you think it's an argument, forget it." I stood up and began to clean up the kitchen. I thought he might just clear out, leave and go upstairs without waiting for me. The two apartments with their separate locks and keys and no inside connection seemed a perfect metaphor.

"Look," Leon said, "you're under a lot of stress." He came over to me at the sink, put his arms around me, turned me around. "I don't think we can even have a reasonable conversation until this business with Olivia's over."

When this business with Olivia's over.

I was beginning to suspect that the business with your kids was never over. That they held your life in their hands, no matter how remote from you they'd seemed to be. If it was true, Leon didn't know it yet. But he'd find out.

I said, "Let's just go up and go to bed. I'll clean up in the morning."

"It's best if you wait out here during the examination," the nurse informed me as Livvy wavered. "Later, Doctor Widner will talk with both of you."

So. No choice to be made. I smiled encouragingly, told Livvy he was nice and she shouldn't be nervous, a phrase which, when directed to me in my youth, had infuriated me. I smiled.

"Unless you feel like being nervous," I said, "in which case it's also allowed."

She smiled back, a polite, scared little smile, and went into the office. After some time had passed, Widner came to the door and invited me to join them. He was a tall, skinny, bearded, and soft-voiced man of perhaps forty. I could see as I entered the office, where Livvy sat in one of the two chairs facing his desk, that she had responded favorably to him, or at least hadn't disliked him. Her eyes never left his face as he told me his examination showed that Olivia was indeed pregnant, and that while we were still in the first trimester, the procedure should be performed as soon as possible. He wouldn't be at the hospital tomorrow, Wednesday, but would schedule her for Thursday morning. She should count on spending a few hours there, between waiting her turn and resting afterward. He rang for the nurse, who gave us each a copy of the instructions and explanations, which were clear and simple. Did either of us have any questions? I asked when Livvy would be able to return to school. He smiled, shrugged, said the next day.

We returned home, where, after a lunch during which we spoke very little and I prayed that Pablo was tied up in some monumental phone job that would prevent him from calling, Livvy went to her bedroom and, leaving the door ajar, went back to sleep. I spent the afternoon and the rest of the night working on the show.

"The year I was twelve, I decided to make my parents' anniversary dinner. I saved my baby-sitting money to buy a ceramic pot in which I'd serve a *carbonnade*, a simple, lovely beef stew made with the kind of red wine that I still had money for after buying the pot. I cooked the *carbonnade* in a cast-iron pot the day before, and on the afternoon of the dinner transferred it to the beautiful earthenware pot, then put it back in the refrigerator and prepared everything else for this dinner of dinners.

"At seven o'clock, having set the *carbonnade* in the oven, I joined my parents for drinks and stuffed mushrooms, then led them to the dining room, where I'd lighted candles and placed a menu on each plate. Both were enchanted.

" 'I can't believe this,' my father exclaimed, and coming toward me to give me a big hug, he added, 'This is the best anniversary!'

"Actually, what he said was, 'This is the best anni—' because as he began the word, there was a terrible crash, a series of crashes, in the kitchen. The ceramic casserole, which I'd taken directly from the refrigerator and set over a stove light, had exploded all over the kitchen and taken the stew with it.

"It was one of those rare crises where nothing at all can be done. There's a book called *The Cook's Advisor* in which the author, Camille Stagg, lists practically any mistake you can make along with the possibilities for undoing it. Some of the stuff I knew or could have made up, but I came across an item that was utterly startling. I want to read it to you. This is about mayonnaise that won't bind: 'Any cold ingredients should be allowed to come to room temperature before beginning the sauce. It is essential to add oil drop by drop at first,' et cetera, et cetera, I don't actually have to read all this. Here we are. 'If a thunderstorm is brewing outside, stop everything and wait until it blows over. It will prevent your mayonnaise from binding. Remarkable, but true.' Isn't that marvelous, whether you'll ever use it or not? She's also got a whole section on weather and how it affects different dishes. Including Hollandaise, for example."

"No, not Hollandaise!" someone in the audience called out. Additional mikes had been installed to help along audience participation. "I'm sick of Hollandaise. Everyone who teaches cooking tells you how to fix Hollandaise."

I laughed. "Oh, well, anything true is going to be said by more than one person."

Sheldon was signaling from the wings, closing his eyes and resting his head on his hands to indicate that he was falling asleep. I was doing the chatty, nonphysical stuff that drove him wild even when he wasn't concerned that Big Brother Network was watching, but I really didn't know what to do about it.

"Does anybody have any good mistake stories? Preferably something with a Hollywood ending? Like when Escoffier accidentally set the dessert on fire and called it *flambé*?"

A woman raised her hand and told some story about the first time she'd cooked kidneys and bought beef instead of veal, and what they smelled like when cooked. I laughed, but in a distracted way. She was pregnant, and my brain had been thrown back to Olivia. The woman sat down. I couldn't think of anything to say. I looked at the counter in front of me, where I had, among other things, some limes. I held up one.

"By the way, speaking of flexibility, I recently made a startling discovery. You'd have thought it would be obvious, but I never heard anyone ... You can freeze lemons and limes! Why not, after all? It's not the texture you're going to care about when you defrost and squeeze them."

"Hey, Teach," a man called out, "what's going on here? I came all the way from Brooklyn, got the day off when you sent me a ticket for the show, and here I am and you're not *doing* anything!"

"Oh, dear," I said. "I'm sorry. I've had a difficult week and I . . . I'll tell you what. Anyone who doesn't feel as though the show's satisfactory today can get another ticket instead of going to the end of the list."

"Maybe you should have had a couple of drinks," the same man said.

I laughed. "That's not a bad idea at all. You know, you just reminded me . . ." I took from the bookcase a lovely little book called *Whistler's Mother's Cook Book*, which my father had found while browsing in a secondhand shop. "Whistler and his mother were apparently both cooks. Whistler said—here we are—he did not expect the standard of sobriety that his mother did and would not employ a cook who claimed that she did not drink. 'All good cooks drink!'

"That's a direct quote, and of course, drinks are more interesting than leftovers. At least, people have said better things about them. In fact, I think the best way for me to conclude this show is by quoting Saint Augustine's final word on drinking, which was that total abstinence is easier than perfect moderation. Something that nobody to my knowledge has ever said about leftovers."

* * *

Sheldon was waiting for me, fuming, as I exited the stage kitchen. Did I remember that this was supposed to be a *cooking* show? Had I made it a point not to do any cooking *or* any "Seymours" in the whole lousy show because I was afraid of making it a little better? I knew They were watching.

"I'm sorry," I said, "but I can't talk now. There's something going on. I'll call you."

"I won't be home."

"Tomorrow," I said.

"Early morning," he said.

"Late afternoon," I said, "if things are okay."

He followed me as I got my coat and bag and headed for the exit, kept saying, over and over again, that he couldn't believe what I was doing, maybe it had all finally gone to my head.

After the third or tenth time I stopped, turned to him, and said, "Let me put it this way. If I have to talk now to keep doing the show, then I'll have to stop doing the show."

I left, hailed a cab, reached home, checked in downstairs. Livvy's door was closed; a note taped to it said, *Hi. The phone woke me up and I stayed up after you were gone. I watched TV and ate practically everything in the refrigerator, so you don't have to wake me up for dinner. I'm very sleepy. Love, Olivia.*

Love, Olivia.

Dare I hope that a little love for me would survive her ordeal?

I didn't feel like going upstairs. I stretched out on the sofa, felt chilly, covered myself with an afghan. Leon might take it for granted that we were doing our normal routine Thursday-night whatever-I'd-made-to-practice-and-watching-my-show routine, or maybe he was hoping I'd stay downstairs with Livvy. Well, whatever he wanted, I didn't seem to be in any hurry to go up.

When I awakened, I felt as though it were the middle of the night, but the kitchen clock said it was twenty past seven. I checked Livvy's door, which was still closed, took the kitchen phone off the hook, and went upstairs to find Leon and Annie reading in the living room. Both looked up and appeared to be mildly surprised to find me there.

Leon said he'd left the answering machine on because the phone had rung at least twenty times, most of the calls from Sheldon.

I nodded. "The show was lousy. I hope nobody saw it."

Leon shook his head, said the kids had been too hungry to wait for me and they'd gotten a pizza and he'd had a slice, so he was in no hurry for dinner. I couldn't have cared less. I was very cold. I locked myself in the bathroom and took a long, hot bath, then put on a sweater and jeans, rather than a robe, because I felt I had to be prepared to leave the apartment at any moment. When I came back out to the living room, Annie was gone. Leon was still reading. I sat down and pretended to do the same, but I was thinking about Livvy. Olivia. Once upon a time I'd thought Leon's children could make up for the virtual loss of my own daughter, and if they all went away, I'd still probably miss one or another of them more than I'd miss Livvy. In the daytime. But I'd never awakened at three in the morning thinking about Leon's children, even Annie, when she'd "left" me. No one of them had given me the intense pleasure my own daughter once had, or left me as desolate as she had more recently.

Leon looked up from his magazine.

"What's happening?"

"We're supposed to be at the hospital at ten tomorrow morning."

He nodded.

"Widner was very nice. She seemed to have a good reaction to him."

Leon shrugged, as though this might have been taken for granted. He was still unwilling to acknowledge the difficulties one might encounter in trying to lead a very young Catholic girl through the erasure of a life that fed on her own unready one. I wasn't up to convincing him that he was wrong, if he could be convinced; in fact, it was my experience that he was more rigid about matters of pregnancy and abortion than any others. Furthermore, the anxiety I felt told me that not only shouldn't we talk anymore, but that I would rest a little easier if I slept downstairs.

I said, "Maybe I should sleep downstairs."

He said, "Try not to make such a big deal out of the whole thing. You'll get her more anxious than she'd normally be."

I went back to the bedroom and got what I'd need for the morning, hoping I wouldn't let him stop me from going downstairs if he tried.

He didn't try.

* * *

My alarm was set for eight. At eight I arose from the sofa, where I'd finally fallen asleep, washed, brushed my teeth, and went to Livvy's room. I knocked lightly at the door. There was no movement under the blankets that covered even her head. I turned on the light, went over to the bed, and only as I sat down on the edge and put out a hand to find her shoulder, realized there was no person there, but only pillows arranged to give the appearance of someone under the blankets.

I pulled them back.

Pillows, towels, a few sweaters. A note on a yellow pad rested on the second pillow down: *I'm sorry. I can't do it. I'll call you. L.*

My phone was ringing. My brain was splattered in its own corners and couldn't make me get up to answer it. The ringing stopped and began again a short while later. It might be Livvy! I ran into the living room, picked up the receiver. It was Sheldon. I told him I couldn't talk but I'd call him back later. He asked what the hell was going on. I hung up. The phone rang again. I picked it up and said hello angrily, presuming it was Sheldon again.

Livvy's voice, small and frightened, said, "It's me."

"Baby!" I cried out. "Where are you?"

The voice, still so low I could barely hear it, said, "I can't do it."

"But why couldn't you talk to me?" I asked. "Why did you have to run away? Where are you?"

"We can talk now," she said.

"Is Pablo with you?" I asked.

"Yes." The voice, which had become a tiny bit more audible, receded again.

"It would be easier," I said after a while, "to talk about it sitting in the same room, all of us looking at each other."

"We're too far away."

"Where are you?"

A long pause.

"Florida."

It took me a while.

"To get married?"

"Yes."

"What about school?"

"I can finish school. There's only a little more than four months left. I can wear jeans."

"Listen to me, Livvy. You're seventeen years old. And you're a very good student. You *like* school. You should be going on with it, going to college, getting a—"

"I can still go to college. Pablo works nights sometimes. We can take turns with . . . with . . . We can take turns."

Be careful.

My brain was back where it had gone often during these days, to the beginning of my time in Italy with Angelo, the time when I'd become pregnant. The difference was . . . There were many differences, including my being older. The common denominator was in marrying the wrong man. Pablo was surely a nicer man than Angelo. And for all I knew, he'd be able to support a family while his wife went to school. But it wouldn't be easy, and I wasn't sure he could handle her, and she didn't love him, and I'd seen no sign at all that she wanted to take care of a baby.

"Even if it all works, Livvy," I said slowly, "it could be very difficult. It could be—"

"Killing a baby is difficult," she said.

"I understand that," I responded. "I couldn't kill a baby. But this isn't a baby yet. It's the seed of a baby."

"It has fingerprints."

"Does it? I don't think so, not yet, but even if it does . . . Why don't you come home, and we can look at a book. Something. Talk about it. And then you can make your decision. I'm not going to force you to have an abortion."

"I don't believe you." Her voice had grown stronger as the conversation continued.

"I don't think I could. There's no doctor who's going to give you an abortion just because I want you to have it. That's not the way it works."

"I don't believe you."

"Well," I said, "then maybe you should check out everything I'm saying before you—"

"We got married this morning."

So. It was over. But how was that possible? Maybe she was only saying it so I'd leave her alone.

"So quickly? Without anyone's consent?"

"I'm seventeen. There're plenty of places where you don't need it if you're seventeen. The judge said we were good people, accepting the responsibility for what we did. Getting married instead of having an abortion."

"The judge?"

"He was a Cuban," she said. "A good Catholic."

"But you're not."

I'd said it without thinking, an automatic response at a time when that was the last thing needed. I bit my tongue, but it was too late.

"I've been punished for that," she said. "But I will be now." And she hung up before I could say another word or ask when she was coming home. Or where home would be.

I've been punished for that.

The phone rang within seconds of my setting the receiver into the cradle. It was Sheldon.

"Don't get hysterical on me," he said immediately. "We have to talk."

"I'm not hysterical," I said.

"What's been going on?" he asked.

"Olivia got married," I said after a long pause.

"You're kidding," Sheldon exclaimed. "How old is she again?"

"Seventeen."

"Oh, Jesus," he said. "What, is she pregnant? Doesn't she know you don't have to do that anymore? Or is it the old Catholic shit?"

I took a deep breath, irritated that his normally limited understanding had come so readily.

"Let's just say she got married."

"Gotcha. Okay, sweetheart." My excuse had made it, particularly the unstated part. "Now, I want you not to worry about the kid anymore. She won't turn out to be so Catholic if she wants to get rid of the guy."

Fuck you, Sheldon.

It was the first defensive reaction to the marriage that I'd experienced.

"We both know the show was lousy, Caroline. Now I understand why. 'Nuff said. But you need to get your head together." A significant pause. "Our dinner with Landy's tomorrow night."

My brain began whirling around, as though it were a dreidel he'd just spun.

"Four Seasons. Eight o'clock."

"I can't."

"Don't be crazy. You have to."

The dreidel stopped spinning and flopped over.

"I can't. I can't leave my house. There're calls I'm waiting for." I needed to be available, though I didn't know for what.

"Do I have to tell Bob to call you?"

"If they want to come downtown, I'll make dinner here." In my own kitchen, cooking, I'd be in some sort of control.

"I don't know if I can get them to schlep all the way down there," he said, as though I were at the South Pole. But he called again a few minutes later to tell me they'd do it.

Normally I'd have started planning what I would make for this important dinner, but I couldn't think about food now. Normally I'd have called Leon to tell him that Livvy had run away and gotten married instead of having an abortion, but I was afraid to do that. If he were to pull one of his lines that suggested I could have done something to prevent her if I'd only tried harder, I didn't know what I might say to him, and I needed him too badly to risk antagonizing him right now.

If only we were married! He'd said we would talk about getting married when this business with Olivia was over, but it was when "business" with your kids or anyone was going on that you most needed to be contained in the way that the idea of marriage contained you, not to feel that you were floating loose, without custom to fall back on, a frame to hold you. Did the Torah have an index with items like Pregnancy-Daughter: Wanted; Unwanted; Married; Unmarried; Mother should do? Three candles for wanted, one candle for unwanted. Must not under any circumstances say or do the following.

I exchanged the skirt and stockings I'd put on—Could it possibly have been an hour or two ago that I'd thought I was accompanying my daughter to the hospital?—for jeans, found my parka and shoulder bag, and left the house without a destination. I would have liked to talk to my parents but I wasn't supposed to do that. I'd told Leon about her pregnancy when I wasn't supposed to, and I was sorry I'd even done that. It certainly hadn't helped anyone. Normally I had a grocery list in my head. The list wasn't there now. Not that it mattered. I'd shop after I decided what to make for the TV people. I headed south on Sixth Avenue, anyway. There was nothing to the north except the flower district, and I was in no mood for flowers.

At Waverly Place, I walked east, toward Washington Square

Park. It was a beautiful day, very warm for February. Below
Twelfth Street, the sidewalks were full of Village residents,
shopping, strolling with dogs, pushing carriages. Some people
wore sweaters instead of coats. Two fully grown males in rub-
berized tights whizzed by on roller skates. At the park I grav-
itated toward an area where mothers sat with their babies in
carriages.

My daughter was going to be a mother. With a baby in a
carriage. She was seventeen years old and wanted to go to college more than she wanted anything else I'd been able to dis-
cern.

I was going to be a grandmother. I was thirty-seven and had
recently wished to be pregnant.

The park was full of mothers with prams and strollers and
students with backpacks. Ahead of me, a tall, slender woman
with a head of long, wavy gray hair wheeled a carriage, looked
for a place to settle. She hesitated near a space at the end of
a bench occupied by two young mothers. They glanced at her
and turned back to the others as though she were of some other
species. Gray panthers were one thing, gray mothers another.
I'd had one or two gray hairs when they'd first bleached me
blonde. For all I knew . . . Maybe I'd have to keep my hair
blonde just to walk Livvy's baby.

May I join you on the bench, ladies?

Certainly. What's your baby's name?

Actually, she's not my baby, she's my daughter's.

*If that scenario felt peculiar, I might try to picture what an-
other one would have been like:*

Actually, one is mine, the other is my daughter's.

It sounded like something a Rick Landy might come up
with. Maybe Rick Landy looked like Sheldon except his hair
was bleached blond.

Wait a minute. The gray-haired woman was pausing at a
bench that was occupied by women with carriages, and a couple of the women had gray hair! In fact, none of them looked
like a child bride. I stopped short, settled in a space at the end
of one bench, listened to the conversation for a while. These
were no nannies I was hearing; these were middle-class wom-
en, academics, doubtless, some of them, and it was their own
babies they were wheeling, playing with, talking to in between
their conversations with one another.

What do you have to say to that, Leon? This is the age that

*women are having children at now. It's not like when we were
getting out of school.*

What Leon would have to say was that women could have
their children whenever they felt like it, he just wasn't becoming a father to one more. I felt a surge of anger at Leon for not
wanting to marry me, and not wanting me to have his baby,
but I quickly talked myself out of it, the second part, anyway.
Actually it was a damned good thing I wasn't pregnant. There
was no way Livvy was going to grow up so much in six or
seven months as not to need a lot of help with her baby. If I
was a little bit old, by the old standards, to be a baby's mother,
and very young, for the new-career-woman-middle-class, to be
a grandmother, I might, in a way, have the best of both worlds.
I thought of the delight my parents had taken in Livvy, the intense pleasure they found now in Rebecca and Max. What was
the old saw? Why do grandparents and grandchildren love
each other? Answer: Because you always love an enemy's enemy. Maybe Livvy and I could turn a difficult situation into
something reasonable. Pleasurable. Her grades would easily get
her into NYU or Columbia at some point. Why shouldn't I
stay with her baby when she was ready to go back? Leon
might not like my new idea of full participation in Livvy's
motherhood much more than he liked the idea of my having a
baby, but at the moment I couldn't consider Leon's feelings. In
fact, I would have to make myself financially secure so I
didn't need to rely on Leon.

I'd have to try hard to think of ideas Bob Kupferman would
like. I could easily imagine preparing a TV show once a week
as I helped in a substantial way with Livvy's baby. While
when I tried to picture baby-sitting and giving classes, it felt
too much like cooking in a restaurant and taking care of a
young child.

Whether I had a network show or a cable show or no show
at all, I wasn't going to make the mistakes with Livvy's baby
that I'd made with her. Not only would I baby-sit as much as
they needed me to, but I'd play with her (or him) as much
as they wanted me to, bake cookies as I had with Leon's kids
but not with Livvy. The upstairs-downstairs arrangement, if it
lasted, might be made in heaven, in terms of my being available when Livvy needed me to take care of my grandchild.
Granddaughter, as I kept thinking of the baby, although I told
myself I shouldn't do that.

The idea of having a tiny baby around after all, the thought that I might redeem myself with my grandchild for the sins, real and imagined, visited upon my child, cast Livvy's pregnancy in a light so different that I had to remind myself that whether or not there were pleasures attached to it for me, it wasn't good for her. Help or no, she wasn't ready to be a mother. There was still time for an easy abortion, and no matter what fantasies I might have about a marvelous little creature in the house, if there was a chance of discouraging her from carrying this baby to term, that was what I had to do.

As far as I could tell, Livvy hadn't spoken to her girlfriends in recent weeks. Shevaun seemed to have disappeared from her life some time back. When I'd asked about Shevaun, Livvy had told me, lips set, that the other girl had gotten early admission to Yale, as though early admission to anything made her ineligible for friendship. Mayumi, Livvy's closest friend, had disappeared since the New Year's party. Mrs. Sakai had pretended not to see me on Open School Night. My suspicion was that Mayumi knew or suspected that Livvy was pregnant.

At home, I listened to my machine. No message from Livvy. I had a glass of red wine with lunch, almost unheard of (for me) in New York. I went through a few cookbooks, finally selecting a Cajun Seafood Gumbo with Andouille Smoked Sausage from the unreformed Paul Prudhomme, whose ingredients usually horrified me so that I didn't even read his recipes. He never used a stick of butter when two sticks could do. You'd get to the end of some recipe with extremely rich components—cups of heavy cream were standard—and find it called for an additional sauce with another whole set of extraordinary ingredients. (When I open the book at random now, looking for an example, I find Fish with Pecan Butter Sauce *and* Meunière Sauce.) I decided to go all the way with Prudhomme: Artichokes Prudhomme, if I could find artichokes in the market, Cajun Seafood Gumbo, Chocolate Pecan Pralines.

It was just past one o'clock and I felt as though I'd been up for a day and a half. Maybe I'd do the shopping, or at least buy everything but the seafood now, and get it over with. That way I'd be prepared for . . . for what? I had no idea, I just knew that I needed to feel prepared.

Leon called to ask if "the procedure" had gone all right.

I said, "They got married."

He yelped as though he'd been cut.

I said, "In Florida."

"Oh, shit," he finally said. "I'm sorry. I never . . . You want to go out and get drunk?"

"Not really. Maybe we can have a quiet dinner and get drunk down here. The two of us."

I didn't want to tell even an apologetic Leon that I felt uncomfortable about leaving the house.

He said that'd be fine, if it was what I wanted.

"Any special requests?" I asked because I didn't want him to get off the phone and had to shop now for both nights.

"Whatever you feel like doing."

Love's first flush having passed, Leon's interest in food was once again confined to eating it.

I decided to do a simple broiled chicken with potatoes and green vegetables. I hardly ever cooked rice; Leon didn't care for it, except with Chinese food.

I mustn't let myself think about Angelo. Thank God Livvy hadn't wanted him to know. I could hear him cursing me out with a vehemence suggesting that it was I, rather than Pablo, who had gotten his daughter pregnant.

Leon arrived late and dog-tired, fell asleep on the near sofa after briefly commiserating with me. I left the food in the oven on low and tried to concentrate on notes that might be useful for the meeting with Rick. After a while, half-awake and amorous, Leon held out a hand, signaling me to come to his sofa. I sat at its edge, but I wouldn't let him pull me down.

He smiled, his eyes still closed.

"I thought you said she was in Florida."

"She was when she called," I said. "I don't know where she is now."

He was aroused, so he didn't get irritable, just said something cute about how she couldn't possibly walk that fast, but let's go into the bedroom, just in case. I let him walk me in there and pull me down to the bed, where I did an imitation of a large fish being boned as he undressed me, pulled off his own clothes, and made love to me (I could feel him checking for my diaphragm). Then we both fell asleep, I so soundly that he had difficulty rousing me when he awakened, very hungry, at ten o'clock.

We dressed. I reheated the vegetables, left the chicken just warm, brought them to the table along with some bread and red wine.

"Even if they're married," he said, "she can still have an abortion."

"It doesn't matter that she *can* have one, if she doesn't want it."

"What is it, the same shit?"

"It's not shit, Leon," I said. "I mean, it might be shit when the Church is doing it, but in her mind it's . . . It's real. Frightening. She's got a baby in there and she's afraid to kill it."

"If you talk to her that way, no wonder she's—"

"Goddamn it!" I shouted. "I don't talk to her that way, and will you please get it out of your head—"

"All right, all right," he said, "I'm sorry."

But we ate in an unfriendly silence until the phone rang. It was Livvy.

"Sweetheart! Where are you?"

There was a pause, as though she had to register that I was still affectionate. Then she said, "On Ninth Avenue. I couldn't sleep in Florida."

"Are you coming home?"

"Can we?"

"Of course you can. Have you eaten? Are you hungry?"

She said, "I don't know." And hung up.

"She sounded about three years old, and very frightened," I told Leon.

He said, "She's right to be frightened. She's taking on something she can't handle."

There it was again, the anger that came on the subject of pregnancy more readily than on any other. I should suggest that he go upstairs before they arrived. Except I wanted his help. I wanted him to play the tough guy, as I could not with my daughter. I began to clear the dishes. He asked if I wanted him to stay and I said I did. Then I remembered.

"You're not supposed to know she's pregnant."

He pointed out that the rules should have changed when she went to Florida.

The doorbell rang. I opened the door. Livvy, so exhausted that she could barely keep her eyes open, said, "I forgot my keys!" and burst into tears.

I hugged her, took her arm, led her in. Pablo hesitated. I told him to come in, too. She was shivering in a cotton dress under the jacket of his suit. He wore a white shirt, a tie, the suit pants. He carried two overnight bags, set them down just inside the door.

"It's so good to have you back," I said.

She searched my face for some expression, then held up her hand to show me her gold wedding band.

I said, "Congratulations."

Nobody knew what to do next. Pablo saw Leon at the table, said hello. Leon nodded. He wasn't going to do any of this congratulations shit. Livvy wouldn't look at him; she understood that he knew.

"Come," I said. "Sit down. There's some chicken. Other stuff. Maybe you'd like some wine. Then you can go to sleep. You must be exhausted."

They went to wash as I reset the table, sliced what was left off the chicken carcass, put back the bread, brought out some cheese, made a salad. Everyone was uneasy. I brought out another bottle of wine and opened it.

Leon said he'd only been in Miami once, for a convention, asked what it was like now.

Pablo mumbled that they hadn't really seen much of Miami.

I poured four glasses of wine.

"To the Cruzes," I said, raising my glass. "I wish you all the best in the world."

"I'm keeping my own name," Livvy said. "I'm not telling anyone. I'll take off my ring before I go to school tomorrow. I'm going to finish out the term."

"How will you manage that?" Leon asked as she began to eat ravenously, Pablo in a more deliberate manner.

"Nine months is the end of August. I'll wear black jeans. That's what a lot of the girls wear all the time anyway."

Doubtless it would be easier for her to get away with it at Humanities than it would have been in a school where all the teachers knew what a pregnant teenager looked like.

"And I'm going on a diet. From tonight on, I'm only eating diet food."

Pablo's eyes met mine; he looked away. A moment later, Livvy announced that she was going to bed, she was more exhausted than she'd ever been in her whole life. She grabbed a piece of chicken and a fresh napkin and fled to her room.

Pablo poured the rest of the red wine into his glass.

I looked at Leon helplessly.

"Do you think," he asked Pablo, "that she's ready to have a baby? I don't see any sign that she wants it even a little."

Pablo shrugged. "The sign is, we made it."

"Being able to make it isn't the same thing as being able to take care of it."

"She'll learn. I'll help her. My mother'll help her."

"Doesn't your mother work most of the day?" I asked.

He finished the wine in the glass, looked at me levelly. He didn't look at Leon again at any point.

"In my family, we're Catholic. We don't believe in . . . you know . . ." He had to force himself to say the word. "Abortions."

I smiled. "I don't *believe* in abortions. I mean, not the way you believe in God. Or democracy. It's a medical procedure. It should be done if someone really needs it. If she's pregnant and she's too young to take care of a baby. If she feels she can't carry a baby inside her for nine months and gives it away to some stranger, something that's part of her. Whatever the reason."

"Olivia's a Catholic, too."

"She never goes to church."

He shrugged. "Me, neither. That don't mean, doesn't mean we're not Catholic."

"I can understand that."

"You can?" He wasn't sure I meant it.

I nodded.

"She didn't want to do it," he said earnestly. "It wasn't just me. She was gonna do it because you wanted her to, and then she couldn't."

"All right," I sighed. "We won't talk about it anymore if—"

"Wait a minute," Leon said, "I'm confused. This guy knocks up your teenager and he doesn't want to talk about it, so you're not going to talk about it?"

Pablo stood up angrily. "I didn't knock her up. I love her!"

"That has nothing to do with it," Leon said.

"It has plenty to do with it," Pablo said. "I married her."

"You think you were doing her a favor?" Leon asked, his voice raised. "She didn't want to get married. She wanted to go to college."

The door to Livvy's room opened. She leaned against the archway, looking about twelve years old in a white flannel nightgown I'd lent her for times when there wasn't enough heat, watching the two of them as though she could really enjoy this movie if only she had some popcorn.

Pablo struggled with himself to be polite, won only to the extent that he kept his voice down as he said, not without a certain smugness, "In our religion, you don't kill a baby because you want to go to college."

"You're not killing a baby, dammit!" Leon shouted. "You're killing an embryo. It's not the same thing. And sometimes you're saving the mother's life when you do it!" He calmed down slightly, went from furious to hostile. "I guess that's one of the things I like about being a Jew. In Jewish law, the mother's life takes precedence over an unborn, an *unformed*, child's. Most people nowadays say what they mean by 'the mother's life' is what's healthy for the mother. And it's not healthy for this young girl to have a baby!"

"You don't know what's healthy for her," Pablo responded angrily. "You're not—" But then he stopped, confused, I think because he'd been about to say Leon wasn't a doctor.

I sat in my chair, frozen between the desire to have Leon continue saying what I wouldn't say, the desire to make him stop, and astonishment at his quoting Jewish law. Livvy was staring at him. The silence at the table grew nearly unbearable.

"Do you understand," I asked Pablo, "that this isn't about you? Or even about being married, if that's what you both want? It's about what's good for you. Both of you, but especially my daughter."

Leon stood up so rapidly that his chair tilted backward and nearly fell. He caught it.

"I'm going upstairs. You're copping out and I can't stand it."

I didn't reply. Or look at him. He'd never yet been in a position where it was cop out or lose your kid. Livvy hadn't grown up with Jewish law, she'd grown up thinking of herself as Catholic. I couldn't make her do what she didn't want to do because the Jews said it was all right; she didn't even like Jews. I could only lose her if I fought too hard.

Leon stalked out of the apartment. The door closed behind him. Livvy came to the dining table like one in a trance, sat down.

"I'm not copping out," I said to Pablo. "I think she's too young to be married, definitely too young to have a baby, and

I still think she should have the abortion. But whatever she's going to do, I'll help her."

"I appreciate that." Clearly there was something else he wanted to say.

I asked if they needed anything from me now.

He nodded, still couldn't look at me or speak.

"Please tell me," I said. "If I can't do it, I'll say no."

"We can't stay with my mother even after tonight," he said. He stood and began walking around the table. "Aside from not having much room, this isn't a marriage as far as she's concerned. Not until we have a ceremony in a church."

My breath caught. I wasn't sure what he was asking of me, but my brain fastened on the easiest part.

"You're welcome to stay here until . . . until . . ."

"We are?"

"Sure. Until you find an apartment. Or until she graduates. That'd be the logical time."

"You really mean it? That's— We won't get in the way. Honest. We'll try to be helpful."

"It won't be that different from the way it's been," I assured him.

He began clearing the remaining dishes from the table.

"You don't have to do that," I said. "Certainly not tonight. How many hours have you been up, for heaven's sake?"

"We really appreciate this, Mrs. Ferrante," he said as though I were some stranger who might have turned them away. "Don't we, O. Tell your mother."

We both turned to Livvy, who, sitting upright in the wooden dining chair, appeared to be asleep.

In the morning, Pablo left me a note saying he hadn't been able to awaken her, and she was going to have to miss one more day of school. I tended to various chores and calls, including a few from Sheldon telling me how important it was for Rick to *like* me, how I had to listen to everything Rick said. I did my shopping and prepared the stock, seasonings, and vegetables for the gumbo. I'd had lunch and I was preparing the syrup for the Chocolate Pecan Pralines, when Livvy awakened, went to the bathroom, then came to the stove, where I was stirring the syrup. It was about two in the afternoon. I explained about dinner for the TV people, told her she and Pablo were welcome to join us. She said she'd love to, Pablo might be working late.

She sniffed the air.

"Something smells wonderful."

"Syrup for candy," I explained. "Chocolate Pecan Pralines, to be precise. If I don't keep stirring, it'll burn."

She didn't move from the stove.

"You want to stir for a couple of minutes?" I asked. "There are other things I can do."

She nodded. I handed over the pot holder and the wooden spoon, which she took eagerly. I showed her how to make certain she was scraping the syrup that tried to collect on the bottom. Then I let her stir while I added pecan halves and vanilla.

"Sheldon was pitching the TV people the idea of a mother-daughter show, among others, and he told them you grew up in the kitchen, learning how to cook from me."

"But I can learn now, if I want to, can't I?" she asked, at once eager to talk and attentive to what she was doing.

"Of course you can," I said. "I told you, I'd love it. Just do it with me and ask questions. After tonight we can cook whatever you want. Diet stuff. Whatever." I told her I was going to add some chocolate chips to the top part of the mixture. Her job would be to keep them from reaching the bottom of the pot.

She nodded. "So they won't melt." With her chin she pointed to the counter, where I had Prudhomme standing in a clear vinyl cookbook stand, a Christmas present from Annie. "I was reading."

"All right, then." I began scooping the mixture onto the baking sheet I'd prepared, showed her how I did the top layer by holding the two spoons against each other, one between my thumb and forefinger, the other between fore and middle fingers, which I opened, then closed, around the gooey stuff. After I'd added the second bunch of chips, she took over from me. We labored intently and grinned as we licked our fingers; there was no choice but to lick them, we assured each other. But then suddenly we—I think it happened to me first—became self-conscious, and the giggly abandon was lost. Livvy continued to dip her finger in the pot and lick it, but I wasn't in the mood anymore. I was more upset than I'd been the first time I thought about it, felt much guiltier. I could remember her first words; the first time, in the dining room of the trattoria, that she'd let go of a chair leg and teetered toward me as I came out of the kitchen; the first time she'd walked up the Spanish Steps without asking me to pick her up; the first morning she'd gone to school; various other moments of excitement, happiness, achievement. What I could not remember were happy moments in the kitchen; there were only those in which, as in the Great Truffle Debacle, something had happened to delay me, disrupt order, mar my control.

I heated a cup of coffee in the microwave for myself, made Livvy a cup of tea. We sat at the table for a while without speaking. I was disoriented. As though I'd not looked in a mirror for years and then, when I did, had seen someone much uglier than I remembered myself as being. Livvy forced me back to the present.

She said, "Pablo's mother doesn't think we're married. I mean, they know we did something in Florida, but it wasn't a wedding because it wasn't in a church."

"Maybe they just need some time."

"No, it's not about time. It's about a church wedding."

A church wedding would be much more difficult to undo if she changed her mind.

I asked, "What are you telling me?"

She said, "We want to get married at their church."

"You're sure?"

She nodded.

"Where is their church?" I asked, more to curb my own panic than for any other reason.

"Fourteenth Street," she said. "La Guadalupe."

I was startled. "Where do they live?"

"Twenty-fifth Street. Between Eighth and Ninth. In the project."

I smiled. "It never occurred to me they were so close."

She nodded.

"I guess we—I—should meet his family."

Another nod, a moment of silence, then, "The bride's parents are supposed to pay for everything."

"Oh, I see."

"Mrs. Cruz doesn't have any money."

I nodded. "Where's Pablo's father?"

"He went back to Puerto Rico a long time ago."

Funny, that I'd never thought of asking any of those questions. More bias? Or the atmosphere's not being conducive to friendly questions? Or just that you asked kids these questions, and Pablo had seemed like an adult even before I knew his real age.

"Well, we'll talk about it. As long as it's something I can afford. If not, maybe I'll talk to your father."

She didn't appear to react to either idea. She'd never had the slightest interest in my show, hadn't ever seen it, to the best of my knowledge. But she'd always been interested in money. Maybe this was the time to tell her about the possibilities, explain what tonight was about. She stood, yawned, and went to the refrigerator, where she found a piece of pepperoni and some cut-up fennel, and proceeded to eat the sausage from one hand, the fennel from the other. If she was really going to try to keep down her weight, she couldn't afford such indulgences, never mind pralines.

"Would you like to know why these guys are coming?"

She nodded, came back to the table.

"I'm not sure there's going to be a show next year, or where it'll be."

"No!" She was startled, concerned.

I smiled. "It won't be the end of the world, I can always give classes again. But if there's going to be a show . . . cable or network . . . The guys who're coming tonight are about network, which pays much more money than cable, which is one of the reasons it would be nice to have a network show. But even for cable, they want me to jazz it up. Do more cooking. I talk more than I cook. I know you haven't seen it, but—"

"I see it all the time with Pablo's mother."

Now it was my turn to be startled.

"You do?"

"Didn't I tell you? When we said she could meet you, she was shy, because you're a TV star."

We laughed at the notion.

I told her about Bob Kupferman and how I'd tried to interest him in the Cucina Casalinga idea, but that I had no idea how this Rick person would react to it. Rick was a writer, an idea man, a Californian. I'd never met him, but Bob thought he was God's gift to television. A good next sentence escaped me, but it didn't matter, because something, perhaps the phrase "God's gift," had put an end to her amusement.

"What's the matter?" I asked.

"Nothing," she said. "I think I'll take a nap. Or maybe I'll look at some of the tapes from the show."

It turned out this was what she really wanted to do. I brought her up to Leon's. None of the kids was home yet, and I settled her in front of the set with a tape she thought she'd missed.

Rick Landy was something else, one of those new hetero— if not terribly sexual—men who found that jogging used up more calories than sex and didn't involve the psychic wear and tear. He wore a jeans jacket and Birkenstocks, which were okay for a New York winter because it never took him more than a minute to get a cab, and he had a tan that looked as though it had been bought at one of the new sun outlets. I'd have been prepared to think he was stupid if I hadn't been told of his brilliance. Actually, the truth was somewhere between. That is to say, his brilliance, if it could be called that, illuminated a narrow tunnel that passed through prime time and allowed sight of little else.

Bob was genial; Sheldon, eager to please in a way that made him even more objectionable than usual; Rick, polite but restless. I served them wine and the antipasto that I'd mostly prepared in advance, though I'd saved the *panelle*, little chickpea fritters that had to be deep-fried a few at a time, for when they were there. Sheldon kept trying to call Rick's attention to my virtues, to the ease with which I talked as I tossed fritters. (At one point I said, "And I can walk, talk, and chew gum at the same time," but neither of them appeared to be amused.) Rick tended to ignore Sheldon, which I could have enjoyed if he'd been a little pleasanter about it.

"Can you just see her doing that with a bunch of kids around her?" Sheldon asked.

Rick shrugged. "You don't do stuff with hot fat with kids, it's dangerous. On the other hand . . ." He turned to Bob. "Maybe it's not little kids she's teaching. Maybe it's, like, See-more."

Bob got excited. "That's wonderful. Like 'The Odd Couple.' "

Rick grinned. "The Food Couple."

Sheldon said, "You're a genius."

Landy looked at the rafters as though he might find a story

idea hanging from them, cut off Sheldon's sycophantic ravings to muse a little further.

"Or she's teaching a class. A bunch of single guys, maybe just divorced, and now they wanna learn how to cook. Seemore could be one of them."

I had begun to understand better Bob's purpose in bringing Rick Landy. I turned off the light under the oil and left the remaining batter in its bowl because I was suddenly afraid of burning myself. I sat down, poured myself some wine, avoided looking at any of them. But Bob saw that I was upset.

"You have to understand how hard we're trying to do something with you, Cara. We love you as much as the viewers do."

"That's why they're looking for a vehicle for you, sweetheart," Sheldon put in. "They think you're wonderful, but they need a vehicle."

I smiled sarcastically. "A vehicle with two passengers, apparently. One of them named Seymour."

"Seymour came out of *your* brain," Rick said.

"So does a lot of crap I wouldn't want to come to life in front of my eyes," I snapped. Then I got nervous. Bob Kupferman hadn't seen the side of me that snapped. Maybe he'd lose interest in me if I turned out not to be this totally benign person who— Anyway, if they were looking for an actress to play half of a Food Couple, she wasn't going to be me, however much I would have liked to be on network.

I started to tell Bob he shouldn't get the impression that I wasn't grateful for his attempts to make me interesting enough for network television, but the words weren't coming out right, and I was relieved when Livvy came from her room, looking older and prettier than I'd ever seen her. She wore the usual black jeans and long black sweater, as well as cute junky-jangly earrings, and she was made up in a lovely fashion, with mascara emphasizing her wonderful eyes, a deep blush that was perfect for her olivey skin, and a bright-red lipstick that showed off her full, well-shaped lips. She blushed happily as I introduced her to all three men and Bob said that we didn't need a story, we just needed a camera to focus on those wonderful eyes for half an hour every week.

Livvy giggled adorably.

"So," Rick said when he'd allowed me to make him up a little antipasto plate to have with his wine, "tell us what it was like, Olivia, growing up in a restaurant."

"Well," she said thoughtfully, "I guess it was like growing up in an old-fashioned home, only more so. Everything is more. The noise. The heat. The work. There's always something going on. And it's not— Our apartment was upstairs, over the restaurant. So even when it was quiet up there, there was always something going on downstairs."

"Upstairs, downstairs," Sheldon said. "Don't you love it?"

"Where was your father during all this?" Rick asked.

"Oh, he was everyplace. He really . . . My mother did the cooking, but my father managed everything. The people, the bar, the money. He was the bartender. I had a little room in back of the bar where I slept and he kept an eye on me. He took care of me when my mother was cooking, which was most of the time."

"How old were you when you started cooking with her?" Rick asked.

"Why don't you all move to the table," I suggested. "So I can hear you better while I get dinner ready."

Rick wanted to sit next to Livvy. I took the end of the table closest to the stove. Bob, whose attention was on Rick, sat across from them, next to Sheldon. I checked the artichokes and brought more wine to the table just in time to hear Olivia explaining something.

"I don't know if my mother's mentioned this, in Italy we have a lovely expression, *la cucina casalinga*. It means home cooking. You can see why it came to mean mother-daughter cooking."

A nearly word-for-word parroting of what I'd said months before. I looked at Sheldon, smiled. He shrugged. It was okay if it worked.

"Cucina casalinga," Rick repeated. "Wonderful. I've always wanted to learn Italian. Tell me more about the kitchen in Rome."

"Oh," Livvy said wistfully, "there was always so much going on. I remember, when I could finally climb up onto a chair by myself, there were always big boxes and sacks on them, and my father had to clear them away before I could sit there. Anyway, I usually sat on the table to eat because I couldn't reach the food from the chairs."

I waited for the story about getting screamed at over the truffles, but apparently those memories were in a compartment that wasn't being opened tonight.

"There was this huge black stove, with maybe eight or ten burners. It gave off so much heat that on a winter's night, we'd leave the kitchen door open all day and it would heat up the dining room enough so we didn't need any other heat." She smiled. "Remember, Mama?"

I nodded. What pleasure! She had good memories of me in addition to the ones I'd heard about. And she'd called me Mama!

Livvy smiled shyly at Rick. "I was there for so long after Mama left us, I'm never sure, you know, what she remembers."

Thud.

"We had a fireplace in the apartment," she said. "Not in the living room. In the bedroom. My father and mother's bedroom. That was where I got dressed on winter mornings. If there was no fire going, my father would make one for me."

"I love it," Rick said, pouring more wine for her and for himself. "Go on." Sheldon, whose glass was also empty, had to reach for the bottle and pour his own and Bob's.

I served the artichokes.

"Jesus," Rick said, "that smells wonderful. I only wish I knew how to eat it."

Livvy said, "Let me show you." She pulled off an outer leaf, showed him how she dipped it in the sauce that had baked in the center of the artichoke and which contained, among other things, oysters, cheese, and heavy cream, and then set it between her teeth and pulled it through them, scraping off the pulp and sauce.

"Oh, my God!" Rick said when he'd done the same. "I'm in heaven."

"Who made the artichokes?" Sheldon asked, innocent to the point of burlesque. I think he was concerned that Rick was losing interest in me.

"Mama did," Livvy said. "You mustn't give me credit for the whole meal, I only made the dessert."

"But you, my dear," Rick said, à la Claude Rains—or was it Ronald Colman?—"taught me to eat them."

"It's wonderful," I said. "A few hundred years after the Jews brought artichokes to the Italians, an Italian, a half-Italian, brings them back to the Jews."

The three of them looked at me as though I'd just gotten off a spaceship from Mars. Even Livvy didn't understand what I was saying well enough to be offended. I was disconcerted, myself, by what had come out of me. I finished my wine. The bottle was nearly empty.

"It's nothing," I assured them. "I just—the Jews were the first people in Italy to cook artichokes."

They went back to eating. I brought another bottle of wine to the table. How was I ever going to make it clear to my grandchild that he or she was Jewish? Partly Jewish? A wonderful part. A mother's life takes precedence over an unborn child's. That was beautiful. Where had Leon learned it? He hadn't had any more religious education than I had. Someone at the hospital must have told him. Unless he'd taken a course: 1001 Reasons That Most Babies Should Be Aborted.

Pablo came in as I was setting up the gumbo dishes. I was glad I'd insisted that Livvy set a place for him. She was talking now about the fact that her father's wife didn't like the business, so he wasn't able to spend as much time at the restaurant as he'd have liked. Rick wanted to know how the wife wanted him to spend his time, if not at the restaurant.

She shrugged. "Maybe in church."

Pablo went to kiss her cheek. She ignored him as she told Rick that what her father's wife wanted was not actually easy to figure out, other than that she wanted everyone in the whole world to do what she told them to. In the ensuing silence, I introduced Pablo as Livvy's husband. Her look of annoyance should have been my first clue to the fantasy that was suddenly dominating her thoughts. Pablo went to wash.

"It's a shame, in a way," I said. "Angelo had a terrific personality for a restaurateur. Sociable, expansive, really interested in people. And wine. He knew everything there was to know about the Italian wines. He'd worked for vintners."

I was surprised to find Rick listening to my words as attentively as he had to Livvy's. And then, as I served the gumbo, I heard him ask Pablo what he did.

Pablo said that he worked for the phone company.

"Oh?" Rick asked politely. "Lineman?"

Not trying to conceal his pride, Pablo said no, that he worked with the Secret Service, checking out hacker fraud.

"That's very interesting," Rick said. "Hackers. Those're computer whizzes, right?"

"Computer nuts is more like it," Pablo said, more than willing to explain. "They sit there day and night, don't do anything else, know every program, talk like ... They know all the computer words, they think it's regular language. Some of them don't know they're not talking English." He glanced at Livvy, corrected himself. "Speaking English. Most people don't understand them when they talk. It could be Chinese. They try to do different things on the computer. Sometimes pretty crazy stuff. Illegal."

"Like what?" Rick asked.

Our lives were being fed into the maw of a monster who, before the evening was over, would file away every detail and discard our blood and bones. "What was that business, the kid who broke into the Defense Department's records?"

"They break in different ways, different reasons. I don't deal with Defense Department break-ins. Wish I did. It's the most interesting part. Anyhow, the access codes on most of the voice-mail systems ... You know what a voice-mail system is?"

Rick confessed that he didn't.

Sheldon looked as if he was trying to figure out how to slip a contract in front of Pablo.

Pablo had to think how best to explain it, but clearly he was absorbed in the subject, happy to have a reason to talk about it. "People who work for a company can make calls, get their own messages. There's a four-to-seven-digit code." He explained how hackers could run up thousands of dollars' worth of long-distance calls they didn't pay for or arrange a "mail-box" for themselves by telling the computer to forward certain groups of messages, which the company whose code was being used would get charged for.

Rick was rapt, interrupting only to ask for some detail or explanation, then urging Pablo to go on. Olivia, at first offended by the shift in his attention, now looked at Pablo with something resembling pride for the first time in my memory. I had the conflicting desires to be drunk and to remain sober to protect myself and my family. The main problem being, of course, that my family did not feel in need of protection.

I made coffee, cleared the table, served the Chocolate Pecan Pralines.

Amidst various exclamations of rapture, Rick said to Pablo, "You know, your wife is in danger of being kidnapped for her Chocolate Pecan Pralines."

"*This* is my wife," Pablo corrected, gesturing toward Livvy.

Sheldon said, "Candy wasn't her specialty, eh, Pablo?"

His attempt to cover would have alerted Rick that something was going on even if nothing else had.

"You don't usually make candy?" he asked Livvy.

She blushed, shook her head, looked down.

"Tell me what your specialties are," he prodded gently. "Maybe they'll give me some more ideas."

She looked up, not at him, but at me.

"There's something I'd better tell you, Rick," I said. "It has nothing to do with Olivia. You know what a wonderful salesman Sheldon is. Well, he got a little carried away. To put it mildly, he exaggerated her cooking experience. She really did mostly make the candy, but we've been trying not to embarrass him by letting you know . . . you know."

Livvy didn't look up, but Rick was smiling. He closed his eyes.

"They wanna sell the restaurant, and the new owner, he has an eye on the daughter. Wants her and the mother to come along as the cooks. He thinks they both cook and she has to learn fast because . . . hmm . . . Maybe the mother gets sick. Or breaks a leg."

Bob said, "You're unbelievable."

Sheldon said, "You're a genius."

I said, "Thanks a lot."

But my daughter was smiling again.

Pablo turned to her and asked, in a low voice, "What's going on?"

She said she'd tell him later.

"Maybe I can explain, Pablo." I took a deep breath. "The basic fact is, everyone feels I don't have enough ideas to keep the show going for another year."

Pablo said, "My mother's crazy about it."

I blew him a kiss. "Well, the producers . . . What we're supposed to be talking about tonight is ideas for a cooking show. Or that's what I thought we were supposed to talk about. But it turns out, what these guys have in mind isn't a cooking show, it's a story about a cook. They want to make a TV story *out* of my life. Our lives. Anyone's life."

"Ever since we began, it's an issue," Sheldon said to Rick. "I always tell her to do more of her life and she acts like I said do a centerfold."

Rick looked at me. I nodded.

"It's not the same as what we're talking about," he said.

"No," I replied. "This is worse."

"Would we get to play ourselves?" Livvy asked eagerly.

Rick took another praline, bit into it, winked at Livvy, suggested I explain what bothered me.

"I know I've been lucky to have a show at all. My classes, then the show. Not just the money. The praise. Being known by some people. I remember how awful it was when I moved down here, from my parents', and nobody knew me. I was thrilled the first time someone said hello to me on the street. Maybe it's the reason people stay in their little towns. Or dye their hair purple. Or wear torn clothes. To be *seen*. But then at some point, when the show had been on for a while, I decided that wasn't what was happening. I wasn't being seen. It's some character they're mostly seeing. And that's when you're being yourself! I went to a book party and Frank Purdue was one of the guests, this funny-looking man who sells chickens, and the next thing you know, he's playing himself at a book party!"

I paused, looked around me. Everyone was listening intently.

Rick grinned. "You're good, kid. You should have a talk show, except nobody's looking for a talk show about food."

"Well," I said, "I guess we're back where we started."

"Nobody's even looking for a food sitcom," Rick said. A warning. "Except Bob."

"I don't know about that," Sheldon protested.

"It's true there've been a lot of tries at a good cooking story," Bob said. "It's also true there were a lot of tries at an airplane before the Wright brothers."

"How'd you feel about making some more coffee?" Sheldon asked me.

Pablo excused himself, saying he'd put in a long day. He looked at Livvy inquiringly; perhaps she'd like to retire with him? She said she'd be in soon and sat back to watch Rick breathe.

"Let's try this one," Rick said to Bob. "Kid grows up in the kitchen. Her mother's Am— No, her mother's Italian. Works in the family restaurant. Marries this American who comes to Italy. He's in the wine business. Vineyards. They could even meet in California, she's an American, cooks in the vineyard restaurant. You know, all these California vineyards have restaurants for tourists. Her father dies, he takes over the business and they have this adorable kid, they keep it in the kitchen, she cooks practically from the time she can walk." He winked at Livvy. "Just like you, sweetheart. As a matter of fact, you could have the same kid play the young mother as plays the daughter, flash forward. Have to figure it out. Be nice if Livvy wanted to do it, actually. It's easier to teach someone to act than to cook."

Bob laughed. "You're a genius."

I said, avoiding Livvy's eyes, "You shouldn't say those things unless you mean them. She's very young."

"Later on," said Rick, who lived in a state where thirteen-year-olds were routinely left on doorsteps to play bit parts in producers' beds, "there're all kinds of possibilities. Father gets homesick. He loves Italy, but he realizes he's bringing up this kid who's part American and she's never seen the place. Or vice versa, depending on whether he starts here or Italy. Or maybe his wife gets fat. . . . No, the kid gets fat, and then they realize she's pregnant."

Livvy stood up so swiftly that her chair was overturned in back of her.

"You told him!" she shouted at me.

"Nobody told him anything!" Sheldon shouted at her.

"You're lying to protect her!" Livvy shouted at him.

"I got news for you, kiddo," Sheldon shouted back. "Nobody has to tell anybody anything when a seventeen-year-old gets married! The whole world's gonna figure it out, you might as well know that right now!"

I began clearing the dishes. There was a moment of raging silence. Then Rick stood, picked up Livvy's chair, spoke to her softly.

"I should've guessed. There's nobody so beautiful as a pregnant woman."

She grew quiet, allowed him to help her back to her seat.

"I should've known," he repeated, softly seductive. "But I would've thought of it sooner or later. Someone else would've been pregnant, and I'd have seen her, or I'd just have needed something to happen, and I'd have thought of it."

They were gone a short while later, saying they'd be in touch, leaving Livvy, who didn't know that they always said they'd be in touch, in a state so high that she not only helped clean up the kitchen, but was wide awake and eager to talk afterward. I was exhausted, and very uneasy. She'd asked Rick for a number where she could reach him if she had a good idea. He'd given her a New York number that was on a service, told her he was out of town a lot, and she shouldn't get upset if she didn't hear from him, he'd get her messages. She hadn't understood what he was saying. I had no feeling at all for the seriousness with which he regarded his own ramblings about show ideas. I did know that if he took them seriously, Kupferman would; Rick had never been associated with a commercial failure. I didn't know how to protect my daughter from the fantasy in which she was obviously immersing herself, of being a TV star. Should I try, gently, to keep her feet on the ground, or encourage the fantasy, daydream, whatever, in the hope that she'd change that ground with an abortion before it was too late? Anything I said might be dangerous, I just didn't know where the greatest danger lay. Should I tell her the truth, that there was no way I could have anything to do with the kind of series they were talking about? That it was barely a matter of choice? One thing to be cooking for fun and profit. Quite another to become a thread in Rick's invisible reweaving process, feeding him pieces of yourself that seconds later turned into a piece of prime-time cloth that wouldn't feel good or keep you warm.

Livvy was moving around the apartment, remembering adventures from her childhood that might or might not have occurred, then altering them in the manner she'd learned so handily from Rick.

"I remember the time Papa and Mirella took me to this café that was right on—no, maybe it'd be a boy instead of a girl, and instead of Sicily—except it'd be so nice to do something about the beautiful part of Sicily. All anybody American talks about is the Mafia. Is it too late to call Rick's number?"

I suggested that she make notes of her ideas, and that way, if nothing came of them with Rick, she might use them to fulfill a writing assignment, but before I was finished, she was looking at me, puzzled, asking whether I didn't want to have a series. I measured my answer carefully.

"It's too remote even to think about. These guys have hundreds of ideas for every one that gets on the air. I just think the best idea is for us to work on things we know're going to happen, and then . . ."

"Oh . . ." She was irritated, didn't want to think about what she knew was going to happen. She went to her room although there was no way she was going to fall asleep in the state she was in.

And I moved around the apartment like some small, hoppity-nervous caged animal that knows there are twenty beasts waiting to eat him but can't figure out if they're in or out of the cage. Pablo, Livvy, and I had all sorts of things to talk about, from the Catholic wedding they needed in order to be considered married by the Cruz family, to whether they wanted to have a wedding party, and if so how they felt about doing it in the apartment, as opposed to some fancy place that would cost a fortune and probably not feel as nice. I went to put on my nightgown, remembered that I lived upstairs. More or less. Leon. What would Leon have thought if he'd heard the conversation tonight? Leon was angry with me because I wasn't willing to risk losing my daughter by pushing for an abortion she was unlikely to have. It was difficult to imagine that his anger would be so great as to make him leave me. On the other hand, I had to be prepared. No. I couldn't be prepared. The best I could do would be to proceed as though I were prepared. I could, for example, push the landlord on the matter of building real walls. Even if Livvy and Pablo were just with me for another few months, it would be good to have those walls. And it could only improve the apartment for the future, for whoever ended up sleeping in the second bedroom. Me. A baby. A baby and me. None of the above. Livvy should have a doctor. There hadn't been the need of a due date when we saw Widner. If she was going ahead with this baby, she should know approximately when it was going to be born. Maybe having a doctor and a due date would make her reconsider. I didn't believe it. I didn't feel anything in the real world would.

I washed, brushed my teeth, and put on an imperfectly clean T-shirt, a practice I'd never thought about twice until I returned to the States and a TV-commercialized culture that had convinced everyone they were dirty if they weren't perfectly clean. Maybe I should've stayed in Italy, lived with Angelo's screwing around and his provocations, allowed Livvy's life to go on without radical change. I'd told myself my leaving wouldn't constitute a serious change, but maybe I'd been lying. Maybe I should've thrown away another ten years of my life to protect my daughter's. The good things that'd happened to me since my return wouldn't've happened, but maybe the bad things wouldn't have happened to Livvy. Not that an unmarried girl never got pregnant in Rome just because the Vatican was there. Not that Angelo couldn't have found the sainted Annunciata, gotten a barely-necessary-because-we-weren't-really-married divorce and married her with me living a few blocks away.

I was very tired. I was going to fall asleep early.

Or I would have, if only Leon were there in bed with me, to talk with, to snuggle, to scratch the spot on my back that itched. To ward off thought with feeling. It was after eleven, too late to call and see if he was still mad. It would be nice to have an inside staircase between our apartments, so I could just sneak up there and crawl into bed with him. On the other hand, it was difficult to imagine a staircase, even one of those round wrought-iron jobs, that wouldn't screw up both apartments, his worse than mine. The only possibility was to take space from his entrance foyer. Actually, you could just close off the upstairs door and everyone would enter what would be a duplex downstairs. Then the downstairs bedrooms would be left for Livvy and Pablo, and their baby.

But what on earth was I doing? Not only was I thinking as though Livvy, all of them, would be here indefinitely, I'd let my brain vault over my problems with Leon to a place where he'd not only accept Livvy's baby but would want to live virtually in the same apartment. Not virtually. With a staircase it would be one apartment. I had to stop thinking about stuff like that for now. I had to concentrate on what I could do without Leon.

The first thing I should do was find a book for my daughter to read. On the phone she had sounded innocent of any reality that might prevent a mother whose baby was born at the end of August from going to school at the beginning of September. If she was going through with this pregnancy, she should have some sense of what was happening within her. If she couldn't tolerate the thought of what was happening, well, there was still time. She also needed to know better what was involved in caring for an infant. This business of thinking Pablo could work a long day and take care of an infant who might be up during a good portion of the night was troubling. Maybe I should try to get her to a therapist who could help her through these difficult weeks, give her the advice she couldn't accept from me. I mustn't be tempted by my own willingness—

eagerness—to care for a baby. Aside from anything else, my fantasies were of kissing its belly when I changed diapers and googling at it in a carriage as we walked to the Village, not of being kept awake all night by a colicky newborn. It was difficult to see how I could do that and function during the day as . . . Of course, I didn't know whether I'd need to function, and as what. It was slightly easier to figure out how Livvy should be handling her life at this point than to know what I should or would be doing with mine. And whether Leon would go along with me as I did it.

No wonder men were always going for twenty-year-olds who weren't toting around the baggage of a lived life, not to speak of the sags and wrinkles. No children of their own to love or hate the new man in the house. No careers that had to be accommodated, unless it was some hotshot New Woman career that earned so much money it seemed for a while real life would be expedited instead of screwed up. No grown children who weren't grown up enough to care for their own babies.

If Leon refused to marry me, maybe he'd like the idea of some stairs, anyway. A wedding ring might not make me feel happy at this moment, but I'd be warmer if I could creep up a little spiral staircase and stick my feet against his back.

I received spoken permission from the landlord to hire people to build real walls around and between both bedrooms, written permission to follow when he saw the plans and approved the company to do the work.

I bought Livvy *What to Expect When You're Expecting*, which someone had told me was *the* current book on the subject. She came home from school, rushed to her room to listen for messages. She came out and asked what time it was in California. When I said it was three hours earlier, she looked at her watch, then asked if I thought Rick had written her number down right.

"Oh, Livvy," I said, "you mustn't torture yourself with—"

"I'm not torturing myself," she said irritably. "I left a couple of terrific ideas on his machine, the way he said I should, and I just want to know if he liked them. You weren't playing with my machine, by any chance."

I shook my head.

"I bought you a book," I said. "It's on the coffee table."

She picked it up and dropped it as though touching it had been a potentially fatal error.

"I just thought it might give you a nice feeling for what's happening to you," I said. "It can be wonderful if you—"

"If it's so wonderful, how come you don't want me to do it?"

"I didn't want you to because I didn't think *you* wanted to." We'd been through all this already. Nothing I said actually got into her brain, it all just rattled around somewhere in the skull, apart from the rest of her thought processes. Useless. Irritating. "Since you say you do, I thought maybe you should have a better idea of what was going on."

"You want me to want not to have it!"

Guilty.

I shrugged. "I want you to do what you really want to do."

"You promised Pablo you wouldn't do this! You promised you wouldn't try to make me have an abortion!"

"I got you a book about having a baby, not about having an abortion!"

But she knew better. She went to her room and didn't come out for the rest of the day, except for food.

I asked Beatrice for the name of a therapist who might be good for Livvy. But when I suggested to Livvy that she might want to talk to a professional, someone "outside the family" about the various decisions she had to make, she said she had no decisions to make, other people were making them for her, maybe I thought there was something wrong with her? I urged her to go just once, see if it was helpful, but she got so angry that I dropped the subject.

Sheldon called to say "the guys" were working on ideas for me. I told him not to throw away the cable people, and he told me not to be nervous, he wasn't throwing away anything. After debating with myself whether to bring up the matter, I told him Rick had started Livvy daydreaming about being on television.

"Well," he said, "tell her to stop. It ain't gonna help. Nothing'd happen even if she *wasn't* pregnant."

"But he was encouraging her, don't you think?" I asked.

"He doesn't give a shit," Sheldon said. "He's a mosquito. He takes a little bite outa you, gets the blood he wants, flies away. Leaves you with the itch."

It was too good for a reply.

"The only reason he didn't fly away yet is Kupferman. The guy loves you. Had a lot of good mail on you. Calls. His wife loves you. Her friends talk about you. He has a spot to fill in September, and he wants you in it."

Me or someone who sounded like me and got my mail. Maybe they could do a cooking show with puppets. I would have to suggest it when, if, I ever saw Rick again.

I kept myself from thinking constantly about a daughter who felt the necessity to bear a baby she didn't want and a boyfriend who didn't feel like marrying the woman he'd once thought he wanted to wed by making notes for a restaurant that would never open, classes that might not have students, and TV routines nobody would ask me to do. I had a lot of good food jokes. Surprisingly, most weren't about Jewish mothers but took place in restaurants.

Three Jews order tea in a delicatessen. One wants lemon, one wants milk on the side, one wants it plain but tells the waiter to make sure the glass is clean. "Okay," the waiter says when he returns with everyone's tea, "who gets the clean glass?" Some of the jokes weren't even Jewish. *Q.* When will there be a worldwide famine? *A.* When the Chinese learn to use forks and spoons. Actually, it would be interesting to figure out why the clean-glass joke had to be Jewish. Maybe because Jewish waiters were traditionally surly, unwilling to please. If they'd been sweet and nurturing, maybe someone would've thought they were Jewish mothers. It would be interesting to figure out why it was funny that the first time Leon's Texan friend at the hospital had been served bagels and lox he'd asked someone which was which. Or why my father had chuckled for the hundredth time as he told me the following golden oldie:

Customer: Waiter, come here.

Waiter: What?

Customer: The soup.

Waiter: You've been having the same soup for years.

Customer: Taste it.

Waiter: It isn't hot enough? I'll heat it for you. Too hot? Blow on it. It's bitter? I'll add a little sugar.

Customer: *Taste the soup!*

Waiter: Where's the spoon?

Customer: Aha!

The Korean hell is a place where everyone is given extraordinarily wonderful food and chopsticks not long enough to reach their mouths. What, aside from the implements, made one joke very Jewish? Partly it was the Yiddish intonation, but there was more to it. I had another category, ALMOST, for jokes that were almost about food and would almost make it for television. (Husband: Honey, business is pretty bad. Maybe we should fire the chef and you can learn to cook. Wife: I have a better idea. Let's fire the chauffeur and you can learn to fuck.) At the moment, none of them amused me, though I'd thought them pretty funny when I entered them in the computer. Anyway, they might not pass for network, as opposed to cable.

I shuddered. Sheldon had me thinking the way he did.

I made a pot of meatballs, some for upstairs, some for downstairs. There it was again: Sheldon's Upstairs Downstairs routine had entered my brain.

I decided to go upstairs and wait for Leon as though it were any normal day in our lives, then I spent a long time composing a note to Livvy. The easy part was telling her I was leaving some meatballs and I'd make enough spaghetti for everyone, they could come and get it later if they wanted it. Then I needed to convey what Sheldon had said about Rick. I decided to do it as though I were the one who'd been anxious for news. I said I'd told Sheldon how Rick had left us all on pins and needles, worrying about what was going to happen next. Then I quoted Sheldon's mosquito line, and told her I'd be upstairs if she wanted me. Or some spaghetti.

I told Leon I'd gotten permission to put in real walls. He said, "Congratulations."

I'd deliberately told him while the kids were still in the living room with us, so it wouldn't sound like a big deal. But Rennie caught his ironic tone and looked over from the TV set to see what was going on. I was rattled. None of the kids knew about Livvy's pregnancy yet. Rennie asked what I meant about real walls. I explained about making two private bedrooms down there because Livvy and Pablo might be staying for a while after she graduated. Rennie asked who would be in the other bedroom, if I was living upstairs.

"Oh, well," I said, rattled, "I'm not sure. They'll have more privacy when I'm down there. In fact, I can use the second bedroom for my workroom, so I'm not out there in the middle of the apartment when they're home. And we can use the space where my desk is for more bookshelves. Or something."

Annie said, "Or maybe Livvy'll have a baby."

I glanced at Leon uneasily. He wasn't helping. I forced a smile.

"Sure. Why not?"

It wasn't a question, but Rennie answered it, anyway.

"Because she wants to go to Harvard, that's why."

"Ah, yes," I said. "Harvard. I forgot."

The phone rang. Annie picked it up and told Leon it was for him. He had a brief conversation, and said he was going to take a little walk. It was clear that he didn't want company, so I didn't offer to go with him, but of course I was curious. By the time he returned, half an hour later, the kids were in their rooms. I asked what was going on.

"Your daughter," he said in a deliberate, somewhat sardonic, fashion, "wanted a private conversation with me."

I said, "You're kidding." She seldom even stayed in a room if he was there, unless Pablo was, too, and then she held Pablo's hand the whole time. I remembered how she'd come out of her room the other night to hear the argument between him and Pablo.

"What did she want?" There was only one likely reason.

"First of all, she wanted me not to tell you she was consulting me."

My daughter was always ordering secrecy, never believing she'd get it.

"Then she wanted to know how late she could have an abortion and whether it could be done without your knowing."

Without my knowing. As though I'd disapprove.

"What did you tell her?"

"I said the earlier the better, but the first three months were always easiest. The second trimester, there were good people who'd still do it. And I said I wouldn't tell you. But it made me nervous. I don't know what the legal implications are, but—"

"Don't worry. As long as you said yes. There's nothing to worry about yet. I wish there were."

"What does that mean?" he asked irritably.

"It means I don't think she's going to do it."

"Certainly not if her mother keeps telling her she doesn't have to!" He was agitated. He'd risen from his chair and he wasn't shouting but his voice was raised and his movements were jerky.

"Have to? She doesn't have to! You and I know she *should*, but *should* isn't the same as *have to*!" I told him about what I'd begun to think of as the TV Dinner, described how Livvy had gotten caught up in Rick's ideas for turning our lives into television crap without benefit of chewing or digestion. "I think the reason she's even considering an abortion is she has some fantasy, she'll be an actress, a character on a TV show these guys'll do."

"Who cares what the fantasy is?" he asked. "As long as she does it."

I nodded. "I agree. Up to a point. But the abortion's not about to happen, fantasy or no fantasy, show or no show. That's my Catholic daughter and her Catholic boyfriend-husband telling you that. Not me, as you seem to want to believe. They're talking about a church wedding."

He said, "Oh, shit." But it didn't have any force to it. A young girl's marrying for life to someone she wouldn't want if any of her other plans worked out wasn't as scary as her being pregnant. He brought out an open bottle of Chianti and two glasses.

"Maybe," he said, when we'd sipped the wine in silence for a while, "you can get them to postpone the date until she hears from the colleges."

The colleges. He also hadn't believed me when I told him about the intensity of her focus on Harvard.

"Maybe." I was exhausted. "If I can get anybody to do anything."

"Feeling helpless," Leon said, "is usually an excuse to not do anything."

I sat up straighter, stared at him as I fought with myself, and lost or won, depending on where you were sitting.

"The only thing I didn't feel helpless about was getting you to marry me."

Not that I'm certain at this moment that I want to marry you.

His grin might have been endearing in other circumstances.

"Your daughter's pregnant, so you get married?"

I didn't think it was the least bit funny. I told myself to keep my mouth shut, this wasn't like television, where more than two seconds of silence could get you banished from the realm.

He said, "I thought we weren't going to talk about all that until after the Livvy business gets settled."

I said, "What if it doesn't get settled? Does that mean we'll never talk about it?"

He said, "I don't understand the sudden urgency."

I said, "It's not sudden. I've been thinking about it for a while. This has been nice, but it's also awkward. I feel it more now because everything's awkward. Unsettled."

"When you think about the future," he asked after a long time, "I mean, let's say the worst happens, she has the baby, a church marriage. Then what?"

"I can't tell yet." He'd put me on guard. "They can't move before she graduates. I'm only praying she gets away with the two-lives bit. She means to wear black sweaters and jeans to school, she's afraid someone'll realize and she'll get kicked out."

"Are you kidding? If kids got kicked out for being pregnant, half the schools'd be empty. As soon as anyone knows they're pregnant, they start getting a hundred different social services, nobody can do enough for them."

"All right. I didn't know that. Let's say she just doesn't want them to know. They mean to look for an apartment for when she graduates, and if they find it, I hope it'll be nearby so I can help with baby-sitting." Maybe he wouldn't think about the fact of which I was acutely aware, that it would be irrational for them to move if their primary baby-sitter was upstairs. If I hedged on that, I'd have to be very straight about everything else. "Livvy's still talking about going to school in September. That's crazy, but for all I know, she'll be able to do it in January. Not Boston, but New York. She'd surely get into Columbia, or NYU would be better, in terms of traveling. Anyway, if she does it, I'll be happy to take care of the baby when she's in school."

"Well," Leon said, "you've got it all worked out, don't you."

It wasn't a question.

"And did you envision a double wedding in this outline?"

I stood up.

"Oh, *va 'ffa 'nculo*. Forget it, Leon. I don't need you for any of it." My voice cracked. "It just would have been nicer. I'm going downstairs."

He slapped his thighs, stood up.

"I'll go with you. If they're downstairs, maybe we can all talk. I need a little leeway here, you know. I'm feeling a lot of lives closing in on me."

They were in the living room, watching television. Livvy looked back and forth between us, trying to divine what Leon had told me. Pablo nodded in my direction, lowered the sound on the TV.

I asked, "What's doing?"

Livvy said, "Nothing."

Pablo said, "Well, something, actually. We found out the first Saturday we can have the church. March twenty-eighth."

I smiled, kept myself from glancing at Leon as Livvy looked back and forth between us. We had the rest of February and most of March to do what had to be done. If it had to be done. I had to pretend, for now, that I had no doubt the wedding would occur.

"Well, now we know that part, and we just have the rest to figure out."

Livvy said she wanted to check her answering machine, she thought maybe it was broken. Pablo said that people who didn't get some call they wanted always thought their machine was broken. Before he could finish, Livvy had gotten up and gone to her bedroom. I met Pablo's eyes; he looked away from me. Leon was thumbing through a magazine.

"Well," I said, "we have a lot to do. Invitations . . . First, I guess, we have to figure out who you want to invite, and where you want to have the party. You want a party afterward, don't you?"

He nodded.

"To me," I said, "the nicest way to do it would be here in the house."

"You mean it?" He brightened up. "You mean, you *want* to do it here?"

"Sure," I said. "It feels nicer than some hall. Or restaurant. And it's cheaper. Maybe your mother and aunt can come to dinner next week, or soon, and we can figure out a menu from both sides."

He looked troubled.

"I don't know if they can do much. You know, my mother works, and my aunt has little kids at home."

"If I need help I can hire someone," I assured him. "I meant, they could tell me some of the dishes from Cuba and Puerto Rico that are right for a wedding. And, of course, they have to tell us who they want to invite. I guess we'll have to send invitations pretty soon."

Livvy didn't come back out of the room. After a while, Pablo checked on her, told me she was asleep, sounding as though he'd been told to say that. He also said that his aunt was going to make Livvy's gown for her. That way we'd only have to pay for the material.

Leon picked up a magazine.

I said, "Don't answer this if you don't want to, Pablo. When you and Olivia are with your family, is she the same as she is here?"

"Oh, no!" he said, then flushed as he heard himself. But he decided it was just as well to go ahead with the truth. "She gets along real good with my mother, all my family. They're all crazy about her."

"How nice," I said. We had both lowered our voices.

"She helps with the dishes."

I smiled. "I promise I won't tell her you told me."

He nodded.

"Is she the same to *you* as she is here?"

He shook his head.

"Why do you think that is?"

He shrugged. "She says it's what happens to her, you know, here. She thinks it's because you left her when she was little."

"She was ten. And I wanted her to come with me."

He was startled. "That's later than my father left."

"She wasn't such a little kid, huh?"

Leon's arm came around my shoulder. He patted me, signaling that I didn't have to defend myself, but I felt more defensive with him than with Pablo.

"I think she felt like one," I said. "I think she feels like one now."

Pablo's eyes filled with tears. "I'll take good care of her."

Leon looked up from his magazine. "You'll take care of her, but who'll take care of the baby?"

Pablo was startled, even more upset. He spoke to me.

"My aunt says lots of young girls, they don't know what to do with a baby. And then they learn."

"Maybe some do," Leon said. "Some of them never learn. They bring them to the clinic if they cry because they don't know that if a baby cries, it usually just wants to be picked up and fed."

"We'll tell her," Pablo said, looking at me. "We'll all help."

"Of course we will," I said, uneasy because I couldn't see Leon's pushing getting us anyplace. "We're just concerned. She doesn't seem to be planning for anything to do with the baby."

"For instance," Leon said, "are you planning to look for your own apartment?"

"We're going to," Pablo said. "Mrs. Ferrante said we could stay here until Olivia graduates."

But he was uneasy; he knew as well as Leon and I that it didn't hang together. In a city where reasonable places were nearly impossible to find, we were talking about their walking out of a half-used one in the same building as their most obvious baby-sitter, immediately before the baby's birth.

"Or until you find an apartment, if it takes longer," I added.

"Which could," Leon said, "be years."

Pablo was silent.

"What do you think'll happen," I asked Pablo, "if Olivia gets into Harvard?"

He shrugged. That part was easy.

"She can't go. That's just talk. Anyway, hardly anybody gets into Harvard."

Finally there was something he and Leon could agree on.

"Look," Leon said after a long time, "I hope you understand, being opposed to the marriage, the baby, it's not about you, it's about what we think's best for Livvy."

Pablo met Leon's glance levelly, shrugged. "It doesn't matter what it's about. God decided to give us a baby. We decided to get married to take care of it."

"Well," I said after a long pause, "I guess it's time to pack it in. This weekend we should have a conference. Figure out the details. The wedding. The guest list."

Pablo nodded. Leon stood and stretched. I thought Pablo had finally won him over a little, or just won, but at the door, he couldn't resist one last word.

"I just hope God decides to give you an apartment and a good baby-sitter."

Pablo turned away from us.

"Let's go," Leon said to me, and though I was tempted not to, I followed.

Upstairs, we prepared for bed and turned off our lights but then lay wide awake, our bodies not touching at any point. When he finally spoke, his tone was sardonic.

"So you're going to have a baby to take care of after all."

I had better be careful. No more hedging. I measured every word carefully before I let it out of my mouth.

"Yes. At first I was so upset about Livvy, I couldn't admit there was anything good about it. I was afraid of encouraging her if I sounded as though I'd do everything. But I'll do whatever the baby needs that she doesn't do. And some of it I'll enjoy. I hope she'll get to a point where she enjoys it. If I can get her to a therapist, maybe. And if she knows I'm right here. Backing her up."

Leon sat up in bed, turned on his night-table light.

"Explain what you mean by 'right here,' " he said in a neutral voice.

I sat up, too. His totally unnecessary exit line had put me on guard and I was feeling no friendlier to him than he was to me.

"Well, that'll depend, I guess. On what happens between you and me. If we're together, 'right here' will be up here. And I guess I'd want an intercom of some sort." I smiled ironically. "Maybe a beeper." He had one, though it wasn't often used.

"Go on." His voice had grown chillier.

"If things are worse, if they're like they are at this minute, or we've broken up altogether, then I'll go back to my apartment, and I guess I'll share my room, my old room, with the baby. Until that doesn't work anymore. I'll probably want them to stay. If we break up, if you leave me, I'll be pretty lonely." My voice trembled but held. He was waiting. I took a deep breath. "And then, of course, if we decided, if *you* decided to get married—most of the time I already know I want to, even if right now I don't—then we could think about other possibilities. Changes you wouldn't want to make when everything's temporary."

"You consider what we have temporary?"

I thought carefully, finally said, "I guess I do. It's not permanent. You were the one who talked about the final step."

"So, if I don't want to take the final step, it means I might want to leave you?"

I shrugged. "More that you want to be free to leave me. If the desire takes you at some point."

Was he going to bother to point out that married people left each other? And then I'd have to come up with something about intention. A ceremony lent weight to people's intentions. I was becoming interested in life's ceremonies. Well, in customs, anyway. Even before Livvy's pregnancy, I'd begun to think about the matter of never knowing who would be joining me for dinner, when, where, even how. What people might expect, as opposed to what they were suddenly in the mood for. It was one thing to cook for anyone who dropped in to your restaurant, another to live your whole life, your *home* life, that way. Or maybe it was just about getting older. The word refuge hadn't been in my vocabulary when I was young. Home, my parents' refuge, was what I'd needed to escape, custom was boredom's best friend.

"All right," Leon said, "so marriage would mean we intended to stay together for life. Then what would these other possibilities be?"

There was a studied neutrality to his voice that warned me to keep my distance. Keeping it, I could more easily answer him.

"For the apartments, you mean? There're all kinds of possibilities. If we didn't want to think about moving if . . . when . . . my kids move out. I need a study. We could have a better kitchen. But the biggest thing in terms of money and work, if we wanted the apartments to get married . . ." I smiled timorously; he didn't smile back. I shrugged. "The obvious thing is, if we were turning it into a duplex we'd need a staircase. Maybe one of those wrought-iron circular jobs that doesn't take up so much space. There're all kinds of possibilities. It depends on how far you want to go, and whether the landlord . . ."

I stopped. On Leon's face, neutrality had been replaced by something else that had given way to incredulity. I shouldn't have been so straightforward. Our wavelengths were too far apart these days.

Finally, he said, "You've got it all figured out, don't you."

I shrugged, but my heart was racing as though I'd just run a mile.

"I wouldn't say that. The other night I was just lying in bed, and I couldn't sleep, and I was thinking about the possibilities."

"The possibilities, indeed," he murmured. Then, after an interminable period, he said, "I'm sorry if I sound like a bastard, but I feel as though I'm being suckered."

At first I didn't quite understand. When it hit me, it did just that. For some time I couldn't move. Or breathe. But eventually I got out of bed and went to the bathroom doorway, standing there, facing him as though he might otherwise come up from behind and hit me again.

"I'm hell-bent on not having any more kids," he said, "and you're dying to have a baby, so you'll just have to raise this baby that isn't yours, that you're supposedly trying to persuade your kid not to have, except you're ready to spend a lot of money, mostly my money, I suspect, to turn this place into a duplex, so that if your daughter doesn't happen to feel like leaving, I'm going to be living with another baby. Which is exactly what I was hell-bent on avoiding."

I nodded.

Let my head hurt as much as it wants to, just let me not cry!

In fact, I was in no danger of crying. My mouth, my head, all of me was painfully dry, as though I were having the world's worst hangover. I wanted some water, but I couldn't exactly remember where the water was. I wanted to be somewhere else, but I couldn't figure out what to do about that, either. Maybe I could just find some kind of blanket, lie down on the sofa, cover myself. I couldn't concern myself, just now, with what Leon's kids would think if they found me there. They weren't my family. Families weren't just people who liked one another. They occupied the bottom line, whether you talked to them or not. Then again, I wouldn't want to have to talk to Livvy or Pablo right now.

"I see your point," I managed to croak.

"What does that mean?" Leon finally asked.

"It means that we should forget it. Obviously. Forget about the apartments, maybe even about living together. There's plenty of room for my family downstairs. For Pablo and Livvy and me and a baby. For as long as they need to stay. As long as it works. If Livvy and I aren't fighting. Whatever. I'd move downstairs now if they weren't there. It would be announcing to all the kids that something's wrong. I mean, something *is* wrong, I just can't tell how wrong, with everything else going on. I don't know why you'd want me around at all if you're worried about being suckered. I guess for meals and fucking. Makes sense. You like one female at a time for both."

"You know perfectly well that you moved up here because we were in love." He heard the past tense, flushed. "You know what I mean."

I knew this and I knew that. I shook my head. At the moment all I knew was that I needed him badly and he didn't trust me. I wanted to cry, but the dryness hadn't loosened its grip.

He tried out, "Am I not supposed to tell you how I feel?"

I shook my head. "What you said wasn't about how you feel. It was about what you think of me."

"All right," he said. "I'm sorry."

It didn't move me. I remained immobile in the doorway.

He said, "It's not what I think most of the time." He got out of bed, came around it to embrace me. I did not respond. "I'm really sorry, Cara. I'm not just saying it."

"All right," I said. "I accept your apology." But I remained dry, wooden, as he drew me back to the bed, got into it, turned off the light, reached to embrace me, led my hand to the beginning of a hardness that just needed some small encouragement.

He gave up quickly.

"What I think," he said, "is that we have to get the business with Livvy out of the way before we can think about the rest of it."

"The business with Livvy isn't going to get out of the way. And even if it does, there's always going to be some other business. With her. With your kids. Rennie and Annie thought it was okay for me to be up here, but I'd bet money they wouldn't feel the same about your marrying me. That's something I didn't think about when I was arranging life and the furniture at the same time. I'm not willing to go through one tiny difficulty I don't have to go through. I'm not even willing to go through anything nice I don't have to go through. I just ... I just ..." I just wanted sleep. No sex, no talk, no warm bodies touching, no nothing, except maybe a drink of water.

Nor did that change much in the days that followed. Leon

was considerate but made no particular effort to turn me on. I was reminded of how civil Angelo and I had been during our last weeks, and I thought maybe Leon and I had come to an end, but I was too absorbed in the wedding and the show to worry a great deal. I had bad dreams but I slept through the night as long as I read in bed until my eyes wouldn't stay open.

Briefly Leon became Livvy's confidante. She described her reservations about Pablo, discussed her girlfriends, continued to ask him about abortions. But at some point he realized her questions weren't going anyplace, and after reassuring her on some point for the tenth or hundredth time, he asked her why she was letting so much time pass if she wanted to have an abortion. She'd just shrugged, he reported to me. He acknowledged for the first time that I'd been right all along, it was hopeless.

As the time for Pablo and Livvy's wedding drew closer, I thought I saw Leon clinging to his kids as he never had, thinking up things they could do together at times when even Annie would have been just as happy to be with her friends.

I dreamed that Pablo and Olivia moved out with the baby because I asked them to pay the rent when I couldn't pay it myself. I woke up as I was trying to explain how I could be so broke, promising that if only they'd stay with me, I'd try to get my classes started again.

Bob Kupferman and I had lunch together and he told me about the ideas Rick was working on. The first was about an Italian family that leaves Sicily because the father doesn't want to climb the Mafia ladder as had his father before him. They open a restaurant in New York, or maybe Boston, and have various adventures, some of which would sound familiar to me. I would play, depending on the mother's age, her or the oldest daughter. This daughter cooks along with the mother but is also the one who's learned English fastest, and serves as a bridge to the community. She might even give cooking lessons. Rick had some wonderful scenes outlined, I could see them if I liked. Bob waited for me to react. When I just kept eating, he told me the second idea, about a family that owns a California vineyard *cum* restaurant. That one would give you more good scenery than a PBS documentary, the problem being that scenery wasn't as lively as the action of a big city. You'd have to find out how many people were turned on by the making of wine, as opposed to the drinking of it. Finally, there was the one they were leaning toward, about a fellow who worked for the phone company, maybe checking out computer fraud. They had a terrific actor to play the guy, whose girlfriend—that'd be me—would run a diner, a kind of rundown place close to a phone company office, like, say, the one on Eleventh Avenue, except the food in this diner is amazingly good, because I took the job when I needed one, then got attached to everyone. The cook wouldn't be the sole lead character in this one, but he didn't think that should bother me because there'd be room for lots of my kind of ad lib quips and kitchen routines. Also, I was going to be crazy about this actor, a sweetheart, Alden Bells, a terrifically handsome blue-collar type, around thirty-five, Bob didn't know if I'd seen him. Anyway, because of the cook's personality and her food, the diner has become a magnet for men who work out of the phone company office. They were really excited about this one, Caroline. They were practically ready to bump something else from prime time if it worked out.

He stopped talking because he noticed that I wasn't eating anymore, and I wasn't talking, either.

"What is it? You're not worried about Pablo or anything, are you? We'll pay him a consultant's fee if we do it. We'll *need* consultants, and . . ."

I shook my head, looked down at the table.

"We've really tried to develop something you'd feel comfortable with. We think you can do any of these roles. And Rick says we can give you a lot of latitude. The diner one, especially. You can ad lib, improvise, the whole— He's got one scene sketched out where they have a power shortage, the whole place goes out, and you figure out what you can do with what you have on hand. You're really going to be able to use your ability, your talent for . . . You know."

I nodded. I knew. I also knew that if he didn't understand by now why neither idea was for me, he never would.

"Are you worried about Olivia? Rick'll find a way to work her in occasionally."

I shook my head, looked down so he wouldn't see my face.

He made some sympathetic remark about the difficulties of raising children. Then, as our coffee was served, he apologized for pressing.

"If there's even a prayer of doing anything next fall, we have a lot of work ahead of us."

I nodded. "I think if you want to do a series with a cook, you should do it, Bob. But I'm a cook who talks a lot, not an actress. It just isn't for me. Anyway, I think I'm going to have to be at home next year, with Livvy."

Sheldon, after several days of yelling that he couldn't believe what I'd done, convinced the cable people that not only had I turned down Bob Kupferman, but I wasn't dying to do another year with them and might forget the whole thing if they didn't give me more money. He was pretty much leaving me alone. He asked me for the names of various cooking schools and, unless I'm mistaken, got busy trying to find a gorgeous actress who could talk and cook at the same time.

I was far from certain I had another season's worth of shows in me. The subjects I was drawn to now were ones Sheldon had already deemed uninteresting or unacceptable for television. Or insufficiently visual. Some time back I'd bought a black-and-white hardcover notebook (nothing to do with television; no electricity required in the daytime), on the first page of which I'd written, *ORDER: How to Find*, then I'd crossed out *Find* and written *Make*. But at the moment it seemed that before I thought about developing order, that was to say, group habits, I would have to know for whom I was developing them. At the moment it was easiest for me to imagine a group whose nucleus consisted of me, my daughter, and a granddaughter, around whom various female friends would gather, eat, talk, and laugh over a time when we'd thought we needed men. I was interested in jokes and folklore that would sustain me in this position. Among my current favorites were, first, the ostensibly true one about the Mafia ex-wife who says that her husband left her because he didn't like her idea for a Halloween costume; she'd wanted to go as a widow. Try as I might, I couldn't link that or my second favorite to food.

Adam: God, why did you make Eve so beautiful?
God: So you would love her, my son.
Adam: And why did you make her so charming?

God: So you would love her, my son.
Adam: And why did you make her so stupid?
God: So she would love you, my son.

"The question of taste is pretty interesting. Part of it's surely what you grew up with, especially for men, many of whom appear to be incurious and unadventurous about food. Whoops! I hope nobody's going to get mad at me for suggesting a difference between men and women. You know, I was thinking of making shortbread today, but I opened my little Scottish cookbook, not one of your bal-uh-back-breaking feminist tracts, and it said that men like shortbread thick, and women, thin, and I was afraid I'd forget and mention this and get into trouble. . . ."

Someone suggested that since I'd brought it up, I talk about the difference between male and female tastes.

"Well . . ." I began, faking hesitation, "in my experience men don't like to gnaw on bones the way women do. I'm not saying it's genetic. And if you walk into a Kentucky Fried Chicken, you're going to see men eating chicken off the bone. All I'm saying is, if you put a bunch of men and women around a home table, the women are more likely to pick up the bones and gnaw at them. I've never seen a man do it except at a fast-food place or a picnic, and they mostly don't like picnics. Of course, I don't like picnics, either. That's where you get into trouble, making distinctions. Any one you make, you can always find exceptions. I'm not sure that means they're not valid. Unfortunately, we're not allowed even to ask these questions anymore. Somewhere there might be men who hate flan and love to eat raisins and nuts and crunchy things, but I don't know them. At least they're not of my generation. The kids now . . . A lot of the rules seem to have changed. Not just food. Sex. Living arrangements . . ."

"That's because the rules didn't make sense!" someone yelled from the auditorium.

"Sometimes, for sure," I acknowledged. "I mean, there're the ones drawn from experience, like men can lift heavier things than women can because they've got a heavier pelvic girdle that doesn't have to leave room for a baby to grow inside. Or, if you let the dough rise for too long, it's going to fall again. But then there're the ones someone decides *must* be true. A lot of those were written by woman-haters like H. L.

Mencken. Mencken said that all the best cooks and dressmakers were men. Tell that to M.F.K. Fisher, Elizabeth David, Julia Child, Shirley King, Alice Waters, Marcella Hazan . . . the list goes on and on. Italy's a country with an extraordinary range of cuisines and a relative lack of rigidly codified recipes. Invention in the kitchen isn't just encouraged, it's the basic way of life. And there are far more women than men cooking in and out of restaurants.

"Oh, well . . . Men want either to keep women in the kitchen or keep them out of it, but they want the choice. Maybe they figure they don't have a choice about whether to have babies. The trick is to figure out where life would be better if we broke down the barriers, and where it would just get dull. I think the world was more interesting when you could tell if it was a male or a female walking ahead of you down the street. But I can't see where professional woman chefs would do anything but increase the competition for good jobs. Today we're going to try two similar recipes, one from a woman's cookbook and one from a man's, and see if we can find significant differences without knowing which is which. . . ."

It wasn't one of my great shows, but it drew more mail than any before, and the cable people gave in to Sheldon's pressure for more money. All they asked for was more of the same. Nobody believed that more of the same would get boring. I couldn't imagine that in the year ahead I would be inventive. On the other hand, there was no way to consider giving up the show when everything else was so uncertain. I told Sheldon I'd stumbled upon a terrific book called Cooking Wizardry for Kids, which had inspired me to try some programs for children. At first he brushed off the idea, but after talking to the cable people, he said they'd like to hear about that, too.

I had the impression Livvy wasn't doing much homework, but until Open School Night, in March, I had no confirmation that she had fallen off in her studies. It could almost have been a hopeful sign that she'd stopped obsessing about Harvard, the problem being the reality element: If she were to go back to school at some later point, her senior year's grades would be more important than they would be if acceptance came before they were in. I urged her to concentrate on getting through this school term with the best possible marks. But it wasn't until she called Sheldon "just to find out what was happening," and he informed her, apparently in the most abrupt possible manner, that she should forget about it, she wasn't going to have a TV show, and she should stop bugging Rick, that she cried hysterically for an hour or so, then began to talk, for the first time, as though the wedding was really going to happen. She also began to ask me about money. She expressed interest in how much I earned from the cable show. I didn't mind telling her, or discussing money in general, except that it seemed to be tied in to the matter of whether she'd need to work while she was in college.

Upon my parents' advice, I urged her more strongly than I had before to talk to a professional counselor. She thought it was dumb to discuss what was going on before she knew what it was. I said she did know she was going to have a baby, and she said that I had a genius for making a big deal out of everything. I talked to a psychiatrist Leon knew at the hospital. I described how the possibilities seemed to be living separately in my daughter's mind, but the baby wasn't there at all. He, too, thought it might be useful for her to talk to a therapist, but meanwhile, I seemed to be extremely agitated; would I like him to prescribe a mild tranquilizer?

I talked to an analyst my sister recommended who got me to urge Livvy one last time to talk to someone about the choices she had to make. She said she had no choices to make; they were all being made for her.

"Hi, everybody. Some of you will remember my show on an Italian wedding feast. Tonight we're going to play with another wedding dinner, this one for a couple of Cuban and Puerto Rican heritage. For hors d'oeuvres, we'll do miniature versions of a sandwich Cubans love. The basic one has layers of roast pork, Swiss cheese, and boiled ham with mayonnaise, mustard, butter, and pickles, all toasted together. On the blackboard I've listed some new ingredients I thought would be interesting. I've got Chinese roast pork and prosciutto, a variety of olives from an Italian grocery, some interesting cheese, and real sour pickles that you can find only in the city's Jewish appetizing stores. Delis, as people call them now, although an appetizing store isn't a deli. Often the opposite, since I understand from my parents that the real, quote, appetizing stores didn't have any meat at all."

I'd needed to get in something Jewish, as well as Italian, and that was the best I'd been able to do.

"In the meantime, we're going to be preparing *Ropa Vieja*, the recipe for which is also on the board. *Ropa Vieja* means 'old man's clothes,' and when I show you the completed dish, I don't think you'll have to ask why someone thought to name it that.

"As you can see, I'm pouring a little oil into the casserole and now I'm going to heat it, then brown the meat on all sides."

I began making the sandwiches, but then the oil was smoking in the pan. I set in the chuck roast, but I was awkward and I had nothing funny to say. I'd planned to point out that dishes like the ones I was preparing were perfect for this cold, wintry March day, although they came from beautiful tropical islands we associated with sunshine and warmth, at least when we weren't thinking about politics; that, in fact, many of the dishes we longed for in the dead of winter, from Indian curries to Cuban black beans and the various thick soups and stews of Puerto Rico, came from places we associated with swimming and piña coladas. But all that was a jumble in my mind and I concentrated on preparing the onions, garlic, and pepper.

Someone asked if I was acting nervous to make it like a real wedding. I laughed and said that was it, it was always an act when I was nervous.

But I couldn't find my normal insouciance, and I breathed a sigh of relief after I'd concluded by showing the audience, with a roast I'd cooked the day before, how I shredded the meat into something they might think resembled a poor old man's clothes.

When I got home, there was a message from Sheldon on the machine that the cable guys wanted to talk to me about *Cooking Wizardry for Kids*. I told him they should talk to the authors, Margaret Konda and Phyllis Williams. We then had an argument which Livvy heard and which disposed her to talk to me. Sheldon's very name had been enough to send her into a rage since their no-show conversation, which he'd reported to me proudly as a lesson in how to handle a difficult kid. He was, she said now, a pig.

"Definitely someone his parents wouldn't've approved of," I said, mock-serious. "Or his grandparents, anyway."

I'd said it without thought. Livvy stopped pacing, asked what I meant.

"Oh, well, it's about pigs not being kosher."

"Kosher?" she repeated. "Oh, you mean, Jewish?"

I explained briefly about the kosher laws, and that "not kosher" had come to have the meaning of not quite right, and that I'd said grandparents because with each generation, fewer Jews obeyed those laws, many of which had lost their everyday purpose, as opposed to their ceremonial one. What was astonishing was that she listened respectfully, asked questions, and at some point interrupted to ask what I'd meant about an appetizing store not really being appetizing.

"Well," I said, "it was really a grammatical point. The Yiddish word *forshpayz* is appetizer, the food you have before the main course—smoked fish, that kind of thing—so it should've been appetiz*er* store, but my father says it never was."

She nodded thoughtfully, asked the name of those wonderful little cakes she'd had at Grandma's, wanted to know whether you could get them in our neighborhood.

I was, of course, pleased by my daughter's first interest in the large group of people who'd given her half of her genes. I said that maybe we could try to bake some *rugelach* at home, even for the wedding party. She nodded, but immediately retreated to her room. When she came out hours later, her mood was distinctly different. She stood on the other side of the counter, watching my hands cut and break broccoli florets as though I were picking fleas off a Steiff dog. I steeled myself, or, rather, tried to think of myself as an endlessly flexible surface, a bow toward Jewish history, a bend backward toward— toward what?

"When you were pregnant, before Papa married you, did you think about having an abortion?"

Take your time, Caroline.

"Yes." I smiled. "Before I married him I thought about having an abortion."

"Why didn't you?" Her voice was calm. Neutral.

"I told you. I wanted to have a baby."

"Did he?"

"Absolutely. He was very happy about it, said that now we had to get married."

"Just like Pablo."

"Mmm."

"You were in love with him, weren't you?"

Thank God for broccoli.

"I liked him a lot. We had a good time in bed."

She leaned against the counter, still looking at the broccoli.

"I don't understand why you never told me any of this."

"Mmm. Well, I guess there was no right time. You were too young, then you were always mad at me, and then, suddenly, you were pregnant yourself."

"Maybe," she said, her voice thick with meaning, "it would've been a good lesson for me."

"You used to get mad," I said, "any time I tried to teach you a lesson."

"You have an answer for everything, don't you," she said, though without the rage of the old teenager facing an enemy. "No wonder I never tried to talk to you." She rummaged in the cupboard for food, found an unopened jar of hazelnut butter, brought it to the counter with some crackers, and began making and devouring sandwiches. "I really should've asked how come, if you're so big on babies, you don't want me to have one."

"It's not what I want you to have. It's what *you* want. If I thought . . ."

"If you thought *what?*"

Her mouth was full, her manner increasingly frantic. I told myself to be very careful.

I said, "*You* tell *me*, sweetheart."

She burst into tears.

Startled, I went around the counter to embrace her.

"Talk to me, Livvy."

"I don't want to get married! I don't want to have a baby!"

I waited quite a while, then I said, "If you're serious, I don't think you have to do either." What month was she in? Fourth? Just the beginning. Barely past the first trimester. Many good obstetricians would still perform an abortion.

"I don't want to have a baby," she repeated, sobbing now.

"Is there something you want me to help you with?" I asked after a long time.

It felt as though she'd stopped crying. She asked if I had a tissue. I gave her a napkin from the counter. She wiped her eyes and nose.

"It doesn't matter," she said after a long time, her voice dull. "Pablo wouldn't let me."

"I don't understand," I said. "Doesn't what you want count? You're the one who's having the baby."

"It doesn't matter," she said again. "Pablo wouldn't let me do it. It's a sin against God." And she went to her room as I called after her that having a baby you didn't want might be a sin against yourself. And the baby.

When Pablo came home, in Livvy's presence, I repeated her words to him, asked if he would try to prevent her from having an abortion or backing out of the wedding if she wanted to.

He was very angry with me, asked what I was doing, with everything set, all their friends and family invited. He'd thought I liked him.

I said, "I do like you, Pablo. This isn't me. It's *her*. We were talking about something else, and she started crying, and then she said it to me."

"Olivia?"

She wouldn't look at him.

"Did you say that to your mama?" he asked.

She shook her head. Then she looked up. "I mean, I did, but I didn't mean it. I was nervous."

He looked at me to see if I was satisfied with this explanation.

"No," I said. "She wasn't just nervous. She doesn't want to have a baby."

"Olivia," Pablo asked, "is there anything you want to say to me or to your mama?"

She looked down again, shook her head.

"It's natural," he said to me, "for a girl, a young woman, to be nervous."

She was such a radiant bride, in her grandmother's crowned veil and the satin Empire-style gown concealing her swollen belly, that nobody could have believed me if I'd reported our conversation. She looked at Pablo adoringly, repeated the marriage oath unwaveringly, held his hand and smiled happily as they came out of the church and we returned to the house and the small mountain of flowers her father had sent. He couldn't come. (He'd asked me if she was pregnant. I'd told him to ask her and he'd hung up on me.)

Now the apartment was crowded and lively with families meeting one another, eating, dancing, Pablo's relatives exclaiming how they couldn't believe I'd cooked the Spanish food as well as the Italian, TV program or no TV program. I'd intended to make chopped liver or do something else Jewish, but in the last mad rush, I'd forgotten. Then, in what could have been the only bad moment of the afternoon, I remembered.

Livvy, having cut the first slice of wedding cake, moved it on the cake knife toward the plate Pablo held for her, but dropped it on the floor instead.

There was a collective gasp.

She stood looking down at the cake as though it were a baby she'd dropped.

The room was quiet.

"Hooray!" I exclaimed. "It happened!" And then, as everyone around me stared, I said that I'd been worried. "The one thing missing from the wedding until now was something a little bad. I mean, they always say, 'for better or for worse,' but at many weddings, there's no *symbol*. At a Jewish wedding,

301

they wrap a wineglass in cloth and the bride and bridegroom step on it. I remember I got upset when it happened at the first wedding I went to. My father explained to me that the broken glass was a symbol of the difficulties in life they'd face together. Well, now Pablo and Livvy have their symbol of life's difficulties. A big mess of cake on the rug. And I say, Hooray, and let's clean it up and go on with the celebration!"

Pablo gave me a big hug, one of the hired helpers brought paper towels from the kitchen, and Pablo's bride dutifully handed him the paper towels, a few at a time, to scoop up the splotched cake. Then he let one of the hired helpers clean the rug. The festivities had resumed.

I drank more than I ever had in my life, picking up half-empty glasses from the counter and tables and draining them without regard for what they contained. I don't remember the end of the evening, when the bride and groom took off for their one-night-and-day honeymoon in the Sherry-Netherlands Hotel, where they'd been guaranteed a glorious view of Central Park. I awakened, lying on my own bed downstairs, fully dressed, extremely thirsty, and with a bad headache. The bedside light was on. The clock said it was ten to four.

My shoes were off.

Leon was not in the room with me.

There was a light on somewhere in the apartment.

I decided to take some aspirin and drink a lot of water before I let my brain work.

The small kitchen light was on. The kids we'd hired had done a good job. The big room and the kitchen were clean. I went to the bathroom, took four aspirin with water, and only when I came back through the nearly dark living room saw that Leon was half-sitting, half-lying on one of the couches, propped up on an elbow. His eyes were open. He was watching me.

I had no idea what to expect. We'd had little to do with each other during the day. The coatrack was upstairs in his living room, and his girls had volunteered to take turns supervising Max and Rebecca, as well as the many kids in Pablo's family, up there. For all I knew, Leon had spent most of the party there, too; I could remember only a brief exchange when he'd asked if I realized how much I was drinking and I'd replied, less snotty than insouciant, or so I'd thought, that I kept trying to realize but I always needed another drink to do it.

Now I told him I needed to change, went into my bedroom, took off the maroon-velvet Mother-of-the-Bride dress I'd almost liked when I bought it, and put on jeans and a sweater, not because I assumed I was going up to Leon's but out of a sense that I needed to be prepared for anything. When I returned to the living room, he was sitting upright but his eyes were closed. I sat down facing him. He began to snore, but gently, not in a way that could take the edge off the sadness just welling in me.

I'd been like one possessed; the possibility of losing him hadn't been in the part of my brain that knew how I was feeling. He'd once accused me of tucking him away for times when it would be convenient to think about him. I'd persuaded him that if I were living upstairs with him, it wouldn't happen. Mostly, it hadn't. But in my postnuptial depression I could feel for the first time how it would be to lose him and I wanted to cry, though once again my mouth and every other part of me was too dry.

After a couple of minutes, he turned and his eyes opened slightly, then, when he saw me, all the way. He went to the kitchen sink, splashed his face with water, and instead of taking a cloth dish towel, grabbed two or three paper towels to dry himself, one of the hundreds of small acts we performed differently since I'd acquired my adult habits in a kitchen in Italy, where disposable goods were not used with the American profligacy that assumed nobody would ever run out of anything. I'd tried to get him to use fewer paper towels, while he'd tried to get me to buy more and store them where he could find them.

He looked toward me. Our eyes met. We smiled.

"So," he said, walking back to his sofa, "you still want to marry me?"

"Not if you think you're doing me a favor," I lied.

"You're a pretty tough broad," he said, his smile a trifle grim now. "Just as well for me to know it."

I shrugged. "I haven't particularly changed since we met."

"You know what's changed."

I knew. Not only did I know, but I thought the changes might be even greater than he feared. It had begun to seem likely that Pablo and Livvy and their baby would be with us, at least with me, for a while. It had already occurred to me that the circular wrought-iron staircase I'd fantasized would be dangerous for a little kid. My brain hadn't specified the little kid's age, but I knew I wasn't thinking about an infant anymore.

"The only thing I can promise is that I won't change." I smiled. "I'll even stay blonde. At least for a while."

"You have a bug about this blonde thing," he said, throwing up his hands. But I was courting him now, and he wasn't really angry. "Anyway, it seems to me we have no choice now but to just do it. Get married. It's such an issue that . . . I don't want to live without you—I mean, I've tried to imagine what it would be like, and I don't want to, and the only way I can imagine things getting back to normal is if we get married."

I said, "If that's a proposal, I accept."

He stared at me for a while. He had to retreat now or forget about it. He ground one heel into the rug as though he were making sure a cigarette butt had no spark left. Then we both stood and came around the coffee table for our first real embrace in a ridiculously long time.

We decided we'd have only family and a few close friends at the wedding, then a party afterward for all our friends as well. Upstairs and downstairs. We'd have a rabbi if we could find a Reform rabbi who didn't remind us of a mortician. If we couldn't, there was a lovely woman judge who'd married two couples we knew. She might spare us the discomforts of measured religion and false ritual without turning the ceremony into a procedure à la City Hall. I'd have to ask the judge if she would let us step on a glass; on the other hand, my current sense was that we wouldn't need any reminder of life's difficulties.

Livvy and Pablo had come home shortly after breakfast at the Sherry-Netherlands. Livvy said she just couldn't sleep there. Pablo grinned uncomfortably, asked, "How do you like that, for a mama's girl?" Livvy looked at him as though he were out of his mind; what on earth did being home have to do with me?

She had greeted the news that Leon and I were getting married with amusement, as though we'd never have thought of it if she and Pablo hadn't done it first. He, on the other hand, thought it was great, told us how happy his mother was going to be. He was flustered when I laughed, said he'd just meant because she was crazy about both of us. (He still barely spoke to Leon.) I had told them we were asking the landlord for permission not only to improve the walls, but to put in stairs, turn the place into "sort of a duplex." Pablo nodded gravely, said stairs would make it easier for everyone. Livvy didn't react.

She appeared to be doing homework again. She never talked about her pregnancy, or about college. But two weeks after the wedding, she began checking the mail before she'd even dropped her knapsack; April fifteenth was when Harvard and many other schools sent word of admission. I grew more tense. One thing to have a pregnant teenager dream about being discovered for television when that dream has been created and fostered by a professional. Another to find her refusing to relinquish the fantasy of leaving a husband and baby for college a week or two after she's given birth. There were moments when it seemed the best I could hope for was a rejection, others when I feared she couldn't tolerate one. I tried again to talk her into seeing a shrink. She turned briefly into someone resembling the old Livvy. Actually, I would have liked to believe she was that girl; the one I saw was more frightening, not all of one angry piece but fragmented, more likely to collapse weepily into herself than to explode at me. The shrink I'd felt was the smartest of the ones I'd talked to thought it would be pointless to push her to see him until she heard from Harvard and we had a better idea of the immediate problem.

On April 17 there was mail from Harvard and Brown. I made certain to be in the kitchen and occupied when she came home from school. She went straight to the end of my desk where I left things for her, grabbed the two envelopes, opened one, then, expressionless, the other. She handed me the letters. She had been accepted by both schools.

I was overwhelmed by pride and dread.

"My goodness, sweetheart," I said, "you should be proud of yourself." I hugged her. "Just being accepted—"

"Do all schools begin at the same time?"

"I guess," I said. "At least within a week or so." She'd been given a due date of August 29.

She nodded.

"Too close for this coming term, Liv. Even if we were talking about New York."

Her demeanor altered; the Sugar Plum Fairy had plucked the magic fruit from her hand as she grasped it.

"In the meantime," I rushed on, "even if you have to delay college, I hope you'll keep working hard at school."

"Don't you understand," Livvy asked, her manner that of a

five-year-old who needs mommy to see that it's not just that she wants some Cracker Jack, she's *really hungry*, "I don't want to lose a whole term?"

"Livvy," I said, "I think maybe we should talk about this when Pablo comes home. Okay? With Pablo here, maybe it'll be a little easier to figure things out."

He came home early. Livvy was sleeping. I told him what was happening, suggested she should see a psychiatrist. Before he spoke to Livvy, his manner was matter-of-fact: Harvard was not happening. By the time I called them to dinner, he was more troubled. (Leon was working late; I'd brought the kids' dinners upstairs.)

Livvy was abstracted, not responding to anything Pablo or I said until it occurred to me to draw her toward the future by way of the past.

"You know, I was thinking today about when I had you, Liv."

She looked at me, expressionless.

"It was the happiest time in my life. In the morning, I'd wake up and I'd nurse you. . . . I don't know whether you'll want to nurse your baby."

Her hands flew to her breasts as though I'd proposed cutting them off. She shook her head adamantly.

"Anyway, I'd feed you, loaf around for a while. Then I usually took you for a walk. When you were little, I just carried you. You weren't just little, you were tiny! I remember when I put the tiniest undershirt on you, I was sure it would be small, and it was much too big!"

She'd grown attentive.

"There weren't all those contraptions they have now for carrying kids, but a tiny baby's very easy to carry; I carried you everyplace in my arms." I smiled. "One arm, a lot of the time. When I was cooking, we had a car bed in the kitchen of the restaurant. But before I went back to work, when we were visiting Anna, she'd sit in the rocking chair and hold you so I could work. Or we made a little bed out of a quilt in one corner of the kitchen, on the floor, and you slept and we both worked. You don't remember Anna anymore, do you?"

She nodded, then shook her head. She was rapt.

"We'd go home, and I'd feed you, and then we'd both sleep for a while. Eating and sleeping. That's what we mostly did the first few months. I felt so lucky to have those quiet months with you. So glad I didn't have to be working all the time."

"See, honey?" Pablo said. "That's what your mom's trying to tell you. You'll need a lot of sleep."

Livvy nodded emphatically. "You can go to school and sleep a lot. Especially college. You take as many credits as you want to and sleep as much as you want to."

An utterly sensible statement unless you had some feeling for the realities. Not to speak of the fact that she appeared to have in mind a college in Boston.

I smiled. "Especially if the baby happens to sleep when you do. In the first few months they're just as likely to be up in the night as the day. That's why you can't just say, 'Well, the baby'll do this and I'll do that.' "

She said, "I thought you were going to help me."

"Of course I am, love. I'm going to help you a lot. I *want* to. But it's still ... I think if you look at that book, maybe you'll get a feeling ..."

"It doesn't have to be such a big deal," Pablo said. "My aunt had my three cousins in the first three years she was married."

I shrugged. "I guess it's different for different people." It was the first time I'd felt irritated with my son-in-law. "Maybe she was older than Livvy. Or just more ready. Livvy's very young."

"My aunt was young."

I decided to ignore him.

"In the meantime, Liv, I think you ought to keep doing just what you're doing in school. For this last term. Then, when you do start thinking about colleges again—"

"Not colleges," she interrupted. *"Harvard."*

It was too much for all at once.

"Well, whether it's Harvard ... or Columbia ... or NYU ... which'd be easier, because they're here in New York, and Pablo'll be here, and I'm here ... Then you'll have the grades to show them, including for your last term."

She looked back and forth between Pablo and me, trying to make up her mind about something.

"You're right," she said, standing up abruptly. "I have to do my homework. Can I have some coffee? No, I mean, tea. No. Coke. Diet Coke. I'll take it into my room with me." She came around the table to kiss the top of my head. "You're absolutely right, Mama. This isn't the time to let my schoolwork slide." She took the roll that was left in the breadbasket and went to her room.

She was eating at least as much as she usually did, and her belly was visibly larger than it had been at the wedding. She wore big black sweaters and jeans to school every day, varying the sweater occasionally with one of a couple of oversized black cotton T-shirts I'd picked up for her because the weather was growing warmer and she'd shown no interest in shopping for clothes.

Because of the recession, we were able to get a good contractor, a friend of Pablo's, who would begin work, the bedroom walls first, right after our wedding. It was written into our two new leases that we (Leon) would be responsible for removing the staircase and bringing both floors back to their original condition if one or both of us moved and the landlord requested that it be done.

We had planned to rent the same big Westhampton house as we'd had the summer before and were surprised to discover that Leon's kids wanted to go back to their old camps. We felt it had to do with their uneasiness around Livvy. We'd told them she was pregnant, but they sensed that more than a pregnancy was going on and they seldom came downstairs without a reason these days, unless they knew Pablo and Livvy were out. Rennie didn't mind that they would use her bedroom while she was at camp and the walls were being done, though Livvy might choose to stay out at the summer house with me. The one wrinkle was that Leon couldn't afford all the renovations, plus camp, plus the substantial rent on that house, so we ended up taking a considerably smaller place in Bridgehampton that would be a squeeze when the kids returned from camp, a week or so before Livvy's due date.

There was no longer talk of Pablo and Livvy's looking for an apartment. I'd told them it seemed just as well for them to remain with us "at the beginning." He'd nodded eagerly, said his aunt had told him that every new mother could use some help. Presumably this was the same aunt who'd had three children without needing any. I didn't feel inclined to ask. Pablo was extremely eager to do whatever he could for us. He had great faith in Benny Torres, his friend who would be our contractor, but he still planned to oversee the men working in the apartment to make sure things went right.

Leon and I were married in my parents' living room with just our kids and families present. My parents were joyous; Larry, congratulatory; Beatrice, pleasant to me, girlish-giggly with Leon; Max and Rebecca, supervised by Leon's kids, lively and agreeable. (If he had problems with his kids over our marriage, Leon spared me knowledge of them. Only in Annie could I see renewed signs of hostility, and she'd reached that age where you could never be certain what was bothering her, or whether you had anything to do with it.) Leon's parents, old and wrinkled and very cranky, came up from Florida for the wedding. They spent most of their time here telling everyone that if they'd known what New York was like now, they wouldn't have complained about Miami. Leon assured me they would complain as much as ever when they went back. We left them our upstairs bedroom, and we slept downstairs.

The judge had turned out to be booked through July, so we settled on the most innocuous rabbi we could find, a bright-eyed, bushy-tailed kid who looked about twenty, and whom I almost asked, before I caught myself, whether he'd gone to Harvard. Rabbi Merker was more than happy to incorporate into the ceremony any nugget of wisdom precious to Leon or me. My choice was the last lines of a beautiful poem by Yeats, the only poet who'd ever left me wanting to take another English class. Its title is "A Prayer for My Daughter." I had loved it long before I knew it would come to have the meaning for me it did now.

> And may her bride-groom bring her to a house
> Where all's accustomed, ceremonious;
> For arrogance and hatred are the wares
> Peddled in the thoroughfares.
> How but in custom and in ceremony
> Are innocence and beauty born?
> Ceremony's a name for the rich horn,
> And custom for the spreading laurel tree.

"Some of you will remember shows I've done on an Italian, and then a Cuban–Puerto Rican, wedding. Recently I had occasion to make a party for an American Jewish couple who aren't religious. They married in a ceremony that was performed by a rabbi and was quite lovely, except that many of the words might as well have been spoken by a Unitarian. Or a Buddhist priest. I compensated by cooking a lot of good Jewish food. But good food that's just Jewish is almost as complicated as good weddings that're just Jewish. Since this will be my last show for a while, it seemed inappropriate for me to do something entirely different from what I've been doing all along. So I've posted a couple of recipes but I won't—please don't tell See-more!—actually cook either dish. Instead, I'm going to talk about the Jews and food. Tonight, my swan song, will be just conversation.

"Both recipes on the board come from Jewish cookbooks. The first, for *spanakopita*, from a lovely book called *Cookbook of the Jews of Greece* by Nicholas Stavroulakis, calls for spinach and feta cheese, among other things, and is to be taken seriously. The second, for lasagna, is a little horror whose origin I won't reveal, but its ingredients include kosher salami and cottage cheese. The lesson to be learned from these two recipes is that Jewish food—any food—is good when it uses well the ingredients that come to it naturally. And that nobody should try to cook foods that have no virtue except to sound like foods he or she would like to be able to eat.

"That much is easy. What's more difficult to understand, at least for me, is what it means to be an American Jew who doesn't practice Judaism. When I try to identify the spirit of Jewishness, I come first to the humor that became part of American culture more rapidly than anything else, certainly faster than the food. Even the bagel, though the bagel is making up now in volume what it lacked in speed of assimilation.

"There is virtually nothing forbidden the Jews as a source of humor. Even God, of whom someone said, 'Of course he has a sense of humor. He created the human race.' Actually, my favorite in that category is 'God will provide—but why doesn't He provide *until* he provides?'

"When I began checking out Jewish food jokes, I thought I'd find more about Jewish mothers than anything else. But there were far more about Jewish waiters and stale food. One of my favorites is about the customer who asks, 'What's that fly doing in my soup?' And the waiter looks down and says, 'I think it's the breast stroke.' Then there's, 'Are you the waiter? By now I expected a much older man.' And the customer who asks the waiter the nature of his offense because, he says, 'I came in here an hour ago and I've been living on nothing but bread and water.' Finally, we have the customer who complains about a piece of fish he's served and is told, 'You liked it yesterday, and it's the same fish.' And the one who asks room service for a glass of bitter orange juice, some blackened toast, and cold coffee. When they say they can't fill that order, he replies, 'Why not? You did yesterday.' Notice that the customer in these jokes is invariably male; the women are home, cooking good, fresh food, and if the men were a little smarter, they'd be there, too.

"As I began reading more serious stuff for this program, the first question that engaged me was what it meant to be a Jewish food. If pita, the Arabic bread that's become so familiar in New York and now throughout the country, is a Hebrew word (pizza comes from the same word), and if falafel is the national dish of Israel and Egypt, then is there anything that really distinguishes Jewish food? Just as the Jews have always picked up dishes from the larger culture and adapted them to fit their own dietary laws, the larger culture has, over the centuries, adapted dishes invented by the Jews to suit those requirements. Cassoulet, that perfect marriage of the earthy and the divine, was introduced to Florence by the Spanish Jews, called Conversos, who'd been forced by the Inquisition to convert to Christianity. It came to represent a sign of faithfulness to Judaism, presumably because it cooked so slowly, and remained hot in its cooking pot for so long, that it required none of the work, like lighting a fire, that was forbidden on the Sabbath. The Spanish boiled dinner called *coçida* was brought to Spain by Jews, and it was Sephardic Jews who taught the English, as well as the Spanish and Portuguese, to fry fish in oil. On the other hand, if those of us raised in Jewish households think of lox—smoked salmon—as quintessentially Jewish, the North American Indians and Scandinavians, who've been smoking salmon for centuries, surely never viewed it that way.

"Which reminds me of the Martian who lands on the Lower East Side and breaks a couple of his landing wheels. He passes a bagel bakery and sees these great little wheels in the window and goes in and asks for two wheels. The saleslady explains they're not wheels, they're a kind of bread, and offers him one. The Martian takes a bite, and his face lights up, and he says, 'Hey, this would be great with cream cheese and lox!'

"The only food I know of that is indisputably and exclusively Jewish is matzo, the cracker made with flour and water, and then its crumbs, called matzo meal, and the various dishes made with the meal, most particularly the delicious dumplings called matzo balls. Have you heard about the curious Englishman who goes into a Jewish restaurant for his first bowl of chicken soup with matzo balls? Having eaten with great pleasure, he asks the waiter, 'Tell me, my good man, are there any other parts of the matzo that can be eaten?'

"In fact, there is no simple way to characterize Jewish food, unless what we're talking about is food that is kosher. For those of you not familiar with what it means to be kosher, let me state the major rules. It is forbidden to eat any animal that doesn't chew its cud, that is, whose stomach does not send back the results of the first digestive process for a second chew. Animals must have split, or cloven, hooves. That is, they must not be pigs, horses, or dogs. Of these, pigs, of course, provide the greatest problem for many modern American Jews. It probably goes without saying that the cassoulet of the Conversos did not contain pork sausage. On the other hand, Converso kids didn't have to pass a stand with pepperoni pizza whenever they went out to lunch.

"All shellfish are nonkosher, as are fish without fins and scales. And various birds, not including turkey or chicken. But permissible meat and fowl must be slaughtered by trained rabbis in a specific ritual which, for most of history, was faster, cleaner, and kinder than the methods used by other slaughterers. I'm told that in this century the world has caught up.

"Another basic rule of kosher is that meat is never cooked or served with dairy products. Milk, butter, cheese, cream. Different plates and silverware are used for eating foods in the two categories, they're cooked in different pans, and everything connected to one is kept separate from the other, even in storage.

"Finally, there's the interesting matter of blood. After the list is drawn about which animals can be kosher and how they're to be slaughtered, there are stringent rules about blood, which is not allowed to reach the dining table. Prior to cooking, raw meat is salted and soaked in cold, running water until all its blood has run out. It's ironic that crazy anti-Semitic stories told over the centuries have the Jews using the blood of Christian children to make matzo, when the kosher laws forbid eating blood in *any* form. A blood spot on an egg yolk makes it mandatory to discard the egg. I doubt it's by chance that early anti-Semites picked matzos to have Jews bake the fantasy blood in. They had to pick something none of them ate. If they started saying the Jews put children's blood in their meatballs, someone might get the idea that they knew because they used it in their own.

"Somewhere, in some layer of the human mind, different layers in different groups and times, there seem always to have been a complicated set of permissions and taboos related to the eating or drinking of blood, and, even more—Jews are not alone in this—to the drinking of blood combined with the drinking of milk. And all but the most primitive of societies, perhaps even some of those, have had rules, explicit or so deep and strong as to be taken for granted, governing the eating of their own kind. One of the differences lies in what the collective mind sees as its own kind. Does 'my kind' mean my family, my group, my sex, my townsmen, my country, my species, or every living creature? Whether the Jews created the most stringent rules because they had the strongest sense of mankind's negative potential, or the strongest sense of mankind's commonality with other animals, few authorities have set down such strict rules for a population that has disregarded them in ever greater numbers.

"Let's see. Fruit and vegetables are never forbidden, and we tend increasingly to look to fruit and vegetables as substitutes for less healthy foods. Too, the number of people you might call 'accidentally kosher' has increased as everyone's become more aware of dietary fat and the meat and dairy products in which so much of it is found.

"But when all is said and done, the people who follow the kosher laws today aren't reacting to their own taste or to health concerns—not bodily health, at any rate—or to any sense that a pig or a shrimp, whatever its habits, can't be made clean enough to eat. They are following custom for its own sake. Perhaps they're saying, 'The messiah has not yet been found who will restrain us, and therefore we must train ourselves in restraint.'

"In planning for this affair . . . for this program about a Jewish affair . . . wedding . . . Oh, dear, I'm going to interrupt myself because I just remembered the one about two women friends who meet on the street and the first one says, 'I'm having an affair,' and the second one says, 'Wonderful! Who's catering?' Anyway, in planning this, uh, wedding party, I considered adhering to a Jewish menu, even a kosher menu, a greater challenge. I was interested to know whether, at this stage in my life, being kosher could take on, even briefly and in a ceremonial context, some significance for me. The closest it came was in a book called *Voices of Wisdom* by Francine Klagsbrun. I'm going to read you a paragraph from it now:

" 'The zeal for human life is reflected in the appreciation shown all living things. Although during ancient times conquering and subduing nature was a major concern, early teachers and sages had a deep respect for their environment. A single biblical command prohibiting the destruction of fruit trees during wartime, for example, led to a wide variety of laws forbidding any kind of wanton destruction. Biblical and talmudic rules deal with air pollution and city planning, with the care of animals and the preservation of species. The dietary laws ... have one core idea throughout. In their prohibitions against eating blood or the flesh of living animals, in their restrictions on the kinds and parts of animals that may be consumed, they set limits on human dominance over the animal world.'

"So, there it was. The rules were there for their own sake. We need rules to limit our unruly impulses, custom to contain us. I flipped through the book and found some other beauties. The one I recall now is from the Babylonian Talmud and says that when a divorced man marries a divorced woman, there are four minds in bed. I couldn't believe it. When had the Babylonian Talmud been written, with this breathtaking piece of sophisticated psychological wisdom? It was the first time in my life that I had to feed people, and all I wanted was to curl up with a good book. To some extent, that's continued.

"I don't mean that I've lost interest in the care and feeding of myself and other humans. As a matter of fact, I'm reminded of the old man who, when asked if he had any regrets about his life, said he certainly did: 'I spent so much money on good food, fine wines, lovely women. And I go crazy when I think of how I wasted the rest!' I love it. But once some idea makes its way to the center of your brain, it becomes a sort of magnet. Other particles stick to it. In the past few years, as sexual obsession has grown increasingly complicated and/or visibly unhealthy, an ever larger number of people seem to have become obsessed with food. Sales of cookbooks far exceed the sales of most works of fiction and nonfiction, many of them interesting or important or just pleasurable for our lives away from the table. It's become a bit much. I need to move on.

"Which is not to suggest that I'm ordering in chow mein tonight. But I find myself less interested in cooking just now than in establishing custom in a life that's been unruly. That has had, for one reason and another, little custom to guide it. I need to find customs that are reasonable for an American Jewish mother . . . and grandmother, as I'll soon be . . . living in New York City at the end of the twentieth century. There's a Yeats poem in which he asks, 'How, but in custom and in ceremony, are beauty and innocence born?' I'm feeling that if beauty and innocence haven't been left on my doorstep, I'd like to go out and find some.

"We've come, for a while, to the end of 'Pot Luck.' Earlier I referred to this last program as my swan song. Now I feel that in a spirit of regard for a set of rules I'd feel unnatural following, I would prefer to call it my farewell.

"Swans, I have learned only recently, are not kosher."

Leon kept saying that I'd been absolutely right, it was much better being married. It would be better yet if I stopped worrying so much.

I could not stop worrying so much.

The kids left for camp, the rest of us moved out to Bridgehampton and the men began working on our apartment. Livvy chose to remain with me during the week when the men went to New York. She had grown attached to me in a way that made me vaguely uneasy even while I enjoyed it. Sometimes she reminded me of Leon when he'd just fallen in love with me, following me from room to room, nodding, mesmerized, when I spoke of the simplest matter. She put on and did not take off again the locket I'd sent for her birthday when she was still in Italy. But there were times when I thought I saw signs of her coming to terms with the baby's existence. If she still had to be coaxed to return to Manhattan for her doctor appointments, and never wanted to put her hand on her belly when Pablo told her the baby was moving, she was willing, once we were in New York, to shop with me for a crib, a Bathinette and a stroller, as well as the essential items of an infant's wardrobe.

On a rainy day in July, as she and I browsed in a Westhampton antique shop, she stopped in front of a very large, old cradle. It was only when I'd been through the store and come back to find her in the same spot that I looked at the cradle carefully. It was very much like the one we'd had for her in Florence. Genevra had lent it to us because there wasn't room for a full-width crib in the room Angelo and I lived in. Later, we'd moved it to the upstairs apartment, and eventually it had gone back to Genevra's.

Livvy was lost.

"Are you remembering your cradle?" I asked. "It was almost as big as this one."

She nodded. "What happened to it?"

"Anthony and Genevra needed it back. It was theirs. But we had it for a long time in Firenze."

She nodded.

"Do you remember the Firenze apartment?" I asked.

"Was there a narrow staircase?"

"Yes."

"And one of the rooms was very dark, and the other was very bright?"

"Absolutely. The one in the front was light, but the back faced another building."

Other browsers had come into the shop and a few crowded past us. Livvy was oblivious to them as she stared at the cradle. It was a shame the crib was already delivered. On the other hand, the cradle was horrendously overpriced, and we didn't have room for extra furniture yet, with only the downstairs walls done. Leon and Pablo had covered all the furniture and moved it against the far walls as the men prepared to cut through the ceiling and floor.

But as Livvy stood mesmerized in front of the cradle, I began the process of rationalization that would allow me to buy it. Leon and I could keep it upstairs for when we were baby-sitting. If he didn't want it there, we could keep it in the big room downstairs. For when *I* was baby-sitting. When the baby outgrew it, we could use it for magazines and newspapers. Or hats and gloves. Or something.

I asked the shopkeeper if she'd come down a little on the price.

Carefully not looking at Livvy's belly, she said, "Maybe if you wait till the end of the season."

"It needs a new mattress," I pointed out.

"I'll find one, Mama," Olivia said, putting an end to my attempt at negotiation. "And I can make a cover. It'll be simple."

We put it in the back of the wagon. Leon's reaction, upon seeing it on Friday night, was, "And this is the woman I've been trusting with my checkbook."

"It seemed to be so important to her," I said. "I figure anything about the baby that she really—"

"Sure, sure," Leon said, kissing my cheek. "But a few more like this and I might want my checkbook back. Or ask for yours."

This actually brought up a touchy matter.

I had, when we got down to the wire, written Sheldon and the producers of "Pot Luck" explaining why I could not sign the contracts. Sheldon had refused to speak to me for a while, but the producers had been kind, assured me that they understood, told me to come back to them when I was ready to do another show.

I had put aside some of what I'd earned. But now that I wasn't earning more, I was reluctant to spend much of it. Leon didn't seem to mind being my virtually sole support (Pablo was paying the rent and utilities downstairs, while I paid for food), but I found it uncomfortable. As the summer progressed, and Livvy seemed happier, I thought more about what I might do when the baby was born if my responsibilities were not so overwhelming as to prevent other activity.

I could return to giving classes; surely the baby's being in the apartment wouldn't prevent that, if Livvy was there and caring for her. Or I could do what everyone else in the world was doing, write a book. I didn't have enough original recipes to fill a cookbook. This didn't bother every cookbook writer, but unfortunately, my brain, so delinquent at other tasks, remembered where every dish I'd ever cooked had originated. Then I had begun to play with the notion of a book called *My Life in Food*. A sort of love story, it wouldn't deal with difficult husbands, impossible children, or any of life's elements that were unsusceptible to reasonable control. It would be, rather, a sort of kitchen romance, beginning with my earliest memories of sitting on the housekeeper's lap to lick batter from the bowl, going on to cooking Italian food with Anna without learning the significance of regional variations until I cooked for Angelo. But there it was already. I couldn't remove Angelo from the *caponata* story any more than I could separate Leon, so to speak, from the matzo balls. So much for *My Life in Food*. It wasn't what I wanted to do, anyway. What I wanted was to take a couple of history classes. Were there people who'd pay me to do that? Was my Columbia tuition freebie good all these years later, as my parents began to think about retirement? I would have to find out, once we were settled back in the city.

Livvy seemed to have forgotten about school. She had refinished the cradle to perfection, and she finally found a sufficiently beautiful blue cotton print to cover its mattress, then did a creditable job of sewing it on. She was so proud of her handiwork that I didn't have the heart to point out that it would be covered by a sheet most of the time. Sometimes she asked me questions about the family, beginning with Anthony and Genevra and the cradle. She became interested in testing herself for memories, wanted to hear funny stories about Salvatore and the other people in the restaurant's kitchen, whom she'd seen more recently than I had and remembered much better. She didn't like to listen to music in the car (hadn't listened to it even at home in some time), but she didn't like silence either, so we had many of the best conversations we'd ever had during the drives between Manhattan and the beach.

She'd seen my last program—the Jewish program, we all called it—as well as the staggering quantity of mail it had brought in, by far the most I'd ever received. She thought it was my best program ever, still repeated some of the jokes. Her favorite was the one about the Englishman who wanted to know if you could eat any other parts of the matzo. Pablo had told her that there was a Jewish guy at work and he was very funny. She asked why I thought Jewish people were funnier than other people. I said that if it was true, the only reason I could think of was that they'd lived outside of the mainstream for most of history and had that dual sense of events from which so much humor stemmed.

As I was trying to think of an example, she asked suddenly, "Will you go to the baptism?"

"Sure," I said. "I only hope, at some point . . . later . . . I hope she'll know, he'll know, he's part Jewish."

Silence.

"Just a little bit?" I asked in what I thought of as a comical voice. "Around the edges?"

"Not *that* edge." She tittered.

So that was the other thing she knew about being Jewish. Angelo had been circumcised as a teenager, something to do, he'd reluctantly explained, when I asked him how come, with *"non-trattabilità d'il prepuzio,"* non-tractability of the foreskin. When I'd used the phrase as a joke after a light argument when he wouldn't take back something he'd said after being proven wrong, he'd been distinctly unamused.

Now I just laughed, said nothing. We'd been getting along so well all summer, it might never be necessary to risk all with a discussion of the aesthetic or possible health benefits of circumcision.

By the third week of August the new staircase was in. A massive but attractive piece of curled wrought iron, it went from the right of the downstairs front door to what had been a large entrance hall. (The children had been upset by this loss of space, but it was less offensive to them than other ideas we'd explored, like having only one kitchen, downstairs. The only idea that had upset them more was closing off the upstairs door, so everyone would enter and exit downstairs.) Leon and Pablo had approved the men's work, but Benny wanted me to see it before the paint job, in case there were touches they hadn't thought of.

The doctor, having inspected Livvy, said it would be all right for us to go back to Bridgehampton, it would likely be two weeks or so before Livvy gave birth. We would return to the city right after Labor Day, as planned.

Leon was meeting the bus bringing the kids home from camp. The apartment's air was still full of sawdust, the bedroom walls, with their white primer coat, already smelled of paint. We would go out to dinner when Pablo came home from work and Leon returned with the kids. We knew what the menu would be. They hadn't had a real pizza all summer, just "some disgusting gunk they put on English muffins and call a pizza." Then we'd drive out to the Island.

Livvy circled the base of the staircase, looking thoughtful. It wasn't a set of stairs you could imagine a kid negotiating. Eventually we'd need a gate. After a while, she gathered up the skirt of her pretty cotton muumuu, one of three I'd found in a little store in East Hampton, and, having tested the railing to make sure it was solid, she very slowly mounted the stairs. There was no need to tell her to be careful. She was being cautious in the extreme. I waited awhile, finally called up to ask her how it was.

She called back, "I don't think I can come down."

"No problem," I said. "Go to the regular stairs. I'll let you in."

A long silence, and then I heard the lock being undone upstairs—Leon and I had never really talked about how it would work, two different entrances, locking and unlocking doors, but because of the kids we'd felt we had no choice—and she came down.

She yawned. "I think I'm going to take a nap. Wake me up when everyone's ready to go out for dinner."

Back in Bridgehampton. Sunday night. We'd all been to one of those movies about ten-year-olds who have terrible things happen to them that aren't sex. Afterward, we'd bought ice-cream cones, then driven home. The kids had gone to their rooms. The rest of us sat around in the pretty living room with its striped-cotton-covered chairs, watching the eleven o'clock news. Pablo and Livvy sat together on one sofa, his arm on the pillow back, his closer hand resting on her enormous belly. (For a while I'd made an effort to help her with dieting, but she fought it at every turn, and I'd given up. She was always eating or asking when a meal would be served. Or both.)

"Hey, there it goes, honey! This is the first time in a week I felt it!"

He'd often felt the baby move, but she claimed not to have.

Livvy was engrossed in the news.

He tried to take her hand and put it on her belly, but she resisted.

"I'm hungry. Could you get me some popcorn?"

Reluctantly, he went to the kitchen, returned with a large bag of popcorn that he handed her. She tore it open and proceeded to stuff popcorn into her mouth as though death by malnutrition were an immediate concern. Pablo excused himself to take a little walk; I think her eating routines had become difficult for him to watch.

Leon stood and yawned. "I'm ready to turn in."

"Mmm." There wasn't much on the news and something in

the air made concentration difficult. I stood, too, went to kiss Livvy good night, a recent habit she hadn't objected to.

Unusual. Suddenly she set aside the unfinished bag of popcorn.

She picked up a copy of the *East Hampton Star*, in which she normally displayed no interest, opened it, appeared to be reading. Then, as I bent to kiss her, I saw that next to where she sat, a dark, colorless stain was spreading on the sofa's striped fabric.

Her bag of waters had broken.

For a moment I was paralyzed. Then I said Leon's name in a low voice. He was in the hall already, didn't hear me the first time. Livvy didn't look up when I called a little louder, but Leon came back. I pointed to the wet couch. He looked at Livvy, then me, looked at the ceiling, whistled softly, and snapped into action. Speaking to Livvy gently past the newspaper she didn't want to put down, he asked her whether she was feeling any contractions. She looked at him as though she didn't know what a contraction was, although the doctor had instructed us on the subject during our recent visits.

"We'll go to Southampton," he said to me. "It's possible we could get to New York, but I don't think we should take a chance. You get her ready. I'll call them."

"Livvy, sweetheart," I said softly, "I think we have to go to the hospital now. Would you like to change into a dry dress, or do you want to go this way?"

As though in a trance, she allowed me to lead her to her room, help her change into another muumuu. Pablo came back from his walk as I was getting the overnight bag we'd long since packed. He was distraught, felt guilty that he'd taken a walk, which I assured him was ridiculous, everything was okay. We would all go to the hospital—all the adults, that was. Leon was telling his kids what was happening. Pablo took Livvy's bag. She didn't want to hold on to him, clung to me.

Livvy said she had to go to the bathroom but came out of it crying.

"I can't go," she said, weeping. "It hurts, but I can't go."

I found the good sense to treat everything in the simplest possible way.

I said, "They'll help you at the hospital." And when she repeated that it hurt, I put my arm around her, grabbed my pocketbook from the table, and led her out of the house to the driveway. Pablo followed us. Leon had already started the car. Livvy didn't want to sit in the front with Leon, she wanted to sit with me in the back. She didn't speak until we reached the hospital, where, in the voice of a little girl who knows she's done something bad but isn't certain the teacher knows, she gave the admitting attendant her name and birth date.

Less than three hours later, she gave birth to a beautiful, healthy girl whom Pablo decided to call Donna until such time as her mother was interested in finding another name.

For a couple of days it was possible for the attending doctor to assure us, if only because Livvy slept so much of the time, that nothing unusual was happening. But by the third day, when she was still sleepily unresponsive, showing neither pleasure nor interest when the baby was set down beside her, he became concerned. He discussed the situation with her doctor in the city, and then with us: If they handed Olivia the baby's bottle, she didn't reach for it, so they placed it on a folded towel near the baby's mouth to make sure it would stay there. After one or two small incidents, they had a nurse remain in the room to pick up the baby in case she began to choke while being fed. Finally they suggested that I be present during feedings.

Back home in the city, Livvy continued to sleep most of the time. Her obstetrician and the various doctors and shrinks Leon and I talked to agreed that more time would be needed to gauge the severity of what was clearly a postpartum depression, and then to decide upon treatment and medication.

My body did everything required of it; my brain was crushed between intense joy and guilty despair. I adored Donna, found no greater pleasure than in holding her, feeding her, feeling her soft skin as I changed her, bathed her, kissed her. But I could not look at her mother when I was holding her, felt guilty if I thought she was watching. Mrs. Borelli agreed to come back for a while to baby-sit with Livvy weekday afternoons so I could take Donna for a walk. Only when I was away from the house, wheeling the carriage on my errands, picking her up for the guys in my markets to admire, sitting for a while in the little park at Abingdon Square because the sight of Washington Square Park was enough to bring me to tears, could I simply enjoy her. There were mothers and children here, too, but it was smaller and it didn't evoke that earlier trip. I always brought a book or a magazine so I wouldn't be drawn into conversation with the mothers sitting nearby. At home I would bring Donna into Livvy's bedroom, set her down on the bed, talk as though something I said might interest Livvy. Nothing did. The world was a movie she wasn't interested in watching.

I began to welcome headaches, other discomforts and difficulties. If I caught myself having a good time, if Leon or a friend had some juicy gossip and I forgot the family for a while, I'd call myself back as though my moment's pleasure could harm my daughter. Where did I get off enjoying myself when the person I'd once loved more than anyone in the world was a husk of the healthy, lovely girl she might be? In the kitchen, I sliced vegetables too close to the hand holding them, grabbed pot handles that might be hot. If I had a lovely time with Donna in the park and came home to find Livvy lying on the sofa, her eyes wide open but not looking at the TV with Mrs. Borelli, I would set Donna in the cradle, go into the bathroom, make a fist of my hand, and bite into it long and hard. Then I would come out and carry on like a normal human being, a mother taking care of a family. The hand never bled but sometimes the tooth marks remained for days. When Leon made love to me, my body performed in such a way that he didn't have to know anything was wrong, but if I was having pleasure, my brain wasn't communicating it to me.

Livvy came to the table for meals, but ate lightly, without interest, though she lost weight slowly because she was inactive. The only object in the apartment that ever drew her attention was the cradle, which stood against a wall near the dining table. Donna lay in it most of the day, at night slept in the crib in the bedroom that had once been mine. If she cried during the night, Pablo took her to bed with him. He told me that he cradled her on the bed's far side, in case Livvy should roll over in her sleep. Pablo was depressed, apologetic, always helpful with Donna, whom he adored and handled effortlessly from the first day.

At first Leon, September-busy with work and getting his kids settled in at home and prepared for school, was sympathetic about Livvy without exactly paying attention to what was going on. He kept wanting to know if I was as happy as he was with Benny's work. He'd ask what the doctor had said about Livvy without exactly absorbing the answer. The girls' hostility to me had vanished. They wanted to do anything they could to be helpful. Anything that didn't involve dealing with Livvy, whose condition was upsetting to them. They played with Donna only if Livvy wasn't around. Ovvy didn't appear to be upset by Livvy, but neither was he interested in the baby. He wanted to be out playing ball with his friends.

As she passed through the living room, Livvy would always stop at the cradle, which was so wide that we'd moved my desk into the bedroom to make room for it in the passageway near the dining table. At first I thought she might be thinking about the space it took up. Then I hoped she was looking at Donna. But at some point I became aware that even if Donna wasn't in the cradle, Livvy still stopped and looked down in the same way.

Our understanding with Pablo was that if the staircase light was on, anyone from upstairs could come downstairs, or vice versa, without a signal. One night, when Leon was watching some awful TV program, I decided to go down to pick up the biography of Eleanor Roosevelt I'd begun. The light was on. I wound my way down the steps, stopped before I reached the bottom.

Pablo was sitting on one of the sofas, holding the baby. He was crying. I didn't see Livvy, which wasn't unusual, since she was most often in bed.

"Pablo!" I went to him, looked down at Donna, who was asleep. "What happened?"

With his head he beckoned toward the cradle. I was momentarily confused. Then I walked over to the cradle and looked down. Livvy was curled up inside it, asleep, her thumb in her mouth, her back pressing against the rail on one side, her knees squeezed up against the other. She wore one of the two white cotton nightgowns I'd bought her. A few toes of each foot stuck through the bars at the bottom.

I went to Pablo, sat down next to him, offered to take the baby. He shook his head adamantly. He had cried so much that the collar and front of his blue cotton shirt were soaked. He was still crying.

"Listen to me, Pablo. I'll call the doctor in the morning. But I think . . . I don't know if this is so different from what's been going on. Maybe it's a little worse. We'll have to get her to a doctor, even if it's difficult. They'll want to give her medication, I imagine. In the meantime . . ."

Maybe it's a little worse.

It was very much worse. When I try to understand why, my brain goes to the television images of Vietnam that moved Americans finally to protest what was happening there. We'd known all along, but it had been possible to know without knowing. With this picture of what was going on inside Livvy it was no longer possible to believe she'd win the battle. There was no reason even to assume she was fighting. She'd lost it. There she was, an infant in a cradle. I had no idea of how long it might take her to grow up again. I just knew that whether or not she wanted help, she needed it.

I put my arm around Pablo and sat with him. When the baby stirred and cried, he gave her a bottle, then, almost reluctantly, brought her to the crib. I took a mohair throw we kept on the sofa and covered Livvy. Then we came back to the sofa and he reached for my hand as though he couldn't go on without touching another human's flesh. We sat in silence until daybreak. Sometimes one or the other of us drifted briefly into sleep, but each time we woke ourselves up as though there were something that had to be done. Now.

Of the doctors I'd spoken to, only Edward Weinberger was an M.D. who could prescribe medication but also sounded competent to treat a patient, didn't expect that everything would be solved by the medicine. Pablo was in the middle of an important job, but with Leon's help, I got Livvy to Weinberger's office the next day. She was indifferent to him and to everyone else we encountered, though she took the medication without resistance. Weinberger warned us that it would be a minimum of two weeks before we saw results, but that didn't keep me from constantly checking the cradle as though some change might have occurred that even he hadn't been able to predict. For three weeks there was no change at all. She slept in the cradle, awakened to eat, curled up again in the cradle. She went to the bathroom as she needed to but never washed unless I went in with her and helped.

There were marks on her back from its pressing against the bars. I had no need now to chew at my hands to feel pain. When the baby was awake I carried her around over my shoulder or on my hip so she wouldn't see my expression, lest it make her cry.

I became aware of a first small difference during an afternoon when I came home with Donna to find Livvy still asleep in the cradle but with a pillow under her head. Mrs. Borelli said she had awakened and asked for milk and cookies. Then she'd gone to the bathroom, walked to her bedroom, gotten the pillow, and returned to the cradle with it.

I looked away from Mrs. Borelli so she couldn't see that I was crying. I think that until that moment, I hadn't been certain that anything would change.

Livvy became more concerned with her comfort. Instead of looking like the figure of a fetus carved by some depressed Impressionist, she began to squirm in the cramped cradle, change positions, occasionally to stretch out on her back, legs over the bottom rail. Soon she was napping in her bed during the day. Finally she abandoned the cradle for the bed.

Pablo's extraordinary patience became spotty as she seemed to be getting better but she wouldn't speak to him (or to anyone), and recoiled if he touched her.

Leon confessed that until she'd begun to sleep in the cradle, he had allowed himself not to know how bad it was. He thought I was wonderful, and when all this was over he was going to take me to "the Caribbean for a week." I couldn't imagine being away from Donna for that long. In my good dreams, Livvy and Donna were my two adoring daughters. In my bad dreams, I was taking care of Donna when she was snatched away and a rag doll was left in her place.

Each week saw some small improvement. If Donna might still have been an object dumped in our midst and requiring a detour, Livvy began to exchange a few words with the rest of us. First me, then Ovvy and the girls, then Leon, and finally Pablo. I told Pablo, who was hurt when he was the last, that maybe it had to do with the order in which she'd known us, that he still mustn't react as though she were grown up. I had almost used the phrase "in her right mind," and of course I was glad I'd caught myself. But it was somehow more accurate. If a stranger might now have spent a little time with her without noticing anything amiss, she was not yet in the mind that a friend or relative could recognize as Olivia's.

* * *

When my parents asked what I'd like for a Christmas present I said, "A menorah." This is the candelabrum the Jews use on ceremonial occasions—or so I'd thought. There had always been one in my parents' dining room.

Everyone laughed.

"Terrific," Leon said. "For Christmas."

My father, with mock gravity, said it was about time I was getting a little religion and Leon was not to make fun of me. Now, which kind of candelabrum did I want?

I looked at him blankly.

He smiled gently. "Haven't you ever noticed, dear, the menorah in my study, the one my parents brought over with them, has seven branches, one for each day of the week? But the one in the living room, the *chanukiah*, which is used for Chanukah, has nine, one for each day of Chanukah and one to light the others?"

What could I say? I had never noticed. I considered for a while, in spite of the difficulty of doing so with Leon grimacing at me.

"I want the everyday kind," I finally said. "I don't like that whole business of being Jewish once a year, for Chanukah."

Leon wanted me to know, my parents were his witnesses, that if this was the first step in a gigantic conspiracy to get him to go to *schul* or observe the Jewish holidays, I should forget it. I assured him that *schul* would feel no less strange to me than to him and I'd never developed much more feeling than he had for the holidays. It wasn't about religion. I was looking for a meaningful way to mark time, physical incarnations of that meaning, other than food. It was about finding a way to live when there was no crisis. A way that had something to do with something else, that wasn't just about that day or week or even year. There was no reason to think Pablo and Livvy would leave soon. We were three adults, one girl hovering between infancy and adulthood, a teenaged girl, an almost-teenager, a boy of eleven, and a baby, and I wanted to find some meeting ground, a way to live that would give us some sort of stability through all their comings and goings during the years. For starters, I wanted to reinstate our Friday-night dinners. Nobody had objected to the idea when I'd first proposed it, but we hadn't exactly stuck with it either. Now I wanted everyone to be there unless there was some really good reason. Friday night was a natural time to come together. The end of the work week. We would eat together downstairs, talk, relax, get things off our chests. If I knew perfectly well that Friday night wasn't simply a logical choice but contained an effortless echo of the Jewish sabbath, this wasn't what mattered the most. If everyone liked the idea of lighting candles, we'd do it. If not . . . Maybe I'd do it, anyway.

When my parents asked what I thought Livvy would like for her present, I said I thought perhaps some clothes, or money for clothes. She still wasn't going out, except to see Doctor Weinberger, but she had to wear either a maternity dress or, more recently, the black turtleneck and jeans she'd lived in toward the school term's end; her pre-pregnancy clothes didn't fit, yet. They decided to give her a check. I gave her a couple of crewneck sweaters and some turtleneck T-shirts she immediately began wearing. She put away the check from my parents. Shopping was not a possibility.

Livvy began going upstairs frequently, though she was still afraid to come down the inside way and used the building's staircase. The first time she went up on her own, I was writing at my desk in the baby's room. Donna was sleeping in her crib. I knew Ovvy was home because he'd come by to get some cookies on his way. (He now favored Coke with his cookies but he'd get the Coke upstairs; I'd explained that my love for him stopped at helping anyone drink Coke with cookies.) I made the decision not to speak or follow Livvy lest I be interfering with some move toward independence. She came down about half an hour later, but in the following weeks spent more and more time upstairs, always after Ovvy had come home.

It became clear that she and Ovvy had a secret. I began to think it had to do with Ovvy's computer; once or twice I heard them speaking that awful language I'd not been able to train myself to use, and then I'd noticed Livvy glancing through a hacker magazine Ovvy had gotten for Christmas, along with his own computer.

She began walking with me when I wheeled Donna around the neighborhood or down to the Village. She noticed a dress she liked in a store window, then became concerned about the weight she'd gained "over the holidays." She began to discipline herself in the matter of how much she ate. She was not interested in seeing how far the check from her grandparents would take her toward buying some new clothes. She had another use for the money but didn't want to discuss it. She began to race-walk and became impatient when I couldn't keep up with her because of the carriage. She forged ahead and waited for me at corners. By a few days later she was taking off on her own and meeting me back at the house. The first time this happened I was frightened, uncertain I would find her waiting there. She became willing, if we were together and I had to go into a store, to stand outside and hold on to the carriage. This, too, made me anxious the first time, and I kept checking her from inside the store, though I didn't let her see me.

By the end of January, Donna was sitting up, Livvy and Pablo were going to the movies together, and I was beginning to feel human. Livvy was spending a lot of time upstairs even when Ovvy was in school, and at a Friday-night dinner, she confessed bashfully that he'd been teaching her the computer.

"She's getting real good at it," Ovvy announced. "I even let her use it when I'm not there."

Livvy smiled, looked down at her napkin.

"Aha!" I said. "So that's what you've been doing upstairs all these afternoons!"

"I didn't want to learn it when I was in high school," she admitted shyly. "I thought it was just for the kids who didn't like real subjects."

"She can type much better than I can," Ovvy said. "She could get a job."

With Livvy's improvement, the other girls had grown a little impatient with the attentions and privileges accorded her. Now Rennie got Annie's attention and raised her eyes to the ceiling to mock the notion that typing fast was a big deal. Leon sent a warning look and the moment ended but the feeling didn't.

I had long since made up my mind that when Livvy was ready to go back to school, I'd do whatever was required of me, as long as she confined herself to New York. It was clear that whatever else was true, she'd be ready to think of herself as a student before she felt like a mother. In January, I added to my parents' gift the substantial amount required to buy her the computer that felt like a first step on her way back to school. To my surprise, she was happy to have me move my own computer from the desk in Donna's room so that hers could occupy it. We moved mine to a small desk outside, next to Donna's playpen, which occupied the spot where the cradle had once been. But we had no reasonable place for the cradle.

This was a weightier problem than it might seem. The stairwell had eliminated more than half of the upstairs foyer. Whatever my old fantasy about a hat-and-glove cradle, there was no place for such a piece downstairs, where there was no entrance hall. It was out of the question to fit the long cradle into the baby's bedroom, which was crammed with my old queen-sized bed and my-now-Livvy's desk (a door-top resting on files) as well as the baby's furniture. Attempting to prepare Livvy for the possibility of moving the cradle out of the apartment, I brought up the matter of space and made some joke about whether anyone had ever seen a cradle rocking on a ceiling.

Livvy shrugged. "All we have to do is get rid of the bed."

It was a terrific idea except it made no sense to get rid of a bed we sometimes used in order to keep a cradle we didn't.

I asked my parents whether it might fit someplace in Westport, but they had no garage and the new rooms, not to speak of the crammed older ones, weren't of a size to accommodate such a piece of furniture.

In the meantime, it had been moved to the space between the downstairs entrance and the circular stairs. And on a Friday night when Rennie was late for dinner, she came running down too fast and, at the bottom, tripped over the crossbar at the foot of the cradle, which didn't quite clear the stairs. When she fell, one elbow banged into the cradle's nearest corner and it was that bang, more than anything else, that made her scream out as she landed on the floor, "Motherfucker! Why don't you get rid of that asshole motherfucking cradle!"

Then she collapsed into tears.

Pablo ran to help her up, Leon and the other kids being momentarily thrown by her language, which wasn't generally heard in the house. Livvy began buttering a piece of bread with inordinate care. Pablo helped Rennie to her seat, on one side of Leon's. She was still crying. When Leon asked if she was all right, she began a tirade about how we didn't need the cradle blocking the stairs, why didn't we get rid of it, we weren't going to have any more babies around.

I glanced at Livvy, who now watched Rennie with the purest sort of hatred on her face.

"I don't know why it has to be there, Daddy," Rennie said,

still crying as he looked at her right knee, which was bleeding.
"We always have to watch out for it so something won't happen!"

He took her to the bathroom, as much to calm her as to
clean her bruises.

Leon was wonderful, although our lives, of course, were different than we'd thought they would be. If he occasionally
chafed at my being so busy with Donna, he grew fond of her,
so that the irony attached to my being a full-time mother substitute when he'd not wanted me to be a mother grated on him
less than it might have. It was Leon who solved the Great Cradle Dilemma by arranging with a young woman doctor at the
hospital who had inherited a huge West End Avenue apartment
and was expecting, that she would use the cradle for her baby,
then store it in one of their three "maids' rooms" for as long
as we wished.

We staged the moment when Leon would announce to
Livvy, not in the presence of his children, that he had found
the cradle a good home. We had no idea of what her reaction
would be.

She appeared not to have one.

By the time he'd explained about the apartment and joked
about visiting privileges, she'd picked up a copy of *Computer
Shopper*, Ovvy's and her current favorite magazine, and was
absorbed in it. The two spent an unbelievable amount of time
discussing the merits of various computers, hardware, software,
networking possibilities, and so on.

But the cradle episode was the identifiable beginning of a
feud between Livvy and Rennie that occasionally threatened to
turn our Friday-night ritual dinners into something resembling
primal scream therapy. Livvy displayed her first sign ever of
interest in Donna when she came out of her room one night to
find Rennie holding the baby on her lap, turning the pages of
Donna's favorite cloth picture book. She came to the kitchen
and said she didn't want Rennie to hold Donna, she didn't trust
her.

I said, looking intently at the plum sauce I was experimenting with for our spareribs, never having succeeded at
making a satisfactory one at home, "Well, why don't you just
tell Rennie you want to hold her for a while."

After a moment's hesitation, Livvy stalked over to the sofa

and, without a word, snatched the baby from Rennie's lap. Donna, frightened as she would have been even if she'd ever had contact with her mother, began to cry. I turned off the light under the plum sauce and moved toward Livvy even as she came to the kitchen, thrust the bawling baby into my arms, and retreated to her room. She refused to come out for dinner, but the next day, Friday, she had a session with Doctor Weinberger, whom she now saw three times a week. That night, at our ritual dinner (I never made pork on Friday nights; Leon teased me about the way "Jewish stuff" was edging into my brain; I always replied that it had begun with chicken soup and matzo balls) Livvy spoke haltingly, as though trying to remember learned words.

"I know ... This has been a very difficult time for me. Maybe for everyone. I don't know. I've been ... sort of ... out of it. But now I think I'm ready ... I mean, the baby ... She's my baby. I don't even want to call her Donna, because I didn't give her that name. I mean, Pablo and I didn't give her the name together." She'd obviously talked to Pablo in advance and now she clutched his hand. He was supportive of her, if slightly embarrassed about the rest of us. Everyone but Rennie was looking at her; Rennie was looking down at her lap. "Now everyone has to get used to the fact that she's mine. And if I—" She'd run out of prepared words and the next ones came out in a frantic rush, their hostile message belied by an increasingly frightened little-girlish manner. "If I don't want her to hold my baby, she'd better not, because I'm her, I'm her—" But she couldn't think of precisely who she was to the baby, or maybe she just couldn't say it, and she ran to her room.

Poor Rennie. Leon had told her we had to be patient as Livvy recovered, but why did she have to be the kid of whom the most patience was required? For a few weeks she refused to come downstairs for meals, and when she began joining us, she made it a point not to be there on Fridays. She told Leon there was no reason to come if she was the only one who wasn't allowed to get anything off her chest. In fact, she seldom came downstairs for any reason and never went near the baby.

Nor did Livvy display further interest in Donna. She began speaking frequently of Doctor Weinberger, the wonderful man who was her therapist. She thought he was probably a genius, certainly he knew everything, though he liked her to find out things for herself. Doctor Weinberger understood her desire to give Donna "my own name," though he hadn't been willing to suggest one himself. What bothered her about the name Donna, she said, was that it didn't mean just woman, after all, but maid. She had this picture of Rennie taking Italian someday and finding out that *donna* means maid and trying to get Donna to clean up her room. When I objected mildly to the notion that Rennie might do such a thing, Livvy ended the conversation.

Barring such moments, it was becoming possible to believe that my daughter was recovering her self. That self wasn't a woman who could care for a child, but appeared to be at least as rational as the seventeen-year-old who had given birth to a baby five months before.

It was during an afternoon in February that I came out of Donna's room and realized that Livvy, on the sofa, was reading one of her old college brochures. Others were scattered on the coffee table in front of her.

It would be a shame if she was getting interested in going back to school just when it was too late for the spring term.

She continued to read the brochures but didn't refer to them, and I was relieved because this suggested that she didn't feel anxious. Her medication had been cut back slightly and the doctor had asked me to be aware of any real changes in her behavior, as opposed to just some increased anxiety.

On Saturday, as I prepared lunch in the kitchen and Donna sat in her playpen knocking two stuffed animals together, Livvy looked up from a magazine or brochure and asked Ovvy, who'd just come downstairs, the date. He said he wasn't sure, so she asked me.

I said I thought it was February 18.

She said, "It can't be. I wouldn't have graduated yet."

I smiled uneasily. Surely she'd noticed the dates on papers and magazines, even if she hadn't paid real attention to them.

"That was last year that you graduated, sweetheart. Ninety-two. This is Ninety-three. Remember?"

She bolted to her feet, extremely agitated.

"No!" she exclaimed. "Doctor Weinberger would've told me!"

Ovvy, frightened, muttered that he'd forgotten something and ran upstairs.

"I guess," I said carefully, "it never came up."

She marched to the phone—I suppose it was a measure of her sense of urgency that she didn't even bother to go to her own room but came to the kitchen—and left a message with Doctor Weinberger's service, then hung up, uncertain of what to do next. She finally settled upon berating me—loudly.

"I can't believe you were letting me read a bunch of stuff from 1992 when we're in 1993! Everything's going to be totally different!"

In her playpen, Donna began to cry.

"Not totally," I said, trying to appear calm. "Some things'll be different, you'll be looking at different schools, but we have plenty of time to get the new brochures and—"

"Plenty of time! I don't believe you!"

And as I stood at the counter watching her, not wanting to pick up Donna because I couldn't tell what would happen next, my daughter stalked out of the room with her old, angry energy, convinced that having been forgiven so many earlier crimes, I had committed the unforgivable one of stealing a year from her life.

Recovery continued, not always recognizable as such. She was like a frostbite victim rewarming and feeling for the first time the pain the iciness had protected her from, then blaming the rescue team that had brought her down from the mountain. She was always upset to discover some specific of the months she'd lost, tended to hold Pablo or me responsible for the loss. After we'd had a minor argument, the little gold locket, around her neck for more than a year, disappeared. After a fight with Pablo because she wanted to go to a movie on a night when Leon and I had a date and he wouldn't ask us to stay home, she took off her wedding ring. It remained off. I had the impression she spent a lot of her time with Doctor Weinberger talking about her husband. She and Pablo would have an argument after which she'd not speak to him, then she'd come home from a session and greet him lovingly, remain affectionate until the next fight. She began to compare Jewish men like Doctor Weinberger with Latino males like Pablo; she could pay her husband no greater compliment than to tell everyone that Pablo was more like a Jewish husband than your average *"mucho macho"* Latino.

Pablo often brought the baby to visit his mother. I'd tried to make her welcome at our house but she was too concerned with imposing to come often. At some point during the early spring, Livvy began to go there with him. Pablo said that during these visits she played the little mother as though it were natural to her, told everybody of Donna's latest achievements, held the baby on her lap, explained how I would take care of Donna when she herself returned to school in September. At home she sometimes watched Donna crawl around or play, but never picked her up or spoke directly to her.

Donna's first sound was "Da," which Livvy took to mean that the baby was trying to say her own name, the corollary being, she and Doctor Weinberger decided, that the name should not be changed. This made Pablo happy because (1) he thought the Da stood for Daddy, and (2) it was he who'd chosen Donna, the first name, he confided to me only now, of his adored kindergarten teacher.

It began to seem that Livvy always had to be mad at one or the other of us. At times when she was particularly fond of Pablo, she'd be irritated with me because she was sure she'd heard me call the baby Nonna instead of Donna; at other times she'd tell Pablo he was "ruining the child," picking her up when "she wasn't even crying." Once or twice Pablo tried explaining that he'd picked her up because he felt like it, but Livvy reacted as though he'd made some absurd excuse. The first time I saw him become furious with her was when he pointed out that she held Donna at his mother's house when the baby was perfectly happy, and she told him that was because the floor was always filthy. He wasn't just angry and upset, he was embarrassed on his mother's behalf because I was there. He drew himself in and coldly informed her that if she worked as hard as his mother did, maybe she wouldn't have time to clean the floor every day. As a matter of fact, he hadn't seen her clean a floor or do anything else in this house. Ever.

She stared at him like a little kid who didn't believe all the warnings about electricity and has just put her finger in a socket. Then she burst into tears and ran into her room. He did not follow her but stood looking after her, furious, unforgiving.

I put a hand on his arm.

"I suppose," I said, "sometimes the recovery's going to be more difficult than the illness."

"I'll pick up the baby and move to Puerto Rico," he said through clenched teeth.

"Pablo!"

He turned to me, saw my stricken expression.

"I'm sorry. I didn't mean it. I just . . ."

I nodded, looked away from him.

"I forgot," he said. "I would never . . ."

But I still couldn't meet his eyes.

"I would never," he said, "take her away from you."

But I began to dream that I came home to find the house empty. Even the furniture was gone.

I talked to Leon about my fear that someday Pablo and Livvy would just get up and go. He said that I had to look forward to the day when she was well enough to do that, though he understood that I wouldn't want them to be too far away. He thought there was no likelihood they would be in a hurry to leave the best set-up two young parents ever had.

I went to the two public schools closest to our apartment to ask about the possibility of tutoring a child who was having difficulty learning to read. If Mrs. Borelli would continue to come in weekday afternoons, there was no reason I couldn't take a couple of hours during one or two of those afternoons to do something useful for someone outside of my family. I signed up to begin in a tutoring program the following fall.

The more Livvy's brain came back to something resembling itself, the more energetic she grew, but there was nothing she cared to do with her energy except play at the computer, where she did whatever people do at computers when they don't actually have anything to do. She signed up for exercise classes at the Y but didn't go to them. She had no desire to care for Donna but was increasingly concerned about who did. If Rennie was in the baby's vicinity, Livvy pointed like some alert hunting dog that smells its prey and is waiting for it to make a move. When I joked about this, Rennie allowed herself to grow a little closer to me. She did a comical routine in which, if she wanted to talk to the baby, she'd first go to the front door and listen for sounds of Livvy's approach.

Livvy began attending Columbia in September, when Donna was one year and one week old. School took her over as it once had, and she fought less with both Rennie and Pablo. She came home exhausted, since on the days when she didn't have a full schedule, she saw Doctor Weinberger. (She'd wanted to take five classes, but he'd urged her to start with four.) Often she went to her room for a nap that seemed to last through the night. Once or twice, when I was downstairs cleaning up the kitchen and assumed everyone was asleep, I became aware that she was working at her desk in Donna's room.

I began using my own computer to record memories of our Italian years as only I would ever remember them.

Twice a week I tutored an eight-year-old named Maria whose family had moved to New York from the Dominican Republic during the summer.

We were well into winter when I took longer than usual, one night after company had left, to clean up downstairs. Everyone else had gone to bed and as I dried some big pots that would be in the way in the morning, I thought I heard Donna cry. I put away the last of the pots, dried my hands and went to her but hesitated at the threshold of the room. Livvy sat at her computer, typing with one hand and holding the now-quiet baby on her shoulder with the other.

She met my glance.

I said, barely breathing, " 'Night, Livvy."

She smiled the old pained smile I'd just begun to see recently and said, "Do you think you could manage to remember, Mother, that my name is Olivia?"

Her other name, of course, was or had been Ferrante, and that was the name she'd registered under at Columbia, explaining that it would be "a royal pain at this stage" to try to get them to change her name on all the records.

Pablo seemed to withdraw from Livvy in a way that made it easier for him to remain even-tempered when she was hostile. He ceased to make any effort to interest her in Donna, with whom her behavior was so erratic that I sometimes wondered if the baby didn't think she was different people: There was the relaxed, reasonably affectionate young woman who cradled her at the computer table or might allow her to climb up next to her on the sofa with a picture book; the anxious student who ignored her as she paced around the living room before an exam, often banging into furniture; and then the

buoyant young woman who'd not only done beautifully on
some test but had been asked out by "the only other Italian at
Columbia," whom she'd had to tell (a coy laugh) that she was
married.

I thought, *And have a baby,* but Pablo said, "If you wore
your ring, you wouldn't have to tell people."

"I know, but it doesn't feel— I think because of the weight
I lost, it could just slip off."

Pablo said, "I told you, they can fix that."

She made a face. "With some awful piece of wire that
they—"

"It's not wire. It's a little strip of metal they attach to the inside."

"Ohhhh . . . please. Leave me alone. I don't like the way
rings feel. Okay? I've never worn one."

I supposed I should be grateful, at this point, that he would
not readily throw away a Catholic marriage. Anyway, the following Saturday, in what had the effect of a response to this argument, although he was startled when I joked about it, Pablo
took Donna to his aunt's brother-in-law's jewelry store in
Queens, where Donna's ears were pierced to accommodate mi-
nuscule gold earrings. He showed her to me proudly. Curls of
shiny black hair dipped over her little ears, pointing toward the
tiny hoops. She reached for me and I took her from him,
kissed each ear.

"Did she cry much?" I asked, wondering what Livvy would
say.

She'd spent the day studying for finals.

He shook his head proudly. "Hardly at all. Charley's the
best."

Donna was sleepy. I told Pablo that Olivia was in the baby's
room, as we still called it, though Livvy spent a great deal of
time in there and often slept through the night on the big bed
that was so close to her desk. Now Pablo brought Donna to
that room and closed the door behind them, so I have no idea
of what transpired within. But on the following Friday night,
when Donna was asleep and the rest of us were gathered
around the dinner table, Olivia announced that she'd joined a
new group at school, Humans United Against Clitoridectomy,
HUAC, which was dedicated to fighting the genital mutilation
of women by the Masai and other African tribes. We stared at
her. There was no way the men were going to say a word,

much less make a joke, as they probably would have liked to. She confronted us all.

"You're not going to try to say it doesn't happen."

As one, we shook our heads.

She turned to me. "Or tell me I have more important things to worry about."

I shook my head again. "I can't tell you what to worry about."

I'm not sure Annie knew what a clitoris was, but she knew she didn't want to hear about its mutilation and she asked Ovvy if he wanted to play cards or something upstairs. He went willingly. But Rennie looked directly at Olivia for the first time since she'd fallen over the cradle.

"What are you going to do?" she asked Livvy.

Livvy told her they were just beginning to make their plans, but someone was drawing up a list of the countries that engaged in the practice along with the products they exported to see which ones people could be pressured to stop buying. In the meantime, if Rennie was interested, Livvy would show her the letter she'd helped write that they were distributing around school. Rennie was very interested. Together they went to find the letter on Olivia's desk.

Pablo said that if we'd excuse him, he'd just remembered something he needed at the drugstore.

There was no ism to bridge the gap between him and his wife. Somewhere along the way he'd stopped calling her O and begun to address her as Olivia. If a certain distance was suggested by anyone's use of her full name, the distance between the two of them seemed a worse portent.

School became a way of maintaining that distance. At first it was difficult to be sure she was doing it on purpose because she was genuinely back in her element there, and it was possible that her talking about little else was simply a reflection of that reality. Then there came the night when she told us she was taking a placement exam in Italian so she could enroll for some advanced literature courses. Pablo, who hadn't spoken during the entire dinner, said that a little Spanish would be more useful to anyone who lived in New York City.

She not only responded that these weren't courses in learning the language, but rather ones where you read great literature like Dante's *Inferno*, but then added, snottily ignorant, that there were no great classics in Spanish.

"Oh?" Pablo said, his face flushed with controlled fury. "Well Señor Cervantes would be very surprised to hear this."

Whether or not she knew of *Don Quixote*, she perceived that she had made a mistake and quickly began talking about her one elective, a course in basic psychology, the teacher of which was, she advised us repeatedly, so stupid compared to Doctor Weinberger that she couldn't imagine ever again taking a psych course.

Pablo excused himself.

He began to do this frequently, though he seldom stayed out late. He made it a point to tell me that he "just hung out" at a club on Fourteenth Street called Tequila's where there were a lot of other Latinos, drinking and schmoozing. It was the first time I'd heard him refer to himself as a Latino without saying "American" first.

Olivia got an A in her psych course and everything else. Apparently she hadn't challenged the teacher in class but just let off steam at home. And of course in her sessions with the doctor. As she entered her second term at Columbia, the phrase "Doctor Weinberger says" was enough to make Pablo leave the table or wherever we were, and more than once he muttered in Spanish, knowing that I could hear, "Ah, yes, the sainted doctor." It was easy to understand his hostility toward the man who occupied his wife's brain so thoroughly as to leave no room for him. I had to remind myself, when I felt too sympathetic to him at her expense, that I had tried to convince him not to push her to get married.

Of course, I had also tried to talk them out of having this baby I adored, who in the second year of her life was acquiring language and holding me enthralled, who had already given me more happy hours than I'd been allowed when Livvy was tiny. I would sit down to record some memory of the past or idea for the future and instead I would make notes of Donna's new words, giggle over a funny gesture, something she'd done at the park.

Sheldon called to say that he didn't know why, but the cable guys still wanted me if I'd come back next year. I told him I would let him know in two or three weeks, but it was difficult for me to focus on the matter, although the cost of Doctor Weinberger alone made it seem like a good idea.

* * *

Donna hadn't begun talking at a particularly early age, but from the time she did begin, she'd strung together sounds and words, and by the time she was a year and a half, she had an extensive vocabulary. She called me Mama, perhaps because that was what most of the kids in the park called the large person who accompanied them. I was always careful to call Olivia "your mama" when I spoke to the baby, but Donna never looked at Olivia at those times and I don't think it had registered. Pablo was Papa, Olivia was Vavava, Leon, Leelee, the kids, Nennie, Nannie, and Novvy. She took attendance at our Friday dinners, asked for whoever wasn't there, had just begun to ask why when we said someone had to be someplace else.

We'd had a gate made to close off the bottom of the wrought-iron staircase, but when the baby reached the age where she wanted to climb steps, they turned into a logistical nightmare. What we hadn't envisioned was the different ways she could get on and fall off them, the worse being from the sides, which had very widely spaced perpendicular rails. Someone had to follow her extremely closely when she climbed them. There was no gate upstairs, which fortified my inclination to serve meals downstairs all the time. (The normal wood ones didn't fit the opening.) Further, once she became accustomed to having someone open the downstairs gate so she could climb up, she discovered she could go around the sides and hoist herself up to the second step without aid.

Olivia got into the habit of studying at the dining table when she wasn't using the computer. She seemed to enjoy being around the rest of us, though she became absorbed in her work and didn't appear responsive to what was happening in the room. On this Saturday everyone else was out and I'd prepared sandwiches for her and the baby and me. When I brought them to the table, Livvy pushed aside her books, but then Donna, laughing wildly, ran to the steps.

"Do you remember when you used to climb the steps at the Piazza?" I asked Olivia as I picked up the baby and put her in the high chair.

"I loved them," Olivia said when the three of us were settled. "More than anything else in Rome. I remember we used to go there all the time. It was the only place . . . After you left, I always wanted to go there with Papa, but he thought I was crazy, wanting to be where the tourists were. Anyway, he only wanted to go, you know, where his girlfriends were."

I didn't speak, nod, eat.

"Sometimes I went with my girlfriends. To pick up Americans. But the ones we wanted to pick up—you know what I mean by pick up, talk to—I don't think we'd even have gone to a movie if they asked us. Anyway, we were scared of the ones who asked. They were too old." She smiled. "I mean really old, not like Pablo's too old. Although they might've been. I was younger. I didn't see them the same way."

I nodded, looked down, saw my plate, forced myself to begin eating.

She said, "If you think I don't remember that you were right about everything, you're wrong."

I looked up, startled. She was watching me intently. There was nothing I could say.

She glanced at the baby, who had already made a fine mess of her sandwich. Donna had begun to refuse the separate pieces of bread and cheese, or whatever, that I gave her for lunch if the rest of us were having sandwiches. She wanted the "rown-up food."

"What I don't remember is everything from the time . . . I hardly remember the summer I was very, you know, just before I had Donna, until I woke up. I mean, I woke up in my own bed one day, and it was as if I'd been sleeping the whole time. Can you believe that?"

I managed to say, "Sure," although it was very difficult to speak. I heard a noise in the hallway and prayed that it wasn't any of our family coming back already.

Just let them stay out for pizza. Please.

"I'm not sure I believe it, but it's true," she said, and went back to her sandwich.

Donna wasn't eating anymore but was pulling crumbs from her nice, firm peasant bread and sort of rolling them in her cheese. Now the cheese dropped and she got mad and began banging the bread and the remaining piece of cheese on her high-chair tray. Finally she said she wanted to go down.

I whispered. "We'll have to watch her if she gets near the stairs."

Olivia nodded.

I wiped the baby's face and hands, set her down on the floor, suggested she look at one of her books.

"Except for that one time ... There's nobody in any of my classes who has a better memory than I do," Olivia said.

"I believe it."

The baby brought over a book. She wanted to climb up on my lap and be read to. I told her she should look at the book for a while, and when I was finished with lunch, I'd read to her.

Olivia said, "The stuff I'm reading is for Physics for Poets."

I nodded, smiled. She'd talked to us about this class more than any other. Actually called "Physics in Historical Perspective," it fulfilled a science requirement for a lot of liberal arts students who took as little science as possible. The teacher was the only one Livvy had had so far who she thought might be as smart as Doctor Weinberger, or at least have as broad a range.

"Do you know who Niels Bohr was?" she asked me now.

"I just know he's a scientist."

"Was," she corrected. "He died in, I think, 1962."

"Was," I repeated.

"He was someone who really changed the way people looked at the world. The physical world."

"How did he do that?" I asked obligingly.

"Well, his first big discovery, when he made his sharp break with classical physics, was when he said that various elements emitted light in discreet wavelengths. Don't get confused when I say elements, I mean chemical elements, like chlorine, not the basic elements." My daughter was oblivious to the fact that she was speaking to someone who'd forgotten the distinction the day she left high school. "Anyway, what Bohr said that a lot of people refused to believe for a long time—it was against all the ideas of classic physics—was that various elements emit light in discreet wavelengths, and you don't get emissions of light unless they're excited in some way."

Her voice had grown louder. Nineteen years earlier I had given birth to someone who was excited by the fact that various elements emitted light in discreet wavelengths.

She began to say that she was thinking of taking more physics classes, but then she stood up so hastily that she frightened me, and ran over to the stairs, where Donna had taken advantage of our absorption to climb by her sideways route onto that reachable second step, and had already managed to reach the fifth or sixth one. She began to teeter dangerously at the narrow side of the wedge-shaped step, looked around for the grown-up who was always in back of her, and began to fall just as Livvy reached the steps and extended her arms to catch the baby, buckling under her weight.

Safe in Livvy's arms, Donna began to cry, "Mama, Mama."

Olivia brought her back to the table and seemed about to hand her over to me, but then changed her mind and instead sat down, holding Donna on her lap as she discussed the matter of when and how she would make up her mind about what her major would be.